Without warning an urgency coursed through her body, to have him not as Josiah Eaton, but as a man. She wanted a man who could make her feel like a woman relieved of pride and anger and disappointment. He was standing before the fire. She admired his broad shoulders, the strong back and narrow hips.

"When you're ready," Josiah said without turning. "I'll take you back."

He walked to the door. The moment is passing, she thought. We shall be forced to become ourselves again, no longer two people without names in a cozy room shut away from the world.

He looked at her, with her tumbled black hair against the pillows. She was smiling, womanly and appealing, as he had never seen her before.

The aristocratic southern beauty and the reckless, handsome man of the world —engaged in a battle forged in passion; explosive as the Civil War!

Stolen Splendor

Evelyn Hanna

BALLANTINE BOOKS • NEW YORK

Library of Congress Catalog Card Number: 78-63050

ISBN 0-345-27216-1

Manufactured in the United States of America

First Edition: December 1978

Stolen Splendor

✥ Chapter One ✥

VALERIA'S SLIM BODY was numbed far beyond the point of discomfort. After three days of sitting bolt upright on various trains, dozing fitfully then rudely waking to interminable jolting and rattling, she had lost all sense of anticipation or direction. She no longer wondered what time it was or how much longer it would take before she reached Arcadia. Her slender fingers had lost their customary dexterity; the embroidery lay abandoned in her lap. It had been morning, then afternoon, soon it would be evening—of which day, which week? Her old life in the South was irrevocably over.

Atlanta and Arcadia, two names that signified an end and, supposedly, a beginning, with this endless journey in between.

Valeria neatly folded the needle work and replaced it in the wicker basket at her side. Retrieving a bottle of cologne from inside, she moistened her hands, then dabbed the refreshing liquid across her neck and forehead. It brought momentary relief. She wished that she had not brought that particular fragrance; Roman Hyacinth; Tante Elize had always used it. She must not allow her mind to wander back. She had sworn to train herself not to remember the early, halcyon days, nor the horror and destruction of the War itself. She must focus all her attention on what lay ahead, on this job that Ford had promised her, on making a success of it, on saving money so that she and Randy could build a new, productive life. She must force herself to believe that all this was possible. Randy was working on the paper; Ford had arranged it. She must work, too, and together she and

Randy could build an enclave in this northern wilderness where at least they could be themselves. Ford had reminded her in one of his cynical yet amusing letters that a good marriage was still her best solution. There were plenty of profiteers who would jump at the opportunity to nab a beautiful, well-born, accomplished Southerner. Even in the North, the fact that she was the cousin of Robert E. Lee meant something. She smiled inwardly. Dear Ford, always so worldly, always offering such sound advice! She had long since ceased to think of herself in any of these terms. A social secretary and housekeeper to Mrs. Henry Brewster was good enough for her. The profiteers could wait.

She peered at herself in the little hand mirror as she tried to tidy up her long black hair. Valeria had never thought of herself as beautiful. Her eyes were too large and strange in their misty greenness and her skin too white. Her distinctive looks had earned her the reputation of being remote and haughty. Even when she was a girl, young men had hesitated to approach her at dances. She had always seemed much older than her years. It was the family nose, with its fine arched bridge, that gave her profile an aristocratic suggestion of disdain. That nose had been passed down for generations, whomever the Lee men married. She was proud of it; her father, like his cousin the General, had been a very distinguished man.

The roles of a secretary and housekeeper were all that Valeria Hortense de la Pagerie Lee must count on. Being well born and accomplished were not attributes for a domestic. But she had no intention of bartering her background for security, as Ford had done.

A middle-aged couple, huddled among their bundles, were unwrapping packages of food. The wife glanced across at the solitary young woman, who seemed so very much alone, staring impassively through the window.

"Shall I ask her?" the woman nudged her husband. He shook his head tersely. He didn't like the looks of her—cold and superior—and what decent young woman traveled without a companion? A foreigner probably. The thought of having to speak to her, of offering to share their meal, embarrassed him acutely.

But his wife's good nature and curiosity prevailed.

Making her way down the car to where Valeria was sitting, she said, "Excuse me. We're just having something to eat. We'd be glad if you'd join us."

She was surprised by the grateful smile that softened the tense, white face and gave it immediate charm.

"Why, how kind! Are you sure that you have enough?"

"Oh, yes. My daughter packed us a basket. There's plenty."

Valeria followed the woman back, thankful for this diversion. She inclined her head graciously to the husband who flushed slightly. "You are most kind, sir."

Southern, he thought. That explains it. He'd known there was something wrong.

The woman held out a package of neatly cut sandwiches. "Chicken or ham. Home cured. My daughter bakes all her own bread. She scorns buying it from a shop."

"She is right," Valeria agreed, selecting a sandwich. "There's nothing so delicious as homemade bread."

"You'd be surprised how many people buy from outside. I always say it just never tastes the same."

Valeria's spirits revived slightly at the taste of the rough barley bread and the sweet yet tangy ham.

"You going to Arcadia, I 'spect?" the woman inquired.

"Yes."

"Your first visit?"

Valeria nodded. "I have never been North before."

The woman smiled with a trace of embarrassment. "Foolish to ask where you're from."

"I come from Atlanta."

"Oh."

A silence fell. The shared memory of the burning of that city hung like a reproach between them.

"My son—" the woman began and then thought
better of it. What was the good of raking up old
scores? Her son had taken part in that act of retribution and had, thank Heaven, got home safely. The
South had been rightfully beaten, but one had to be
charitable; not all Southerners had been to blame.

"You have friends in Arcadia?" the woman pursued.

"My brother. He works on the paper there."

The woman's eyes opened wide. "Why, mercy!
That's Mr. Eaton's private car back there. It was
hooked on at Cincinnati. He's traveling on this train."

"What a coincidence! I have never met Mr. Eaton."

"Everyone in Arcadia knows Josiah Eaton. He
owns *The Courier* and the branch line of this railroad
that goes on through to Chicago. He's a very prominent man."

Valeria detected a hint of disapproval in the
woman's voice.

The husband added, "Some talk of his running for
Governor. Can't say I'd vote for him myself." He bit
self-righteously into a sandwich.

"Well," the woman ventured, "people do say—"
She wiped her mouth discreetly. "Of course, in a
town like Arcadia folks like to gossip." She managed a
timid laugh. "But I 'spect your brother knows all
about Mr. Eaton. Has he worked on the paper long?"

"Three months."

"Oh well—" she smirked. "I 'spect he'll have lots to
tell." She opened a paper bag and offered it to
Valeria. "Black plums. Best for jam, but still good
eating."

"Eaton and Sam Garvey," the husband pronounced, "between 'em about run Arcadia. Town
grew up around the Garvey mills."

"Of course, you've heard of Mr. Garvey," the
woman said. "He's one of the richest men in the country. Old now, but his mills are the biggest in the state.
Arcadia was just a small place before. My mother can
remember when there was just fields and a few farms
and one store. You should see it now. All the big
houses on The Heights and the town spreading out!"

she nodded her head in wonderment at such progress.

"Steel and iron ore," the man said, munching. "Boomed in war time. All them big guns and rifles—now the railroads. They say Sam Garvey's worth a hundred million, some say more. Gettin' richer every day."

"And he's only got one daughter. She lives in the biggest house on The Heights, right above the town. Mrs. Henry Brewster."

"My brother has mentioned her, I think," Valeria said carefully.

"Everyone knows Mrs. Henry Brewster. And *she's* only got one son and a daughter. Imagine! They'll inherit everything." The woman shook her head, awed by the thought of such an avalanche of wealth. "You'll like Arcadia, I'm sure. It's growing all the time."

The tasseled shades of Josiah Eaton's private car were drawn.

In the golden lamplight that pooled the red plush parlor, Josiah was lounging naked in an arm chair, admiring the opulent nudity of Rosie Delmar who was reclining on the sofa, balancing a glass of champagne between her breasts.

These two handsome animals had been making love all afternoon and were now frayed and disenchanted. But it amused Josiah's sense of the incongruous to see her lying there, a splendid and vulgar odalisque, lazily rocking one foot in its blue satin slipper that was adorned with a sequined butterfly. Rosie was still superb with her powerful thighs and generous breasts, and mass of auburn hair. She would have been a great beauty but for the wide and loose-lipped mouth that, unlike the rest of her, betrayed her origins.

Rosie's sensuality was unbounded. She had the appetites and aptitudes of a born whore. But she was good-natured, even amusing. Her only pretension to virtue was her absence of pretensions. She was an organism devised for rutting. But he had had enough of her for the day.

"All the same, you're a beast, Jose," Rosie was

saying, holding out her glass for more champagne. "You won't take me serious."

"God forbid," Josiah laughed, bending forward to refill her glass. "Why spoil a good thing? You're perfection, Rosie."

"Oh yes, on my back. The moment I'm on my feet I don't exist for you." She drained the bubbling drink into her mouth. "It don't occur to you that I have thoughts and feelings. I'm not as dumb as you suppose."

She sat up abruptly, leaning her elbows on her knees, spread wide like a washerwoman's. A heavy coil of Titian hair swung forward down one breast. Her normally brilliant eyes were bloodshot.

"It may surprise you to know, Josiah Eaton," she announced with determination, "that I've got a good head on my shoulders."

"A very good head," Josiah conceded, "on the finest shoulders I ever saw."

"I'm good for six or seven years," Rosie judged realistically. "Ten, maybe, if I don't drink too much." She stood up, defiant in her flamboyant sexuality. "You think about that and do something more than have me arsing around on this God-damned train."

"What do you have in mind, Rosie?"

"Set me up in Chicago," she challenged him. "I'd like something a bit more steady. I can do a lot for you, Jose. I know what you are. I can run that side of your life and save you a lot of trouble."

"I don't need you to procure for me, Rosie," Josiah replied coldly. "Besides, since you know me so well, you ought to know I like variety."

"If you go into politics," she reminded him, "you'll have to watch your step. Rosie can be very discreet. Rosie can cover up a multitude of sins and we know how many of those you're in the habit of committing.

He was not interested in her suggestions, but instead fell to considering his body, still in very good shape for a man of thirty-seven, his belly flat and firm, no extra fat on his hips and not a single varicose vein on either of his legs. His face was still classically handsome. Only the curly hair on his chest betrayed him; it was turning gray in contrast to the blond hair on his head.

Rosie landed a well-aimed prod at his scrotum with the toe of her slipper. "Stop admiring yourself. I know you think you're God's gift to women and I dare say a lot of 'em think you are. As it happens, I've a soft spot for you myself, though I know you're a bastard at heart." She sniggered. "That's a laugh! A heart's the one thing you haven't got."

She put her hands on his shoulders and leaned over him, so that her massive breasts were close to his face.

"Come on, Jose, be good to Rosie and Rosie will take care of her great big handsome lecherous beast."

Her mouth came down on his while his hand reached up between her thighs.

"Stop that!" Rosie smacked his hand down. "Be serious for once! You'll ruin your career if you get elected, carrying on the way you do. I can give you a front. People don't mind if a man has a mistress. It's understood, as you're not married. They won't inquire who she entertains. Rosie can be very understanding."

Josiah placed his foot squarely on her belly and thrust her back onto the sofa. "I can handle my career," he warned, "however many women I choose to see." He stood up, towering over her, arrogant, self-indulgent and self-assured. "How about earning your keep instead of giving me advice?"

Rosie flung herself back horizontally on the sofa. She hated him for refusing even to discuss her proposition. "I may be a whore," she said fiercely, "it was men like you who made me one, but I was trying to be your friend."

"Thanks, Rosie. Let's keep things the way they are."

He went to a writing desk and took out a small bag filled with coins which he rattled over Rosie's blue-slippered feet. "Silver dollars! All fresh from the mint."

She kicked out at him. "Get away from me!" She covered her eyes with her arm.

"Why, Rosie!" he mocked. "What's come over you? I never knew you to refuse good cash before."

"No!" she cried into her arm. She was half willing to indulge him, but resentful of his refusal to consider what she believed was her better self.

"Come on, Rosie!" he coaxed, sneaking a dollar onto her stomach.

"I'm sick of your games," she said without resisting him. "It's always the same with you. You take everything from me and you won't ever think of me as a . . . a decent person. And I am."

"I never thought virtue was exactly your strong point. But in every other feminine attribute you excel."

She watched him, glowering, as he placed the silver dollars, one after another, all over her body. This was the game at which Rosie Delmar was the unchallenged champion.

"Oooo," she squirmed. "They're cold!"

They were laughing, but with ill nature, irked at each other. "You could make a fortune if you took this up professionally," Josiah suggested.

After some suspenseful moments the bag was empty. "There! Now you know the rules," Josiah said like a ringmaster. "Drop one and you lose the lot."

Rosie lifted her arms with elaborate care. If she dropped one coin while trying to embrace Josiah she'd lose every dollar. "It's not fair," she protested petulantly. "This damn car lurches so and I'm half drunk."

"You can make it," he said in a husky voice, then began to probe the soft recesses of Rosie's mouth with his tongue. Expertly, Josiah touched every part of her creamy flesh, trying to make her as excited as himself. He gently stroked her inner thighs with his deft fingers, sending burning, shooting sensations to the inner region at the top of Rosie's legs. Just as she was beginning to respond, Josiah stopped and lifted his blond head to give Rosie a mischievous grin. Then he started to tease the pinkish tips of her breasts with his full lips. With practiced care he avoided each dollar, only caressing the warm areas of skin between.

The train was jolting badly causing Rosie to move

more than usual and a silver piece fell to the carpeting.

"Never mind," Josiah laughed. "I'll give you a handicap. You can lose five because of adverse conditions."

Several more dollars slid to the floor as Rosie could no longer stem the tide building inside her. She turned slowly. Her rich hair had fallen across her face. Rosie was crying and trying to cover her eyes with her hands.

"Oh, I hate you," she whimpered. "I hate you and your rotten games."

Josiah was amused by her sudden misery. "You're losing your grip, Rosie. What's the matter? It's all in fun."

She thrust him savagely away, showering coins over the carpet.

"It's not funny. I'm sick of being treated like a circus animal. I give you the pleasure you want. But I deserve some . . . something—"

She stumbled past him to the door.

"Rosie! Come back here."

She swung around, sweeping the mass of tawny hair from her face. Her sense of outrage gave her a grotesque and pathetic dignity. "I hope you get elected and then someone exposes you. I hope they drag you in the mud where you belong. And if they want any details of what a low-down beast you are, let them come to Rosie Delmar. Christ, will I tell them plenty!"

The door swung violently behind her.

He was taken aback and then angered by this outburst. He caught sight of himself in the mirror. His dissolute nakedness seemed to justify her contempt. He put on a burgundy dressing gown and sat down.

The champagne tasted bitter. He had drunk too much and wasted the whole day playing games with a slut whom he cared nothing for. It was not what passed for love-making—and was no more than the discharge of excess male energy—that he now resented. Rosie's prescribed role did not include the right to confront him with the truth.

It was not, of course, entirely the truth, but she had struck uncomfortably close. As he sat there alone in the lamplight, in that over-upholstered, over-ornamented parlor, the train rattled on into the dusk. A sense of some personal failure, deeper than mere dissatisfaction, returned to plague him as it often had of late after these bouts of sexual indulgence. He had everything; he was rich, successful, admired, on the brink of what promised to be a brilliant new career. Apart from his unresolved feud with Sam Garvey, fate had persistently showered him with blessings and rewards. He had boundless good health, good looks and good fortune. Only one thing had been denied him.

Rosie was a whore, a woman of no mentality, but a woman. She had sensed the essential lack.

"A heart," she had sneered, "is the one thing you haven't got."

Dark had fallen when the train pulled in to Arcadia.

It rumbled into the gas-lit station and, with a great grinding of brakes and a tremendous sigh of steam, dragged to a halt.

Doors swung open as weary passengers, released from their long confinement, clambered out.

Valeria hauled her suitcase and the wicker basket onto the platform. She saw at once the two beloved figures waiting. Randy started toward her with a cry of "Val!"

She ran forward and flung herself into his arms. He was there. He was holding her. They were together. The long ordeal of separation was over.

She clung to him. "Oh Randy, I thought I would never get here."

He was kissing her, laughing, delighted, "The train was two hours late."

Her sense of self, of her own individual life, rushed back to her. In the next instant Valeria was hugging Ford. She hardly saw them or heard what they were saying. The indestructible trio was reunited. That was all that mattered.

"Welcome to glorious Arcadia!" How reassuring to hear Ford's easy, ironic voice! "You're staying with us at Fairlawn. My sainted mother-in-law isn't here yet, so tonight we'll celebrate."

Randy was picking up her suitcase. Ford took charge of the wicker basket. "Is this all you have?"

"I brought all I had that was decent."

"Never mind. Althea has dozens of dresses she never wears."

Randy's arm was round her. "You have to adjust to the fact that our friend Mr. Hollister is now a bloated plutocrat."

"You're damned right!" Ford laughed. "So will you be if I have anything to do with it."

Valeria linked her arm with his. "Darling Ford, have you found me a profiteer?"

She was barely aware of the tall man in gray with the gray fedora nonchalantly tilted on his golden head, as he came abreast. She noticed instead the statuesque woman overdressed in ruby velvet and a hat with many plumes. They had been fighting, Valeria saw.

"Why, hello there, Josiah!" Ford greeted him.

The stranger paused for a moment. Too complacently handsome and full of himself, Valeria thought.

"Ford Hollister! And Randolph Lee! What are you doing here?"

"This is my sister, Mr. Eaton. She's just arrived from Atlanta."

The pale blue eyes took her in at a glance and dismissed her. He said formally, "I'm sorry I didn't know you were on the train."

He made no attempt to introduce his companion who hung back as though ashamed.

"Can I give you a lift?" he offered. "I'm going out to my place."

"No, thanks. Valeria is staying with us at Fairlawn."

Josiah nodded and touched his hat. "I'll see you then. And meet you at the office tomorrow, Lee."

He barely glanced at Valeria. She smiled at the woman, so abashed despite her finery. Rosie ventured a timid, grateful smile.

Josiah strode off, leaving Rosie like a piece of unclaimed baggage.

"Perhaps we can help this lady," Valeria suggested.

"Oh no, I can manage. Thanks." Rosie picked up her suitcase.

"One of Josiah's dubious conquests," Ford murmured as they followed her down the platform.

"That is my new employer," Randolph explained. "A man of many parts, too many some might say."

Valeria noted the athletic, well-shouldered figure as, with an air of casual authority, he vanished into the station, forlornly trailed by Rosie, dragging her velvet skirts, her red feathers nodding.

"What a very ill-mannered man!"

The Brewster mansion stood at the crest of the hill that rose from Arcadia to the wealthy residential district known as The Heights. The house was a hideous pile of dark red brick in the Gothic manner with enough turrets and crenelations to withstand a siege. It confronted in glum defiance the shabby, industrial town below.

Valeria's heart sank when, two days after her arrival, she stepped down from Ford's new buggy. This ostentatious mansion repelled her. It was the glaring proof of Northern power, of wealth amassed by destruction.

Together they went up the steps to the front door. "Don't be alarmed, my dear," Ford reassured her. "Ida Brewster is far more likely to be frightened of you than you need ever be of her."

A butler opened the heavily carved entrance, and Ford announced them. "Mrs. Brewster is expecting us at three."

They entered a huge, dark hall from which an ornate staircase rose cumbersomely to the floor above. The house had no air of being lived in. It might have been ordered *en bloc* from a catalogue as a testimonial to its owner's financial worth.

When they were shown into a parlor Valeria was astonished. It was the ugliest room she had ever seen.

"Try not to look too appalled, dear," Ford cautioned her. "As you see, there's no need to describe the mistress of this *outré* establishment."

Valeria looked around. He was right. It was an outrageous tribute to bad taste.

Maroon-flocked wallpaper, a crimson Turkey carpet, vermilion velvet curtains held back by immense gold tassels, Japanese screens with embroidered cranes flying in stiff formation, Capo di Monte urns stuffed with pampas grass and, hung indiscriminately, a panoply of murky landscapes in heavily gilded frames. Over a liver-colored marble mantel that had been imported from Carrara via Grand Rapids, cramped by a scrimmage of fans and vases, hung a picture of a huge cow gazing balefully, with swollen udders, from a farmyard scene. Valeria smiled, "It's an achievement in a way. There's not a single thing—"

"Oh, surely this—?" Ford placed a forefinger on the nipple of a simpering virgin holding aloft a torch of opaque glass.

"Or this—?" Valeria patted a porcelian sphinx in a dust cap. "Amazing! To have gathered so many hideous objects together in one room."

"This is the grandest parlor on The Heights, my dear."

"Are they all like this?"

"Worse, mostly."

Valeria sighed.

"Think you can stand it?" her old friend asked.

She moved over to the window, gracefully avoiding the potted palms and *étagères* cluttered with bisque figurines and bud vases, and looked out onto the terrace with its bleak concrete balustrade. Below The Heights, a brownish haze blanketed the town.

Briefly, she saw a cool gray room with tall windows, dusk shadowing the mirrors. Tante Elize was playing the piano. In a moment Eugene would soundlessly carry in the tea tray laden with gleaming silver.

"It's no use remembering or comparing." She turned to face him; they were fellow exiles and survivors. "This is the North and it's today."

Ida Brewster had for years taught herself to sail into a room in the manner of "the" Mrs. Astor. In-

stead, being physically unwieldy, she barged through
doorways like a battleship cleaving a breaker. With
her large head, burdened by a mass of russet hair
that was held in place by a bun as flat as a cow turd,
and with her prominent bosom dislodging the space
around her, she thrust herself forward like an affront.
She had developed the habit of staring defensively,
and her smile, which she imagined to be gracious,
bared her alarming teeth. She was doubly ill-at-ease
and overbearing now because she recognized in Ford
Hollister and his protégé products of a social order
to which, however great her wealth, aggressiveness
and power, she could never quite belong.

"My dear Mrs. Brewster," Ford shook the coarse,
square hand with too many diamond rings.

"Charmed, Mr. Hollister. And this, I presume—?"

"My dear friend, Valeria Lee. As I told you, we
grew up together."

The paw passed to Valeria who barely touched the
fingertips.

"How do you do, Mrs. Brewster?"

"Miss Lee." Ida refrained from adding that she was
delighted to meet her. Valeria, having come to obtain
a position, must be relegated to the status of a servant.
"Do be seated."

Valeria positioned herself in a high-backed chair.
Why, she wondered, does a woman that size wear
tweed? She looks as bulky as a sofa.

Ida, viewing this cool intruder, thought in turn,
how dare she give herself such airs in that worn out
coat and skirt? Ida noted the casual way the sable
scarf was draped around the young woman's shoulders; the relic, she guessed, of some coat long since
discarded. The small tricorne, quite out of fashion,
was tilted becomingly forward with its veil discreetly
raised. It set off the well-bred face which fell short of
great beauty because of the high-bridged nose. The
unusually large, disturbingly green eyes were too
steady, too aware of social shortcomings, Ida decided.
But she was forced to admit that any women would
envy the luminous pallor of that skin. A snob, far too
conscious of her background. And what did that

amount to any more? They were all destitute, these stuck-up Southerners, except Ford Hollister who had sold himself to the Haverfields in return for taking that half-witted daughter off their hands.

"When did you arrive, Miss Lee?" she asked.

"The day before yesterday."

"She's staying with us at Fairlawn," Ford put in. "My wife has become quite fond of her."

Ida's lips curled. She was well aware of the implication—that this woman—a nobody—should be allowed to stay at the one house in Arcadia to which she had never been invited! No, Miss Lee would decidedly not do.

"I'm sure it's a welcome change," she said unkindly.

"I've been telling Valeria so much about you," Ford proceeded to business. "Not that one needs to tell anyone about 'the' Mrs. Brewster. You really run the town."

Ida, slightly mollified, gave her smile. "I try to bring a little culture here. The West doesn't have the advantages of New York or Boston. But we endeavor."

"Anything of interest in Arcadia happens in this house," Ford said blandly to Valeria. "It's the Mecca of social climbers. I had the pleasure of watching Mrs. Brewster preside over the musical committee. General Grant couldn't have organized it better."

"I had asked Mrs. Haverfield to join us," Ida reminded him.

"Oh, she will, I'm sure. I merely deputized."

Ford's maneuvers on Valeria's behalf were becoming patently clear.

"The town owes you a great debt," he persisted, "I really don't know what it would do without you."

Ida apparently accepted this blatant flattery as her due. "I like to entertain," she said more easily. "And someone has to take the lead. We do manage quite a lively season here."

"That's where I thought Valeria might help. She could take so many of the boring details off your hands."

Ida was not going to be coerced into making a decision quite so easily. She asked bluntly, "What experience do you have?"

Valeria, acutely embarrassed at finding herself the prize in this contest between snobbery and expedience, looked down at her gloved hands. "I ran our home, did the catering and the flowers, sent out the invitations. My aunt," she hesitated, "liked to have people in."

Her qualifications sounded meager, so she added, "I believe I know how to arrange a menu." She raised her eyes to meet Ida's uncordial scrutiny.

"She plays the piano—beautifully," Ford interposed.

Ida stared. This girl might pretend to be demure and unassuming because she needed the position, but Ida could detect, with the instinct of an ambitious woman, that under that composed exterior lurked a coiled determination. Her voice had a veiled smoothness that irritated Ida. She was by no means subservient enough. She'll cause trouble. There's too much hidden, Ida thought. "I have a chef," she announced. "He's French. He came to me highly recommended. I give dinners three nights a week."

"I speak French," Valeria ventured modestly.

"There's a lot else to see to in a house this big." Ida was determined to establish that by postwar standards, Southern pretensions meant less than nothing. Her social position was, after all, unassailable, buttressed as it was by her father's millions. Why, then, did this penniless creature, begging for employment, nudge her insecurity? "How many servants did you have?" she asked.

"It was . . . a little different at home."

"Oh," Ida retorted with contempt. "You had slaves, I guess."

The interview was going badly. Ford intervened, steering Ida back to the main issue. "My mother-in-law so much wants to meet you. It's really absurd that Arcadia's two leading ladies don't know each other."

Ida stiffened. It was insulting the way this upstart kept reminding her that, however hard she had tried, she had never received an invitation to Fairlawn. Mrs. Haverfield might be an ambassador's widow and might move in the highest circles, but *she* was Sam Garvey's daughter. The Garveys were far richer than the Haverfields, and she was not going to abase herself openly.

She asked coldly, "How *is* Mrs. Haverfield?"

"She's on her way back here from Europe. I must bring you two together."

Ida's resolve wavered. "Perhaps she'd come here?" she plunged. "To one of my concerts."

"I'm sure she'd love to."

He was forcing her to decide. But she would not capitulate without a show of strength. "I envy her freedom," she said grandly. "I'm so tied down. What with arranging our musical season. I had Madam Patti here last winter and Mrs. Langtry came to tea. And then there are my committees and clubs and charities. Sometimes the days are so full, I wonder how I manage to get through them."

"All the more reason," Ford pointed out nonchalantly, "to have a social secretary. My mama-in-law insists she can't get on without one; in New York, that is. Of course," he added, "Valeria's welcome to stay with us as long as she cares to. But I'm afraid she's too independent. We Southern folk have learned to be so."

"No doubt you found independence a great asset when you came North, Mr. Hollister."

"It was different in my case," Ford countered. "I was lucky enough to meet Althea and, as we know, 'love conquers all.'"

Valeria gasped at his audacity.

"I'm glad to know you're a romantic," Ida nailed him. "So few people are today."

It was no use prolonging this fencing match. She gave Valeria a last dispassionate stare. If this was the price of meeting Mrs. Haverfield, she supposed that she could put up with this girl for a short time. Once that contact had been established she could get rid of her. "If you'd like to come on trial—for two weeks, say," she offered ungraciously, "we'll see."

She stood up, dismissing the applicant. Ford rose to escort her.

"I understand," Ida boomed, as she forged through the doorway, "that Fairlawn has such glorious roses. They must be coming out right now."

"The gardens are quite a sight."

"I hope to see them," Ida announced firmly.

They crossed the dark oak hall. A suit of armor tilted inappropriately by the front door. Valeria followed, thankful that this disagreeable interview was over.

"You can start Monday," Ida said. "There's a room on the third floor. Of course, you'll eat upstairs. We can discuss payment later."

Valeria responded to this insolence by a slight inclination of her head, an unnoticed gesture of sarcasm, and went outside.

Ford raised his hat. "It's been a pleasure, Mrs. Brewster. I'm sure this meeting will prove a boon for both of you."

They exchanged smiles of mutual dislike and Ida shut the oak door.

She was disagreeably aware, as she went upstairs, that she had not impressed them as forcefully as she had intended, but she was too realistic not to know that it was one thing to lord it over what passed for society in Arcadia—people had no choice but to acknowledge her supremacy since her father had practically built the town—and quite another to be accepted in the sphere that Mrs. Haverfield moved in and to which she passionately aspired. She had a great deal of money; she had drive and she had endurance; but she needed the right contacts. One Mrs. Haverfield was worth the whole of Arcadia. She held the key to that glittering world of New York and, later on, of London and Paris.

It was humiliating to use a mere secretary as a stepping stone, but it was not the first time in her social career that Ida Brewster had had to swallow her pride.

Meanwhile, as they went down the steps, Valeria

said, "Really, Ford, you're incredible! I felt like a
darky in a slave market!"

"You have to deal with these people on the terms
they know," Ford said as he helped her into the
buggy. "She's a horror, but she'll serve a purpose." He
pressed her hand. "I don't intend for my children to
spend their lives in Arcadia."

Ford climbed in beside Valeria and flicked the
whip. The horse shook itself and started.

"It won't be easy," Valeria admitted. "She hated me
on sight."

"Because you're a lady, my dear, and she's a miner's daughter. Besides, do you care?"

They passed the red brick pile. Even the Virginia
creeper seemed reluctant to scale those walls.

"I suppose we're no better than they are really,"
Valeria admitted. "We're all climbers or trying to be.
At least you married into a civilized family."

"Who knows, my love," Ford patted her arm
fondly, "lurking among the smokestacks may be some
well-heeled charmer. Don't despair."

She closed her large eyes, remembering how they
used to linger over tea. The blue agapanthus lilies in
the tubs outside would turn the color of lapis lazuli.
The dusk would be haunted by the singing of the
darkies returning from the fields. Tante Elize would
say, "I think I'll give a little dinner next week. Let's
see—whom shall I ask?"

She thought of the blackened shell of Whitebriars
as she had seen it last. It had been torn down following the War, the gardens flattened. Cheap houses
were replacing its beauty.

Would the pain of that lost world ever leave her?

She forced herself to look around at what the present had to offer. They were driving down Tremont
Avenue that was bordered by the mansions of the
newly rich; stolid, pretentious, untouched by charm.

❧ Chapter Two ❧

Dinner at the Brewsters' was not an occasion for celebration. It was an ordeal that the family endured, impatient for the moment when Ida would ring the hand bell and rise to release them for the evening. Ida waved the silver bell commandingly, as though summoning up the spirits of generations of serfs to do her bidding.

She sat enthroned in a forest of silver; six sterling candelabra on the long refectory table, centered by a silver epergne, overladen with alabaster fruits, a quartet of shimmering salt and pepper shakers, and several glinting artificial pheasants whose heads bowed over silver bowls filled with nuts and candied ginger. Every item of Ida's collection crawled with figures, pouting angels, nymphs with flowing hair, and leering satyrs semi-concealed behind rocks and foliage. Ida insisted on not less than four crystal glasses with filigree stems beside each plate. The sideboard groaned with silver trays, tureens, more candlesticks. An immense Venetian chandelier cast a blinding glare over this aggressive display of wealth.

Ida always dressed for dinner. She considered it a mark of breeding and was arrayed in royal blue which antagonized her russet hair. She was wearing a parure of diamonds as though she were going to the opera, and her squat hands were ablaze with rings. She had, notwithstanding her ostentation, a brassy power. She was impressive because of her size and her features, which while too large, were regular. She belonged atop a pedestal on Main Street and there, in later years, she fully intended to have herself commemorated. Had she not personally raised this backwater to a cultural center where artists such as Adelina Patti were pleased to stop on their Western tours? She had a number of unpleasant photographs in gilt frames to testify to her acquaintance with the artistic great.

She ate steadily, plowing her way through the seven-course dinners she considered *de rigueur*. While the others floundered after the roast, Ida stoked her appetitite from the turtle soup to the Scotch Woodcock. She had introduced the English custom of ending a meal with a savory. It was an innovative touch that showed her easy familiarity with European ways.

At the far end of the table Henry Brewster limped in his personal limbo. He had sloping shoulders and a bedraggled moustache. Everything else about him was indefinite. He was like a business suit that came and went, consumed meals, retired behind a paper, and drooped its way to bed. Ida, staring through the mass of silver, wondered why she had ever married him. He was a liability and an impediment in her rise to social fame. He seemed to become vaguer and duller and more unsatisfactory as the years passed. Once Nancy was married and Hank established in the banking business, Ida had it in mind to close the house, pay Henry off, and find some more socially profitable spouse in Europe. She could divorce Henry. Who would ever know in Paris that she was not a widow? Her money would cover up the rest. There were plenty of impoverished noblemen who would be glad for shelter behind the Garvey millions. A duchess, maybe. Having reassured herself about the future, Ida rang the bell.

The English butler, Haddock, supporting himself by one gloved finger against the sideboard, his brain awash with port, indicated to Roberts, the footman, that he should remove the plates.

Hank Brewster, fresh, personable and buoyant, on vacation from his freshman year at Harvard, was examining the bosoms of the nymphs on the candlestick before him, comparing them in size and shape with those of Milly, the parlormaid, with whom his attentions were currently engaged. Hank was having difficulty in persuading Milly to let him take her breasts

out and caress them freely. He longed to suck her
round pink nipples. But she was coy and fearful and
had, so far, only allowed him to feel them through her
stays. It was a pity, Hank was thinking, that artists
covered up the lower regions of their creations with so
many flowing draperies. What was Milly like down
there? He had succeeded in getting his hand up her
skirts a few times, but she had cried out in alarm and
threatened to tell his mother. If only he could induce
Milly to meet him on Tremont Avenue. They could
drive out into the country. He saw, with sudden vividness, Milly—quite naked, gleaming against the grass
—and felt himself stiffen agreeably under the napkin
laid across his lap.

"You've hardly eaten," Ida admonished her daughter Nancy. "I don't know how you think you'll keep
up your strength if you only peck at things. Sit up.
Don't slouch. It's unbecoming."

Nancy, a wispy, washed-out blonde with ringlets
that never hung straight, forced herself to sit upright.
She never knew where to look. Her eyes found refuge
on one of the silver pheasants. She wished devoutly
that her mother would stop staring at her, that Hank
would say something to relieve the tension or that her
father would just for once come to her rescue. He
never did. Nancy dreaded her mother. She was so
forceful. She seemed to devour all the oxygen, leaving
Nancy faint and helpless. If only Hank would really
be her friend, but he treated her with no more than
amused condescension. She was his kid sister, not
worth taking seriously. After all, Hank was a boy; he
went out with girls and got drunk in bars. And what
could he understand of her *passionate* involvement
with the characters in the books she read? How could
she ever explain that she *knew* how Jane Eyre felt
about Mr. Rochester because she felt it with the same
intensity? She was so filled sometimes with the need to
love, to devote herself utterly to someone, that it made
her dizzy. She would come to and the loneliness
would engulf her and she would cry. But what was the
use of all these despairing tears? No one would ever

rescue her from Ida and the house and the town. The future appalled her. She was *doomed*.

"Mr. Hollister told me that Mrs. Haverfield is on her way back from Europe," Ida announced. "I'm having her to a musicale. I do wish you'd study harder, Nancy. It sets a tone if the daughter of the house can show some talent."

"I try," Nancy squirmed, her eyes glued to the tail of the silver pheasant.

"Well, I'd like to see some progress."

Hank took a pear from the fruit bowl offered to him. "Who's this woman you're hiring as a secretary?" he asked.

"She was recommended to me by Mrs. Haverfield," Ida said offhandedly, spitting out the pits of a Concord grape into her hand. "Mrs. Haverfield says a social secretary is essential if one is to have any time to oneself at all. The girl is Southern." This was one step above saying, in Ida's parlance, that she was black.

"I can't stand Southerners," Hank said. "They never want to admit they lost the War."

"I'm only taking her on trial," Ida said, sluicing out her mouth with water from the finger bowl.

"What's her name?"

"Valeria Lee. She's supposed to be related to the General. But all those people who've lost everything pretend to be related. She most likely won't work out."

She spat vigorously and wiped her mouth.

"How old?" Hank swallowed the last of his Burgundy, "Some antique crow, I guess!"

"It's no concern of yours how old she is," Ida said tartly. "She's not coming here to amuse you."

"It would be a change to meet one good-looking woman around here," Hank said with the air of a practiced Lothario.

"There are plenty of nice girls. You just don't look."

"I look." Hank was the only member of the household who was not afraid of Ida. "I look plenty, Mama, and I don't much care for what I see."

He leaned back, expanding his chest. Hadn't Charlie Hammond told him that he was more attrac-

tive than most guys and that any girl was bound to
fall for him?

How handsome he is! Nancy thought, timidly glancing up to see his wavy brown hair and laughing eyes
and that cleft in his chin that was so romantic.

Henry Brewster surfaced like a carp from the
depths of a stagnant pool, slowly wiped his mouth
and regarded his firstborn with distaste. "Spoiled
brat!" he said.

Ida insisted that Nancy run through her repertoire
after dinner. It was the worst torment of anything
Nancy could imagine because, all the time she was
fumbling at the keys, she could feel her mother's gaze
upon her. Ida's eyes seemed to tangle up her fingers.
The notes danced before her and she could only hear
what she was playing from a distance. She was
trapped in a fog of apprehension.

Hank, leaning against the mantelpiece, watched her
with amusement. Poor old Nancy! Thank God he
didn't have to parade her before his college chums!
He wondered, shifting his stance, how he would ever
get through the month he had to spend at home. He
had to stay until he could wheedle the old woman into
handing over a few hundred. Then he would meet
Charlie Hammond in New York. Charlie knew the
ropes. They would visit a few select houses. Boy, what
fun! Meanwhile, in this wilderness, there was nothing
for it; somehow or other he had to get Milly into bed.

Henry Brewster had read *The Courier* from cover
to cover, including the ads for rented rooms. He was
wondering how he could manage to get away to visit
Helen Tennant. It was awkward, the old excuse of going to the club. But Ida would know if he took out the
carriage. Useless to say he wanted to take a walk. He
never walked and Helen lived on the other side of
town. He concentrated on an ad illustrating a new
kind of automatic cleaner. It was a box with a long
stick attached that you pushed back and forth over the
carpet, guaranteed to gather up the dust.

Nancy stumbled and then, panic-stricken, hit a

wrong chord which seemingly crashed right at her mother's feet.

"You don't seem to have improved much," Ida observed sourly. "I shall have to talk to Madam Paul. It's because you don't practice. The piano's there. Why don't you use it?"

Nancy blundered on. Her fingers were losing control. Her mother's voice resounded in her head like a sledgehammer.

"I can't impress on you enough how important it is for a girl to have some social accomplishment. You're pretty, but you're no great beauty. It's useful to have an asset like the piano. Later on when you marry you can play to your husband in the evening."

Henry glanced up from the paper. The thought of Ida pounding the piano when they were alone together horrified him.

"And when you entertain, if there's a lull in the conversation, a hostess can always fill in with a number or two—just to keep things going."

Suddenly every nerve in Nancy's body tightened. She knew that something catastrophic was about to happen and that she could not prevent it. Her hands flew to her ears and a shudder ran through her. She heard herself shout, "Why don't you let me alone!"

She got up somehow, cheeks flaming, and fled, slamming the door, rushed blindly across the hall and up the stairs. Mr. Rochester would be waiting. Dear Mr. Rochester! She would run into his consoling arms.

But there was no Mr. Rochester. There never was. Only the bleak emptiness of her room and the tears that wracked her to no avail.

Hank was saying, "Why do you bully her so? If you'd leave her alone she might gain confidence."

"I don't pay Madam Paul to teach her confidence," Ida retorted. "I pay her to teach Nancy the piano." She turned her attention to her son. "And if it comes to social graces, you might make more effort. You're supposed to be able to sing, but I don't ever hear you. Why don't you and your sister practice a few duets? I don't know what you do all the time at Harvard, pretending to learn a lot of nonsense that won't get you anywhere in the world."

"The purpose of Harvard, Mother, is precisely to meet chaps who may prove useful. Charlie Hammond's father happens to be the president of the Westlake Insurance Company. He takes care of men like Jay Gould. I suppose you've heard of him."

"If you know the sons of those kind of people," Ida snapped, "why don't you bring them home?"

"I don't fancy they want to come all the way to Arcadia just to hear me and Nancy sing 'O, for the Wings of a Dove.'" He cut the argument short. "Well, I've some reading to get through—Gibbon's *Decline and Fall*. Quite spicy stuff." He bowed mockingly to his mother and then to his father.

Henry, besieged behind the paper, was rereading the Lost and Found ads. "A bracelet of sentimental value lost somewhere between Vine and Maple about six P.M. last Thursday." He grunted at the closing door.

They were alone. The gulf of their alienation gaped between them.

Henry slowly and methodically folded the paper and stood up. He took off his glasses, folded them, placed them in their case, and neatly slipped them into his inside pocket.

"I think I'll go to the club," he said in his colorless voice. "I have to see Joe Armitage about that second mortgage on his store."

"Why waste your time?" Ida snorted. "Joe Armitage can't do a thing for you. He'll never amount to anything."

"Well," Henry replied lamely, "he wants the bank to back him. It'll save time if I know the score."

Ida looked at him with contempt. "Why don't you just say you want to get out of the house, instead of making up such tame excuses?"

Henry drooped.

"Oh, get along! I don't care where you go."

The door closed behind him.

Deprived of anyone to dominate or denigrate, Ida felt the room around her become immense and hostile. She hated to be alone. Everything that threatened and

mocked her, that made her feel grotesque and unwanted and inadequate loomed up and confronted
her. She tugged the bellpull and waited impatiently,
tapping her foot on the fake Aubusson carpet.

At last Haddock drifted in. He could only see Ida as
a distant blur, but managed to preserve his dignity
at the angle of the Tower of Pisa. "Yes, Madam?"

"Have someone light the fire."

"At once, Madam," he said, exiting quickly.

Ida sat feeling angry until Milly came in with a
bundle of kindling, knelt before the grate and lit the
fire. Ida dismissed her with a nod.

Ida stared at the logs as the flames flickered at first,
then caught and spread, licking the thick logs,
turning them crimson. The memory she hated most in
her whole life leapt into her mind. She struggled
with it, but the fire hypnotized her, tormenting her
with the image of herself and Josiah sitting on the
wicker sofa. He was beside her on the porch with his
athlete's frame that never seemed to be decently covered by the clothes he wore. Josiah was too madden-
ingly handsome and he knew it. He mocked her with
his perfect white teeth and sensual smile. It was his
mouth that tempted and aggravated her the most, the
wide lips too knowledgeable of kissing, and those
strong, perfectly shaped hands that had caressed too
many girls far more desirable than she.

She had wanted him so badly, with such an aching
longing. But he just lounged there, challenging her
with his insolently half-closed blue eyes. Ida had
leaned forward, impelled by some foreign energy, and
touched his chest. The power of Josiah's body shot
through her fingers like an electric current. Suddenly,
as though propelled out of her uncouth, unwieldy self,
she had thrown herself on him and pressed her moist
mouth to his.

His hand was fondling her breast, probing under
her dress, reaching for her nipple. A shudder of desire passed through Ida. She had thrown herself back
and ripped open her bodice, and grasping his hand
had forced him to squeeze her. Ida wanted him to
crush her, to cause her pain. She wanted the madness

of love to erase the knowledge that she had always been rejected.

But Josiah had pushed her gently away. "We'd better watch it, Ida. We musn't go so far—not yet."

"Yes, now!" she had insisted. "I want it now."

He had kissed her formally on the lips and murmured, "No, Ida. Not yet."

Josiah had left her there, dazed, in an agony of frustration and embarrassment, with her torn dress and her heavy red hair fallen about her shoulders.

All night, Ida had tossed in her bed repeating, "Not yet. Not yet." She couldn't wait. She had to marry him. Josiah was her savior, her most passionate need, her release, her chance for life.

Next morning she had gone downtown to buy material for dresses. Ida wanted to transform herself; to shed her awkwardness, her plainness, her lack of poise and charm. She would have dresses made to beguile Josiah, to entice him beyond the point where he would be able to say "Not yet." He would call again that evening after work and she would force the issue. Somehow she would get him to propose and, once that was settled, they could make love with total abandon.

She had opened the door of the milliner's on Main Street and stood there—riveted. Josiah was draping a silk shawl around the shoulders of a whore, a pretty, pink-cheeked, golden-haired whore. The girl had on a dreadful vulgar hat with feathers. They were laughing; Josiah was laughing as he kissed her neck.

Ida couldn't move. An avalanche of horror buried her. It was the end of trying to be a woman, of trying to be desirable, of getting married. It was worse than an affront—a crime—against *her*, against what she was in her heart.

Somehow Ida had forced herself to walk away. She was stupefied by the knowledge that he cared nothing for her. She was nothing more than an *object* he had courted because of her father's money.

In this shock of wounded pride, this total debasement of her self-esteem, Ida had shut herself up in her room and refused to see Josiah. She refused for three successive days. Two weeks later she had announced that she would marry Henry Brewster, a traveling salesman of no account.

Staring into the fire, nineteen years later, she knew that those few moments on the porch with Josiah were all she had ever known of love. He had been lost to her forever out of stupid, vain defiance. The finality of her folly would torment Ida all her life. She was an ugly, bitter, unwanted woman whose ambition and wealth could never satisfy the hunger that Josiah had awakened.

She got up, filled with hatred and self-loathing. She locked the door, went to the bookshelves and found the hidden bottle of whiskey. Ida steadily filled a glass almost to the brim. She must blot that memory out. Only if she could never think of Josiah Eaton could she endure the empty charade that had become her life.

CHAPTER THREE

MR. HADDOCK WAS INDISPOSED the next morning. It was Milly who let Valeria in.

She was surprised by this elegant stranger and, not seeing a suitcase, thought Valeria had come to call.

"Good morning. I am Miss Lee."

"I'm afraid the Madam's poorly," Milly hesitated. "She's not receiving."

"I am Mrs. Brewster's new secretary," Valeria explained.

Milly gaped. "You? Why, I never—"

"Could someone bring up my bag?"

Milly was quite flustered. "Oh, sure. I'll do it. Or I'll get Keith. Please come in, Miss." She busied herself hauling in the tattered luggage and then straightened her cap, gulped and managed, "I'll show you to your room, Miss. It's next to Monsieur Emile. Oh dear!" She was by this time covered in confusion. "I do hope it'll be all right."

The house seemed weighted with an oppressive silence as though all the doors were purposely shut against each other, thought Valeria as she followed Milly to the third floor.

Here, abruptly, the furnishings were strictly Spartan. There was no carpet on the passage floor, no pictures on the walls. Milly led the way to the last door and opened it into a bare little room with blue wallpaper spotted with yellow stains. A narrow iron bed, a painted dresser and a wicker chair constituted the furnishings. There were no curtains at the window and the shade was broken.

"I'll get you a new shade, Miss." She turned apologetically. "It's not so grand."

Valeria thanked her. "It'll do."

"The madam said you was to see her right away." Milly wavered at the door. "She's having one of her spells." Valeria took off her gloves, the tricorne hat, smoothed her hair at the dusty mirror and turned to Milly. "Will you take me to her, please?"

As they went down the passage Milly pointed to the doors. "That's Monsieur Emile and that's Roberts, the footman, and that's Mr. Haddock, the butler." Heavy snores confirmed these introductions. "And that's Pinky and Mabel. They share, being sisters. And that's Bartlett, the coachman. He does odd jobs, too. And that's me. I'm Milly, Miss." She was genuinely shocked that Valeria had been relegated to this company. "I think there must be some mistake. I mean there's lots of empty rooms."

She led Valeria down to the floor below where the hall was once again thickly carpeted and where the dark walls were covered with a multitude of lithographs. When Milly cautiously knocked on Ida's door, a thick voice summoned.

"It's Miss Lee, Madam," Milly said, showing Valeria in.

Ida was lying in a disordered heap in a huge French bed that rose behind her to support a group of dubious angels enmeshed in ribbons. Yards of lace cascaded from the windows, festooned the dressing table, clung around the lamps, and the chaise longue. In the dim light that filtered through the half-drawn curtains, the room seemed a wilderness of cobwebs. On the dressing table lay Ida's diamonds, cast aside like glass. There was a smell of stale whiskey and female fleshiness. Valeria waited.

The bedclothes moved. Ida's voice, rasping from the effects of a night of drunkenness and vomiting, grated, "Come over here."

Valeria determinedly approached the bed. She was aware of the mass of Ida's hair spreading like seaweed across the pillows.

"I'm ill," the voice informed her. "One of my migraines." Ida turned and stared at her.

Valeria was struck by a reluctant pity for that bloated, ravaged face.

"There's people coming. Can you manage?"

"Yes, of course."

"Talk to Emile. There's twelve."

She rolled over, aware that Valeria knew precisely what was wrong, and despised her for it. She wanted to bury herself deep down beyond shame, beyond her own despair.

"Will you allow me to make you a tisane?" Valeria inquired gently. "I suffer from headaches and I find it helpful."

"What's that?" Ida demanded, speaking into the sheets.

"It's an old-fashioned herbal remedy. Please rest, Mrs. Brewster, and don't worry. I'll see to everything."

Ida turned her head to watch Valeria leave with her effortless grace of carriage. Patronizing bitch! Ida's head throbbed like a swelling boil and she lay back, staring at the ceiling. The abyss of the day gaped before her, a void till six when she would have to drag herself up, dress, put on her jewels, and go down to face them. Who was coming? The same second-rate climbers who envied her for her money, flattered and hung around her because they wanted favors from her father. She hated them all. Most of all, she hated Sam Garvey for being her father. He had made everything himself, wrested a fortune from the grasp of all those petty speculators and prospectors, outfoxed them and crushed those who had dared to cross him. How they feared and hated and respected him! She would make them respect her, too. She was "the" Mrs. Brewster. She'd make them grovel. She'd see to it that Joe Armitage never got that mortgage. Let him go bankrupt. She turned her throbbing head toward the window. Why was it that, having everything, nothing satisfied her? Why wasn't it enough?

She was aware as she lay there of the useless bulk of her body. Why hadn't she been born slim and graceful and elegant life— She would block any schemes that adventuress might be hatching. Arcadia was Garvey territory. Miss Lee would soon find out.

Ida thought of Mrs. Haverfield, secure in a social enclave that was beyond question. Somehow she must get her to the house and then Mrs. Haverfield would be forced to ask her back to Fairlawn. She needed to find out about the something extra people of quality had, that meant style and ease and being accepted and doing everything the right way. Later on when she went to Paris . . .

There were men you could hire there, men built like Josiah, who came in for a night and made love to you. It was as low as any woman could sink, but she would welcome that particular degradation.

Having extracted the tin of herbs from her suitcase to make the tisane, Valeria found her way downstairs, through a maze of passages to the kitchen. It was a large, low-ceilinged room with small, high windows running on a level with the base of the house.

Seated at an immaculately scrubbed table, Monsieur Emile, a trim Parisian with a waxed goatee, was consoling himself with a French newspaper, already two months old. What appeared to be a blond wig on the floor beside him seemed to spring to life at the approach of a stranger, and barked shrilly. Monsieur Emile scooped up the tiny Pomeranian in an attempt to quiet it. *"Tais-toi, DArtagnan!"* He was as surprised at Valeria's appearance as though suddenly confronted with a French patisserie on Main Street, filled with *babas au rhum, milles feuilles* and *gâteaux royaux,* all confections unknown in this savage town.

"Monsieur Emile? I am Mrs Brewster's new secretary. She asked me to go over the plans for tonight's dinner, if you won't think it an intrusion," Valeria said in French. "Mrs. Brewster is not feeling well today."

Monsieur Emile's astonishment turned to joy. To meet a lady was sufficiently unexpected, but to meet one who spoke French was quite unprecedented. He bowed crisply and drew up a second chair.

"May I ask how Mademoiselle speaks such excellent French?"

"My mother was French," Valeria explained.

"We spoke it at home. But mine is no longer good. One loses the habit."

"*Tout au contraire,* Mademoiselle, you speak with the greatest charm."

These amenities exchanged, Monsieur Emile offered Valeria a cup of coffee which she accepted. They embarked with the hushed respect of clerics debating some delicate question of theology on that most subtle and complex of all problems: the devising of a menu. It required sensibility and tact, a feeling for the aesthetic balance between taste, color and substance. It was a work of civilized art to which Monsieur Emile, parched for gastronomic appreciation, responded with alacrity. His imagination, stifled by thick soups and roasts, mountains of boiled potatoes, acres of string beans, and that most horrid of anticlimaxes, the boiled pudding, revived, took wing and soared. Enchanting vistas of *Ortolans Feuilletés, Truite à l'Impératrice, Cervelles Du Barry à l'Estragon,* bloomed like rare flowers in a border overgrown with weeds. Who in this barbarous country understood the care and patience and concern required to create a *Sauce Armoricaine?* The cream must be coaxed to thicken slightly, the stock kept absolutely clear, even a hint too much of Courvoisier could vulgarize the whole effect. And the tincture must be no pinker than the blush of a ripe peach. Monsieur Emile sighed.

"*Inutile,* Mademoiselle. There are no lobsters here." In Paris those sublime creatures awaited their destiny in tanks of illuminated sea water to be selected by connoisseurs escorting beautiful women in *grandes toilettes.* "It is a pleasure to discuss such matters, but one has to admit it is a wasted effort. The palates of the Garveys are not awakened. For them food is nourishment. They eat, but do not dine. The art of haute cuisine—" he shrugged expressively, "Mademoiselle, do not bestir yourself. We give them the tomato soup, the boiled fish, the roast of pork, the potato mash." His voice ebbed to a note of doom. "The apple pie."

"Might it not be possible all the same," Valeria suggested, "to compromise? After all, you have a mission,

Monsieur Emile. You are a messenger of the gods bearing promises of joy. You must educate them as one educates children. First they must read and write and then, little by little, they will arrive at Racine and Molière."

They laughed. Monsieur Emile bowed gallantly, "Command me, Mademoiselle."

"Might I suggest a *Petite Marmite, sole Véronique* with *pommes nouvelles,* perhaps *entrecôtes minutes* with *Sauce Béarnaise?"*

Monsieur Emile nodded, "Yes, the first lesson. For the children." Leaning forward he confided a fact almost too dreadful to speak aloud. "Do you know, Mademoiselle, that Madame wishes to emulate the English who, distinguished mariners though they may be, *du point de vue de la cuisine,* are somewhat primitive. She wishes," he whispered this most sinister of accusations, "to end every dinner *with scrambled eggs!"*

At last, the menu settled and the tisane brewed, they shook hands. Henceforth they would be allies. A ray of hope lit Monsieur Emile's solitary confinement. In honor of the occasion he presented D'Artagnan with a cube of sugar dipped in coffee. *"Voilà, ta bonne bouche!"* he said tenderly, caressing the tiny dog.

As Valeria crossed the hall, it struck her that there was something extremely odd about the running of this household. None of the servants were in evidence. Mr. Haddock was presumably still recovering from the excesses of the previous night, the maids had vanished and where were Roberts and the coachman? The house had succumbed to a heavy and reproachful silence. As she went upstairs she heard someone picking out a popular tune on the piano. A youthful tenor attempted a few notes and broke off, as though discouraged.

There was no answer when she knocked on Ida's door. She went in cautiously. Ida was asleep, breathing heavily with her mouth wide open. A rank odor hung over the bed.

Valeria put down the cup on the bedside table.

Turning to go, she noticed Ida's diamonds strewn among the silver toilet articles. Lying on the floor near the flounced skirt of the dressing table was a ring of three large Brazilian diamonds in a gold setting. Retrieving it, she put it down beside a necklace and some other rings, but in doing so Valeria caught sight of herself in the beveled mirror.

A little too tall and a bit too thin, Tante Elize had always said. Her wide forehead was outlined by smooth, glossy, dark hair pulled back in a chignon. The style revealed small, shapely ears and the curve of Valeria's graceful throat; both features Tante had conceded were good ones. Other people had commented that Valeria's pale shoulders and enviable waist looked well in an evening gown. She modestly accepted these attributes, secretly wishing intelligence and sensitivity might be considered more important.

Gazing directly at her reflection, Valeria was surprised by the new disdain in the carriage of her head and the cold, calculating expression in her large veiled eyes. Was she already becoming so hard, so filled with resentment and distaste? She mustn't let them see what she thought of them. She must learn to be more guarded. What was it she really wanted? Money? To escape, to buttress herself against an alien world, to buy protection? Could she really sell herself for that? Were these her only weapons, a cool brain, a distinctive presence? Little did these parvenus know how often she had grubbed for food with her brother in the remains of the vegetable gardens at Whitebriars, sold trinkets to buy meat, and burned furniture for fuel. Yes, enough money to forget those years. She must be harder, more determined. She was prospecting among the vulgar rich just as men fought and struggled in the wilderness to strike a vein of gold. She must stop looking back, stop thinking of times before the war that now seemed so innocent; she must never allow herself to think of the dank evening when she had driven down the arbored avenue for the last time, so blinded by tears that she couldn't see the azaleas and the giant magnolias that had scented the whole house each summer. Money to seal away the past. Could she find it here?

"What are you doing?" the harsh voice accused her.

Valeria spun around to find that Ida had struggled up in bed and was glaring at her. Ida's heavy hair had fallen about her shoulders making her look like an over-painted, crudely carved figurehead.

"I was wondering if I should put away these jewels."

"That's not your business. Have you seen Monsieur Emile?"

"Yes, Mrs. Brewster, the dinner is all arranged." She was surprised at how even and remote her voice sounded.

"Then send Kitty with a convenience." Ida noticed the tisane. "What's that?"

"Please try it. I'm sure it will ease your headache."

Ida glowered at the cup. "See if the parlor's tidy and ask Emile about the wine."

Watching her secretary leave, she realized she would very soon grow to hate this self-satisfied intriguer. Staring at her diamonds! Had she stolen anything? Ida forced Valeria from her mind and began to wonder if it were true that Mrs. Haverfield's daughter had fits during which she became violent and attacked the servants. And there were rumors about Ford Hollister. Tabitha Grey, her father's housekeeper and her chief source of gossip, had heard that he—or someone very like him—had been seen going into a house near the railroad depot with a youth notorious for servicing the stockyard hands. Southern scum! That would ruin anyone if it were known. If only she could be sure!

Valeria corralled the three maids after luncheon. They had taken advantage of the hiatus in their daily round to go out shopping.

Milly was only too happy to carry out Valeria's orders. The two sisters, Pinky and Mabel, red-cheeked, giggling girls, were sent to dust the parlor, while Milly was assigned to cleaning the dining room silver. Roberts, the footman, who had won three dollars from the coachman after five hours of serious play, was dispatched to the only florist in town to buy all the yellow roses available and any white flowers in season. A gangling youth named Keith, who had a loose mouth and acne, and who lurked around the basement, polished Mr. Brewster's boots and ran errands for Monsieur Emile, was equipped with rags and instructed to polish the brass on the front door, the staircase banisters and the tilting suit of armor in the hall.

When Valeria went into the parlor to see how the maids were doing, it was clear that Ida Brewster knew very little about housekeeping. Although Pinky and Mabel were laboriously circling the objects on the mantelpiece, their dusters were having no effect.

"That's not the way," Valeria told them. "You must take everything off. I'll show you."

She lifted up the fans, the vases, a French clock with a diamond-encrusted pendulum that didn't work, and laid them carefully on the sofa.

"Oh, Miss," Pinky exclaimed in wonder, "I wouldn't dare!"

The mantelpiece was filthy, pockmarked with stains and circles. But with Valeria's guidance the marble was duly washed and shined.

Valeria replaced the bric-a-brac, but in more aesthetic order.

"Now," she said, "take all those objects off the stands and wipe them carefully."

Pinky trembled. "Mrs. Brewster don't like no one to touch her treasures."

"I'll take the responsibility," Valeria offered. She proceeded to remove the cushions from the sofa and the chairs, shake and plump them. When she shook out the velvet curtains a veil of dust filled the air. "These plants," she further instructed, "all have to be washed with a damp rag."

"Wash the plants?" both girls questioned, astonished.

"Of course. They can't breathe when they're so dirty."

"Breathe?" Their mouths dropped open.

"Come along now," Valeria encouraged them. "We have a lot to do."

The sisters proceeded willingly. It was a new experience not to be shouted at and muddled by conflicting orders. Their new instructress worked alongside them, swiftly and with precision; dusting, replacing, rearranging. Neither of the maids could understand just where Valeria fitted in and eyed her surreptitiously. They hated Mrs. Brewster; but she was their mistress. Miss Lee was obviously a lady. Why was she doing their kind of work?

While they were thus occupied Hank strolled in. He was flushed from riding, handsome in his tan breeches and forest green corduroy jacket. He had come in search of Milly but stopped when he caught sight of Valeria as she rearranged the pampas grass in one of the Capo di Monte urns.

She looked around and smiled. "You must be Mrs. Brewster's son," she said amiably.

Hank, taken aback by what struck him as one of the most beautiful women he'd ever seen, nodded, tongue-tied.

"I am Valeria Lee, your mother's temporary secretary."

"Well," Hank gulped, "I never expected anyone like you."

"I'm sorry if I'm a disappointment."

"Oh no—I mean—I thought secretaries were all—"

"Old?"

"Well, sort of. I would never have thought—" He looked at her in open amazement. What a figure! What grace! Those eyes the color of dark jade!

Valeria was amused by Hank's obvious admiration. His bright good looks and bearing, a distinct cut above his mother's, charmed her. Apparently money was already having its effect on the younger generation. Hank had the makings of a gentleman, a social stamp that Ida, too close to the crude beginnings, would never have.

Hank lingered, striking his riding crop against his thigh, watching Valeria as she moved about the room. He clumsily handed her things and helped her put the chairs back in place. She thanked him with smiling glances that seemed to cause his solar plexus to dip unexpectedly.

He noted the elegant slope of her shoulders, the appealing nape of her neck where the hair, brushed up so carefully left a curl which he longed to kiss. Of course one would never consider Miss Lee's other attributes. He avoided looking at her bust. He forbade himself to consider her extremities. Miss Lee inspired chivalry. By the time she had reinstated the bud vases, replaced the sickly ballerinas and shepherdess figurines on the étagères, he was willing to ride in any tourney with her kerchief tied to his lance. Miss Lee was the realization of a dream. Charlie Hammond might know about the seamier side of the demi-monde, but what could he possibly know about a reincarnated goddess who could turn a man into a knight at arms, albeit tongue-tied and helpless, ready like Sir Walter Raleigh to lay his cloak across any puddle or preferably to offer himself as a doormat to be blissfully trampled by those swift, decisive feet? Idealism obliterated his instincts. He followed Valeria about the room finding it impossible not to look back, to admire and wonder.

She considered him; her head tilted slightly back, her eyelids half lowered, with a quizzical and ironic expression. "Will you help me tidy the study?" she asked.

He was ready to fall at her feet.

Valeria's conquest of Hank Brewster was compounded when he discovered that she could play the piano. He summoned up the courage to ask her to accompany him.

"I really shouldn't. There's so much to do."

"Please." He blushed crimson at his temerity, then glanced away.

He handed her the sheet music, and Valeria found she could not resist the temptation of running her fingers across the keys. She started the accompaniment lightly, easily. He was enchanted by her delicate hands as they barely caressed the keys. His throat had gone dry and, although he knew the song by heart, he choked on the opening note, sputtered and broke off.

"Sorry." He covered his acute embarrassment by coughing into his handkerchief.

"Never mind. Let's try again."

She recommenced, and this time with great effort he managed a wobbly E flat. But something had gone wrong with his voice. It sounded breathy and hoarse. After the first verse, maddened by his wretched performance, he stopped. "It's no good. I can't today. I don't really sing well anyway. I've not been trained."

"You should be," Valeria said. "You have a charming voice."

He was leaning dangerously close to her across the piano lid. She looked so lovely and serene sitting there with those mysterious, clouded eyes raised to his. Was she laughing at him? Probably. He didn't care. "Please, Miss Lee, play something for me. I'd much rather hear you than my own ridiculous efforts."

"Something short, then. I still have the dining room to do."

She played Schumann's "Prophet Bird" with the ease of a professional. He was really very good looking, Valeria decided, not unlike the boys who came to Whitebriars before the war, with the same bashful ardor and innocence. She thought of it as the charm of dawning manhood. She glanced at him, smiling. What a pity he wasn't a few years older! She was twenty-five. Too old, by far, for him.

At the finish of the piece she stood up. "There! Now I must get back to work."

He was thunderstruck by her. Hank was certain this was love at first sight. *It had actually happened to him!* For a moment they stood there, entranced, on some remote planet, outside of time. So close! He felt as though he was drowning in her eyes.

She stepped aside and, with a slight inclination of her head, moved past him. He watched her, spellbound, as one follows a white bird skimming away across the sea.

Ida Brewster's native brawn enabled her to throw off the effects of her drinking bouts. When she sailed into the parlor to greet her guests that evening, she was as formidable as ever; encased in an unbecoming shade of orange, encrusted with topaz and gold like an Indian idol, a lorgnette glinting ominously on her bosom. Her smile announced the opening of hostilities.

The condemned for the night's dinner consisted of three businessmen, two of whom had served prison sentences for embezzlement, a third who had made a successful career of fraud, a lawyer expert in the machinations of illegality, and the pastor of the Methodist Church who had amassed a fortune, albeit carefully concealed, by grabbing up land leases from the widows of the recently departed.

Their wives were a variety of parodies of the current mode; beribboned, feathered, shawled and laced, their hair curled in remarkable contortions. Ida knew the matrons were dedicated to concealing their suspect pasts under various masks of gentility and pretension. One woman, wearing purple taffeta, was the daughter of a San Francisco madam, while another of a saloon keeper. A third, with a dyed black pompadour and, at her scrawny neck a jet choker, had married a dry goods salesman who had died under questionable circumstances. This same matron later had married a prospector who had died after striking it rich; and she was now married to the lawyer, Nathanial Shawcross, who was grimly determined to outlast her.

All that these good Western folk had in common was an abiding hunger to be wealthy, jealousy for those with more than themselves and contempt for those who were not rich at all.

The men were already discussing business, their shrewd eyes hard with avarice, pinpointing hints that might give them an advantage in future dealings. Their wives were readying themselves for the main business of the evening, the shredding of reputations; eager to pronounce the forthcoming ruin of their friends, to impart scandals concerning daughters in the family way, sons with drinking problems, husbands likely to be caught for illegal practices, and wives whose past activities made them unacceptable in polite society of which they considered themselves fine examples. Pillars of salt, they supported the temple of the newly rich who had risen to The Heights from the Sodom and Gomorrah of the town below. They were as respectable as black crepe at a funeral, and completely narrow-minded.

What more suitable excuse for gathering at Ida Brewster's than the enhancement of the Methodist Church with a new stained glass window!

Ida observed that Roberts was handing around glasses of champagne on a silver tray. She glanced at Henry, wilting in his evening suit. Could this conceivably have been his idea? Then it occurred to her that it must be an innovation introduced by Valeria Lee. Such effrontery would certainly not go unchallenged!

"Champagne!" exclaimed Mrs. Almira Bancroft. "Why, how elegant! I declare, Mrs. Brewster, you always lead the fashion in social niceties."

"It makes a change," Ida said loftily, "from the usual fare."

But the room, she now saw, was changed in some subtle way. There were white flowers on a stand before the vermilion curtains and fresh rosebuds in the vases on the mantel. Could it be possible that stuck-up interloper had been rearranging her priceless art? Miss Lee would be castigated and dismissed.

Unexpectedly, she caught Josiah's name. The men were talking of his decision to run for governor. He was using *The Courier* which he owned to stir up popular opinion on his behalf.

"It's unwise to give the men notions of higher pay," Mr. Bancroft was saying. "No use endangering profits. Fourteen dollars a week is as much as anyone is worth. More than that becomes a threat to commerce."

"Besides," Mr. Shawcross added, "Josiah would be cutting his own throat. If your father," he directed to Ida, "was forced to pay his men more money, Josiah Eaton would be forced to do the same. They would

increase operating costs for both. Sam depends on
Eaton's railroad to ship his stock back east and
Eaton—"

"My father," Ida cut in sharply, "doesn't depend on
anyone. He could buy up Josiah Eaton any time he
has a mind to."

"No doubt, no doubt," Mr. Shawcross conceded.
"All the same it would set a precedent. Once you start
monkeying around with wages there's no guarantee
where you'll end. Anyone who aims to get rich can
strike out on his own. Hard work and imagination and
a nose for a good deal—that's the keystone of free
enterprise. There's an opening for anyone in this
country who's got the guts."

These sentiments expressed the vigorous individual-
ism which was these predators' greatest pride. Their
methods of amassing fortunes were incidental to their
greed. They felt in their blood the pulse of enterprise,
as insistent as the throb of the great machines that
resounded through the factories and the mills, echoed
down the mines, or roared along the great arteries of
the railroads. It was a time of dizzying expansion
when an untamed continent promised limitless rewards
for the sharp-witted, the ruthless and the corrupt. As
Genghis Khan had swept down with his wild armies
through the dust storms of Mongolia to level a continent and build an empire on its ruins, so these no
less rapacious pioneers were determined to conquer
the world's greatest empire of hard cash.

"Strikes me," Mr. Bancroft offered his opinion
through a cloud of cigar smoke, "that Josiah's cutting
off his nose to spite his face. Setting himself up as the
champion of the underdog may get him votes, but his
money comes mainly from the railroad. Loading and
unloading freight and keeping the tracks in order ain't
done by campaign promises."

It was a cause of bitter irritation to Ida that, whenever people got together on The Heights, the conversation invariably turned to Josiah. His financial activities
were a source of constant conjecture in business circles. No one exactly knew from what source his money

came. The branch line of which he was managing
director, that linked Arcadia to the Great Western
Pacific and thus to Chicago, did not appear to produce
outstanding profits. This led to the assumption that
there must be considerable manipulation of the books.
The railway primarily served the Garvey steel mills
which constituted the town's sole industry. There was
something ambiguous here also, for it was well known
that Eaton and Garvey were deadly enemies while,
at the same time, they were, too a large extent, financially dependent on each other. The railroad
seemed to be the only thing they had declared a truce
about.

The Courier, which Eaton had bought when it was
no more than a four-page rag, had been built up under
his ownership into a paper equal in quality to many
in the major cities. But it still had a circulation of less
than fifteen thousand. How was it, then, that Josiah
grew steadily wealthier and was, by Arcadia's standards, now very rich indeed?

To the women on The Heights he was a maddening,
indeed an unforgivable, enigma. He had never married, carrying on numerous affairs with women—often
quite openly. Josiah gave lavish entertainments on his
estate out in the country near the Haverfields, but always for people from other places: railroad magnates,
copper kings or financiers like the great Thaddeus
Brownlow, president of Brownlow's Bank. Ida found it
infuriating that the Haverfields accepted him, invited
him to their soirées, and went to his. With his resplendent good looks and expansive manner, dressed by the
best London tailors, he was an asset to any gathering
because of his ease in society. He had a magnetism
that both men and women found difficult to resist.
Scandalized whispers circulated on The Heights concerning his sexual excesses such as reports of orgies
arranged for visiting millionaires with women of the
lowest character imported from Chicago. It was
claimed that once he had ridden around naked on his
grounds with a carriage full of screaming harlots. As
McGiver, the chief of police, was an old crony whose

gambling debts Eaton was rumored to have paid, nothing was ever done against Josiah.

These lurid tales, endlessly embellished by shrewish matrons, would have ruined anyone less formidably established. They seemed not to affect Josiah's career at all. He was also noted for his contributions to charities, officiating at local ceremonies, and making speeches at civic dinners that were praised for their caustic wit. Josiah was known for being extremely shrewd in business, brazenly taking advantage of anyone less adept at chicanery. As this was the accepted standard of the day, on that score his competitors and critics reluctantly accorded him respect.

"In my opinion Josiah Eaton is quite unsuitable to be the governor of this or any state. I shall do everything in my power to oppose his nomination," said Mrs. Almira Bancroft.

"Decidedly one must expect some moral standards from public servants," Mrs. Craddock echoed. "A man with his reputation," a censorious sniff curled her lip like a dog's scenting the effluvia of a lamppost, "should be barred from holding office."

Ida thrust her capacious bosom forward like a barricade. "I don't care to discuss Mr. Eaton in this house."

An asp of malice uncurled in the breast of Mrs. Shawcross. The old scandal of Sam Garvey's involvement in the shooting of Josiah Eaton's father had been endlessly debated. What was less well known was that young Josiah had plotted his revenge by trying to marry fat, clumsy, unattractive Ida. "I can quite understand," Mrs. Shawcross said with a calculated edge to her voice, "why *you* should feel that way." She gave Ida a look as sharp as a pinprick. "And I must say *for reasons of my own*," the jet choker glittered dangerously, "I quite agree."

Mr. Haddock appeared at that moment, having navigated the wine-dark seas of the Brewster mansion and announced in honied tones, "Dinner is served, Ma'am."

Ida led the cortège into the dining room. She was outraged to discover that the alabaster fruits had been removed from the epergne. In their place was a perfectly arranged display of yellow roses.

CHAPTER FOUR

AFTER RECEIVING an unusual number of compliments on the elegance of her dinners, Ida decided to bide her time before discharging her social secretary. While she treated Valeria with ill-disguised hostility, Valeria deferred to her wishes with studied grace. Her politeness gnawed at Ida's confidence. Every alteration in the arrangement of the dinner table, in the sending out of invitations, or in the more salutary treatment of the servants, Ida took as a subtle reflection on her own shortcomings. It rankled her to admit that a paid employee could be her superior in taste and manners. She was uncomfortably aware that Valeria despised her and probably mocked her behind her back. Ida became grander, more overbearing, but nothing that she could say, no calculated slight or small indignity appeared to ruffle Valeria's marble self-control. As Josiah Eaton and Sam Garvey were forced to tolerate each other because of the railroad, so Ida Brewster gradually steeled herself to bear with Valeria because of a certain noticeable tone that she was adding to the house.

The servants were relieved to be under Valeria's orders. She trained them to perform their duties with greater efficiency and ease. Monsieur Emile's reawakened confidence in his culinary skills resulted in a series of fantastic dishes. Cakes rose like cathedrals, embellished with turrets of spun sugar and porticos glistening with crystallized fruits. He created in Valeria's honor a soufflé as light as a summer cloud.

Hank Brewster's life, however, had become a daily torment of anticipation and frustration. He spent hours before the mirror brushing and pomading his hair till he moved in an ozone of Bay Rhum. He would change his suits several times before venturing downstairs, tie and retie and fidget with his cravats to achieve just the right air of jaunty sophistication. Although he was well aware that he was a handsome fellow, he knew that mere good looks were not sufficient to captivate so rare, so superior a person as Miss Lee. He was far less confident about meeting her intellectual standards than about matching any physical expectations. Hank had never got more than a C-plus in any subject.

Daily, he would lurk in the parlor with the door open so that he could catch a glimpse of her crossing the hall while she was about her duties, or would dash after her with some absurd excuse to detain her. Then he would find himself blushing foolishly, offering his services should she happen to want to drive downtown or to the country. Well, he would explain, to buy flowers or vegetables perhaps, or simply to drive because it happened to be such a fine morning. She treated him with amused friendliness, but her attitude, he was painfully aware, was that of an older, more experienced woman toward a youth who had not yet become a man. He could devise no way of making her aware of *him*.

He daydreamed endlessly of what her reaction might have been if he had kissed her in that enchanted moment by the piano. Would she have rebuked him? Over and over he reenacted exactly what had happened, how close they had been to each other, and how inept his hesitation had been. He dramatized situations in which he dazzled her with puns and witticisms or awed her with insights into politics and art. He saw himself beside her—oh with what blissful clarity—driving down Fifth Avenue in New York in a shining new carriage, receiving envious greetings from gentlemen in gray top hats. Although he encountered her half a dozen times a day, and was acutely aware of her presence about the house, she seemed to grow ever more unattainable. Once he had sent Pinkey upstairs with a large bouquet of roses for

Valeria's bedroom and had waited on tenterhooks all afternoon for her response.

The next morning Valeria had thanked him warmly, offering him her hand. But it was no more than a gracious social gesture, and he despaired.

But Hank was not Valeria's only conquest. One day she knocked on Nancy's door, bent on seeing if the room had been properly cleaned and dusted. Instead she found Nancy, in one of her spells of dejection, crying on her bed.

Nancy looked up, her poor eyes red and swollen. Valeria felt an immediate sympathy for this unhappy and embattled girl. She sat on the side of the bed and asked what was the matter. At first Nancy was tongue-tied with embarrassment. How could one possibly explain to a total stranger the absolute hopelessness of one's existence? She had just finished Charlotte Brontë's *Villette.* She was willing to admit that people might live happily ever after in books, but circumstances were quite different in *her* life as Nancy Brewster, condemned forever to be imprisoned in The Heights in this *dreadful, unromantic* town where nothing ever happened. No Italian tenor, falsely wanted by the police, nor English lord, disguised as a poor gardener, was *ever* likely, indeed could *never* possibly appear. What hope was there? And, besides, she hated herself that day, hated the way she looked and the clothes she was forced to wear and was disgusted with her awful hair. These stupid ringlets that bobbed about and would never hang straight. Weren't they just the most *futile, agonizing,* things? Oh, she wished she had never been born! She couldn't see a single point to anything.

This incoherent confession was blurted out between gulps and sniffles and fits of crying while Valeria waited patiently. When at last Nancy could find no more despairing and disparaging things to say, Valeria suggested gently, "Suppose we make a start by doing your hair differently?"

Nancy sat up, aghast. "Oh, Mother would never agree. She likes it this way. She *insists.*"

"I think it's worth a try."

She sat Nancy down at her dressing table and slowly, carefully, started to brush out the offending ringlets.

"Life does seem impossible sometimes to all of us," she said consolingly. "I remember when the War started and we were left alone, my brother and my Aunt Elize and I, not knowing what each day would bring and never being able to sleep at night for thinking of what was coming. And, later on, when the worst *did* come and we lost everything . . . We were so poor, Nancy. We had nothing to eat. Everything we loved had to be sold—just to survive. I cried and cried because it all seemed hopeless. But no matter how bad things are, people have to go on, Nancy. The days unfold and events happen. Situations one never imagined.

"I thought that everything was over then, but I came North, and here I am doing your hair. Everyone has a destiny. We can't see it, but we have to trust in it. You have yours, Nancy; it's there inside you. You must have patience and let it develop and lead you into the future. It will—without any doubt, my dear."

She bent down and gently kissed the astonished girl on the cheek. Nancy's eyes had grown larger and larger as she stared at the beautiful pale image in the mirror. There was something so soothing in the way Valeria brushed out the horrid curls, something so deeply kind in her voice with its soft Georgia drawl. Oh yes, with a lifting of her heart she began to see that Miss Lee was straight out of a romantic novel. She *was* Jane Eyre who had been forced to earn her living as a governess, only far more mysterious and lovely.

"Please. Tell me about your home, Miss Lee," Nancy managed to ask.

As Valeria stroked out the curls and reset Nancy's hair in a simple, becoming way that seemed to change the whole contour of her face and brought out its fragile prettiness, she told her about Whitebriars; the tall rooms and the spiral staircase, the great chandelier with a thousand crystal prisms Papa had brought back from Paris, the gardens with the lilies and magnolias, and how Tante Elize put herbs under the rugs, between sheets of newspaper, to keep the moths out and scent the rooms with mint and lavender and sweet geranium.

When she had finished, Valeria said, "There! Isn't that better?"

Nancy looked at herself, incredulous at the transformation. She stared, unbelieving, at herself and then suddenly seized Valeria's hand and kissed it.

They were friends.

It was not long before Valeria discovered that Ida Brewster's pretensions to being Arcadia's social arbiter —which caused her to be strenuously engaged in a round of burdensome obligations—were largely the figment of Ida's need to be important, feared and respected. Apart from formal dinners and an occasional committee meeting, Ida had little to occupy her days. Now that Valeria was managing the house there was even less to do. In fact, Ida blundered about like a bull in a field, keeping a weather eye out for someone to criticize and humiliate. When she climbed into her barouche and descended upon Arcadia, ostensibly to attend a luncheon, she actually drove around for an hour or two, paid a few visits to local shops, ordered a lot of merchandise to be delivered, and lorded it over the tradesmen who wanted her patronage and were forced into the obsequious attention that satisfied her pride.

Many were the evenings when she sat, a self-appointed queen in the wasteland of the parlor while Henry, drooping in his corner, read and reread the want ads in *The Courier*.

News reached her through Mrs. Bancroft that Mrs. Haverfield had returned from Europe and was in residence at Fairlawn. Consequently, Ida decided to give an important affair in order to lure her rival into her social net. But what bait would have sufficient class and sophistication? She could bring an orchestra from Chicago, fill the house with ferns and carnations, and give a ball. Or perhaps a fête in the garden with lanterns and fireworks and buckets of champagne served inside a tent. She could invite the whole gang of crooks and hangers-on from The Heights to come in fancy dress. Her mind faltered between sides of beef, whole venison on spits, suckling pigs with pineapples in their mouths—or was it oranges? Suddenly Ida had an inspiration. She would offer Madame Patti a thousand dollars to entertain!

Common sense and insecurity warned her that such extravaganzas were not sufficiently *bon ton*. She grudgingly decided to consult Valeria.

To her surprise and chagrin, Valeria tactfully dissuaded her from such grandiose entertainments. "Might it not be more agreeable to give a small family dinner? Mrs. Haverfield has not had the pleasure yet of knowing you. With the Hollisters, Mr. Brewster and your son, that would be six."

"Six!" Ida exclaimed in shock. An alarming vision of half a dozen people marooned amidst the silver candlesticks, forced to make conversation across abysses of candied ginger, prompted her to rebuttal. "Never! I would never consider a dinner for less than twelve."

"That means three couples, then," Valeria said, unperturbed. She handed her an embossed address book.

Ida wavered. It appeared to her that the more guests there were milling about the less apparent their social shortcomings might seem. She reviewed her acquaintances and found them wanting.

"I could ask the McGraws. He's the President of the bank. Mr. Brewster's a partner there." The Craddocks—? They hardly qualified. The Shawcrosses? Not with his record. Almira Bancroft? Too pushy and overdressed.

"Might I suggest, Mrs. Brewster, that since your father is Arcadia's leading citizen—"

Ida gave her a scornful look. "My father has no interest in society," she said firmly. "He cares for nothing but business." With a shudder she thought of Sam Garvey expelling a jet of tobacco juice into a cuspidor, making his customary caustic remarks, and showing them all how little he thought of them. That would be the end of any future relations with Mrs.

Haverfield. Her father had only one thing to recommend him; he knew how to make money.

"Mr. Garvey," Ida concluded, "is quite out of the question. I could ask Madam Paul," she considered doubtfully. "She's French."

After an hour of uneasy deliberations the guests were selected, the invitations written. Valeria rose to go.

"I hope you have no objection, Mrs. Brewster, but I am going out this evening."

"Out?" Ida queried, amazed. "Out where?"

"It's my brother's birthday. Randolph has asked me to dine with him."

"Your brother?" Ida repeated as though social secretaries had no right to be encumbered with relatives. "I didn't know you had one."

"He came north before me. He's been here three months."

"Doing what?" Ida demanded. Really, the duplicity of which these Southerners were capable!

"He works for *The Courier*."

Ida sat bold upright and confronted her. *"The Courier?* Are you telling me he works for Josiah Eaton?"

"He's only a cub reporter."

A hot surge of anger rushed to Ida's brain. The full extent of the conspiracy hatched by Ford Hollister was immediately clear. Valeria had been planted in the house to report on all her doings to this brother who, in turn, would relay every detail to Josiah. It was part of Josiah's lifelong campaign to humiliate Ida and ruin her father. She had been used as a dupe and as a tool against Garvey.

Ida checked herself on the brink of an outburst because it suddenly occurred to her that Josiah was a close friend of the Haverfields and probably of Ford Hollister. Could it be possible that living so close, Hollister had been a party to those infamous debauches? Men with such depraved appetites usually drew together. If it were true that Hollister consorted with young men . . .

An idea, Machiavellian in its cunning, leapt into

Ida's mind. If she could ever prove there was some connection . . . A man of Josiah's unbridled sexuality might well have become satiated with women and experimented with obscene perversions. Was it conceivable that not only women were smuggled late at night into Josiah's house? The enormity, the totality, of the revenge that such a piece of information might place within her grasp thrilled and staggered her. At one blow she could utterly destroy Josiah, bury him in shame so deeply that no amount of influence or money could ever rehabilitate him. Didn't crimes against nature carry a life sentence? Men shot themselves . . .

She must put Tabitha to work.

"Your brother," she commented acidly, "had better find other employment. No decent man would be caught dead working for Josiah Eaton. He's a blot on the whole town."

She was grimly determined on one point. The day after the Haverfield dinner Valeria Lee would go.

To be with her brother was so great a joy, such a longed for relief, that Valeria's spirits rose as she hurried down the dismal street. The clapboard houses, shabby from enforced economies and worn by the ordeal of survival, hid their decrepitude behind drawn blinds. It was the subcontinent of poverty in which the majority of urban dwellers eked out their doomed endeavors—a limbo that struck dread in Valeria's heart. Every instinct in her rebelled against the threat that she might be dragged down to such a hopeless level. There must be, must be, must be some way out.

She ran up the steps and rang the bell. After some moments a jaundiced mask peered through the cautiously opened door.

"Mr. Lee, please? I'm his sister."

The mask receded. A miasma of cabbage and hamhocks pervaded the hallway, clinging like dry rot to the walls. She hurried upstairs to the front room. Just as Valeria reached it the door flew open.

"Come in, sugar cup!" Randolph hugged her tightly.

Oh, how she adored him! He was the embodiment of strength, of reassurance, of everything she still believed in and wanted life to be. She stood back to look at him, filling herself with the happiness only he could give. The pallor of the skin they had both inherited from their mother was striking in a man, set off by his wild black hair. He had once closely resembled the bust of young Brutus that had stood on the bookcase in Papa's study. Randolph was thinner now. There were two sharp lines beside the clever, ascetic mouth. But the classic features, which might have been cold in a man less vital, had a vividness and distinction that set him, in her mind, above all others. With him, her guarded heart, chilled by the horrors of the War, recaptured its youthful fervor. "You'll never let yourself fall in love," Ford had once twitted her. "You'll always be in love with Randy." Brushing back the wayward lock that strayed across his forehead, she would gladly have admitted that evening that Ford was right.

Ford rose to greet her. She kissed him warmly. "How good you came! But where's Althea?"

"Indisposed," he grimaced slightly. "She suffers from convenient migraines. They relieve her of the burden of going out."

"I'm sorry. I'd so looked forward to seeing her again!"

"Oddly enough you are the one person she has ever expressed any desire to see. I'll fetch you on your next day off. I suppose you're allowed one?"

"Supposedly twice a month. Otherwise I'm on duty and in the evenings I'm required to perform."

"How is your ogress?"

"Ogreish as ever."

"No likely prospects? No rough millionaire begging you to make an honest man of him?"

"After two weeks at the Brewsters'," Valeria confessed as she took off her coat and hat, "I'm doubtful if there's one civilized man in the whole of Arcadia. They are gross and ignorant and unmannerly and talk of nothing but money. Even Mr. Garvey's millions wouldn't compensate me for one of them."

"Hang on awhile." Randolph was reaching the critical point of extracting the cork from the champagne without an explosion. "I'll be earning enough soon. We'll get a place of our own and forget this abysmal town."

"Arcadia is only a stopgap," Ford reminded them. "Your ol' protector won't let his children languish in the sticks forever."

The two friends had arranged the table for this occasion with roses brought from Fairlawn and candles stuck in wine bottles. But it was not these festive gestures that warmed Valeria. They were together; the three who had braved and endured so much and depended on each other as survivors of a vanished world whose treasured memories they shared.

She held out a hand to both. Their love for each other was a never-to-be-broken pledge, whatever fate might bring.

While Randolph poured the champagne into tumblers borrowed from his landlady, Ford was unpacking a hamper of delicacies rifled from the Fairlawn kitchen; a terrine of foie gras, veal in aspic, and hothouse peaches.

"What a luxury, Ford!"

"An improvement on our usual fare in Atlanta, wouldn't you say?" There had been many occasions when they had been grateful for cheese and a hunk of sausage and stale bread.

They raised their glasses, but the gladness of this reunion was touched by an older sorrow. Each wanted to make a toast, but no words, however gallant, seemed appropriate. They smiled and drank in silence.

Valeria was watching them, fondly questioning and reappraising, hardly listening to what Randolph was saying. How many times, in how many dismal rooms, had they sat like this while Randolph harangued them on the iniquities of the War—the criminal greed and barbarity of the North! His hatred of the North had become his passion, then his cause. He had poured his rebellious youth, his idealism and pain and anger, into firebrand schemes for rousing his dispirited countrymen, resurrecting their broken pride and their tarnished honor. Unify and rebuild the South! But the ruins had swiftly engulfed them as they had everyone, spreading like the waters of a swollen river. The restraining banks had subsided, and the river had swept away homes and landmarks and then the whole structure of their lives. She had feared for Randolph then. The anger had turned to bitterness. He drank to forget defeat, hurled anathemas at his compatriots, at their weakness and obstinate refusal to face facts. He lacerated himself for his own failure and futility and floundered, drowning, with the rest. She had maintained enough sanity from day to day to keep him from going under.

It had been Ford who had adapted best to the Aftermath. Shrewder and more realistic, he had discarded standards that had become anachronisms. He had seen survival was the one imperative. It was he who, by all sorts of borrowing and badgering, had produced the rent money and somehow procured the food. Whatever compromises and contrivances he had resorted to, Valeria could never forget that Ford's unwavering loyalty had saved them time and again.

Looking at Ford now, Valeria realized he had hardened. Money had given him a casual contempt for a society whose pretensions he had quickly recognized as no more than a facade. With the few well polished weapons at his disposal—charm and wit and a civilized instinct for insincerity—he had challenged the entrenched caste system of Knickerbocker society and found it a surprisingly easy conquest. After four months in New York he had married Althea Haverfield and had thereby bought his freedom from the peonage of being poor.

Valeria had been jealous of Ford in her girlhood because of his possessive devotion to her brother. Even as a child, he had followed Randolph like a pet dog; eager to do his bidding, hungry for the least word or gesture of approval. She had come to realize, as time passed, that this idealized obsession was, in some way, the focus of Ford's life. Caring for no one else, accepting her because she was Randolph's sister, he had manipulated and exploited anyone who could provide whatever was needed to sustain and protect his hero. It had been through Ford's efforts with

Josiah Eaton that Randolph had been hired on *The Courier*. The Haverfields spent part of each summer at Fairlawn and thus Randy would be close at hand. There had always been something in the intensity of that attachment which Valeria had never quite understood.

Ford's marriage, she had seen in the few days she had spent at Fairlawn, was not without its penalties and pitfalls. There had been something strange, even a little sinister, in the way that spacious mansion revolved around Althea. Ford's watchful attentions had given Valeria the impression that his wife was being guarded like a royal prisoner or an overprotected invalid. Althea was odd, high-strung, and spoiled, intelligent in a way that made one uncomfortable; and she lacked any feminine allure. Her prominent bulging eyes had a constant look of apprehension as though some shameful secret about herself might be revealed at any moment.

Valeria felt sorry for Althea. She was vulnerable and ungainly and so pathetically eager for both Ford's approval and for the establishment of friendly relations with other people. It was not hard to see why Mrs. Haverfield had welcomed a penniless Southerner as a son-in-law. Most men would have shied away.

Would Randolph, she wondered, ever marry? He was probably too cerebral, too self-involved, too driven by his passion for righting wrongs that never could be corrected. She thought of the girls who had swooned over him at home. Yet, after a few meetings, they had bored him with their simpering chatter and hesitant advances. How could one talk to these gingerbreads who knew nothing but needlework and tinkering on the piano? He came closer probably to loving her than anyone. Randolph accepted Ford because of his loyalty; he was Randolph's only friend.

But then one knew so little about the people one supposedly knew the best. Perhaps he had had secret loves as she had had her brief affair with the Yankee captain when Randy lay wounded and delirious at Whitebriars. Despite everything, though, Valeria had never thought of that episode in terms of love. It had been the need for refuge in a time of peril. It remained in her memory as a blurred experience like something from a half-remembered novel.

"You're not listening, Val!" Randolph accused her. "Don't you see that this may be the turning point for me?"

"I am listening, darling. Please go on."

"This town," he was explaining, "is divided into two armed camps—Sam Garvey's and Josiah Eaton's. Their feud goes back to a time before Josiah was even born. His father and Garvey were partners; Eaton the geologist, Garvey the prospector. It was Eaton who discovered the iron ore deposit, Garvey who set up the company. Once the money was rolling in, Garvey took the precaution of having his partner murdered. Old Eaton was shot one night, ostensibly over a poker game. The assassin was sprung from the local jail by some unknown accomplice, only to be killed himself a year later in San Francisco under highly suspicious circumstances.

"After he was relieved of his closest friend, the man to whom he owed everything, Garvey appropriated the entire enterprise. Of course, he took care to see that Eaton's family got next to nothing. They lived in genteel poverty, until Garvey, as a sop to public opinion, had Master Eaton educated and later gave him employment as an accountant at the mills—half of which, incidentally, should have been his by right. But Josiah was no pacifist. He had no intention of turning the other cheek. He quit the works and vanished into the hinterland. In a surprisingly short time, he returned with cash lining his pockets. No doubt he'd enjoyed his full share of double dealings. They have long memories, these Western elephants. Little by little Josiah gained control of the railroad Garvey depends upon. Next, Josiah bought up *The Courier;* the only weapon with which local opinion in Arcadia can be swayed. He's quite a formidable foe, is our Josiah.

"And now, my friends, Act Three of this drama of greed. It seems, I have been cast for a minor role in it. At last Mr. Eaton is marshaling his forces. He's preparing for his invasion of the Garvey empire. He

plans to run for governor. Under what better aegis
than as champion of the people! Eaton plans to agitate
for higher wages and shorter hours. That should guarantee him votes and rile Garvey beyond endurance.
He's conceived the notion of running a series of articles
on sweatshop labor conditions; depicting in lurid
terms how these supposedly free citizens are forced to
earn their daily crust of bread. But all this, you understand, is only a preliminary maneuver before the
major offensive. And I, my dear Val, have been appointed cloak and dagger investigator. My duties are
to riffle through the archives, dig around the grave-
yards, bribe and corrupt the lowly to disgorge any
scrap of scandal, any hint of malfeasance or corrup-
tion, crime or immorality—though on that score the
old tyrant seems about as promiscuous as a cigar
store Indian."

"I can't imagine," Ford objected, "that stirring up
the workmen will help Josiah get elected. Every busi-
nessman will band against him. Besides, Randy, he
and Garvey depend on the railroad. They're forced to
parlay."

"Methinks Mr. Eaton has other plans for the
railroad. I suspect he is not averse to letting it deteri-
orate; even, perchance, to liquidating. That may be his
last trump card. Eaton is not without other resources;
mysterious and multiple interests in a variety of
concerns. And meanwhile, resplendent and persuasive, he'll woo the populace who will take him at face
value and cheer him on to the governor's mansion."

"But, Randy, once you've gathered all this information, is he going to allow you to write the articles?"
Valeria asked.

"That, my sweet sister, is my intention even if it is
not yet his."

Valeria laughed, unconvinced by her brother's
analysis of this involved vendetta. "I fancy I shouldn't
mention a word of this to Mrs. Brewster."

"You're absolutely right, my darling." Randolph
laughed as he sliced his veal. "Mrs. Brewster, who
bought her husband—an erstwhile salesman of ladies'
underwear—a partnership in the local bank, and re-

ceives from her accursed sire an annual stipend of a hundred thousand. By the way, did you know that Mrs. Garvey died of malnutrition and went unmourned, it seems, by the founding father or by winsome Ida? One could scarcely come across a less devoted family."

Ford had been watching Randolph, rather than listening, beguiled by the old attraction which vitalized him like an electric current. This was the same irresistible Randy of the early days.

"But what Garvey and Eaton do not realize," Randolph continued, while refilling their glasses with champagne, "is that they may both be hoist by the same petard. The working men will undoubtedly support the Eaton ticket. But to win concessions they will have to agitate, backed, of course, by the Knights of Labor and countless other ill-paid drones. Hopefully, a strike will result. What may have started as a feud between two ruthless opportunists—if I am permitted so to qualify my respected employer—could well explode into a major confrontation. Even newspapers are run by hand." He raised his glass. "I drink to the forthcoming revolution. A pox on Northern industrialists and all their tools and vassals!"

They talked and argued until midnight, avoiding, as though by mutual consent, all reference to the past.

At last Ford peered through the curtains. "The carriage awaits, Mademoiselle."

Valeria was loath to leave. This shabby little room had become home for an evening. Her heart sank as she put on her hat and coat.

"When shall I see you, Randy?"

"Soon, honey pie."

She kissed him, clinging to him for an extra moment. But he was no longer with them. Instead Randolph was already soaring away on the wings of impassioned, impossible ideas.

Ford also kissed him. It was an intimacy that Randolph tolerated from their childhood.

While they were making their way down the malodorous stairs, Ford asked, "How will you get in at this hour?"

"My friend Monsieur Emile is waiting up for me."

It was a humid, pitch black night. As they crossed the dirt sidewalk to Ford's carriage, Valeria hesitated. "Do you think it's safe for Randy, digging up all these scandals? If Garvey finds out he might retaliate."

"I'll have a talk with Eaton. He's coming to the house next week," Ford reassured her, opening the carriage door. "Besides, it's only an interlude. I'll find something better for Randy when I get back from the East."

She climbed in and settled back, surprised that Ford made no move to follow her. Instead he placed the hamper on the seat beside Valeria and closed the door.

"Aren't you coming?"

"I'll walk awhile. I have things to think about."

"Walk! All the way to Fairlawn? It's miles away."

"You know I never sleep. I have plans to make— for all of us."

She knew that he was embarking on something connected with the hidden side of his life which she preferred not to inquire into. She leaned through the window and touched his arm. "Ford, please take care."

He kissed her hand, then signaled to the gillie and the carriage started.

Valeria sank back against the plush cushions, depressed and obscurely apprehensive. It seemed impossible that anything worthwhile could result from the unstable circumstances of their present lives.

Turning up the fur collar of his coat Ford walked at a steady pace. He was coldly determined to risk another meeting. Every time, the danger of being recognized became greater and thus more tantalizing.

He crossed Main Street with its stone bank and the marble courthouse standing stolidly between the one-story frame facades of the stores and hash houses. Here a few gas lamps cast a wan glow on the deserted sidewalk.

Turning up a narrow side street Ford passed a saloon that was still open. A tuneless ditty jangled from a dispirited piano. The inevitable drunk sprawled in a doorway. House after house, blacked out like a row of tombstones, hid the brief oblivion of Arcadia's sleepers.

His nerves tensed like a stalking cat's. He felt singularly alive, with a sharp and controlled alertness. Balancing on this tightrope, stretching across disaster, afforded him an excitement unequaled by any other.

He had left the business section and was entering the slums that struggled around the railroad depot. Occasional dim lights in the stockyards glimmered without casting shadows. Not even a train rumbled through the silence bearing with it the lonely message of the prairies.

Ford had reached a huddle of shacks without stoops or porches, match-stick dwellings held together by the habit of misfortune. Taking a coin from his pocket, he reached to a window, tapped twice, then twice again. Furtively, he looked up and down the street for anyone who might be following. The door opened a crack and Ford slipped inside.

He followed the silent figure into a small room, lit by a single light, turned low. The cubicle was stark in its poverty, but meticulously neat. A youth wearing a thin dressing gown opened a door into an adjoining room, barely large enough to accommodate a double bed.

Without glancing at his client, the boy took off his robe and laid it carefully across the foot of the bed. The youth got into bed and lay there waiting, while Ford undressed.

The white sheets were cold but clean. Ford had provided them on a previous visit. But as he clasped the body, it felt icy, as though the blood had been drained away. Ford thought suddenly of Randolph. They had been walking in the woods one evening— fireflies among the branches—something had almost happened. But that was the dream never to be realized, the lost fulfillment.

The youth turned over, according to routine, and Ford drew him against his groin.

"Can't you send me someone?" the youth asked in a hollow asthmatic voice. "I can't manage on what you give me."

"I'll give you money," Ford said as he eased into him. "You can move from here and get a better room."

"I'd like that," the youth said as Ford started the rhythmic movement. "Only I owe rent here and I'd need a suit. I don't like to show myself in town; I look so shabby."

"All right."

"I'd stick with you," the youth offered, "if you'd give me enough. I don't need much."

Ford thrust and withdrew and thrust again.

"We'll see."

ᏃᎩ Chapter Five ᏁᏙ

Sam Garvey marched up the steps of Ida's mansion and pulled the brass bell.

Among the trials of life at the Brewsters' none was more dreaded than the bi-monthly Sunday luncheons for which Sam Garvey pried himself loose from the old house near the mills and drove out to spend two hours castigating his family. He kept them on the rack, opened old scars, inflicted new wounds and generally lacerated their egos. It was the price they had to pay for depending on him for everything.

He was a rough old tyrant of seventy-odd, wiry and vigorous, with a squat, sinewy body and calloused hands. He always wore the same black suit, the same black hat, the same black boots. He had never been known to possess duplicates for any of these items. From his appearance and style of life no one would have guessed that, single-handed, he had built up one of the greatest empires in the Midwest. No one knew exactly how much he was worth. Some said a hundred million, some said more. He had no intentions of allowing anyone to know the extent of his fortune, nor would he have admitted that even he was not exactly sure. He carried the vast record of his enterprises, assets and investments in his head. By any account he was not only exorbitantly wealthy, but also one of the toughest and most disliked men in the Middle West. Power had isolated him from his fellows. He despised the majority of men as weaklings and incompetents, respecting only those who could equal him in rapacity and guile. And there were few.

Haddock opened the door. Steadying himself at the

sight of the old tycoon, he took Garvey's hat and ushered him ceremoniously into the parlor.

"Madam will be down shortly, sir," he announced with suitable deference. "May I bring you a whiskey and soda before luncheon?"

Sam grunted and went in.

Valeria had been putting the last touches to a bowl of coral-colored gladiola and turned to find herself confronted by a pair of sharp and very shrewd blue eyes.

"Good morning, Mr. Garvey."

"Who are you?"

"Mrs. Brewster's secretary. I hope you are well this morning."

Garvey scrutinized her. Women played no part in his scheme of things. He never dealt with them in business. But he recognized that this young woman differed in some way from the addle-pated creatures who occasionally crossed his path. She seemed unusually self-possessed and calm, no more impressed by him than by any of the other nonentities who gathered at Ida's house.

"Didn't know she had one," he remarked gruffly. "What does she need you for?"

"I help Mrs. Brewster with her social engagements," Valeria explained, not the least flustered.

"Well, if it keeps her busy!" He stalked over to his usual chair and repossessed it. Valeria was leaving. He noted the slim line of her back and her graceful walk, as though her feet hardly touched the floor.

"What's your name?" he demanded.

"Valeria Lee."

"You're Southern," he said, as though this were a demerit.

"Yes." Valeria surveyed him from the door.

"Most Southerners with any sense got out," he pronounced sentence. "The South won't recover for a hundred years."

The old man's calculated insolence prompted her to retort. "I'm sure that's a source of great satisfaction in the North."

"The South was bound to lose. You counted too long on slave labor." He was implacable in his lack of even rudimentary consideration, his absolute disregard for manners.

Valeria said sharply, raising her head so that the high-bridged nose equaled him in disdain, "Don't you?"

Sam Garvey was not used to being challenged, least of all by a woman. "I pay my men what they're worth, but I don't own them."

Stubborn pride refused to allow her to give in. "Poverty is a kind of ownership, isn't it?" she found herself saying. "Our slaves were part of our family. Are your men part of yours?"

Suddenly her heart was beating with an icy rage. There, facing her, was the enemy, the Northern Juggernaut that had ground her world to dust; he was infinitely more repugnant than Ida with all her silly pretensions.

"I know all about poverty," he said bluntly. "I worked for seventy cents a day, sometimes less, until I was thirty. I made what I have. No one thought I was part of their family."

"Not everyone has your capacities, Mr. Garvey." For greed and murder, she was tempted to add.

The old criminal's eyes narrowed. Her sarcasm pricked and then amused him.

"I hope Ida's paying you more than I got." He inquired slyly, "Does she think you're part of her family? Maybe you'd rather not be. I wouldn't blame you." He was laughing at her.

Valeria was flustered. He was evil personified, uncouth, uncivilized. There was no way of hitting out at him. Any blow vibrated back like metal against stone.

"You took everything from us," she flung at him. "But pride you didn't take."

He chuckled. "How much does pride put in your pocket, Miss Secretary?"

Garvey had made her appear ridiculous. Valeria quickly went out, too confused by anger even to slam the door.

Sam Garvey's silence was far more alarming to the Brewsters than his usual acerbity. He munched stolidly, his sharp eyes shifting among the silver. What cruel plan was he devising to decimate them all? Nancy, in abject terror, glued her eyes to her plate. Hank ate mechanically, not daring to glance at his grandfather. Henry had shrunk into himself. And Ida fingered her rings nervously.

They waited expectantly while he cleaned his plate with a piece of bread. Their immediate fates hung in the balance as he mopped up the gravy and transferred the bread to his mouth. Even the servants moved like robots. Mr. Haddock seemed to have turned to stone.

Sam Garvey filled his mouth with whiskey, swilled the food around and swallowed. He sucked his teeth, as though considering the right moment to launch his broadside.

Finally he sat back. He did not consider them. They did not exist for him that day. He turned the searchlight of his dreadful authority on Henry. "You heard any rumors about Josiah?"

Henry trembled like an insect impaled on a pin. "No, sir. I've not heard—" his voice faltered. "It says in *The Courier* . . ."

"I know what it says. What do people say when they come to do business at the bank?"

"He'll never be elected," Ida shot in, fiercely.

"Think not?" Sam Garvey looked at his daughter as though daring her to challenge him. "He's personable and rich. No worse than any other."

"You mean," Ida exclaimed, outraged, "that you don't *care?*"

"Politicians are all the same. You buy them when they're out of office, you buy them when they're in. Only Josiah don't need money, and he's ambitious."

"He's just trying to get at you with all this talk of higher wages."

"If the men think they can get more, let 'em try. Plenty of others to fill their place." He smiled. It was a grim recognition that he took Josiah Eaton seriously. "The bank owns stock in the railroad. "I want to know any rumors," he delivered his command to Henry who quailed. "Josiah plans ahead. I don't intend he should catch me napping."

Ida and Henry Brewster were well aware that the old tyrant had revealed nothing of his intentions. He was up to something, like a sly and malevolent spider slowly and steadily spinning a new web.

"Who's that girl from Georgia?" Sam asked unexpectedly.

Ida was startled, "Miss Lee?" She took a deep breath. Her bosom expanded like a bellows. "Mrs. Haverfield suggested that I should have a social secretary."

Her father's mouth twisted in a sardonic smile. "Yeah, I guess you need someone, Ida. Well—?"

"I'm trying her out. Her brother works for *The Courier*," she admitted. "I didn't know that when I hired her. She probably won't stay."

The old man spat accurately into a finger bowl. "No," he agreed, "I wouldn't be surprised if she don't stay."

Hank, enflamed with the desire to defend his idol, blurted out, "She's a superior person. A real lady." His face was crimson from the effort of asserting himself before his grandfather.

Thrilled by her brother's daring, Nancy managed to gasp, scarcely above a whisper, "I think she's wonderful."

The old man looked at them for the first time, as though mildly surprised that they possessed identities.

Very much put out by this impertinent defense of a paid employee, Ida glared at her children. "You know nothing about her."

"Seems like you don't know much about her yourself, Ida." Sam Garvey pushed back his chair and stood up.

The ordeal was over.

Unaccountably he sent for Valeria. Ida, to her indignation, was dismissed and the others voluntarily fled. Garvey sat waiting in a high-backed chair like an old inquisitor, wrapped in spiraling cigar smoke.

When Valeria entered she was determined not to let

him see that he had put her at a disadvantage on their first encounter. She stood stiffly, drawn to her full height. Sam understood why the children, used to the shoddiness of Ida's friends, admired her. She was worth playing with, worth taunting.

He kept her waiting. It was an old game that seldom failed to undermine his adversaries' confidence. The noxious fumes rose and twisted around him. He watched patiently for the first indication of insecurity. At last she inquired, "You wished to see me, sir?"

He put out his cigar, crushing with deliberateness the soggy butt into an ashtray.

"You got any money, Miss Lee?" he asked abruptly, intent on shocking her.

Valeria was momentarily taken aback.

"Well, have you?"

She tried not to be flustered by the unexpectedness of this attack. "I don't think that's any of your business, Mr. Garvey."

"Money is my business. I know about it. How it's made. You got any?"

Using all her willpower Valeria controlled the instinct to lash out at him. But it was useless to fight with this old monster, she saw suddenly. One could only match him in bluntness. That was all he was capable of understanding, perhaps the one thing he could respect. "No, I haven't."

"Not a cent?"

But, really he was outrageous! "I don't see that I have to discuss—" she began. She looked straight into those very bright small blue eyes and detected a gleam that was not altogether as wicked as she had thought everything about him must be. "I work because I have to."

He nodded. "I didn't ask what Ida pays you. I mean money of your own."

Her head high, the family nose as arrogant as it was capable of looking, she retorted, "When the War was over we were left with nothing. I fail to see why that should be any concern of yours."

"You think you'll get somewhere, running other

peoples' houses?" Miss Lee's defense of social superiority annoyed him.

"I don't plan to stay here forever," she snapped back.

"Where will you go without a cent?" he demanded. "You don't belong in this town. Nothing but ordinary, commercial folk live here. Not worth considering."

Valeria's finely arched eyebrows rose in surprise. "You think I'm different?"

"Don't you?" He gave his sardonic chuckle.

"What does it matter to you? You don't know me." She was baffled by his intentions. Why had he sent for her? Why was he asking her these questions?

"I'm seventy-three," he said impatiently. "I know something about people."

Valeria realized that Sam Garvey was more than just a machine for making money. Beneath his arbitrary crudeness, there was an individual core formed by his long, harsh struggle against a world untempered by social conventions. It was a society about which she had no knowledge.

"When you're in my position, Mr. Garvey, you don't have choices."

"Women like you are brought up to marry," he said frankly, as though inferring that to be married was all she was good for. "You want to settle for my foreman or a salesman like my daughter? Or maybe you'd prefer a man who owns a cigar store on Main Street? That's all you'll find here."

"I don't intend to sell myself to anyone," she countered hotly. "And I do not intend to discuss my future in this way."

He smiled craftily. "I could work." Sam held up his gnarled hands. "I could fight other men. I was smarter than they were though some would say more dishonest. You don't have that opportunity."

Before she could retaliate he got up. They were exactly the same height. Suddenly Valeria was no longer afraid of him. She was too astonished to be angry. He was outrageous, but in his own way, extraordinary. He had forced her to recognize in him his own brand of incongruous honesty.

"Get hold of some money, Miss Lee. Not less than five hundred. When you've got it, come and see me. I'll show you how to make money work. Then you'll have choices."

Garvey walked past her, as though he had already dismissed her and was about his usual business.

She was bewildered by this offer which seemed so totally out of keeping with everything she had supposed a man of this kind could be. "Why should it matter to you what becomes of me?" Valeria directed to his retreating back, half in defiance.

Pausing by the door without turning to look at her, he said, "I had a partner once. He knew more than I did. If he hadn't, I'd still be a penniless prospector." Then he stomped out into the hall.

Hank had driven himself into a state of nervous exhaustion in his pursuit of the unattainable. Although Valeria was always charming to him, she had never once indicated considering him as a serious suitor.

His male ego had been frayed by daily contact with her indifference. In desperation, he decided that the only way he could win a respite from this obsession was by possessing Milly.

He was lying naked under crisp sheets, waiting for her to bring up his shaving water.

When Milly knocked at last and came in with a copper kettle Hank pretended to be asleep.

She placed the pot in the wash basin and laid a towel across it. As she started to draw the curtains, Hank threw back the sheets. Milly blushed scarlet, and exclaimed, "Mister Hank, you cover yourself! That's shameful!"

As she made a dash for the door Hank sprang out of bed and pinioned her against the wall, almost winding her. His hand was up her skirts in an instant dragging at her knickers. Milly struggled, whinnying. "Don't, Mister Henry. Stop that! I'll scream!"

Her layers of aprons, skirts and petticoats were a jungle that kept getting in the way of his half-erect member. The cheap fabric of Milly's knickers tore and for a moment he felt her wirey brush. She tried to scream, choked, and flailing from side to side, managed to dig her knee into his groin.

Unexpectedly, they heard someone coming down the passage. For a moment they were arrested—panting, their faces close. Panic stricken, Hank thought of Valeria and stepped back as the footsteps drew nearer. In a flash of wild disorder, Milly was through the door.

He sank back on the bed, shaking and hot with shame.

Hank lay back with his hand over his eyes. Had that madness really happened? What a total mess he had made of it! Charlie Hammond would laugh himself sick at such ineptitude. Tears of anger and frustration pricked his eyes. He hated himself, hated Milly and, above all, hated Valeria for not giving him a chance.

What was the use of this emotion that uplifted and distracted him and constantly reminded him of his defects? Why couldn't he have waited and been content to visit the houses in New York with Charlie and enjoy himself with whores he didn't care about? Valeria had inflicted the hopeless desire in him to be finer and nobler than he was, a man of the world with all sorts of qualities that were far beyond him. He was just a mediocre youth. His good looks were no advantage without the character and intellect she looked for. She was right to despise him; he was nothing.

All that was left was to try to expel the futility of lusting after Milly, drain himself of this incessant daydreaming about Valeria. How else would he still this uncontrollable hunger in his heart?

Hank beat love out of himself, and loathing his body for responding, spent across his chest. It solved nothing. In the aftermath of dull depletion, he thought of Valeria at the piano and of those mysterious sea mist eyes, so disturbing in their shadowed depths, raised ironically to his.

When Hank came downstairs an hour later, he was filled with apprehension. Had Milly talked? Would there be some awful scene with his mother? Worse—

if Milly had told Valeria, she would never speak to him, never look at him again.

As he reached the hall Ida sailed out of the parlor, caparisoned for a sortie into town. Her head was flattened by a millstone of a hat with a raven crucified across the brim, and she was entangled in an unmanageable feather boa.

Hank thought, She looks like an old cart horse done up for a country fair.

"A fine time for you to come down. It's after ten."

"I didn't sleep last night."

"Mrs. Haverfield is coming to dinner a week from tomorrow," she announced proudly. "I shall expect you to attend. Are your evening clothes in order?"

"Except for pressing."

"I want you to look your best," she ordered and marched out.

What a great bullying bore she was! What a bore the whole place was! At least Milly hadn't blabbed.

Hank wandered listlessly into the study, went over to the piano and leaned across the lid. Suddenly the painful reality of his love for Valeria hit him with fresh impact. It was there, inescapably, a life within his own.

He had never felt so wretched and so alone.

Valeria was meanwhile in consultation with Monsieur Emile, making preparations for the great event that had galvanized the household since the morning. A *Guide Gastronomique* was open between them like a Bible at a wedding ceremony. Nancy, who now rarely left Valeria's side, was seated by her, gazing adoringly at her heroine.

Monsieur Emile was saying, "Since the husband of this lady was Ambassador to France, we shall devise a dinner of which even the great Escoffier would not be ashamed."

He was tremendously excited at the opportunity to demonstrate his skill. With rapid gestures he outlined a series of astounding dishes guaranteed to inspire raptures in any gourmet.

"Monsieur Emile," Valeria tried to temper his

enthusiasm, "we agreed to build the menu round the pheasants, omitting the usual meat entrée."

"We have agreed." Monsieur Emile returned to earth. "And preceding the pheasants will be *Truites de rivière à la genevoise.*"

"Can we be sure the trout will be absolutely fresh?"

"Assuredly. I will have them caught not later than the day before. When fish is fresh it is better for the sauce to be delicate and simple. Preceding the fish, Mademoiselle, the *Oeufs en gelée à l'Imperatrice Catherine.*"

"And the vegetables?"

"For the pheasant a *mousse aux marrons,* the newest of new peas and, naturally, *pommes soufflés.*"

"And for the fish?"

"*Céléri glacé au jus* and, unless you consider it excessive, perhaps a *croûte aux champignons.* As to that one must bear in mind that nothing must disturb the flavor of the trout."

"You may not approve, but I would be grateful if you would consider with the pheasant an English bread sauce."

Monsieur Emile received this suggestion with admirable self-control. But he was shaken. To include in a dinner entirely French an invention of that gastronomically insensitive race across the Channel—! Gallantry prevailed, however. "Anything you recommend, Mademoiselle."

"If you would allow me, I could make you a sample," Valeria offered. "Of course, the decision must be yours."

Monsieur Emile bowed to this compromise and suggested they discuss the wine selection.

The Brewsters' cellar was limited. Only the champagne was to be recommended and that was to be reserved for Monsieur Emile's crowning achievement, a *gâteau royal* surmounted by strawberries, surmounted by a swan in spun sugar, surmounted by *cygnets* in blanched *angélique,* surmounted by . . .

Valeria inquired what color scheme for the flower arrangements he would consider the most suitable. "Not yellow with eggs, I think," Monsieur Emile advised. "Red is too sudden. Blue, would you agree? Pale blue like a spring sky that will make the pheasants feel at home. Blue induces light pleasantries. It is *un peu coquette*." His eyes had a wistful look. He was thinking of the sky over the roofs of Paris, that dear canopy that promises romance and joy to couples embarking on adventures in *la haute cuisine*.

"I hope, Mademoiselle, this lady will understand that, deprived as I am of truffles, the sacred ingredient, I cannot achieve perfection." He picked up the Pomeranian and kissed it on the tip of his shining nose. "Ah, *mon cher* D'Artagnan, what you and I would not give for a white truffle!"

Valeria left him dreaming of the day when, having saved enough money in this backwater, he would return to his beloved city and open a restaurant for a discriminating clientele.

Happiness burst like a meteor into the self-condemned purgatory where Hank Brewster lived. Valeria had asked him to take her driving into the country in search of flowers. For once Ida made no objection. She was closeted with her dressmaker, beset by anxiety as to how many flounces, frills and ribbons should be added or subtracted from an elaborate gown of magenta satin which made her look like an overly lush bougainvillaea.

Hank was beside himself. He changed his suit three times, brushed his thick brown hair till it shone like metal, tugged and twisted his bow tie till it perched at his Adam's apple like a jaunty butterfly. An agony of hope possessed him.

As he burst out of his room he encountered Nancy, dressed for an outing and twirling a parasol.

"Where do you think you're going?" he demanded fiercely.

"Out driving with you and Miss Lee."

"Oh no, you ain't." He blocked her way. "I'm taking Miss Lee. You're staying here."

"She asked me!" Nancy protested in dismay.

"Go back to your room," he hissed. "I don't want you messing things up."

"Miss Lee invited me! I'm all dressed up."

He pinched his sister's arm, twisting the skin till she squeaked with pain. "Then get undressed. You're not coming." He gave her a shove. "Get back in there."

Nancy stood dejected, her mouth quivering. "You're a beast, Hank. I love her as much as you do."

"Don't be a cow, Nancy. You're not wanted."

He raced downstairs to find Valeria already waiting. She was all in white with a straw hat, encircled with a pale blue ribbon. The wide brim cast an enigmatic shadow across her green eyes. She was holding a tiny white sunshade with a silk fringe. He had never seen anything so lovely.

"Nancy begs to be excused," he gasped. "She has a headache."

"Oh, but she was looking forward—Are you sure?"

"I just talked to her." He hurried to open the ornate front door.

It occurred to Valeria that if she went driving unescorted with Hank Brewster it might lead to gossip. But his anxiety to be alone with her was so apparent and so touching that she gave in and went outside.

He was breathless with excitement as he handed her into the pony trap and sprang up on the seat beside her.

It was impossible not to be charmed by such eagerness. He was the epitome of youth and innocence and first love, a summer world Valeria had only briefly known.

It was a perfect day. The sky hung softly over the gardens that modified the ugliness of the mansions along Tremont Avenue. The crepe myrtles of pink and puce, the yellow green of willows, and the jade green of elms lent a riot of color to the backdrop of velvet lawns.

Valeria opened her parasol and leaned back, relaxing in the pleasure of giving happiness to this young man who stared proudly ahead, not venturing to look at her.

"Do you know the way to the Hotchkiss farm?" she asked.

"Oh sure. It's out along the creek, past the Eaton place."

They smiled at each other. The pure delight of being with her, perfectly alone, of knowing that he had a whole afternoon in her company, banished Hank's nervousness. He had no desire to touch her, nor even to speak. It was sufficient that she was there.

"You'll be going back to college soon. Shall you like that?" she inquired.

"Not now." The thought of college, of being separated from her, was impossible to contemplate.

"What are you studying?"

"Oh, not much. I'm supposed to go into banking, but I'm not sure."

"Doesn't that appeal to you?"

He shook his head.

"What would you like to do?"

"I'd like to travel, I guess." Hank had a blissful vision of being on some great vessel with billowing sails, traveling with her to Europe, to the Far East, or to other places he had only dimly heard of.

"Yes, that would be lovely," she agreed.

Hank was encouraged by her interest. "What are you aiming for, Miss Lee? You aren't going to stay on at our place, are you?"

"I don't know yet."

"You shouldn't," he dared to suggest. "It's not anywhere good enough for you."

Her gaze wandered along the lawns. She couldn't think of the future that afternoon. The problems of her life eased away like the dappled shadows that drifted over them. She sighed placidly.

"I imagine in the end one must simply let things happen."

"You belong in New York," he said stoutly, "or Boston, maybe. This place isn't even on the map. It wouldn't exist except for the mills."

"So your grandfather said." She thought of the old steel king in that high-backed chair, holding up his hands to show her how hard he had worked all his life. "Why are you all so afraid of him?"

Hank had never discussed his grandfather. He was

a dreadful *fact*, like God. Nor had Hank ever considered him as a person like his mother or Nancy or his friends at school. He was the omnipotent force that ruled their lives, the source of all their money and their position in Arcadia. He could never remember talking to him except for the few words exchanged at those Sunday luncheons they all dreaded. Of course men at college had heard of him because he was a magnate in a class with Carnegie and Gould and Morgan. That gave one prestige and allowed one to run up bills. People knew that one day Hank Brewster would be rich. It suddenly occurred to him that being Sam Garvey's grandson was an important weapon he had never used to any great advantage. It might even influence Valeria. It made up for a great deal he didn't have himself.

"I hardly know him," Hank admitted. "He comes to the house twice a month. He's only interested in business. He runs everything himself."

"Have you never known him?" she asked, surprised.

He shook his handsome head. "He settled money on us when we were born, shares in Garvey's Steel, so it isn't really ours." Hank shrugged. "He is not a man anyone knows. I don't think he sees anyone. I guess he never has."

The mystery of Sam Garvey's life intrigued Valeria. The sudden baffling interest he had shown in her, the peremptory, half-caustic offer he had made, seemed more bizarre than ever. "It's a pity," she said. "He must be an extraordinary man."

They had come to the end of Tremont Aveue and were jogging along between stretches of open country and small farms. Soon fences and trees announced the Haverfield estate. Valeria glanced up the driveway of sycamores at the pink brick mansion, faced with gray stone. On the terrace the stone urns were filled with scarlet flowers.

It would have been nice to call on Ford and Althea, to savor, for a few moments, the atmosphere of that leisured, more civilized world. But she knew that day was something special for Hank. She did not want to spoil it for him and, besides, she would see the Hollisters at the party the following night.

"The Haverfields were here before any of us," Hank was saying. "They own a mass of land in this state; more than a million acres. The whole of Arcadia and the steel works, all of this, belonged to them."

These immense fortunes and the limitless power they gave were staggering. It was incredible how soon the resources of this country had passed into so few hands. Her own modest desire for enough to secure independence had no relationship to money in the way Sam Garvey spoke of it. She could not grasp its value beyond what it could buy in terms of ease and security and freedom from worry. Beyond that it became a commodity of its own, complex and undefined. Valeria wondered what she would do if she possessed Garvey's millions. What would it mean to know that she could buy up Arcadia, put thousands out of work, transform the landscape? But these were recognizable power games. Napoleon and Alexander had used money, as they had used human life, to feed ambition. It was the abstract aspect of money that escaped her. What satisfaction could it give Sam Garvey to know that he was worth a hundred million?

"That's Eaton's place," Hank pointed out. Massive iron gates and a flagstone wall protected a property surrounding an ornate and sprawling mansion of no particular style.

"He's not married, is he? What would a man alone need with a house that big?"

"He entertains a lot." Hank could not tell her any of the tales he had heard about Josiah Eaton's frolics.

"Is he as rich as your grandfather?" Valeria inquired, brushing aside a few stray locks of ebony hair from her eyes.

"Oh no. But he's rich. No one quite knows how much he's worth or how he made it. He's a clever man, I guess."

They ambled on. A little way down the road, Hank turned off onto a dirt track between fruit orchards. They came to a farmhouse surrounded by vegetable patches and clumps of flowers.

There was a slow, somnolent enchantment about this farm where human beings lived at the service of growing things.

Bent double in an enclosure of scarlet runner beans was a woman in a faded cotton dress and a denim bonnet.

"Mrs. Hotchkiss is the sister of my granddad's housekeeper, Tabitha," Hank told her as he drew up. He tied the reins and came around to help Valeria down.

It was a true country spot. One could almost feel the sap pulsing through the stalks and leaves and the swelling of pods and rinds. Things grew here; refulgent in their season.

Mrs. Hotchkiss straightened up and shaded her eyes. Who was this queen-like creature advancing along the path with the handsome young man, so dapper in his summer outfit?

"Good afternoon, Mrs. Hotchkiss. I've come on behalf of Mrs. Brewster. This is her son, Hank. She wondered if you would allow us to buy some flowers?"

Mrs. Hotchkiss bobbed a curtsey. "You may indeed, Ma'am," she said in a sing-song voice. "Take whatever you please. Shall I get you a bas-ket?"

"We're looking for blue flowers to decorate a dining table."

"Blue, is it? There are forget-me-nots by the million along the creek, if they would suit you. And the delphiniums." She indicated a clump of tall blue stems just coming into bloom.

"You have such a beautiful place here," Valeria complimented the smiling woman.

"We have good soil, Ma'am. They come up splendid year after year. Please help yourself, will you?"

Without waiting for their response, Mrs. Hotchkiss fetched a wide wicker basket from the tool shed and handed it to Hank.

Mrs. Hotchkiss watched them as they wandered off toward the creek. What a handsome couple now! So Mrs. Brewster's son had found a wife, had he? Such a gracious lady!

Behind the house, where chickens clucked and

scratched about the grass, the land dipped down to a stream. Along the banks were patches of forget-me-nots peeping among ferns, moss, and a few late-blooming flags. Dragonflies darted across the water and two geese bestirred themselves and waddled off, twitching their tails. The silence embraced small sounds.

Valeria stood gazing at the rippling water, her face reflecting a new joy. Was it possible that such peace could still exist in the world?

He stood beside her, so filled with love that he felt he was dissolving into the green, soft air.

They started to gather forget-me-nots, moving back and forth along the bank, returning to place the bunches of tiny flowers in the basket. He watched her stooping to feel among the moist leaves for the stalks. Valeria had taken off her hat and a strand of dark hair had drifted loose. She seemed no more than eighteen.

When he rejoined her and they had placed their offerings in the basket, they paused for a moment in contentment. It seemed the most natural thing in the world to tell her how he felt.

"Miss Lee, I guess you have realized it by this time, so there's no point in holding back. I've loved you from the first day I saw you. It's not an ordinary thing."

He had spoken with such simple dignity that she could not put him off with the usual coy disclaimer.

"You're sweet, Hank. But you must not say such things to me."

"I never thought I could feel this way. I love you more than anything in the world."

Valeria saw in his face the strength and poetry of his early manhood. He was ready to give her anything, to be anything she desired.

They were caught up by his emotion in a closed stillness more compelling than that moment when they had stood so close by the piano.

"I am much older," Valeria said softly. "And besides, you know nothing about me."

"I'm twenty next month. I think I know all about you I need to know."

How could she possibly explain that she was so much more mature, not merely in age, but in experience, and that she could never feel with the spontaneity and freshness of his nineteen summers? Her youth was already over. That dawning vision had been torn from her by tragedy and loss and the grim realities of war.

Valeria was surprised that there were tears welling in her eyes as she bent down to pick up the flowers. She realized that what she had thought of as a youthful infatuation had become a painful reality to him.

"I want to marry you, Miss Lee—if you think you could consider me."

She looked up at him in amazement. Marry this boy who could never be more to her than a younger brother?

"Hank, you must not," she cautioned gently. "It is not possible."

"Why not? I can leave Harvard. I'll ask my grandfather to release my money." He saw her again on the deck of some great sailing ship with the salt spray blowing through her loose hair. "We could travel. I could show you the whole world, Miss Lee."

It was all so absurd and touching and for a moment she loved and pitied him.

He mistook her emotion for compliance and put his arms around her. And suddenly Valeria felt the need to be loved and protected, to escape into some dream of happy foolishness and ease. He was good and kind and simple. Did it matter that he was so naive and knew nothing whatever of the world?

Reluctantly, she disengaged herself.

"Please—" he insisted, "Will you think of it?"

She touched his arm and said in an attempt to end it, "Dear Hank, yes, I will think of it."

She handed him the basket and moved away to pick up her hat with its blue ribbon from where she had left it on the grass.

CHAPTER SIX

ON THE EVENING of the Haverfield dinner Ida was
in paroxysms of apprehension over the magenta gown.
There were too many frills across her bosom and an
adipose flounce at the rear stuck out like a buttress.
More importantly, there was nowhere to pin her diamonds. She tugged and twisted, but the dress refused
to accommodate her demands. It appeared to have
taken a dislike to her. Ida was enraged. After so much
preparation, the main focus of her appearance was
determined to be unsatisfactory. In despair she sent
for Valeria.

In the kitchen Monsieur Emile was putting the final
touches to his masterpiece, the *gâteau royal*. The atmosphere was electric. The maids had been banished.
The Pomeranian dog avidly watched the great artist,
waiting for a single false move by his master so he
could ruin the entire effect.

Hank had taken an hour to dress. He had examined
himself at every stage in the long pier glass. First, he
looked at himself after his bath, turning sideways to
make sure that not the slightest untoward bulge
marred the flatness of his bare abdomen, flexing and
unflexing his pectorals; then repeating the actions in
his snow-white drawers; then in his vest, shirt, and
perfectly creased black trousers. His heart was singing. She had not refused him. She was considering his
proposal. He must present the flawless image of a
consort fitting for a queen.

In the dining room Valeria and Nancy were com-
pleting the table decoration. The epergne was filled
with white roses encircled by forget-me-nots. Strands
of maiden hair fern, entwined with tiny knots of blue

flowers, strayed the length of the *point de Venise* cloth. Cut glass bowls of roses and forget-me-nots nested between the candlesticks. A single blue scabius floated in each of the fingerbowls. And by the window were Chinese vases filled with delphiniums. It was as though the summer sky had strayed into the room and changed its complexion.

"It's lovely!" Nancy exclaimed. "And when the candles are lit—!"

Before Nancy could finish, Milly bobbed in. She was more flushed than ever since her wrestling match with Mister Hank. She couldn't seem to remember what she was doing, dropped things and was forever crying in corners. "Mrs. Brewster wants you," she said to Valeria. "She's having fits."

Valeria found poor Ida angrily confronting herself in a mirror.

"I just don't know what's wrong with this dress," she said as though the dress itself had been guilty of some misdemeanor. "I can't get it to feel *right*."

Valeria saw at a glance that this particular dress was a lost cause. "May I speak frankly, Mrs. Brewster?"

"Well, say what you think, but I can't change it," Ida said defiantly. "I've got to wear it now. I had it specially made."

"It is not the dress, but the color," Valeria said with a solemn tone. "You have beautiful hair." It was not too great an exaggeration. Ida's Titian hair was her best feature. "That particular shade of red does not do you justice."

Ida glared, torn between outrage and disaster. "I won't change it," she barked. "Can't you *do* something?"

"May I look in your closet?"

"Oh, I can't start changing." Ida was suddenly close to tears. She waved an arm like a general ordering a retreat. "Well, look!"

Among the least gaudy of the evening gowns in Ida's wardrobe was a celadon green velvet. She brought it out. "This would be perfect."

"I haven't worn that for a year. And I never liked it. It's too plain."

"Please, do me a favor, Mrs. Brewster. Try it on. If you decide against it, you can always wear the magenta."

"Change? Now? It's almost six."

"I will help you. There's plenty of time."

Ida allowed herself to be unhooked and dismantled. The awful thought occurred to her that Valeria was purposely trying to make her look ridiculous in order to ruin her chances with Mrs. Haverfield. Why was she allowing this scheming creature to interfere? But, as she stepped into the green garment Ida experienced a sense of relief. It might be simple, but it came from New York. It made her feel more normal.

"I don't say I'll wear it," she said grudgingly.

"It's beautiful, Mrs. Brewster. You couldn't be better suited."

Ida surveyed herself. At least there was room for all her diamonds.

"Will you allow me to make another suggestion?" Valeria asked.

Mollified, Ida nodded. Valeria selected from the open jewelcase a diamond spray of flowers with wired petals that shivered slightly when moved. She pinned it to the center of Ida's bun of heavily coiled hair.

"And the pearls—may I?"

Ida was suddenly too exhausted to battle any more. She allowed herself to be decked out by her secretary. With the double rope of pearls and her large lavallière of diamonds, she looked quite imposing.

"Shoes?"

Ida pointed to a closet.

Valeria rummaged and found a pair of Nile green slippers with diamond heels. Ida kicked off her red satin slippers and, propping herself on Valeria's shoulder, wiggled her square feet into them.

"Do you have—perhaps a stole? Something diaphanous?"

Ida was not sure what the word meant, but it sounded vaguely sophisticated. She remembered that there had been some sort of scarf that had come with

the dress. She had never worn it. "I don't know—
maybe in there."

In a drawer filled with unused Paris-made gloves
still in their boxes, feather trimmings and shawls,
Valeria found a stole of green tulle embroidered with
pale flowers. She draped it over Ida's shoulders. The
effect softened her massive head. Looking at herself,
Ida detected some vestige of lost femininity and for
a moment the hard core around her heart softened.
"I'll admit, it does look better."

Feeling calm again, she turned to Valeria. "You may
borrow something for the evening." She indicated her
jewel case. "I'll send Milly up when the ladies leave
the table. You can play then. Not loud. Something
that won't interfere with the conversation."

Ida rose to greet her guest of honor. She advanced
with measured steps, extending her arm in what she
thought was a grand gesture. As Mrs. Haverfield was
quite small, she had to reach up to shake the bejeweled
hand.

"Charmed, I'm sure," Ida proffered a smile. "It *has*
been so long."

Mrs. Haverfield was slightly startled by this formidable figure and not knowing to what lapse of time
her hostess was referring, murmured, "Yes, hasn't it?"

Millicent Haverfield was a lady of watery distinction.
She had undefined manners and features. She was
dressed in gray silk with a train and also wore a
gauze stole that drifted about her like a cobweb. She
had a general air of having mislaid something. But she
was gracious and soft-spoken and often forgot whom
she was speaking to.

Breaking through the awkward introductions was
the entrance of Althea Hollister who was leaning on
Ford's arm. She was striking, if for no other reason
than she was obviously well bred. Althea was wearing
a jet-colored satin gown from Worth accented by a
necklace of blood red garnets. The dark colors heightened her staring eyes, which betrayed uncertainty and
apprehension. Anyone more perceptive than Mrs.

Brewster would have realized the young woman was consumed with fear.

Ida did not notice, however. "Mr. Hollister, good evening. I'm so charmed to meet your wife," she announced, giving Althea a critical going over.

Althea froze in mid-step. Who was this dreadful woman dominating the group?

"Good evening, Mrs. Brewster. So nice to see you," Ford greeted, noting at a glance the improvements that Valeria had effected in the room.

"I am sure you know everyone," Ida made a rapid round of introductions. "Do be seated." She waved an arm.

As Althea sat down, slightly stunned by this encounter, she exclaimed with inappropriate candor, "Poor Valeria!"

"Don't talk so loud," Ford cautioned, smiling at the assembly.

"I thought she was your friend," Althea responded, adjusting a fold of her skirt. She inquired in a loud whisper, "Who *are* all these people?"

"Be quiet and drink your champagne," Ford hissed in her ear.

Ida had meanwhile forced Mrs. Haverfield to a sofa and planted herself firmly beside the woman she envied.

"What seasonable weather we are having for this time of year," she pronounced as she beckoned to Haddock.

Mrs. Haverfield was not sure whether she had heard seasonable or unseasonable and murmured politely as she took a glass of champagne. "Yes, isn't it!"

"And how are your roses?" Ida boomed.

"They have been very plentiful this year," Mrs. Haverfield said timidly, beginning to feel ambushed by this Amazon.

"I hope to see them," Ida said, administering a verbal nudge.

The thought of Mrs. Brewster marching among her rosebeds presented an alarming picture to Mrs. Haverfield, but she managed to escape behind a vague, "Oh yes—"

"I am also fond of roses," Ida announced, making it plain that she too belonged to the hierarchy of horticultural connoisseurs.

"Indeed?" her victim asked politely.

"Are yours French? So many are, I believe!"

It had never occurred to Mrs. Haverfield to consider the nationality of her roses. She ventured, "I suppose —occasionally."

"The French are great exponents," Ida bared her teeth. "I am not at all sure that roses were not first thought of in that country." She glared across the room at Henry who was beginning to fade into a corner.

Suddenly Althea Hollister exclaimed loudly, "How red this room is!" She looked to Ford for confirmation.

"Yes, dear, it *is* red," he said soothingly.

"I think red adds tone to a salon," Ida declared.

To her relief, conversation quickly broke out on all sides. The men, as usual, started talking of business. She overheard Mr. McGraw, the president of the local bank, speaking of an impending visit of the great financier, Thaddeus Brownlow, the American partner of the Rothschilds. Mr. Brownlow was making a western tour and there was much conjecture in business circles as to the purpose behind it. Was he planning a great new merger, a coalition of lesser railroads? Were there new mining interests or the floating of some colossal loan? Mr. Brownlow had, single-handed, financed the French government, currently in desperate straits at Tours, with a loan of two hundred and fifty million francs.

"I heard a rumor," McGraw turned to Mrs. Haverfield, "that Mr. Brownlow might be staying with you at Fairlawn."

"Yes," that lady modestly admitted. "We are expecting him."

"Mr. Brownlow is an *old* acquaintance of my father's," Ida remarked. "They have been much involved in business over the years. I must try and arrange a musicale."

"I'm afraid Mr. Brownlow is tone-deaf," Mrs.

Haverfield said, trying to avoid another evening with Mrs. Brewster for whom she had conceived, if not an aversion, a sort of dread.

"Mr. Brownlow," Althea Hollister said shrilly, "can't tell a French horn from a kettledrum. It's all noise to him." She gave a sudden strident laugh.

"He once stood at full attention, hand on heart, when a band started playing what he thought was the 'Stars and Stripes,'" Ford interposed. "It turned out to be 'Waltzing Matilda.'" A burst of laughter greeted this apocryphal tale.

"How unfortunate!" Ida said. "I find nothing so good for the nerves as a good cantata. I do hope," she tilted her bulk toward Mrs. Haverfield who shrank into her corner of the settee, "that you will add your name to my musical committee. We are planning quite a festive season. Madam Patti has promised to return. There will also be a quartet from Chicago and a Welsh choir and recitals of one kind and another."

"I should be pleased," Mrs. Haverfield stated, "but I am also a little deaf."

"I'm thinking of starting a fund to build an opera house," Ida persisted. "The present building is quite unsuitable. We must do our best to raise the level of culture here. It's a responsibility I take much to heart."

"Everyone in Atlanta used to play some instrument," Ford recalled. "It was pleasant to meet with friends of an evening and make music."

"My daughter plays the piano," Ida responded. "And my son Henry sings. I am not endowed in that direction. I lead the applause instead." She gave her smile.

"Schopenhauer played the flute," Althea remarked to no one in particular.

"Perhaps," Ida persisted graciously, "we can persuade him to perform here."

"I'm sure," Ford replied. "that he'd fit perfectly into the musical life of this town."

Fortunately for Ida, Haddock threw open the door at this juncture. On Valeria's tactful insistence he had resisted the temptation to deplete the Brewsters' supply of port that day.

"Dinner is served."

Ida rose, marshaling her guests forward.

There were exclamations of delight from the ladies at the sight of the dining table. In the soft glow of the candles it had a fairytale beauty. "How charming!" Mrs. Haverfield declared.

Hank remarked proudly, "That's Miss Lee. She has such wonderful taste."

"Miss Lee is my secretary," Ida explained. "She's quite clever at carrying out my ideas."

The dinner, indeed, was perfect. The *Ouefs en Gelée à L'Impératrice* lay like great bees in the palest of amber, softly embedded in a still life of vegetables that would have done credit to a Dutch master.

Ida's confidence soared. She felt that she had indisputably arrived as a hostess. Her voice grew louder and more grating as she enumerated the social obligations that kept her chained to Arcadia. "I so long to get away to Europe. I understand the London season has been more brilliant than usual this year."

"The season in Paris has been hilarious," Ford injected, "what with bombs bursting in the Tuileries and the supply of rats runnning low. They've been selling off the animals at the zoo, did you hear? *Entrecôte d'éléphant* is quite the *pièce de résistance* at Grand Véfour."

The irony of this statement was lost on Ida who was not *au courant* with events in France. "The poor Empress!" Mrs. Haverfield sighed to the man beside her whose name she could not recall. "Luckily she got out in time."

"I believe you are acquainted with the Empress," Ida's voice rang down the table.

Mrs. Haverfield started like a parishioner caught napping during a sermon. "Years ago when my husband was stationed there—," her voice trailed off.

"I am a great admirer of the Empress," Ida stated. "So much more colorful than Queen Victoria."

By the time the pheasant was being served, Hank who was seated next to Althea Hollister had become aware that there was something strange in the way she kept fingering the cutlery. Her fingers were straying to the knives as though drawn by a magnet.

"Do you do much riding when you're here?" he asked, trying to draw her into conversation.

Althea had begun to feel that the muscles inside her head were expanding, pressing against her skull. The room was blurring. The flickering of the candles merged as though she were seeing them through rain. Haddock hovered at her side with the tray of pheasant. With a shaking hand she picked up a knife. Althea looked pleadingly across the table, trying to catch Ford's eye. She felt suddenly frightened and alone.

"Don't you want any pheasant?" Hank asked.

Was Ford still there? She could hear his voice, but could no longer make out his face.

"Mrs. Hollister,"

Hank's voice brought Althea back to the meal. She shivered and dropped the blade. What was required of her?

"It's pheasant," Hank repeated.

She realized where she was and quickly helped herself. She picked up the knife again, gritting her teeth.

"I ride quite a lot," Hank went on bravely, "I'm at Harvard. They hunt up there."

Althea made a great effort to laugh. It was an ugly, discordant sound which at once attracted Ford's attention. He darted an anxious look toward his wife. "I don't like horses," she said loudly, "they frighten me . . ."

"Oh, then," Hank replied, defeated, "it's not much use."

Cries of wonder greeted the arrival of the *gâteau royal*. It was a thing of splendor, far exceeding Ida's expectations. As one of the servants carried it ceremoniously down the room, the spun sugar swan glittered and the *cygnets* quivered as though eager for flight. Over their nest arched a hoop ornamented with tiny forget-me-nots.

As Ida wielded a silver cake cutter, cries rose from all sides. "Don't hurt the swan! Save the little ones!" "Oh, what a pity!"

The evening was an unqualified success, Ida preened herself.

Only Hank's apprehension grew at the decidedly odd behavior of his dinner partner. With one hand Althea repeatedly clenched her napkin while, with the other, she fumbled with the remaining silver. She was bent slightly forward. Her mouth stretched as though in pain.

"Are you all right?" he asked softly.

Althea felt like her head was swelling. The glare of sterling blinded her. She looked wildly across the table, seeking help.

Ford was telling an elaborate anecdote about an eccentric aunt of his in Georgia. He interspersed this account, greeted by bursts of laughter, with "Remember, Althea?", "Wasn't that true, Althea?"

He was throwing life lines across the table which she wanted to grasp, but failed. She was sinking away beyond rescue. The pressure inside her head grew to an unbearable ache.

Althea was dimly aware that Ida had risen and was saying something about the ladies' leaving. Where could she go to? Where could she hide?

Hank was helping her up. He had realized her distress and said in her ear, "Can I get you something?"

Suddenly Ford was beside her and Althea finally found the support she needed. His voice sounded blessedly close. "I am going to break the tradition and join the ladies. I have heard all the impolite stories you gentlemen are likely to tell and I have no head for business."

Objects swam toward Althea and then receded as if she was crossing an immense space. Somewhere in the distance there was a babble of voices.

"We must stay to greet Valeria," Ford whispered. "We'll go right after."

"Where is she?" Althea asked vaguely. She remembered suddenly that Valeria was the sole reason she'd agreed to attend this dreadful party.

"She's to play now." Ford guided her firmly toward the parlor.

Mrs. Haverfield was not aware that her daughter

was having one of her "spells" and idly trailed out at Ida's side. She was surprised by the quality of the dinner considering the vulgarity of the hostess and rightly surmised that Valeria Lee had been responsible. Ford had spoken so highly of her and Althea had echoed his praises. It had been purely to please them that she had accepted this invitation.

Althea found herself on an overstuffed love seat in the parlor with Ford beside her. What was she doing there? Oh yes, they were waiting for Valeria of whom in the three days she had stayed at Fairlawn she had become so fond. Althea rarely took to people, but that cool and lovely creature, so distinguished and considerate, had charmed her. "Why is Valeria living here?" she asked too loudly.

Ford leaned over toward her. "She's working as Mrs. Brewster's secretary. Remember?"

"But why here?" She looked round the unfamiliar room. The walls seemed to be dripping blood. She felt herself falling and clung to Ford's arm. At that moment the door opened and a tall apparition in gray came in.

Ford rose at once and went to her. He said quickly in a low voice, "Thank God, you came. What an ordeal! Please come and greet Althea."

As Valeria approached, Althea suddenly held out her arms like a drowning person reaching for a raft. She clasped Valeria's hand in both of hers. "What are you doing here?" she asked in deep concern. "You must come back with us. Ford, I want her to come back with us. Valeria can't stay here."

Taken aback by this intensity, Valeria bent forward and said gently, "Dear Althea, I promise to come and see you the first chance I get."

But Althea would not release her. It seemed to her, in her general confusion, a matter of the greatest urgency to rescue Valeria from this hateful house and that disgusting woman.

Valeria saw the panic in her eyes and said in the same soothing voice, "I have to play now. I'll play the barcarolle you liked."

Althea's arms fell back like a puppet's. "The barcarolle—yes—from Venice."

"Play, Val. We can't stay," Ford said quickly.

On her way to the piano she was greeted by Mrs.
Haverfield. As she paused to say good evening, Ida
gave her a warning stare.

"I'm so pleased to meet you," Mrs. Haverfield said
warmly. "Ford and Althea have spoken so much of
you. I do hope you'll drive out to see us soon." She became aware of Ida's accusing presence. "You must
bring Mrs. Brewster, of course. I mean you must come
together."

"Thank you so much. I should be delighted."

Ida was seething with ill-concealed resentment.

Valeria inclined her head with the grace which Ida
mistook for condescension and went to the piano. She
glanced with a twinge of alarm at Ford, who was sitting beside Althea like a keeper behind an untamed
animal, and commenced to play.

Althea relaxed a little as the first cascade of notes
brought an end to the ladies' chatter. If only she could
absorb these cool and soothing sounds! She wanted to
be close to Valeria because Valeria was good and
could ease this burning sensation in her head. If only
she could sink down slowly and rest under these
waves of flowing sound. But she was losing her balance
again. An abyss was opening before her.

She gripped Ford's arm in panic. "I must—I can't
—" she shuddered.

Ford managed to catch his mother-in-law's eye. A
distress signal flashed between them. As Valeria
came to the end of her first number, Mrs. Haverfield
rose and said with quiet intent to Ida, "I do hope
you'll forgive us. My daughter is not feeling well.
Could you please call for our carriage?"

Ida was too astounded for a moment to feel outraged. Leave? They couldn't leave? The whole evening would be ruined. "She can lie down," she said
firmly. "I'll have someone take her upstairs. My secretary can make her tisane."

"I'm afraid we must go," Mrs. Haverfield said with

polite finality. "I do hate to interrupt your perfectly charming party."

Valeria was aware that a *contretemps* was about to erupt and that the other ladies were aware of it. She boldly struck the opening chords of a Chopin ballade to compel their attention.

Mrs. Haverfield had gone over to Ford and together they managed to get Althea up.

"I want Valeria to come with us," Althea pleaded, resisting their united pressure as she was half-guided, half-forced into the hall. "She must come with us," she wailed. "Don't you understand? She can't stay here."

Ida followed them into the hall and purposefully closed the parlor door.

"Surely she can take something. I'm sure if she lay down . . ." She was angry and baffled and wanted at all costs to keep Mrs. Haverfield there.

"I'm so sorry," her guest of honor said as she and Ford bundled Althea into her evening cape. "But we really must get home."

Ford said in a peremptory tone to Haddock who had appeared unexpectedly, "Bring our carriage around—at once."

Althea was sagging. Her body seemed suddenly bereft of coordination. An inarticulate, protesting sound escaped her.

"Mrs. Hollister can take her home," Ida persisted. "He can take my carriage." She actually took Mrs. Haverfield's arm in an attempt to restrain her.

"You don't understand!" Mrs. Haverfield said sharply. "My daughter's ill." She opened the front door herself.

Ford shunted Althea out. Her head sagged. She moaned like some animal cornered by a hunter.

Appalled, Ida watched them go.

Ford maneuvered Althea down the steps. She was tugging at the bodice of her dress. She wanted to tear it off so that the night air would cool her body. She wanted to be totally naked so that her tortured body could be free.

After what seemed an interminable wait the carriage rolled up. The Italian coachman sprang down from the box.

"We have to get home," Ford told him. "Help me." To his mother-in-law he ordered, "Get in."

Mrs. Haverfield did as he told her and sank into a corner. Together Ford and the coachman hoisted Althea into the carriage, where she collapsed on the floor.

Ford climbed in, stepping over her. "Hurry!"

He pulled down the blinds.

Ida returned to the parlor. She could not believe what had happened. The entire evening, all her plans, were ruined. Her crowning achievement had collapsed in a landslide of anticlimax. She had been made a fool of, insulted, by these people who thought they were so far above her. They had come to her house, eaten her food, mocked and insulted her. That horrible girl had been drunk. She had purposely made herself drunk. Ida sat down, her face livid. If she had had a weapon she would gladly have killed Mrs. Haverfield, a stupid, vapid nobody who had not said one worthwhile thing all evening.

Valeria continued playing, trying to restore normalcy.

When the men returned from the dining room they saw at once that Mrs. Haverfield and the Hollisters had gone. What had happened? They saw Ida's face, purple with indignation. Had she driven them away?

"Mrs. Hollister was taken ill," Ida explained in self-defense. "She suffers from the family weakness, you know." A significant pause followed this statement: "It is the cross Mrs. Haverfield has to bear."

But Ida was thinking, that despicable Ford Hollister. Nothing more than a paid nurse for a madwoman. He had sold himself into that tainted family so that he could bugger young men on the sly. She would get all the evidence and publish it. Oh yes, she grimly decided, she would expose them all.

After half an hour, embarrassed by the glowering silence of their hostess, the guests made polite excuses and drifted off. Ida barely acknowledged their fare-wells.

At last she stood up, ugly and tragic in her defeat, and marched out, slamming the door.

Valeria and Hank were left alone.

"Well!" he grinned. "What on earth was all that about? I knew something was wrong at dinner."

"Mrs. Hollister was upset. I'm afraid she's very high-strung."

"I don't envy him, married to such an odd duck. She's bonkers, if you ask me."

"Don't say that, Hank. It's so sad."

But it was true. That was the mystery she had sensed behind the studied calm and all Ford's watch-ful solicitude at Fairlawn.

Valeria was depressed and worried and wondered if she should ask Hank to drive her out there. There might be something she could do. She felt desperately sorry for Althea. Under that distracted manner Vale-ria had sensed her pathetic need for a woman friend.

She fingered the keys and said, to divert her thoughts, "Why don't you sing something?"

As he was finding his music, Hank said, "You looked wonderful tonight. Those old crows could have killed you. I don't know how you do it. They deck themselves out like Christmas trees and there you are in that plain gray dress, looking so regal."

She was wearing the severest of gowns which she had made herself. Valeria's only adornment was a white opal brooch, the one relic she had never parted with because it had belonged to her mother.

It was a relief to play.

Hank sang well, his tenor clear and lilting. He looked his best that night, flushed with the vigor of youth and well-being and happy to be acquitting him-self well before his goddess. But her mind was on Ford and his luckless marriage. What was happening to the three of them, after all their struggles and heartaches? How endlessly difficult it seemed!

After a while Nancy crept in, bundled in her dress-ing gown, with her hair in crimpers. She curled up like a cat in a chair by the piano where she could watch

the light as it played on Valeria's deft and delicate fingers. She thought her friend more beautiful that night
than anyone she had ever seen.

In spite of the debacle that had ruined the party, an
aura of domestic peace gradually enfolded them.
Nancy was thinking, how lovely it would be if our lives
at home could be like this, with just Hank and me and
this dearest and truest, most perfect of all friends.
Hank was thinking, if only my married life could
always be just like this.

Valeria loved them then. They seemed to her like
her own children in a charmed life that could never
be. She thought of what money was doing to Ford, of
what it had done to Ida Brewster and Sam Garvey and
of what the lack of it had done to her. Could there
ever be enough money to recapture peace of heart?
Did such peace exist any more, anywhere on earth?

She played and they listened, beguiled by the old
songs of her childhood, the songs that her mother and
Tante Elize had remembered from their childhoods in
France. The memory of those long soft evenings at
Whitebriars seemed to rise from her fingers. How innocent and secure they had been! How long, long ago
it seemed!

And how much longer, she wondered, would she
have to endure this household; arranging dinners and
bearing with Ida Brewster's crassness and bad manners? Where could she go if she went away? She
looked up and caught Hank's adoring gaze. Could she
bring herself to marry this boy for the money he would
one day inherit? Could she use him as a means of escape as Ford had used Althea? And would the outcome, in terms of happiness, be the same? Probably
she wouldn't hurt him more than he would be by life
itself.

Her thoughts turned to old Sam Garvey, shut away
in his house near the steelworks, alone with his millions. Only a man as rich and as callous as he could
have taunted her with that proposition. Where could
she get five hundred dollars? A typically tasteless joke!

ᏣᎤᎲ Chapter Seven ᏁᎥᏨ

THE FOLLOWING MORNING Sam Garvey stomped into
the Brewster house. It was the first time he'd ever
broken his visiting schedule to the mansion. "Tell Mrs.
Brewster I want to see her," he said to the astonished
Milly.

"She's still in bed, I think, sir."

"I don't give a damn. Tell her to come down at
once."

Ignoring Milly's terror, he went into the parlor.
There was a look of grim resolve on his face as he stationed himself in the high-backed chair and lit a cigar.

Still shaken by the events of the previous evening,
Ida had no desire to start the day. It was too much to
ask her to grapple with the humiliation, to review the
dreadful incidents that had brought the evening down
like a house of cards. However she looked at the dinner, it had been a disaster. And she well knew, The
Heights would be buzzing with defeat this morning.

Thoroughly flustered, her cap askew, Milly knocked
on her mistress's door and peeped in. "It's Mr. Garvey, Ma'am. He wants to see you."

"Mr. Garvey?" Ida was startled. "But it's not Sunday."

"He's downstairs, Ma'am, and he said to come right
away."

As she struggled up, Ida wondered what crisis could
possibly have caused her father to make such an unprecedented break with tradition. She rarely saw him
other than on alternate Sundays. It was more than
sufficient for both of them.

Ida made her way downstairs with her hair still in

disarray. Her heart sank when she saw him. She knew that look.

"Sit down, Ida. I've got something to say to you."

Obediently, she sat down, but on the opposite side of the room.

"Thaddeus Brownlow will be here next week. We have a deal to talk over, something of prime importance. I've asked him to dinner here."

Normally, the prospect of entertaining Thaddeus Brownlow would have released a waterfall of Ida's social juices, but this morning she could not bear the thought of another important dinner.

"I don't want other people; just you, Henry, Hank, and Miss Lee," her father went on.

"Miss Lee? But she's a *servant*. I can't ask her!"

"I want her. She has class. Brownlow likes pretty women."

Ida set her jaw. "I will not have her sit at my dinner table."

Sam Garvey pierced her defiance with a look like a jab from a stiletto. "You'll do as I say. I've embarked on the biggest deal of my life. It's important to get Brownlow in a receptive mood."

"What makes you think she can help to do that?"

"Because she knows how to behave," he said cuttingly. "Brownlow is used to women of her kind. None of us qualifies."

Ida was stunned, though she managed to stammer, "That's a wrong number. Four men—"

"I want Hank to meet him. If he goes into banking it'll be a very good contact. I want the best dinner possible, the best wine. Tell Miss Lee to arrange it. She'll understand."

Ida summoned the full force of which she was capable. "This is my house. I won't be told what to do. Take him somewhere else. Take him to the hotel," she sneered, "you and your Miss Lee!"

"This will make you a very rich woman, Ida. Wealthier than you ever dreamed of being—even with my money."

"What are you up to?" she demanded. "What is this deal?"

Garvey exhaled an ominous cloud of cigar smoke.

"I'm going to build a railroad. One of the biggest in the country. I need Brownlow's money—at least twenty million."

Ida was not the daughter of a tycoon for nothing. The moment she grasped the enormity of what he was contemplating, she asked, "A railroad? Where?"

"The details don't concern you. I'm sick of playing Red Indians with Josiah."

At the mention of any maneuver against Josiah, Ida rallied. "About time. You should have done something years ago."

"Maybe," the old man conceded, his ice blue eyes glinting. "And you'll keep your mouth shut, see? I don't want a word of this to leak out at one of your damned soirées."

They had joined forces on the eve of a battle, Garvey against Eaton. "What night is he coming?"

"Next Thursday. He'll be staying out at the Haverfields." He filled his lungs with smoke. "Now get Miss Lee." The smoke poured from his nostrils like a dragon's in a Chinese painting.

"Don't trust her," Ida warned. "Her brother works at *The Courier*. She probably tells him everything."

"She'll do as I tell her. I know what she's after."

Ida hesitated. She was jealous, and perturbed. "She's after money," she said. "What else?"

The old man dismissed her with a gesture. His mind was already seething with schemes and figures. A map spread out in his mind across which trains roared, laden with steel and iron.

When Valeria appeared Garvey did not greet her. He played his old game of keeping her waiting, watching her discomfort and annoyance through half-closed eyes.

"Get that money, Miss Lee?"

"I didn't think of it again," she replied coldly.

He smiled, not believing her. "How would you like to earn it?"

She waited, stared straight at him without blinking.

"Will you sell me an evening for five hundred dollars?"

He had spoken to her as though she were a harlot. He seemed to find it amusing to offend her. She turned away, the family nose at an angle of utmost scorn.

"Miss Lee," he called her back, "I need your help."

"There's nothing I can do for you."

"There's a great financier coming here to dinner, Thaddeus Brownlow. Mean anything to you?"

She nodded.

"I have business to discuss. I want you to charm him."

"How much charm do you consider is worth five hundred dollars?"

"Not much. Just talk to him, get him in the right mood. He's used to the best society, the real stuff, not the riffraff that comes here."

"Mr. Garvey, I have now met you three times. You're a blunt man, so perhaps you'll understand. I don't like you. In fact I dislike you intensely. This is the second offer you've made now. I decline them both."

"It seems to me that five hundred dollars is a good figure," he argued, "for doing what comes to you naturally. I'm paying you a compliment."

"That is your idea of a compliment, not mine."

She went to the door.

"A thousand."

"Not for ten thousand. If you'd asked me as a favor or simply invited me, I would have considered it out of respect for your daughter, if nothing else."

"You respect Ida? That's something," he guffawed.

"She employs me. I live in her house."

"Oh yes, I remember. You want to be part of her family."

"You are uncouth and uncivil," she said icily, her hand on the doorknob.

"Don't go, Miss Lee," he said in a quieter, more reasonable tone. "Thaddeus Brownlow is a very important man, one of the richest in the country, a genius in his way. When you go to New York he might be of use to you. He's done many kindnesses for people he likes, especially women."

"I didn't know you included pimping among your other activities."

"God damn it!" he exploded. "I'm trying to help you!" He stumped out his cigar.

"I can do without your help, and without your insults, too."

"You're a fool!" He got up and came across to her. "All right; I said it wrong. I forgot women are short on humor. Will you do this for me, with or without the money?"

They were facing each other, antagonists who in a strange, involved way respected each other. She seized her advantage.

"No."

As Sam Garvey was leaving, now in a very bad temper, he said to his daughter, "Talk to that girl. She's obstinate. It's that damn Southern pride. I want her at that dinner."

He clamped on his hat. "Give her a piece of jewelry. Anything." He stalked out.

Ida was thunderstruck. Had Miss Lee the effrontery to refuse an invitation to meet one of the most important men in the country, when there were millions at stake? Yet, she was dimly aware that barriers existed in good society that could not be crossed by money or the position that money could buy. Mrs. Haverfield—a thoroughly stupid woman—and Valeria Lee shared a code of attitudes and conventions that, try as Ida might, she could not completely fathom.

Later, when she sent for Valeria to discuss the dinner for Thaddeus Brownlow, she said with a circumspection unusual for someone so crudely outspoken, "I understand that you don't want to attend."

"It was the manner in which your father asked me," Valeria explained. "I told him that I would have been happy to accept if it had been for you."

Ida was more baffled than ever by this explanation. It suggested, which she found impossible to believe, that Valeria liked her. Having no friends and never in her life having had a woman friend, any expression of cordiality was immediately suspect. What was Valeria angling for? An increase in pay?

"I don't understand," she said.

"Your father offered to pay me for coming to this dinner. I am not used to being given money for accepting an invitation. Do you think Mrs. Haverfield would have enjoyed your dinner more if you had sent her five hundred dollars?"

But that was rank impertinence. Mrs. Haverfield was rich and Valeria Lee was penniless. Besides, Mrs. Haverfield had come on sufferance to please that disgusting Ford Hollister. "I'm sure my father meant no offense. He is not a tactful man," Ida admitted.

"No, he doesn't need to be," Valeria said before she realized the implied sarcasm, "he is so rich."

Ida had entered a realm of manners where she felt totally lost. "He wants this dinner to be *bon ton*. Mr. Brownlow is used to the best of everything." It was annoyingly obvious that without this high-handed Southerner who refused to know her place, the table would be hopelessly lopsided; one woman and four men.

In some perturbation she went to her jewel case and rummaged through the drawers, looking for some insignificant brooch or pendant. But, really, it was outrageous that one should have to bribe a secretary to appear at a dinner, not merely for anyone, but for a man of Brownlow's prominence.

Valeria watched her, amused. It was one of the rare occasions when she felt sorry for Ida Brewster.

Ida had come across a gold locket on a chain. It was one of the first pieces she had ever owned and she never wore it. All the same, she hated to part with it. She was in the habit of weeding out her less important jewels and exchanging them for something larger and flashier, or using them as a first payment on something she really wanted. But a railroad! Her father had said she would be richer than she had ever dreamed of being. She held the locket out to Valeria.

"You can have this," she said, "instead of the money my father offered you."

"Mrs. Brewster, it is extremely kind, but I never wear jewelry."

"Well!" Ida exclaimed. Was she mad? "You haven't any to wear, have you? Except that brooch you had on the other night."

"I kept that because it belonged to my mother."

The locket was dangling between them. It occurred to Ida that long, long ago perhaps Josiah had given it to her. Was that why she had kept it? She said testily, "Will you take it or won't you?"

"It is very kind, but no," Valeria said as gently as possible.

Ida glared. "Your manners aren't any better than my father's, it seems to me. When someone offers you a gift—"

"It is not a gift, Mrs. Brewster." Valeria's voice was smooth as silk. "It is a bribe."

"Who do you think you are to give yourself such airs and graces?" Ida exploded, reverting to her usual manner. "Just because you were born on some kind of plantation and had slaves—" She dropped the locket angrily back in her jewel case.

"I will discuss the dinner with Monsieur Emile," Valeria ended the interview with perfect politeness, "and bring the menu for your approval."

Ida struggled with herself. She saw an untold fortune from the railroad sliding out of reach. As Valeria was going through the door, she forced herself to say, "You said you'd come if I asked you. Will you come to this dinner?"

Valeria bestowed on her the most gracious of smiles. "Since you are kind enough to invite me, of course I shall be delighted to attend."

She left Ida bewildered, but smarting.

Thaddeus Brownlow was more than a great financier; he was a legend. Unlike Sam Garvey he had come from a family used to wealth and had had the advantages of a European education. He traveled about the country on his private train with the velvet pomp of a Medici. But Machiavelli would have had little to teach him in the conduct of great affairs. He

was familiar with courts and kings and the wielding
of influence in the corridors of power. He had been
the *éminence grise* of Washington throughout the War.
He lived in splendor, surrounding himself with the finest of Renaissance art. His soul responded to rare
bindings from princely families, furniture made for pal-
aces, and carpets looted from sultans. He wore on the
little finger of his left hand not a mere signet ring, but
a pigeon's-blood ruby rifled from some sanctuary in
Ceylon. Queen Victoria, who was not easily impressed, had offered him a barony. He had declined.
To have become Lord Brownlow would have been a
condescension for an emperor. At the mention of his
name, hotels opened their grandest suites, headwaiters
ushered him to the most secluded tables. The casino at
Monte Carlo flung open its doors, but the ivory ball
skuttled in vain against the spinning wheel. Thaddeus
Brownlow made money. He never lost it.

He was a sensualist who had possessed many
women. He distributed jewels and largesse among his
mistresses. They never resented his change of appetites and remained his friends.

Brownlow walked with the tread of a panther advancing on its prey. Not prepossessing; with small,
lugubrious eyes, heavy eyebrows and little humor, his
frown could destroy, but careers had blossomed from
his smile. He was not unkind.

He brought into Ida's parlor an aura of the great
world. At a glance he dismissed his hostess as a fish-
wife, her husband as a nonentity. Hank he appraised
as a personable youth. Sam Garvey, whom he would
never have entertained, he respected as a rough
diamond with a shrewd head for business. This
experienced eye rested on Valeria. She was wearing
one of her severe dresses of unrelieved black which
made her skin appear whiter. At her breast was the
white opal brooch. The elegance of her shoulders, the
slenderness of her arms, the poise of her head, finely
carved as an intaglio, struck him as unusual. What
was such a creature doing in these surroundings? She
offered him her hand. It was perfectly shaped with
nails like almonds. Quite unusual.

He paid no attention to Ida's inane remarks. The fold of Valeria's skirt had fallen aside to reveal an aristocratic ankle. He could always judge a woman's breeding or lack of it by the definition of her bones.

Thaddeus Brownlow had long since dispensed with commonplace civilities. He concentrated on what he found interesting. He had come upon Valeria as a connoisseur might discover by chance in a provincial junk shop a rare work of art. He was intrigued. He could not remember a young woman with such large and strangely clouded eyes.

"You are from the South," he said, seating himself beside her.

"From Atlanta."

"I have kind memories of that city. Let us hope it will be restored to its former beauty now that that wasteful war is over. I am a great admirer of the South. Much that was valuable to our country was lost in that conflict. It should never have happened in my opinion."

"You are the first Northerner who has ever said that to me. Or at least, the first who ever dared to."

"All wars are senseless, but civil wars are a great iniquity. In a country as vast as this and with the resources we possess, there was plenty to sustain both ways of life." He spoke slowly as though reading from a prepared text. "Greed is to my mind not so much a deadly sin as an unforgivable stupidity."

"The issue of slavery," Valeria said, "would have been settled in the course of time anyway. Many plantation owners had freed their slaves and many more were doing so."

"Wars are not fought over issues, my dear, but over money."

"But surely, in the case of great conquerors like Napoleon—"

"Behind every Napoleon there is a Talleyrand. They feed the ambition of the conqueror while *they* make money. The conquerors come and go, but the moneymakers remain."

Sam Garvey was watching with satisfaction. He had

rightly estimated the effect that Valeria would have on the great financier.

Thaddeus Brownlow was charmed by the courage of a young woman who dared to speak her mind and to appear in the evening unadorned by jewelry except for a single brooch.

"What a beautiful brooch you are wearing," he complimented her.

"It is not an affectation," Valeria confessed, "but I have always had a strange dislike for jewels. Opals are the only stones I care for."

"I have some brown opals in my collection. If you are ever in New York I should like to show them to you."

Ida had, for once, the common sense to hold her tongue. She recognized that Thaddeus Brownlow would not be impressed by the usual account of her social obligations. She was unaware of how greatly silence enhanced her qualities as a hostess.

Dinner was announced and they went in.

Valeria had decorated the table with dark red roses. The Chinese vases by the window were filled with vermilion gladiola. The dinner was rich and perfectly cooked. Monsieur Emile had made a special trip to Chicago to select the Burgundy.

Hank was disturbed by the attention Brownlow was directing exclusively to his beloved. The others might as well not have existed. He realized that Valeria had found her level in this multimillionaire, and felt her slipping away into a realm of intellect and culture where he could never hope to follow. They were discussing some of the paintings Brownlow had recently acquired; a series of Fragonard panels from Versailles, that had been dismantled after the Revolution.

"You must add my favorite to your collection," Valeria insisted. "Watteau's 'Embarkation for Cythera.'"

"How strange that you should mention it!" Brownlow smiled. "I have been trying to obtain it for some time. It belongs to the Duc de Broglie who will not part with it."

The large room seemed pleasantly calm as the two conversed. Valeria had not once glanced across the table at Hank whose heart filled with misery and apprehension. He felt certain that he was losing her and that in comparison to this imperial personage he could only seem to her ridiculous. He rapidly finished off three glasses of Burgundy and his head grew hot and clouded. He did not know how to attract Valeria's attention, to remind her of his presence and of how much he loved her. Hank hated Thaddeus Brownlow as he had never hated anyone before.

"It is so tragic about the Empress," Ida managed to put in. "How lucky she was able to get out in time! Mrs. Haverfield was only saying last week how very tragic it was. I do hope that Mrs. Hollister is better."

Brownlow was not aware of what was wrong with his hostess's daughter. She had been confined to her room since his arrival with some unspecified complaint.

"The Empress at one time had great beauty, but she never had much sense." Brownlow fingered his wine glass. He turned back to Valeria. "And how did you acquire your knowledge of painting?"

"My father often went to Paris. He met my mother there. She was French and had studied briefly with Meissonier. We had a few French paintings, a lovely little Delacroix, but they were burned during the War."

"I should love to show you my Fragonards," Brownlow said, observing the curve of Valeria's full breast. She would make an agreeable companion on his next trip to Europe.

By the time the meal was over, Hank was dizzy. He managed to follow Valeria and his parents into the parlor, but things were beginning to sway and swim around him. He was only aware of his agonizing love and how he must somehow win Valeria back. He wanted to take her in his arms and force her to love him again, as he was sure she had on that afternoon when they had gathered forget-me-nots. He bitterly regretted having drunk so much.

Ida stationed herself in her usual chair to await the outcome of the all-important conference. Henry Brewster retired into his corner and reached for *The Courier*. "Put down that paper!" Ida snapped.

She was biding her time. Her burning resentment at Valeria's success with Mr. Brownlow was tempered by the thought that, if her father succeeded in building this railroad, she could leave Arcadia for good. First she would go to New York and buy a mansion on Fifth Avenue among the Vanderbilts and Whitneys. Next she would get rid of Henry, silence him for good with an income of ten thousand. He was certainly not worth more. Her plans shimmered before her like a marvelous, seductive mirage. Then, she would go to Paris, install herself in a lavish apartment and, by entertaining royally, would meet that impoverished duke and marry him. She saw herself riding down that main avenue—what was it called?—with a coat of arms emblazoned on the carriage door. And, in such a way that no one would ever know, because she would never be seen with him in public, she would keep a virile lover of not more than forty who would be available whenever she needed him. French dukes were notoriously thin-blooded and could only manage, at suitable intervals, to add a twig to the family tree.

Hank made his way unsteadily to Valeria. "Won't you play for us, please?" he begged. His eyes had the wounded look of an abandoned spaniel. He longed to throw himself at her feet, to bury his head in her lap, to feel the caress of her consoling arms.

She smiled in a formal, kindly way, "If Mrs. Brewster would like, of course."

Ida nodded. What did she care if that cheap adventuress played? It was her last evening anyway. She had served her purpose and tomorrow she would be gone.

Hank followed Valeria to the piano and stood abjectly beside her. She saw the agony in his eyes and tried, by a gentle movement of her head, to reassure him. He must not be so distressed, her jade eyes told him. She was still his friend.

"Would you like to sing something?"

He shook his head. He was perilously close to tears.

In the dining room Thaddeus Brownlow had made a few discreet inquiries about the Brewsters' charming visitor. "She is unusually cultivated."

A portentous silence fell between these two great opportunists who had, each in his way, plowed a furrow through the world.

"You wrote that you had a proposition," Thaddeus Brownlow opened negotiations.

Sam Garvey exhaled an impressive cloud of smoke.

"I want to build a railroad that will service the main centers of the Midwest; linking this town with Cleveland and Columbus and joining up with the Great Northern Pacific in Oregon. I'm ready to put up twenty million of my own money; I shall need a loan of twenty more. The rest can be raised by floating stock. The existing line from here to Chicago is inadequate and badly run. I reckon we can put it out of business inside a year. The Midwest is expanding fast. It's a great opportunity."

Thaddeus Brownlow's small eyes became smaller and sharper until they were gleaming gimlets. "An interesting idea. I should need to know the facts and figures."

Sam Garvey went to the sideboard and, from the compartment usually reserved for a chamber pot in which gentlemen relieved themselves after a heavy dinner, extracted a bundle of maps and papers. Pushing back the glasses and candelabra, he spread them across the table.

The others waited in the parlor.

In due course Haddock appeared with a tray of whiskey, soda and glasses. Hank, now in despair, poured himself out a large drink. His world was crumbling and, drunk as he now was, he resolved that only a desperate stand could save him from defeat.

At last Thaddeus Brownlow and Sam Garvey returned from the mysterious hinterland of high finance. Ida saw at once that the conference had been successful.

Thaddeus Brownlow took Valeria's hand. "It has been a pleasure. I hope I shall have the opportunity to see you again."

"One day," Valeria smiled, "you must show me your Fragonards."

He gave her hand a slight pressure that promised

an early reunion. "An agreeable evening," he brushed Ida off.

The great man made a stately exit. Waves of grandeur closed behind him.

Sam Garvey beamed with satisfaction. "Miss Lee, you surpassed yourself. You turned that old tiger into a tame tomcat."

Valeria said coldly, "I did no more than any guest would have done. He is a charming man."

Ida snorted. "You were lucky to have the chance to meet him. You can leave us now."

"Don't talk to Valeria like that!" Hank suddenly said too loudly.

Ida was astonished by his tone. "When did you start calling her—" But the ferocity of her son's expression caused her to break off.

He went unsteadily to the door, turned and leaned against it. "You can all stay where you are because I've got something to say to you."

Valeria saw what was coming and tried to silence him with a gesture. But Hank was not to be put off.

"I want you all to know," he announced, his voice ringing across the room as though he were addressing an assembly, "that I love Miss Valeria Lee, and that I'm formally asking her to marry me."

After a split second of silence into which the whole house crashed, Ida rocketed to her feet. Her fury exceeded a tornado. "Hold your tongue, you idiot! You don't know what you're saying."

"I know very well. I know exactly." Hank struck back at the enemy. "Valeria, will you marry me?"

Before Valeria could avert the disaster, Ida advanced on her son and gave him a stinging blow across the cheek. Suddenly they were all involved in a scene out of a slapstick farce. Hank beside himself, delivered a kick to his mother's shin that would have done justice to any goalkeeper. Ida yelped and rocked back against an étagère which tilted precariously. "Shut up or I'll kill you!" Hank shouted. "I'll kill you!"

Ida clutched for support at the étagère, precipitating a landslide of bud vases and ballerinas. "My art!" she screamed.

Hank stumbled over to Valeria. "Say you'll marry me," he implored. "I can't stand it any more." He burst into tears.

Moved by his wild distress, Valeria put her hands on his shoulders. "Oh, Hank, you know, you must know, it isn't possible."

Ida, juggling madly with figurines, yelled, "Get out of this house, you Southern whore!"

Hank swung 'round. One side of his face was crimson from Ida's blow. "I'll never forgive you for saying that. Never!" he shouted with despairing rage.

Valeria turned to Sam Garvey who had been watching this eruption of lunacy with a detached amazement. "Why don't you help him? He's your grandson. Don't stand there smirking!"

She went out quickly. Hank ran after her into the hall.

Valeria had reached the stairs. "Hank—dear Hank —you must know that I cannot marry you, now or ever. Please, don't torture yourself like this."

He clung to the newel post as she ran upstairs. "I love you," he wailed like a wounded animal. "Can't you understand?" His whole being was rent by the agony of rejection.

She paused long enough to say, "You must put me out of your mind. It can't be—ever."

Meanwhile Ida, trampling through the wreckage of her art collection, had started after her son, but Garvey had moved before her and shut the door.

"Sit down, Ida," he said authoritatively. "There's nothing you can do."

"I want to speak to him. That—" In her fury and confusion she could not seize upon a strong enough epithet.

"It's not your affair."

"You—you dare to tell *me!*" Her bosom heaved; a lifetime of antagonism flared up. "You who never felt a moment's love for anyone."

"Maybe," he said calmly. "Now, sit down."

Hank clung to the post. He had ruined everything.

He felt a sudden agonized desire to vent his despair on something. Staggering to the tilting suit of armor, he sent it crashing to the floor.

He ran out of the house, down the steps, onto the road. He ran toward nowhere. If he ran all his life through a night that never ended, Hank could never find anything to console him for this loss.

"There's something about her," Henry Brewster told Helen Tennant as he recounted the incident, rocking slowly in a chair by the window in her frowzy little sitting room.

"But what? Is she so beautiful?" Helen had only two uses for her protector: he paid the rent, and he occasionally regaled her with gossip from The Heights.

"Not exactly." He considered, undecided. "She's different."

"She must be—to cause such a ruckus."

Gazing impassively into the darkness, Henry said, "Funny thing the way Brownlow took to her. I guess she has something."

"*What?*"

He couldn't answer, couldn't define his thoughts. "She changes things. Ida hates her. She makes Ida feel small. Anyone who can do that . . ." He thought of his spouse as some marauding killer whale that occupied the region of the deep in which he was forced to dwell. "But she's nice, you know. She plays the piano." He thought about this and just how Valeria, in a few weeks, had changed the atmosphere in the house and made it, in some way, more tolerable.

Helen gave up. She was never able to make Henry specific. She sat down and picked up a blouse she was mending. Henry bored her because he would never give details and because he went to bed in his socks and underclothes. Henry's love-making was nothing to write home about. He was a fumbler who was frightened of nakedness. At least she had Donovan who worked at the slaughterhouse and barged in after work and simply dropped his pants and plowed into her. Donovan was awful, but he gave her a good time. She would soap herself in a hip bath afterwards and her body would glow with satisfaction. Helen wished she could get rid of Henry Brewster, but it was difficult in a town this size to find a regular who would pay the rent and occasionally give her money.

Henry made a statement after long thought. "She doesn't belong here."

"Well, you don't *tell* me. You say this happened or that happened." Helen bit through the thread. "You don't tell me why."

"I don't know why."

Another silence followed while Helen examined the blouse. It would have to do a while longer. She wondered if Henry would give her any money tonight. She really needed a few things for the flat. It was getting to look so shabby. Disgusting, really, when you thought of it, that a man who was married to the daughter of the richest man in town and who worked at the bank should be so stingy. What rotten luck she had with men! If only she could get her hands on a sizable sum, say a thousand dollars, she could leave Arcadia and try Chicago. There were a lot of well-to-do men there. She was quite pretty still, if she could buy some decent clothes. Donovan said she was the best lay he'd had in a long time. Of course, any woman would go for him because of his size. He had other women all the time, Helen knew. But in her position, tied to a man who was no good in bed, what could she do? At least she didn't have to pay Donovan. A good time and a plate of ham and eggs was all he asked for.

What was Henry thinking about, sitting there by the open window, just looking out? She could have understood if the street had been full of people. She often sat there and watched people come and go, children playing, horses and carts, and things being delivered. But Henry stared out when there was nothing. Just the night. And silence.

"Do you want something to eat?" she asked.

He shook his head.

"There's some wine left."

He didn't answer.

Helen took a deep breath. "I want to get some material to make new drapes and cover the sofa. I saw some at Milner's. Pink with flowers. Not expensive. I'd need about ten yards."

Henry continued to ignore her.

"What are you staring at?" she asked impatiently. "Thinking."

"About that woman? I believe you're soft on her. You and your son. . . . I must say, for à boy that age!" she laughed. "Kicking his mother! I bet she was surprised. I bet she deserved it, too."

After a silence, Henry said, "Yes, she deserved it."

He rocked slowly. Finally, out of desperation, Helen asked, "D'you want to go to bed? It's late."

He didn't answer.

"You know, Henry, you don't have to come here if you don't want to. I can have other men. I mean if you don't like coming here," Helen said levelly.

"I like it," Henry said without expression.

"Well, what are you thinking about?" she asked, exasperated. "You come here and sit by that window. I can have other men who'd take me out and give me things. I could be having a good time if it wasn't for you."

As though he hadn't heard her, he said at last, "I sometimes wonder. All that money. Those millions the old man made. What does anyone get out of it? Ida. The old man. He's onto something now. A big new deal. More millions. What will anyone get out of it? There's something wrong."

"I don't see anything wrong with money," Helen said, wondering if he would give her enough to buy what was needed to make the curtains. "It's just that people who have it don't know what to do with it."

It occurred to Henry that Valeria Lee would know. She would know how to make things pleasant and beautiful and easy. But then, she was different.

"Well," Helen got up decisively, "I'm going to bed."

Henry didn't move.

"Are you coming?"

He nodded.

He was impossible. She went into the bedroom and started to undress. Talking to her about all those millions! It was disgusting and it was cruel. She hated him.

Henry Brewster sat for a long time at the window, rocking a little now and then. It seemed to him that the answer to what life was all about must be hidden somewhere out there in the darkness.

ℭ✗ Chapter Eight ✗℈

VALERIA SAT ON THE IRON COT in the tiny attic room of her brother's boardinghouse. There was no chair and only one chest of drawers with a broken, lopsided drawer. There was nothing she could do until Randolph returned from work. In spite of the fact that she had no money and no prospects, she was relieved to be free of the Brewsters and pleased not to have waited for Ida's inevitable firing. She was sorry for Hank and Nancy. Hank, she knew, would recover. They would send him back to college and after a while he would forget her. For Nancy it would be harder. She had so few defenses and no friends to confide in or console her.

Valeria would have to find work. Perhaps she could give piano or French lessons or teach deportment. She was fully aware of how ill-equipped she was. Such aptitudes as she had were all in the realm of social amenities that were of little value in Arcadia. She was an anachronism who belonged, if anywhere, with Thaddeus Brownlow and the sphere he moved in. She had felt at ease with him because he understood the standards and attitudes and tastes she had been brought up to respect. But there was no way out of her present circumstances back into a civilized world. Valeria had been cast up in this backwater and the grim reality of survival faced her like an insurmountable wall.

She lay down on the hard, lumpy mattress and stared at the ceiling. It was grimy. Everything in Arcadia was covered with a film of dirt that poured, night and day, from the chimneys of Garvey's mills. It was as though Garvey wanted Arcadia to remember that, but for him and his greed and enterprise, the town wouldn't exist. He was the great master and Arcadia's inhabitants were his unwilling slaves. There was not a woman who didn't daily curse him as she struggled to keep Sam Garvey's dirt out of her curtains and sheets and carpets. There was not a man, woman or child who didn't breathe in Sam Garvey's air. The water they drank, cooked with, and washed in was tainted by the refuse of his millions. The mills hummed and roared. The smoke billowed from the chimneys and the dirt settled into every chink and crevice. Valeria felt a certain satisfaction in having refused his money as though, at least, there was one small area of her being that his overweening will and ambition had not despoiled.

She went down to Randolph's room and waited for her brother's return. Dusk fell. She was hungry. Valeria had eaten only a brioche and a cup of coffee which Monsieur Emile had given her early that morning. It was he who had helped her to escape. "Ah, Mademoiselle," he had lamented, pained to see her go, "for someone like yourself to live with such people! *C'est le comble!*" Bartlett, the coachman, had carried her bags to the trap and driven her into town. The girls had cried. They all regretted her leaving. She must write to Nancy.

Valeria dozed in the hard little chair and was woken by Randolph's gently shaking her. She gave a cry of relief and threw herself into his arms.

"But, sugar cake, what are you doing here?"

He looked shabby and unshaven, in a state of nervous abstraction. She was so glad to see him that for a moment, Valeria could only remember that with him she was temporarily safe and free.

She told him about the absurd and painful scene that had transpired the previous night.

"Well, I can see," Randolph conceded, "there was nothing for you to do but leave."

But Valeria saw that he was not altogether pleased. Her presence added another problem to the present difficulties of his life.

"Don't worry, I'll find something to do. I shan't be in your way," she assured him.

"Of course you're not in my way," Randy said without conviction. "It's just that I'm wondering what you *can* do in this accursed town. We must put our heads together and think of something." He brought out a half-empty bottle of wine and found two glasses. "We'll ask Ford. He knows everyone."

"I don't want to bother Ford now that Althea's ill. We'd have heard from him if she was better."

Randolph tried to focus his mind on the question of what to do with his sister. "I wonder if Josiah Eaton would give you a job on the paper?"

"But what could I do?"

"I don't know. Hints for harassed housewives, a religious column in rhymed couplets, recipes, some sort of rubbish that women read, *if* they can read here. It might be worth trying."

She suddenly saw him with a clarity which she had not had on her previous visit. He was an unsuccessful hack, fearful for his own tenuous position in life. Her beautiful brilliant brother, with his wild pride and enthusiasm, was already bowing to commonplace need.

They sat at the table, a corner of which he had cleared of papers. As they finished off a loaf of bread and a hunk of cheese, Randy told her about the latest discoveries he had made about Sam Garvey.

"*At least* a hundred men have been killed or maimed because of faulty equipment which Garvey will not replace. Compensation? Oh dear, no! For the death of a breadwinner, the head of the household, he graciously pays the bereaved the sum of three hundred dollars. For a mutilation, one hundred. Many of the men have had their hands or arms lopped off and weren't able to find other work. Does he care? There are always others. In the mines, boys of fourteen work ten hours a day for the munificent wage of seventy cents a day. Many of them develop consumption or go blind, but they must work. How can any family of six or seven survive on eighteen dollars a week? But that's nothing to the numbers of friends and foes he's ruined above ground. He's floated shares that were valueless, cheated investors, stolen millions from fools who trusted him. You understand, in the most barefaced way. There's no ruse or maneuver he hasn't indulged in, no promise he hasn't broken."

His sister told him of her meeting with Thaddeus Brownlow. "I felt for the first time in years as though I were talking to someone I understood. Of course, he's terribly grandiose. He pontificates like the Tzar. But he liked me, Randy. He wanted to show me his collections."

"I'm sure there's nothing in his collections he wouldn't be glad to show you, Val, but don't deceive yourself. He's just Sam Garvey in a better suit of clothes."

She was exhausted. She was aware that Randy was not really interested in what had happened to her. Only abstract ideas meant anything to him. At the back of her mind she realized that he was doomed and that all his energy and intellect and wit were not enough to combat the world they were forced to live in. It required a much deeper duplicity and hardness of heart than Randolph could ever muster. One had to pay the obscene price that Ford had paid. He had forfeited his integrity to marry a demented girl, but he was materially safer than Randolph would ever be.

"I'll take you to the office in the morning. If you have the same effect on Mr. Eaton that you had on Mr. Brownlow perhaps something may result. Who knows?"

Valeria wanted, with sad tenderness, to remind her brother of all the selfless and noble beliefs he had once had and for which he had been so eager to give his life. But they no longer mattered. Randy was trapped in a second-rate industrial town and could only survive by adopting the standards of Arcadia. Idealists were a lost cause in a world ruled by men like Sam Garvey.

She kissed him good-night. He had already forgotten her and was sorting out papers on which he must work that night.

Josiah Eaton had erected a three-story brick building with marble facings to house the offices of *The Courier*. He had reserved the top floor as an apartment where he sometimes stayed overnight when he felt disinclined toward the long drive home or when he was entertaining friends in a poker game, or some lady of more than usually doubtful virtue.

The main floor was cluttered and noisy. Typesetters, editors and reporters worked in subdued bedlam. It seemed unlikely that out of that sustained confusion a neatly printed paper would emerge six times a week.

Mr. Eaton was not in his office yet; he was still upstairs so Randolph deposited Valeria in a chair and hurried off to his desk. He had to write a report on a fire that had broken out in the stockyards the previous night.

Reporters were scribbling away, subeditors running back and forth with sheets of paper. "Hey, Mack, set this up!" "What the hell is this garbage?" "Get out of my way, punk." There was a rough camaraderie among these men who worked all day under constant pressure, united in the single purpose of getting their paper out on time. They barely gave Valeria a glance as they hurried about their business, always seemingly late, always making a last-ditch effort to finish their copy. A scruffy boy came in with a tray of coffee and doughnuts. Men grabbed cups and sipped while they worked. The presses thumped and clattered in the adjoining room.

A door opened and Josiah Eaton came in. She recognized him at once by that air of casual authority she had noticed at the station. He greeted the men with condescension as he made his way between the desks. "Morning, Farly." "Morning, Mr. Eaton." "Morning, Terry. How's that story coming?" "Fine, Mr. Eaton. Have it for you in half an hour." He paused by Randolph's desk. "Good morning, Lee. Got anything for me yet?"

Randolph looked up with the subservient smile of an employee which pained Valeria to see. "Plenty, Mr. Eaton. I'll just get this report ready about the fire and then I'll be in." He was absorbed in the routine of his profession and had forgotten Valeria.

Her initial impression of Josiah was confirmed at this second meeting. He was too bluntly an advertisement for his own success, with his expensive, tight-fitting suit that displayed the lines of his massive but well-proportioned body. He extended a spurious charm perfectly suited, she thought, for winning prospective voters. He was the cliché of a politician on the eve of a campaign.

He noticed her dark beauty as he reached his office door and bestowed a smile as professional and disinterested as that of a streetwalker. "Are you waiting to see me?"

"I am Randolph Lee's sister. I think we met at the station when I arrived."

He appeared not to remember and said offhandedly, "Oh yes. Come in."

She followed him into his office. There were a number of framed testimonials on the walls and an array of silver cups won by his racehorses. Among these trophies she noted a photograph of Thaddeus Brownlow in a silver frame.

Eaton took off his blue coat and vest and hung them on a carved stand. Ignoring Valeria, he went to his desk and started to look through the morning mail. He stood there, showing himself off, she was sure, his white silk shirt clearly outlining his torso, his trousers smooth across his slim buttocks and powerful thighs. She had the unpleasant feeling that within that well-nurtured frame there was nothing but that creamy substance with which Monsieur Emile's elaborate cakes were filled.

He was reading a letter, studiously forgetting her presence. Valeria continued to examine his face. His features were perfectly regular and for that reason, to her, lacking interest. His hair, too patently gold for a man, was parted at one side over a broad forehead. His wide-set pale blue eyes had the slightly glazed look that follows a night of sexual indulgence. It was his mouth that she most disliked. The lips were too pink, almost feminine in their fullness, but they were balanced by a square, aggressive chin and the throat of an athlete. A fine specimen, she supposed, of a man in early middle age.

Eaton dropped the letter on his desk and looked at her without interest. "What can I do for you?"

"I feel a little embarrassed," she faltered. "My brother suggested that we should meet. He thought that perhaps there might be something I could do on your paper."

Josiah did not take kindly to Valeria's manner. She appeared unimpressed by his importance. He was used to a degree of deference due to his position, especially from women.

"I don't employ women," he said coldly. "What gave him that idea?"

"He thought perhaps a column that would be of interest to housewives. I have done some writing for our paper back home, *The Atlanta Sun*."

While they talked, not liking each other, Josiah was looking her over. She was not his type, too tall and too slender and altogether too self-sufficient. Frigid probably, he judged, though good-looking enough in her way. He was put off by the expression in her strange, cloudy green eyes that struck him as haughty and unyielding. She was not a woman he cared to imagine undressed.

Randolph knocked at that moment and came in. He was taken aback to find that Valeria had gone in ahead of him and was already being interviewed by his boss.

"Oh, you've met," Randolph said, placing his report on Josiah's desk. "My sister has been working for Mrs. Brewster as her social secretary. I was thinking—"

"Ida Brewster?" Eaton smiled, showing his regular white teeth. "Did she give you a reference? If she did, don't show it to me."

"I left Mrs. Brewster on my own accord."

"I don't blame you. How is the old termagant?"

Valeria didn't reply.

Randolph persisted with a shade of anxiety, seeing that Josiah was not in the best of humors. "I thought perhaps, sir, you could use a column or two on local events, theater and dressmaking—things like that."

Eaton gave her a hard look. "You've had experience?"

"My sister wrote some articles on French art for *The Atlanta Sun*," Randolph put in quickly. "They were very well thought of."

Eaton was not impressed. "There's not much interest in art here." He decided that he disliked this young woman and the way she sat there, meeting his eyes steadily. There was an ingrained insolence about her. Probably a virgin. She needed a strong man to break her down.

"Perhaps if you'd let her try something, you'd be able to judge what she can do."

Eaton picked up a copy of *The Courier*, unfolded it, and glanced through the pages. Randolph was beginning to regret having brought Valeria to meet his employer. Eaton had obviously not taken to her; it might reflect on his own position.

At last Eaton said from behind the paper, "There's a performance at Brown's tonight. William Somerset's company. You can write a review." He lowered the paper and said to Randolph, ignoring Valeria completely, "See that she gets a seat." He nodded. "Bring me three hundred words by tomorrow morning."

The interview was over.

"Thank you, Mr. Eaton." Valeria inclined her head. He had already returned to opening his mail.

Josiah glanced up as they were leaving. She walked as though she were wearing a ball gown. He was used to voluptuous, well-fleshed women. Nothing for him there.

Brown's Opera House was a shabby building, scarcely more than a barn. There were benches downstairs and a row of narrow boxes above. It was painted a dull green. Even the gaslights failed to enliven a canvas curtain depicting a forest glade in autumn from which not only the leaves, but also the paint, were falling.

When Valeria seated herself in her box, the theater was already nearly full. The benches below were crowded. People were wearing their Sunday best; men in thick, ill-fitting suits with high starched collars that made them look as though they were peering over a fence, women in much worn dresses and tawdry, feathered hats. A theatrical performance was an event in Arcadia and was always well attended. The audience, starved for color and variety, responded with equal enthusiasm to Shakespeare, pantomimes, or the current blood-soaked melodramas such as "Maria and the Red Barn." The villain was roundly hissed, the hero cheered; tears flowed freely at the misfortunes of the virtuous heroines who suffered, in the space of an evening, rape, motherhood, destitution and repentance. The program that night offered "Macbeth" with William Somerset and Evaline Banff as Lady Macbeth, followed by a drama of seduction entitled "Little Nell or the Revenge of the Lighthouse Keeper's Daughter."

There was a stir two boxes away as Ida Brewster, accompanied by Mrs. Almira Bancroft and Mrs. Shawcross, all decked out like barnyard fowls, their hair frizzed and curlicued, made their portentous entrance. They were determined that the hoi polloi below should be aware that the upper echelon of Arcadia's bank accounts was patronizing this cultural event. Liberated from Valeria's restraining influence, Ida was ablaze with diamonds, her bosom encrusted with brooches, an ermine stole flung by design over the edge of the box and her fleshy arms embalmed in Paris gloves. She swept the hall with a pair of mother-of-pearl opera glasses as though expecting to find the Empress Eugenie, Queen Victoria and other familiar faces in that night's audience. There was no one present worthy of her attention

Mrs. Bancroft wielded a red lace fan like a flyswatter, while Mrs. Shawcross was half smothered in a cape of cock feathers which had arrived only that morning from Chicago.

These three society ladies were exceedingly pleased with themselves, bolstered by their sense of superiority, and were secretly contemptuous of each other's appearance.

"Every time I come here," Ida stated, "it is brought

home to me how much we need a new opera house. We can't hope *to raise the level* in a place like this."

A number of people turned to glance up at Sam Garvey's daughter in all her finery. She looked, the women whispered, a perfect fright, but the men noted her diamonds. She was flaunting more value on her bosom than they would ever make in the whole course of their lives. To be that rich, you needed to have a dyed-in-the-wool bastard for a father.

Valeria had withdrawn into the shadows of her box, but she could hear Ida's voice outlining her plans for a new cultural edifice that would suitably commemorate her patronage of the arts.

The gaslights dimmed and flickered. An elderly violinist with hair like a feather duster, stationed at the side of the proscenium, scraped out a mournful ditty. He was accompanied by a female gnome in glasses who tinkered ineffectively with a piano badly in need of tuning.

In due course the forest glade was wound up. An actor in tin armor clanked out onto the darkened stage over which, from a hidden smudge pot, smoke was drifting. Execrable as the acting was and rudimentary the scenery, the old magic soon cast its spell. Uneducated as most members of the audience were, and unfamiliar with the language, they were spellbound by events that seemed to them more real than the tedium of their daily lives. In the outside world, these audience members were cast in meager roles on a wider and duller stage; but here they shared in the high ambitions, dark passions and haunting terrors of these mighty shadows—echoes of their own lost dreams. The audience saw itself transfigured and ennobled, driven by circumstances no less fatal than those in the saga of the mythical protagonist, struggling to grasp a crown; as they struggled to ward off penury, raise children, and keep a roof over their heads. They shared in this grander vision because they felt themselves to be with Macbeth, victims of a common fate.

By the time the play had reached the murder scene, Brown's Opera House had the stillness of a tomb. The audience trembled at Macbeth's indecision, shivered at his wife's resolve, crept with her along the passages of the castle, shrank as she daubed the faces of the sleeping grooms with blood.

William Somerset had preserved into his sixties a presence, a ruined profile, and a voice. But his gestures were those of one long confined to an asylum. He struck ludicrous attitudes, rolled his eyes, clutched his throat and salivated copiously.

To the audience he was a king.

Miss Evaline Banff whose natural forte was tearjerking—she was later to appear as Little Nell—skittered about the stage as though in flight from the police. She, too, wrung her hands, bit her nails in dreadful agitation, tugged at her long blond wig as though it were a bell pull. On the wrong side of fifty, she was made up like a soubrette of seventeen.

Thanks to the magic of the theater, the audience thrilled with anticipation when she admonished her husband; *Leave all the rest to me.*

The forest scene rolled down, the gaslights flared. The audience woke as from a dream. It had been participating in a mystery and was reluctant to resume the pallid obligations of daily living.

Valeria left before the melodrama. She found Randolph immersed in a sea of papers.

"You can work here if you like, Val. The light is better."

"Shall I disturb you?"

"Not in the least. I am assembling the data that will cast Sam Garvey into the Gehenna of public odium."

"Is Mr. Eaton going to let you write the articles?"

"I am to bring him an example. An indictment of slave labor so terrible that waves of shock will be felt throughout the industrial North. Mr. Garvey will be strung from a lamp post and I shall be acclaimed as the Danton of the American working class. I can hardly wait."

"What do you really think of him?" she asked as she sat on the side of the bed, cupping her glass.

"Josiah?" Randy asked, pouring the wine. "Vastly ambitious, ruthless, vain as Narcissus. But a man of no mean intelligence. Capable of loyalty and consideration for the men who work for him. They all adore him."

"Why has he never married?"

"He has all the women he wants. I think," Randolph admitted, "in his way he's a lonely man, although he's always surrounded by people. He gives enormous routs at his country place. But I have detected occasionally a sort of—well, it's hard to explain. I doubt if he has any real friends."

"Perhaps he's not human enough to have any."

"He can be very charming," Randy admitted, "and generous, too. These self-made men become hardened. Sometimes, I think, they would like not to be. He has all the attributes to make a success in politics and I'm sure he will."

"He's the sort of man I instinctively dislike."

"Well, mask your feelings, Val. If he takes you on we can get an apartment and live like gentry again."

"I'm afraid he dislikes me too."

"He's not used to women who don't instantly make themselves available."

"Was I supposed to offer myself this morning?"

"You were supposed to exhibit signs of susceptibility—which you didn't. Frankly, I was surprised that he gave you an assignment."

Randolph returned to working at the table. Valeria used her knee. At two o'clock she looked up, finished. Randolph was still erasing, rephrasing, transposing. She watched him fondly.

How often she had sat silently, watching that dark head bent over his writing desk! She wished that she had money enough to free him from this unworthy labor. He should be working in some handsome library, not on articles for a second-rate paper, but on some classic biography or history. She wanted him to be admired for all the qualities she saw in him which had no place in a provincial town like Arcadia. Money! It always came back to that. There seemed little likelihood that either of them would ever have enough to be more than dependents, scavengers in the byways of an alien world.

She kissed him lightly on the neck and smoothed his glossy hair.

He glanced up, smiling, and took her hand. "Don't fret, my darling. There'll be a turn for the better soon."

She lay for a long time on her truckle bed staring through the mean little window. Even the moonlight was filtered through a veil of yellowish smoke.

Should she humble herself and ask Sam Garvey to pay her the five hundred dollars he had offered her and go to New York and present herself at Thaddeus Brownlow's door? If she became his mistress at least the humiliation of selling herself to a man she didn't love would be cushioned by his cultivated tastes and great possessions. He would not vulgarize her and perhaps she could legitimize her position in some way.

Valeria dreamed that he was showing her his Fragonards in a sumptuous room, lit by immense chandeliers. As Brownlow led her over to these masterpieces, she discovered to her dismay that they were portraits of Ida Brewster and Sam Garvey, young Hank and poor Nancy. Thaddeus was laughing in her ear.

"Did you really think you could escape, Miss Lee?"

The next morning Valeria presented herself at the offices of *The Courier*. It was as though she had never left. The same men hurried back and forth, waving the same sheets of paper. The same clouds of heavy smoke hung over the desks. There was the same general air of urgency and confusion. In the next room the presses thumped evenly. And, Valeria waited on the same simple chair by Josiah Eaton's office.

He was late that morning. She was grateful when the office boy offered her a cup of coffee.

At last he appeared, impeccably dressed in navy blue with a blue and white bow tie. Randolph was right, she had to concede, he was affable and considerate to his staff. He paused by one desk to ask an editor if his wife had given birth yet. The man had obviously been up all night and was harassed and exhausted. "Take the day off, Terry. We'll manage.

You look done in." The man thanked him profusely and hurried off.

Eaton passed her with a brief glance as though not remembering who Valeria was and then paused at his office door.

"Have you done your review, Miss Lee?"

She stood up and held out her paper. Josiah motioned her into his office. While he was removing his coat and vest, she laid the article on his desk.

He read it in total silence. From his lack of reaction Valeria felt certain that Eaton thought what she had written amateurish.

To Josiah's astonishment, he saw at once that this young woman was potentially a much better journalist than her brother whose style was too convoluted and literary. Getting one of Randolph's articles into shape for publication required major editorial work. His sister, however, wrote with simplicity and directness. There was a certain incisive use of words that put her opinions clearly before the reader and an understated wit that pleased him. Miss Lee had emphasized not the performance, but the audience. She did not neglect to pay tribute to the power of the play which had been able to surmount such a tawdry showing. Josiah read the article twice looking for flaws. Without comment he reached for the bell on his desk and rang it, ignoring her completely.

After a further silence in which Valeria became convinced that she had failed completely, the chief editor, Mack, came in.

"Print this as is. It's fine."

Mack took the article, glanced at her with surprise, and went out.

She was incredulous and relieved. "Thank you, Mr. Eaton."

Josiah leaned back in his swivel chair with his hands behind his head. She was disagreeably aware of his physical presence and of a magnetism that she was loath to acknowledge. His shirt, tight across his chest, outlined his nipples.

She was still standing, less at ease than she had been the day before.

"Sit down, Miss Lee."

Valeria took a chair as far from him as possible.

He leaned forward abruptly, with his elbows on the desk. "Have you any ideas? Anything you'd like to write?"

She was taken aback by the sudden change in his attitude and by the unexpected acceptance of her article. "I thought perhaps something to do with arranging rooms, color schemes—entertaining," Valeria managed to say.

"Most of my readers don't have the money to entertain." He thought for a moment. "Are you willing to face a few shocks?"

She waited, not knowing what he could mean.

"I'd like you to take a walk through Shacktown. That's the area around the Garvey mills where the workers live. You won't like what you see. Talk to anyone you can. Get inside their homes. Women especially. Don't be frightened to put down the worst. It's ugly. I want to know just how ugly it seems to you. I'd like to know how it strikes a woman of your sort. Write as much as you want. We can edit later."

She was more than ever at a loss. Wasn't this infringing on Randy's territory? "I thought my brother—" she began.

"I want a fresh point of view. You're the first woman I've ever thought of for such an assignment. If you find the subject too unpleasant, we'll look for something else."

Eaton was civil and matter-of-fact, without being cordial. Before she could ask for any more details, he had turned to his morning mail. Valeria went uncertainly to the door.

"I don't want it at once. Take a couple of days, more if you need."

Outside the office, Valeria discovered Randolph was not at his desk. The scruffy boy was ushering a group of men in black suits to Eaton's office.

She went slowly downstairs into the street. Two men were hoisting a sign across the front of the building.

"Eaton for Governor. The People's Friend."

She went into a stationery shop and bought a notebook and pencil. It was a cloudy, torpid day. Arcadia looked duller than usual, more desultory, cheap and provincial. The absence of trees or grass sharpened the drabness of the buildings. Valeria walked in the direction of the great chimneys. There was no need to ask the way.

As she came closer, the dirt on the clapboard houses became thicker like a coat of paint. There was an unpleasant odor in the air. There were no sidewalks, no street signs, no gas lamps. Something worse than squalor, a sense of unrelieved depression, hung over this conglomeration of mean houses, shacks and leantos, some with gaping boards and corrugated tin roofs. There were piles of refuse on empty lots where mangy curs scrounged and where the fetid air was loud with buzzing flies. Some ragged children with pinched faces were dragging a wooden crate through the dirt. A woman came out of a shack carrying two slop pails that were obviously too heavy for her. Slowly, she made her way to a grating in the lane and emptied first one and then the other load of excrement. In some of the doorways old people sat. They appeared to have died long ago and existed in an inanimate limbo. Their expressionless eyes followed her as Valeria picked her way through the refuse that littered the way.

Near the works, in grim defiance of the poverty around it, stood the house. It was unabashedly black with grime. A square of black ground was enclosed by an iron fence. A few soot-encrusted trees had bravely put out leaves in the spring. The house was solid, with gables and a mansard roof. As she drew closer she saw that there were still a few long-dead laurels in what had once been an attempt at a garden. They had turned the color of black tea. The shutters on the upstairs windows were drawn. In the midst of dereliction the house stood, a monument to entrenched indifference.

Could this possibly be where Sam Garvey lived?

At this proximity to the mills there was a continual droning and rumbling as though an army were at work demolishing the interior of the earth. The chimneys seemed monolithic, pillars of an industry dedicated to the despoilment and degradation of all living things that fed their energies into its huge, remorseless maw.

At this hour of the day, when the men were at work, there were few people about. Valeria came upon a woebegone store where, among a meager display of merchandise, deal coffins tilted against the wall. A group of women were gathering by the entrance in aprons and faded cotton dresses. She shrank from approaching them. They watched her with dull, half-resentful surprise. They were prisoners of Sam Garvey's leper colony, disfigured by industrial blight. People from the other part of town rarely ventured into this nether region.

Valeria made her way down an alley that had long since abandoned the intention of becoming a street. She held up her skirt to save it from dragging in the refuse. A child was standing alone in the middle of this shack-lined tunnel, watching her approach. Valria had the feeling that it made no difference to him whether it were a dog or a strange woman coming towards him. He stood in his rags and watched without interest. He was small, expressionless, with the bleak lack of identity of the very poor.

The Courier's newest reporter greeted him, but he made no response. There was something chilling in his immobility and indifference. Valeria saw that his eyes were covered with a gummy discharge. Why did he stand there looking and not caring if he saw her? What was he waiting for?

She leaned towards him. "What is your name?"

No answer was forthcoming. The small peaked face was turned toward her, but his gaze was directed beside her head.

"May I wipe your eyes?" As she gently moved a handkerchief around his eyes Valeria saw, with a start, that his head was covered with lice. The dried discharge came away like the crust from an old scab. The child neither responded nor withdrew.

He was blind.

A shiver of horror went through Valeria. She wanted to run from this appalling example of neglect.

She fumbled in her bag, found a dollar and some change, pressed them into the grimy hand and closed the small fingers 'round it.

As she hurried away, Valeria found that she was crying tears of anger, futility, and shame.

By the time she had reached the other part of town, the theme for her article had become plain. The child and the house. They told everything. There was no need to talk to anyone, to explore any further.

She climbed the ill-smelling stairs of the boarding-house. The relief of escaping from Shacktown was so intense that even Valeria's shabby cubicle under the roof seemed bearable. She found, on opening her bag, the handkerchief with which she had wiped the eyes of the child. It filled her with disgust. She folded a sheet from her notebook round it, and not knowing what else to do with it, flung it as far as she could through the window. Then, Valeria scrubbed her hands.

She sat on the edge of the bed with the notebook on her knee. She thought of Sam Garvey, entombed in his mausoleum, counting his millions in that wasteland of human filth; of Ida Brewster decked out in one of her hideous gowns, ablaze with diamonds; of Thaddeus Brownlow with his great ruby ring and his cultured pronouncements; of Ford with his disgraceful marriage; of her own weak longing for money to arm herself against the world, even to the point that she might surrender what, out of vanity, she had prided herself on as her integrity; and all this hypocrisy and greed built on the degradation of a child. It was all perfectly clear what money and the abuse or lack of it did to people. If it were true that wealth was the root of evil, it was also the innermost cause of what was far worse, indifference.

Impassioned, Valeria started to write. The words came quickly, sharpened and clarified by this new awareness. She wrote steadily until the light failed and she could no longer see the paper.

She found that she was not tired. On the contrary, Valeria felt enormously alert. Suddenly she wondered what had prompted Josiah Eaton to entrust her with this mission. Why had he, who disliked her, thought that she was capable of grasping what was, in fact, the antithesis of everything Arcadia and his own life stood for? Valeria had wrongly imagined that she had glimpsed a more human element in Sam Garvey. Was Josiah Eaton merely using injustice and misery to further his own ends?

Next morning, she waited again outside Eaton's office. As before, Randolph was not at his desk. He was out gathering data for the articles on slave labor. He had not received the news that her theater review had been printed without alterations. He suffered too much at the hands of editors who bastardized his work and reduced it to a common level of mediocrity.

When the office boy came 'round with the coffee, Valeria asked him where Mr. Eaton was.

"Upstairs, I guess."

"Could you tell him I'm here? Valeria Lee."

He seemed doubtful. No one disturbed Mr. Eaton in the upper regions. They were his sanctuary and what went on there was not the concern of the staff; though they had their notions.

"Then could you take this up?"

She handed him her manuscript.

He didn't like to exceed his usual duties, but finally agreed. He vanished through the door marked PRIVATE.

Valeria waited, undecided whether to go or to stay. She had made up her mind to leave when the office boy came racing through the door.

He called across the room, "Miss Lee!"

As she made her way between the desks, various men looked up. Quizzical glances were exchanged behind her back. Lee's sister was making rapid progress.

"You're to go up, Miss Lee."

Not pausing to think of any possible ramifications, she went up a flight of carpeted stairs. There were etchings of Paris along the walls. Eaton was waiting for her, holding open the door of his apartment. He had on a maroon dressing gown over his shirt and charcoal brown trousers.

"I hope you don't mind coming up. I'm not properly dressed yet. I've had a lot of business to attend to."

He led her into a well-furnished sitting room. It was solid and masculine with leather chairs, mahogany furniture and sporting prints. On a table were the remains of breakfast.

"Help yourself to some coffee. It's still warm."

Valeria sat at the breakfast table disregarding the offer while he lounged in an armchair reading her article. Even at this hour of the morning and not yet shaven, Josiah was handsome. She found that his good looks were less distasteful to her than they had been. Nor did his prolonged silence dismay her as it had before.

He was nodding his golden head, impressed. He looked up, smiling warmly. "You've nailed the old bird all right. You've nailed him beautifully, without even mentioning his name."

She was pleased by his approbation.

He looked at Lee's sister as though considering her fully for the first time. "You're quite surprising, Miss Lee. I thought the first time I met you that you were a supercilious Southern belle who'd fallen on hard times, and were determined to make me feel that I was far beneath you."

"I don't think you would allow anyone to do that, Mr. Eaton."

"You think I'm a big show-off. Well, it's true."

They laughed spontaneously.

Josiah came over and sat down across from her. "It needs some cutting for our purpose. By and large, you've done exactly what I wanted. Frankly, I didn't think you could do it."

"Why did you ask me then?"

"I'd a notion it would be pleasant to see you come a cropper."

"I hadn't so far to fall."

He lit a cigarette. He was the first man she had met since her sojourn in Arcadia who smoked cigarettes, generally considered less masculine than cigars.

"Can I be quite honest with you? Without causing you offense?"

Valeria waited expectantly.

"I like your brother. He's well educated and well read. He has a fine grasp of things, and he writes well. Unfortunately his style isn't really suited to a newspaper. It's literature, but not journalism. Ford Hollister told me something of your situation. I want to help him. I want to keep him on. But, frankly, I don't know—"

"Randy hasn't worked on a newspaper before. It will take him a little time."

"He's obstinate. Most real writers are. The point is we don't need writers, we need reporters. I don't know how it has come about, but you're a natural, Miss Lee. You say what you have to say. You report what you've seen. And you don't waste words. I'm impressed by what you've done."

"It means a great deal to Randy to work for you. He's learning all the time," she said loyally.

"I guess he's told you about the series of articles I'm planning—an exposé of conditions in the mills." Eaton was pouring himself another cup of coffee. "I daresay you've heard a good many stories about me since you've been here; that I'm out to ruin Sam Garvey and a lot of similar fables. I'm not denying I'm ambitious. I want to be governor. But I'll tell you something; I worked in the mills as a young man and only in bookkeeping, so I didn't get the worst of it. But I never forgot what it did to the men. I saw a man sawed in half by one of the furnaces. One half of him went into a steel rail, the other half was thrown into Potter's Field. Now I'm not saying a man hasn't a right to make money. We all want that. But I am saying that if you run mills as big as Garvey's or any business for that matter, you have an obligation to the people who work for you. And that is what Sam Garvey has never recognized. He's a remarkable man in many ways, but he's hard as his own steel and a good many dead bodies have gone into its composition, believe me."

He drank the bitter coffee slowly. "I'd like to see those conditions changed. Of course, my motives aren't entirely pure; none ever are. I'm after votes and the men at the mills will vote and, if I champion their cause, they'll vote for me. All the same, as far as I'm capable of an altruistic notion," he smiled, "I want to see changes made, big changes. And I don't care what they cost, to Sam Garvey or to me."

Valeria was aware that she was being subjected to the full display of his charm. His wide smile was embracing, boyish, not quite convincing.

"Will you help me, Miss Lee?"

"What could I do? I know nothing about working conditions."

"Your brother is gathering the material. Will you collaborate with him?"

Valeria knew at once that this was one proposition she could not accept. "Randy has counted on these articles. They mean a great deal to him, not only for the work, but because he believes in the same things you do."

Eaton said flatly, his voice hardening, "I can't trust him with those articles alone."

"There's no one here or anywhere who can write them as well as he can. You said I surprised you. Believe me, Randy will astonish you." She went on with a sudden intensity, her luminous green eyes flashing. "You don't know Randy. He's a fighter and an idealist. He saw his whole world, everything he believes in, brought down in ruins. But he never gave in. He fought and wrote and exhorted people to stand up for what was left. Oh, if you knew how he battled to get people to stand together and rebuild the South! I wrote a silly little article that anyone could write. Randy will write you a series that will have an impact all over the United States. All he needs is the chance."

She was beautiful in her defense of her brother. Josiah saw that she was not a cold woman after all; Miss Lee could be passionate when her convictions were challenged. Her loyalty and fire made her astonishingly desirable. She might be a different sort of experience, someone worth waiting for, someone to cajole and subdue.

"You are very persuasive. Is it only for your brother that you feel so intensely?"

"I feel intensely about many things, but chiefly about my brother."

"Then you won't do as I ask?"

"I would not presume," Valeria said, firmly setting her full lips.

They were back on the footing of their first meeting.

"You have made me late for a director's meeting," he said, looking at the clock. "Will you come here tomorrow after the office closes? We can go over your article together."

She understood perfectly well what he implied.

"Mr. Eaton, I would prefer to edit the article downstairs during office hours."

He smiled, showing his perfect teeth.

"Why, Miss Lee, are you implying that I might have untoward intentions?"

"You were kind enough to ask me to write an article."

"You're trying to put me in my place."

"I think we both know our places, Mr. Eaton."

He threw back his head and laughed. "You sound like an English governess."

She was not above playing the Southern belle when it served her purpose. She lowered her thick lashes.

"You have a reputation to live up to. I only have one to lose."

Valeria heard nothing the next day or the day after. On the third morning an envelope was delivered. It contained forty dollars for two articles and a note.

Dear Miss Lee,
    Would you please call at this office at five o'clock this evening. I would like to get your article into final shape.

                                        Yours truly,
                                        Josiah Eaton.

She showed this peremptory summons to Randolph who was at home sorting through the mass of data he had gathered.

"Val," Randy said solemnly, "I rather fear the mat-
ing dance of the peacock has begun."

"Should I go, then?"

"I will station myself at the office door with a shotgun. At your first cry for help—"

"Be serious, Randy!"

"If you want further employment on *The Courier*,
relying on your razor-sharp tongue to protect you—
yes. If you cherish your virtue above rubies—no."

Valeria was undecided. Unquestionably, it was the
only desirable way to earn a living in Arcadia. And, if
she were truthful with herself, Valeria would have to
admit Josiah Eaton had managed to spark certain
magnetism that was difficult to resist.

At four o'clock she made up her mind, put on her
black coat and skirt along with the tricorne hat and
presented herself at *The Courier*. Most of the desks
were still occupied so he wouldn't have the audacity to
try anything compromising. Valeria stationed herself
outside Josiah's office on the hard little chair.

She noticed several of the men glanced at her knowingly. Was she already considered the boss's new
flame?

The office boy hurried forward. "He wants you to go
upstairs."

"Will you tell Mr. Eaton I'll come back when he
has time to see me here?"

"He's been working. He says you're to come up."
The boy hovered uneasily.

Valeria was on the point of leaving. Why wasn't
Randy there? It occurred to her that Eaton had sent
him on some mission so that her brother could not object to her going upstairs alone.

The men were watching her slyly, amused. Should
she go? Perhaps she was imagining things. Valeria
didn't want to jeopardize Randy's chances of getting
the series to write. She decided it was too risky to see
Eaton in his apartment. But on her way out, she
abruptly changed her mind.

The knowing glances followed her as she went to
the private door and found herself going up the thickly

carpeted stairs. The door to the apartment was wide open. Valeria hesitated and then went in.

Josiah was working in his shirtsleeves at a big mahogany desk. He said over his shoulder as his pen scratched away, "Please sit down, I'll be with you in a moment."

She sat down and waited. It was a pleasant, reassuring, well-ordered room. Dusk was falling.

He drew in a long breath and turned to her. "Please forgive me, Miss Lee. Planning a campaign entails a lot of work. I have to solicit support from so many people. Would you like some tea?"

"No, thank you."

"A glass of champagne?" He grinned. "Or would that endanger your reputation?"

"I'm afraid being here at all will do that."

"You mustn't believe all the stories you hear about me. Unfortunately," he assured her, "most of them are not true."

Josiah went into a small kitchen and returned with an ice bucket in which a bottle of champagne was already cooling. Had he planned it like this? It annoyed Valeria slightly that he had assumed without question that she would come. It had doubtless not even occurred to this conceited man that any woman would refuse his summons.

"I like champagne at the end of a day's work. It's refreshing."

He drew the cork, caught the froth neatly in the ice bucket and filled two glasses. He sank down in one of the big leather chairs. "Your health, Miss Lee."

Josiah Eaton had the special ease and freedom of a bachelor used to satisfying his own needs and whims. Valeria saw that for a man of his disposition, essentially selfish and self-indulgent, unused to compromise for the sake of others, marriage would only be an encumbrance. He had all he wanted and did whatever he pleased.

"I have decided to take your advice. Your brother can write the articles. I'll work on them with him myself."

"Thank you." She was vastly relieved. "You will not regret it."

"He is lucky to have such a persuasive advocate."

In this peaceful hour before evening the barriers between them eased. In his own surroundings, without the immediate need to perform and impress, he was agreeably relaxed and natural. He was not, Valeria saw, an ordinary man. He had a certain distinction and, if he employed his Nordic good looks and physical presence as a deliberate weapon, he was nonetheless charismatic. Perhaps, after all, he had genuine qualities that his public manner belied.

Eaton started to talk, not about her article, but about his ambitions. He had grown up in Arcadia and despised it. It had taken him twenty years to reach a plateau of security sufficient to allow him to embark on a new career. He had squeezed Arcadia dry. There was nothing, not even *The Courier* or his country place, to hold Josiah there. He was in the prime of life and ready for his big thrust into politics. He had sufficient experience and confidence and, being financially independent, did not need to form alliances that would lead to compromising entanglements. Josiah could function more or less as a free agent. Of course, all political ventures entailed a good many favors given and promises made and all the subtle varieties of blackmail that won support from key men. The state was owned and run by a handful of landowners and industrialists. He had carefully cultivated them over the years and would, so to say, tolerate their schemes and overlook transactions that might, on too close a scrutiny, infringe upon the law. However, Josiah still needed the popular vote, but that he could win by pressing for obvious reforms. There would be objections at first from entrenched interests, but these could be offset by concessions and unspecified understandings. One had to maneuver for power. It was a game that required cool tenacity, shrewd objectivity and an instinct for where his opponents were most vulnerable. Everyone had his price. His personality and self-confidence would do the rest.

As she listened, Valeria realized that this was the

kind of man most women would find irresistible. They would be eager to surrender to someone so virile and so ambitious. They would only too gladly share in the excitements of his career, the glory of his achievements, proud to take their place, if not at his side, at a suitable pace behind. What was it in her that would soon rebel against such unabashed self-satisfaction, that would cavil at such absorption in his own aggrandizement? Valeria noted that he had not even considered the disadvantage of being single in a position that would require a good deal of entertaining and public appearances. Apparently, Eaton did not feel the need for the assistance of a clever and attractive woman behind the scenes.

Probably women had never been more than objects to satisfy his desires, or mirrors in which to display his charms. Men of such overweening egotism had few real relationships. They were not aware of women as human beings, or concerned with their needs and feelings. Women were accessories like his London suits, his country house and horses.

For many women this would be sufficient. They would settle for the position and the security and the occasional ardor of his bestowed embraces. They would learn to look the other way when his vagrant desires led him to infidelities, nursing their wounded pride in the reflected glory of being the Governor's wife.

Would she be capable of such a worldly adjustment in exchange for enough money to keep the world at bay, exchanging one set of humiliations for another? Valeria knew she could never conquer her core of resistance to being subservient to a man of Josiah's driving will and prodigious vanity. Was it true, as Ford had once twitted her, that she would never allow herself to love anyone? That there would always be some area of her heart that would remain aloof and critical? Only love could override her doubts and resistance, transform her pride of self into selfless giving. Perhaps in the final count she was less materially minded than she imagined. Love? For a man like Josiah Eaton? It was the blatancy of his unopposed masculinity that affronted her, that would soon overshadow whatever tolerance she might develop for his defects.

She observed him closely, his handsome frame lounging at ease, loose-limbed, in a leather chair. Josiah's agreeably resonant voice, well suited to addressing crowds, to cajoling voters, to making plausible excuses, to concealing lies, was directed not at her but at his future. He wished her to see him as a man on the eve of greatness.

Valeria found that the earlier stirrings of attraction for Josiah Eaton were quickly diminishing.

The room had grown dark with the advancing hour. Josiah turned up the lamps, smiling down at her as though he had bestowed some valuable information for which she should feel grateful. He refilled their glasses. Would he ever start to discuss her article, she wondered?

"I apologize for burdening you with my plans," he said graciously. "It's not often that I have the chance in this town of talking to someone who can understand what I'm aiming for."

She was amused by his vanity. She had hardly spoken at all.

He glanced at his watch. "Miss Lee, you may think me unforgivably forward." He was being his most persuasive. "I've had some dinner sent down from my country place. Will you share it with me?"

"I should have gone long ago. My brother is waiting."

"You won't take pity on a lonely bachelor? I swear never to reveal that we partook of a cold chicken."

"Mr. Eaton, I came here to edit my article."

"We can discuss it over dinner."

Josiah accepted Valeria's consent without her having given it. He brought in a tray of food and fetched another bottle of champagne.

She was aware of a certain feline grace of movement, both in the way he walked and in his suppleness as he bent to arrange the plates and glasses. It was apparent to Valeria that he, like many handsome men, took a womanish pleasure in self-display. Eaton was too obviously proud of his tight buttocks and broad shoulders, of his tall, still youthful body. In a subtle inversion of roles, he was like a concubine parading her charms before a sultan.

Although Valeria could feel her pulse quickening, her resistance to him hardened.

Continuing with nonchalant confidence, Josiah offered her food. The cork of the fresh champagne popped and Valeria could not help noticing his strong hand as he proffered the drink.

"No more," she said, knitting her brows slightly.

"Just one glass, Miss Lee."

He sat down opposite her, shaking out the linen napkin and draping it across a well-muscled thigh.

The lamplight gleamed on his thick blond hair. She noticed the fullness of Josiah's lips as he ate, the perfectly matched white teeth. His aggressive good looks annoyed Valeria unreasonably.

She could feel the vibration of a sexual magnetism across the table like that of a stallion circling a mare.

He was talking affably of his last trip to Europe. "London is a man's town. I was taken to dinner at the Reform Club. Very splendid. No intrusion by women allowed. Englishmen know how to arrange things for their comfort and peace of mind. One always feels in Paris that women have a hand in everything. In London women are excluded, except from where they belong."

"And where is that, Mr. Eaton?" she inquired with an ironic tilt of the head.

"In the home. The Englishman's home is his wife's domain. His castle is at his club."

Thereupon, Eaton launched into another monologue on the people he had met in London; titled people with country places and racehorses and shooting boxes in Scotland. "They were very surprised that a mere American could knock down their pheasants as fast as they could. Once they discover that you're not a barbarian, they like to show you off as a sort of amusing freak. Most Englishmen barely acknowledge that America exists. They are in for a big surprise in the next few years, as the center of business shifts from London to New York. They like making money, as long as it's made for them by someone else. One mustn't soil one's hands with trade."

He was laughing as he refilled his glass. He gazed at her steadily over the rim as he drank, his lids half lowered.

Valeria was oppressed by his performance, by this continuous outflow of his charm. She wanted to escape from the heady aura of his male allure.

"Mr. Eaton," she forced herself to interrupt during an account of some peer's daughter with whom he had started a flirtation.

"Cool," he was saying, "unapproachable, haughty . . . and very willing. I was expecting to storm the citadel. Her mother was very anxious to know exactly how much money I had. You have to be enormously rich to carry off even the unattractive daughter of an established family. A good match is very expensive. I decided that I was not quite rich enough."

"Mr. Eaton," she repeated, "my article."

Josiah leaned back in mock distress. "I see that I am making no headway. You Southern belles are just as unromantic as your English counterparts. You are, first and foremost, women of business."

"I didn't come here to discuss romance," she said levelly. "You were kind enough to ask me to write something for your paper."

"You are so stern, Miss Lee," he said coaxingly.

By this time Eaton had nearly finished drinking the second bottle. Almost any other man would have been hopelessly drunk or unconscious, yet the only effect on Josiah that Valeria could detect was an ever broadening, more flamboyant manner. As he gesticulated, she observed how well formed, possessive were his hands. She wanted to leave.

"Very well," he bowed. "We shall discuss business, since that is your wish." He stood up. "But before we begin, there's something I want to show you. Your brother said you were interested in art. Tell me what you think of these things. I bought them from Mrs. Haverfield whose husband found them in Paris."

From a drawer of the breakfront Josiah took a linen portfolio, untied the tapes and brought it to her. Valeria felt the great stretch of his arms as he brushed against her, and the energy exuding from the proximity of their bodies.

An uneasy anticipation filled her and forced her to look at some drypoints by Charles Meryon, scenes of Paris, darkly dramatic and incisive.

To her vast relief Josiah broke the tension by leaving in order to pour out the last of the champagne.

"These are very fine. You should have them framed."

"I know nothing about art, but I liked them, too." He watched her with an appraising, lubricious smile.

She turned over some sanguine studies in the manner of Charles de la Tour, heads of charming women, gracefully seductive. "That looks like Madame de Pompadour," she observed. For a brief moment she was released from his physical presence and could enjoy the simplicity and wit of another century, more civilized than her own.

She found herself staring at an oversized picture of a naked man, in a lewd act with a woman, clad only in a black lace corset. Another man only partially dressed, stripped from the waist down, was crouching before her.

She saw it and turned to ice.

Valeria was too shocked to speak. She managed to pick up the painting and drop it, like some contaminated bandage, across the table.

"Did you buy that from Mrs. Haverfield?"

As she was blindly picking up her bag and gloves, she heard him exclaim, "Oh God, I am sorry! I had no idea it was there."

She found herself at the door.

Anger enabled her to say, "I'm surprised that a man of your colossal conceit would resort to such methods."

Valeria was convinced he'd deliberately tried to titillate her the same way he did his whores.

She hurried down the darkened stairs into the office. Two men, working late, looked up as she fled past. She no longer cared what they thought. She was trembling with anger and disgust.

There was no air in the street.

"Of course, *c'est un voyou,*" Randolph said after she had recounted this incident. "I should go and batter his brains in, though it is *just* possible he'd forgotten the thing was there."

"He knew. It's part of his game to entice women. He's used to the kind that responds to that kind of filth."

Still shaken and angry, she saw that Randolph had no intention of confronting his employer. He would not defend her. To him, the episode was an embarrassment and nuisance.

"Lots of men," he rationalized, "especially bachelors, collect erotica. It seems unlikely that he'd have deliberately gone so far as to use it with you."

She was discouraged by Randy's weakness and lay down on the bed with her hands over her eyes.

"My poor Val," Randolph tried to console her, "I'm afraid you are destined to cause waves in this backwater. This town is definitely not for you."

"Don't tell me that!" she protested, tears turning her eyes to a brilliant green. "You know that I have no choice. I have to live. I have to try and find work somehow."

Randolph was ashamed of his lack of chivalry, and of having to swallow, for the sake of his job, the dishonor done to his sister. He poured out a glass of wine and offered it to her.

"Here, sugar. Forget him. We'll find a way."

She shook her dark head angrily. She had heard that too often. There was no way as long as they were poor. Poverty forced one to accept these endless humiliations. Pride only made them more bitter. They belonged to a doomed race.

Randolph sighed heavily and sat down at his disordered table. Val was a problem. There was some uncompromising quality about her that always led to trouble. Even as a girl she had not been popular. Other girls had found her stuck up and strange. She had never shared in their games and giggling confidences, going her own way, doing things better than they did. Boys looked at her from a distance, with diffidence and admiration, timid of making advances for fear of some sharp rebuff. He thought of her courage and endurance during the blackest days of the War, of how selflessly she had nursed him after the night when the Yankees had broken in and shot him. Her cold pride in the face of adversity had encouraged him to imitate her stoicism and grit. She had set off alone in the dead of winter to sell the last of Tante Elize's trinkets only to be robbed by a deserter on the way home. Instead of weeping or complaining, she had somehow made a broth of herbs and roots to sustain him.

It would have been better if Val had stayed in Atlanta until he was established. At least there she could have held up her head and not minded sharing her poverty with what little remained of a world whose standards she understood.

He must get hold of Ford. Perhaps Ford could find her a position in New York as a companion to someone who would appreciate the superior qualities she had.

When Valeria came down next morning she was greeted by a box of red roses which had just been delivered. Randolph watched her quizzically as she opened the accompanying note.

Dear Miss Lee,
   I apologize for the embarrassment I caused you. Believe me, it was quite unintentional. Please don't hold it against me.

Sincerely,
Josiah Eaton.

She was not mollified nor had she the least desire ever to see him again.

⚔ CHAPTER NINE ⚔

THE PROSPECT of looking for work filled Valeria with dread the day ahead. As she arranged Josiah Eaton's long-stemmed luxuriant blooms, it occurred to her that perhaps Althea Hollister would enjoy them more. Taking the roses to the Haverfield mansion would be an excuse for talking to Ford. But Valeria was reluctant to bother him. She had heard nothing from him since the night of the fatal dinner. Her letter, offering her sympathy and help, had remained unanswered.

Randolph was putting his notes in order. He had now assembled the data on the accidents and deaths that had occurred at the Garvey Mills. On the one hand he felt ashamed for not confronting Josiah with his behavior to Valeria, yet on the other he could not resist a sense of exhilaration because he knew that Josiah would be pleased with the results of his research.

Carefully, Valeria brushed his old blue suit, straightened his frayed tie, and kissed him. He looked the picture of the intellectual off to deliver a lecture. It was surprising, she realized then, with that fine classic head, the brilliant eyes, and the strong and thoughtful brow, how little real strength Randy had.

Left alone, she studied the want ads in *The Courier*. There were few openings for women. A seamstress to embroider childrens' garments for a store on Main Street. A doctor and his wife required a cook. And the last one was for a washerwoman at twenty cents a load.

Returning to her room, Valeria put on a blouse with openwork sleeves which she had made the year before. It would serve as an example of her work. She went over her frayed black coat and skirt and mended a small tear in the veil of the hat. She hated these clothes. They were so old and shabby.

She set out first for the doctor's. There were worse things, she encouraged herself. After all, cooking was often fun and creative.

It was a small, dingy house in a narrow, dank street. Dr. Mortlake's consulting room was on the ground floor. The house smelled of liniment and carbolic soap. Making her way upstairs, Valeria was confronted on the upper floor with a small scarecrow with pin-point eyes. The doctor's wife seemed to have shrunk inside her skin which had puckered into folds and wrinkles that hung over her meager bones.

"I've come about the notice in *The Courier*. You're looking for a cook?"

"You?"

"I've had quite a lot of experience," Valeria smiled bravely.

The woman seemed annoyed, as though this were some kind of joke. "We want an ordinary cook."

"I can cook simple food. You would just have to tell me the things you like."

"Can you bake?"

"Oh yes, and I make good biscuits and popovers and spoon bread."

The woman sniffled, sensing a trap. "We don't want Southern. Just honest food."

They were caught in a pocket of hesitation outside the door. At last the woman said grudgingly, "Well, come in."

Valeria followed her into a small parlor that had the hapless respectability of a waiting room at a mortician's. The windows were closed. A moribund cat lay on a horsehair sofa. There were daguerreotypes of men frozen by the horrors of rectitude, and their women embalmed in black.

"You can sit," the doctor's wife acknowledged, perching on the edge of a chair.

"I can't see your face." The wizened woman peered at the beautiful stranger with suspicion. What was she? A fallen woman in disguise?

Valeria removed her hat.

This applicant was far too superior and haughty to be a cook, the woman decided. What was she after, taking up people's time?

"Where did you work last?"

"At Mrs. Brewster's."

"Mrs. Henry Brewster?" The woman's sharp little eyes opened wide, as though scandalized. Was this creature trying to make a fool of her? "What was you doing there?"

"I supervised in the kitchen," Valeria confessed.

A liar, too. "No . . . I don't think—"

"I am a good cook," Valeria said firmly. "I can make anything you want."

The woman had reached the conclusion that there was something decidedly untoward about this applicant.

"I can make pies," Valeria volunteered.

Of course, the doctor was used to women in a professional way. Nonetheless with a fallen or divorced female like this—certainly with a past.

"No." She got up. "I can't cook because of my hands." She held out hands like roots. "My husband's tried everything. It's congenital." She went to the door. "Mrs. *Henry* Brewster? How did you ever get a place there?"

It was useless to explain. The woman did not want her. Valeria went quickly out.

The doctor's wife peered after her as she went downstairs. Didn't even say thank you or good-bye.

It was a heavy, airless day.

Valeria walked, relieved to have escaped from that crushingly dismal house, and made her way to Main Street. It was a long stretch of commonplace buildings that offered nothing to look at. She passed the one hotel, a shabby establishment with a hash house and bar at one side. It occurred to her that she might work as a housekeeper or help with the catering. Marshaling her courage, she went in.

The owner was lounging in a chair beside a dispirited potted palm, picking his teeth in a desultory fashion and watching the door.

He observed Valeria as she entered and looked around. "Want something?" he asked, not stirring, but removing the wood chip from his mouth.

"I would like to see the manager," Valeria replied, piqued by his refusal to stand up.

"I don't cater to women who ain't escorted." He resumed the excavation of a cavity.

"I'm looking for employment. I thought perhaps you might need a housekeeper."

"Ugh?" His mouth opened as though he had never heard of such a personage. "Nah."

"I'm experienced in catering."

He considered her as though she were a plate of leftovers.

"I could use a waitress. Two a week and food and you help with the dishes."

The degree of humiliation was more than she could face. Valeria thanked him and went out.

She continued along Main Street until she came to the store that had advertised for a seamstress.

A salesman approached her brightly.

"I'm looking for the person who put a notice in the paper for a seamstress," Valeria explained.

The salesman, deprived of a customer, said with a shade of contempt, "Mr. Weisberger. Back there."

Valeria went into a dingy office behind a glass partition. It was piled with bolts of material, cardboard boxes and children's clothes. An elderly man with a nasal drip was poring over a ledger. A drop of moisture clung forlornly to the tip of his red nose.

"Ech?"

"You advertised for a seamstress."

He squinted up at her as though she had said something in a foreign language.

"I would like the work, if you think I'm suitable."

"You can make hole embroidery? Flowers?" Mr. Weisberger pinched the drop between his thumb and forefinger and ran his fingers along the seam of his trousers.

Valeria took off her coat and held out her arm. "Is this what you want?"

"You did this?" He pored over her sleeve, examining it intently. "Very fine. I want not so fine. I show ya."

He fetched a child's smock. Around the neck were a few crudely stitched flowers.

"Provide your own thread. Twenty-five cents a piece. Give ya dozen."

I might as well be doing this in the evening as nothing, she decided. Valeria nodded agreement. "When do you want them?"

"Next week. Early. I fetch ya box."

He corkscrewed into a corner, lifted a pile of smocks and placed them in a flimsy box.

"Name and address?"

She wrote them down.

"Not seen you before. New in town?"

"Yes."

"Where from?"

"Atlanta."

He hummed in surprise. "Hm hmm. Long way. Well, bring me next week. I give ya more." Another drop had found its way to the end of the nasal stalactite.

On her way home Valeria passed an Italian food shop and went in. It was brightly lit and smelled pleasantly of cheese. She bought a sausage, provolone, a loaf, and butter. Under a glass lid a litter of cannoli awaited adoption. She selected two.

"Buon appetit," the cheerful shopkeeper said, stuffing the purchases into a bag.

He was robust and simple. Not even this stultifying town had dampened his natural good nature.

When Randolph returned in the evening he found his sister placidly sewing, the dinner laid out on the table.

"But, sugar, what have we here? A scene of domestic tranquility? Miss Valeria de la Pagerie Lee wielding her dainty needle, a charming dinner in readiness for the weary breadwinner?" He kissed her. "Well, we are under way. Mr. Josiah Eaton, your would-be seducer, was in an exceedingly chastened mood. He approved of all my ideas, commended my diligence, and gave me an increase in salary, albeit a slight one. He is evidently bent on making amends."

"So long as you get the articles to write," Valeria said with a touch of sarcasm, "I guess that's all that matters."

"Oh yes, my sweet sister, he gave me practically *carte blanche*. Though I have to report now and then to present him with stages of my blistering exposés of Sam Garvey, bless his revolting bones. I am confident, however, that I shall not be invited into the private suite."

"One can't say that you're the epitome of the Southern gentleman out to defend the family honor." She looked at him cooly, her green eyes taking on a dark cast.

"If you could stand a few more Parisian artworks, my dear, we could afford an apartment."

"Don't be disgusting, Randy!"

"Evidently Mr. Eaton was astounded to discover that he has a conscience. I am truly convinced that he didn't mean it."

"I'm not," she said tartly. "Open the wine."

Randolph chattered through their simple meal, enlarging on the dire discoveries he had made about Sam Garvey's past. It was a subject Valeria was growing tired of. When she had cleared the dishes away and Randolph had lit a cigarette, he announced expansively, "I think the de la Pagerie Lees deserve an evening at home. We have observed them facing the exigencies of hard labor. We shall now observe them, oh, so charmingly, at leisure!"

Playing the attentive brother, Randolph arranged the pillows behind her head, augmented by several folded coats and a traveling rug. "Recline, my lady, whilst your favorite reader delights you with Jane Austen. Which shall it be? *Pride and Prejudice* with its elegant and lofty heroine who so resembles you? *Sense and Sensibility?* Or perhaps, *Persuasion?*"

She lay there, sewing, while he read.

Little by little there came to her, as she allowed herself to drift back into Jane Austen's world of polite contrivances, an echo of a sort of peace that was no longer hers, but that Valeria could still savor reminiscently like a lingering perfume. She was an outsider recalling the pleasure of belonging. The meanness and ugliness of Arcadia and her present precarious circumstances faded and an old, warm, reassuring sense of being herself returned.

When Randolph paused at the end of a chapter to refill their glasses and light a cigarette, he said, "You know I really think you should go and see Ford. He always thinks of something. Why don't you take Althea those roses? They're still quite fresh."

"I've been thinking about it," she admitted. "If Althea's too ill to see me, at least Ford and I could talk."

"What do you think is the matter with her?"

"I don't know. She had some sort of nervous crisis that night. You remember how high-strung she was when we dined at Fairlawn?"

"I thought her an impossible creature, though I will say she's the only woman I ever met who could quote Sappho in Greek."

"There's a mystery about that family. Poor Ford carries everything off in his debonair way; he has his own sort of gallantry, but it can't be easy."

As Randolph resumed reading, she thought suddenly of the five hundred dollars that Sam Garvey had promised her in return for "charming" Thaddeus Brownlow. Even if she divided it with Randy there would still be enough to take her to New York. Probably the old wretch had forgotten that he ever made the bargain. Being candid with herself, Valeria could not remember exactly what had finally been said.

It was nearly eleven when Randolph closed the book. Valeria had finished three smocks and had thus earned seventy-five cents.

Would Josiah's roses last till morning? She doubted it; half the buds had already opened. She kissed Randolph good night and climbed the rickety stairs to her tiny room.

Perhaps Ford would be agreeable to the suggestion of her coming to look after Althea. She could read to her, play for her, and take his wife for walks in the park. After all, she had nursed Randy for months.

Althea had obviously liked Valeria and it would not be easy to find anyone more suitable in Arcadia. Later on, it might be a way of getting to New York.

As she folded her clothes, Valeria thought how degrading it was that she was perpetually forced to consider ways and means. It cast a blight over personal relationships, cramped her natural impulses, distorted her whole view of life.

She blew out the flickering candle and climbed into bed. She thought again of Sam Garvey and of how he had exploded at her recalcitrance. "God damn it, I'm trying to help you!" She would rather do anything than be forced to turn to him.

When she came down next morning in her white summer dress with the broad-brimmed hat, Randolph had already gone. As Valeria had feared, the roses were now fully open. They would never last all the way to Fairlawn and she couldn't afford a cab. She sighed. Oh well, Ford would understand!

She felt mildly elated at the prospect of a walk in the country. The open air and the exercise would do her good.

The day, however, proved to be far hotter than she had expected. The town was stifling, with drapes drawn and awnings lowered. She made her way down Main Street, and started up the long hill to The Heights. Everything about Arcadia—denied any relieving shadow by the relentless light—seemed uglier than before. The Brewster mansion glared down at the muddle of sweltering buildings.

She would have welcomed a cup of Monsieur Emile's iced tea. Valeria pictured him at his immaculate kitchen table, rereading the *mondanités* of Paris, already three months old, with pert little D'Artagnan at his side. No doubt poor Hank, in disgrace, had been bundled off early to Harvard. Nancy would be shedding tears over some romantic novel and Ida would be plotting for her rivals some deadly ambush, disguised as a musicale. She wondered if the menus had reverted to thick soups and roasts, ending, to Monsieur Emile's despair, with scrambled eggs on toast.

By the time she reached The Heights Valeria was
drenched with perspiration. How many miles was it to
Fairlawn? She had scarcely noticed on her drives to
and from the Brewsters' in Ford's buggy. She regretted that she had not risked the extravagance and
taken a cab. She passed one mansion after another
with their turrets and porches and porticos, somnolent
behind lowered blinds. The crepe myrtles were turning
brown already. Here and there a leaf floated from a
branch. Tremont Avenue seemed interminable. And
the sidewalk shimmered with heat.

To Valeria's immense relief a cart and horse ambled out of a driveway. It had been delivering hay for
the stables. She hurried forward and accosted the carrier as he turned into the road.

"Are you going as far as the Haverfield place?"

The burly carrier, mopping his face with a red
handkerchief, nodded.

"Could you give me a lift?"

The man indicated the cart, empty but for a few
drifts of straw.

She climbed on thankfully. Taking off her hat, Valeria lay down, gathering what handfuls of the sweet-
smelling hay remained for a pillow. It was a blessed
relief to lie there and watch the branches passing overhead between glimpses of hazy sky. Feeling heavy
with heat, Valeria dozed, drifting through daydreams.
Soon there were no more trees, only the sky. Mountains of sunlit clouds were piling up, opulent and fair.

She fell asleep, hardly aware of the sun on her
face, the hardness of the cart and the jolting. She was
traveling across some immense country without any
destination, moving away from nothing toward nowhere.

With a start she woke. The cart had stopped.
She heard the carrier say, "That's it. Down there."

She climbed down, dusting her skirt. She felt dizzy;
her face was burning. There was the sycamore avenue
and, serene and protected, the great pink house with
the urns filled with scarlet flowers on the terrace.

She started down the tree-lined avenue, grateful for
the dappled shade. What a relief it would be to see

Ford; he always managed to find a way out of every emergency. He was adept at swift solutions.

Valeria was aware of the crunching sound of her feet on the gravel as though the place were deserted like a stage setting after the performance of a play.

In an attempt to make herself more presentable, she straightened her black hair, in which a few strands of straw had become enmeshed, put on her wide-brimmed hat and rang the bell.

After a long wait the heavy oak door was opened by the Italian coachman. He was buttoning up a white linen housecoat as though hurriedly assuming another role. He seemed guiltily taken aback at the sight of her. "Oh, la Signora Lee!"

"Is Mr. Hollister in?"

He hesitated, undecided as to whether he should admit her. He had the bronzed, classic looks of southern Italy. Pools of hot oil—this was how Ford had laughingly described his eyes.

"I will see—" He stood aside for her to enter. "If you will wait in here."

She went into the cool hall. The light gray walls and gray and white marble floor offered a degree of coolness, but she sensed as before something strange and unnatural about the house. The Italian preceded her to the drawing room where, on her previous visit, they had sat in the evenings. There was something in his manner that seemed to her more casual and familiar than was customary in a servant, as though he were used to having the run of these downstairs rooms.

The shutters were closed. The French furniture and tapestries were veiled in shadow. The Chinese vases bereft of flowers. The room apparently had not been dusted in some time.

Vaguely disturbed, Valeria turned to see the coachman closing the door. A heavy silence encompassed the whole house as though it were under a glass shell. Where, she wondered, were the other servants? Were Ford and the Italian coachman alone with Althea? Her uneasiness increased as she waited. There had been something furtive and conspiratorial about the

Italian's masquerading as a houseman. Valeria did not feel inclined to sit down.

She noticed that the cushions on the sofa were crumpled. On a lacquer coffee table glasses with dregs of whiskey remained uncleared. An ashtray was littered with cigarette butts. A faint rank odor pervaded the room. It occurred to her that the shutters were closed for some other reason than the excessive heat. Perhaps Althea was far sicker than she had supposed. She had intruded into a well-guarded private ward.

The door opened suddenly and Ford came in.

It was not the Ford she knew. The polished, debonair charm was gone. He was flustered, untidy, in his shirtsleeves, without a tie, and with a feverish flush that did not become his usually pallid cheeks. It was the first time his lifetime friend had ever seen him unshaven.

"Val! What a surprise!" He hurried forward and kissed her, but she could tell that he was not overjoyed to see her. "I've been meaning to write. I'm afraid things have been rather disjointed here."

He urged her to sit down. "Would you like something? I can ask Antonio to make some coffee or iced tea?"

"No, Ford dear," Valeria said, disconcerted by his staccato manner. "We've been worried about you. I thought I'd stop by just to see how you are."

"I'm all right, I suppose," he said jerkily. "I hardly know at this point. We've been having a difficult time. Are you well? How's the ogress? Are you bearing up under the strain?"

"I've left the Brewsters," she confessed. "But it's a long story and that isn't why I came," she lied.

"Left? Why? What happened?" Ford was startled and, with his quick, intuitive mind, guessed that she had come for help or advice.

"That doesn't matter now, Ford. We've heard nothing from you. I wanted to know how Althea is and if I could help in any way."

He seemed to subside inwardly and said with an unbecoming grimace, "She's not well. We're hoping to take her to New York, but she can't be moved yet. No, my dear, there isn't anything you can do."

He was on edge, peremptory in his forced politeness, listening all the time for sounds from the floor above.

On a sudden impulse of sympathy Valeria went to him and laid her hand on his cheek. "Oh, Ford! . . ." She bent and kissed him and was dismayed by his burning skin.

Ford took her slender hand and held it for a moment, seeking some lost reassurance or forgiveness. "Thank you for coming. I've wanted so much to see you. Is Randy all right?"

"He's fine. Immersed in his articles. He and Josiah Eaton are getting on very well, it seems."

He was greatly relieved, as though any good news counted as a blessing, and asked, "Why did you leave the Brewsters?"

"Oh, there was a drama over the son. He conceived a foolish infatuation for me. I had no choice but to go."

"My dear," Ford exclaimed with a flash of his old opportunism, "You should have accepted him. He'll inherit millions."

"Hank's only a boy." She returned to her chair sensing a need for some distance between them. "I thought perhaps I could help you nurse Althea. You know how long I looked after Randy at Whitebriars."

He shook his head, "You don't understand what the trouble is. Or did you guess?"

"I knew she was very upset that night!"

"Upset! She's mad. Quite mad. It's a question of this or an asylum. That's why we're here," he flung at her, impatient with her good-natured persistence.

Ford started to talk rapidly in a sharp and unfeeling way, as though discussing some bizarre affliction that had befallen someone they didn't know.

"She seemed so much better. We thought it was worth risking an evening out. I should have known better than to take her to Ida Brewster's."

"Oh Ford, and you did that for me!"

"Althea was very much taken with you. She

wanted to go. She's been perfectly calm for nearly six
months or as calm as she ever can be. That evening was
her Waterloo. I don't know exactly what set her off
. . . perhaps too many people she didn't know."

"How long has she been like this?"

"How long? Always. It wasn't apparent until she
was grown up. She was a brilliant girl. It's the result
of her distinguished father who had a not so distinguished mistress in Paris. A heritage for which Althea
is in no way—no way—to blame."

Valeria was appalled at this Greek tragedy. "But
didn't you know? I mean—?"

"Before? Not entirely. I knew there was something
wrong; some form of neurasthenia, I thought. It wasn't
so apparent. Althea's mother, who is not the vague
little creature she seems, made a positive beeline for
me. I was out of funds, I had no prospects—as you
know. I was grateful for those invitations. It's a very
old New York name. On the surface everything
seemed well ordered. They entertained, always the
same family friends, people Althea knew. I liked her.
We got on. She's extremely intelligent, far more
learned than I am. I thought her disinclination to
meet people was an inhibition . . . because she'd been
overprotected. I thought it would be possible to make
some sort of a civilized life. Oh," he confessed, "I don't
exactly know what I thought. It seemed the best solution then."

He was telling her as much as he dared, in order
to justify himself.

"I thought that with care and encouragement she'd
improve. We went abroad on our honeymoon. At
first we had a very good time. She was quite content
to go to the opera or to go out driving, as long as we
were alone. The old lady came with us, of course.
She always hovered around. We were in Venice, at
the Danieli. One night as we came into the lobby—"
he broke off.

Valeria saw that something had happened which he
did not care to reveal.

"She became hysterical. There was a scene. A doctor was sent for and through him I discovered the

truth. The old lady admitted she'd hidden it from me. Mrs. Haverfield was frightened, you see, that if anything happened to her, Althea would be left unprotected."

He got up abruptly, lit a cigarette and moved in a jerky, abstracted way to the sofa where he straightened the cushions, avoiding Valeria's eyes. He was not telling the whole truth, she knew.

"The old woman has found a new doctor, a Mesmerist who studied with Charcot in Paris. He thinks he can do something. I doubt it now."

"But surely it can't be incurable. That would be too cruel."

Tapping his forehead, Ford said harshly, "The damage is here!" He turned to Valeria suddenly and exclaimed with complete sincerity, "I wouldn't have brought you both here if there'd been anything I could have done in New York. I planned it quite differently. But you see it's impossible there. We don't go out or see anyone. How can we? And the old woman's very tight with the purse strings. I fancy she thinks if I got my hands on a lump sum, I'd be off. And perhaps now," he admitted abjectly, "I might be. This is hardly the sort of life I'd have chosen. I was better off in Atlanta, poor as we always were."

Unexpectedly, voices broke out upstairs. Althea was shouting; the Italian was trying to reason with her. Ford darted to the door. Valeria instinctively followed. Althea was on the stairs struggling with the coachman. Ford ran up toward them.

"Althea, go back to your room!"

A distracted figure in a stained nightgown, her hair in disorder, Althea broke free as Ford reached her and, raising her arm, struck out at him. Her features were wildly distorted, a savage mask. Ford seized her, and together he and the Italian forced her back onto the landing. She managed to grasp the banister, and, clinging to it with a manic force, caught sight of Valeria in the hall below.

"Help me. They're killing me. Help!"

Ford struck his wife sharply across the face. Althea's head jerked back and she lost her grip. As the two men dragged her along the landing, Ford shouted down, "Don't wait. There's nothing you can do."

"Help me. Don't let them—please—," Althea screamed.

Horrified and incredulous, Valeria went back into the drawing room to retrieve her hat. As she crossed the hall a wild scream from above was cut short by a slamming door.

She let herself out and found herself, trembling with shock, in the torpid sunlight. The tubs of scarlet flowers, the motionless sycamores, the day itself, seemed totally unreal.

Ford and the Italian had forced Althea into her disordered bedroom and, while the Italian held her, pinioning her as she thrashed and wailed, Ford poured a sedative into a silver mug, added water, and gripping Althea's sweat-drenched hair, dragged her head back. Her eyes were staring with terror; her jaws clenched.

The Italian climbed over her, gripping her between his knees, and brutally forced her mouth open. Ford poured the contents of the container down her throat. She choked, sputtered and fell back, spent.

"I want Valeria," she moaned.

Ford smoothed back her sodden hair.

She twisted away her head in bitter defeat. "Why did you send her away?"

"Try to sleep now. Please try."

They left her in the darkened room, rank with the unpleasant miasma of lunacy. Ford locked the door.

He went into his bedroom, poured out a glass of whiskey, took a long drink and handed the glass to the Italian who shook his head. They were both exhausted from this latest outbreak of violence. Ford nodded to his confederate who unbuttoned his rumpled white linen coat, revealing a naked torso, banded with black silk suspenders. He undressed slowly with a calculated indifference. They were resuming a scene that had been interrupted by Valeria's unexpected appearance.

Valeria found herself on the road, blinded by noon-day heat. She was overwhelmed by the nightmare that had engulfed her oldest friend.

She would have welcomed tears, but instead she felt stunned and helpless. Behind her distress Valeria knew that no more help would be forthcoming from Ford. He had bravely and loyally done all he could. They were alone now, she and Randy, at the mercy of this hateful town.

Suddenly, on the point of turning back, she remembered the Hotchkiss farm and the nice country woman bending over her string beans; the stream with the forget-me-nots and the feeling of sun-drenched peace. Anything would be preferable to the soul-destroying drudgery that was all Arcadia offered. Perhaps Mrs. Hotchkiss would take her on. She could work on the farm, put up jams, do the household chores. She knew about vegetables, having spent long hours coaxing them from the ruined gardens at Whitebriars.

It was a wild notion, but Valeria had no choice but to clutch at straws and she was already halfway there.

She tried to put Ford out of her mind as she trudged along. There were things about him that Valeria did not want to consider. Whatever might be the ambigu-ities in his personal life, which she had sensed long ago, they paled before the price Ford had paid for the security they had all three hungered for.

The heat enveloped her like a blanket. She could hardly breathe.

She passed Josiah Eaton's place. A typically par-venu home, badly designed, elaborate in the wrong way. But the lawns looked invitingly green. From the carriages lining the driveway and horses nuzzling the grass under the trees while their drivers dozed, Valeria concluded he must be having a luncheon.

It seemed an endless stretch from the Eaton place to the farm. She was drugged in a mirage of scalding heat.

When, finally, Valeria turned off the road between the orchards, now laden with apples and pears, her head was swimming and she was forced to sit down by the side of the dusty road.

She was overcome by a sense of depression, by the futility of her life stretching before her without prospect of money or release. What was the purpose of endlessly forcing herself to face up to circumstances? Valeria felt doomed to flounder in one fruitless endeavor after another. Her burden of being well-bred, and her Southern manner which these Northern people seemed to resent so were part of a useless heritage. Perhaps she should have grabbed Hank Brewster's offer, absurd as that marriage would have been. It would have been better, at least, than either the fate that had befallen Ford or the one that lay before her now. It had been pure folly to have flounced out of Josiah Eaton's flat, flinging back words of contempt, as though she were a woman of means who was in a position to defend her dignity. He might have given her more work.

Would there ever be a corner where she could hide in blessed anonymity and eke out a livelihood, ridding herself, day by day, of that self-esteem or vanity or pride or whatever it was in her that impelled her to strike out at what repelled and offended her? Everything she was and no longer had any right to be was a hindrance. Could she learn to subdue herself sufficiently to fade into the crowd, to accept meanness and ignorance and vulgarity without question? What did standards of decency and taste matter?

Resigned, Valeria pulled herself up and went on down the lane toward the Hotchkiss farm. Mrs. Hotchkiss was working in a patch of marigolds, in the same blue cotton dress and old poke bonnet. Valeria envied her freedom to fulfill her duties with self-respect, unharassed by the world.

Mrs. Hotchkiss looked up, not at first recognizing this stranger in the dusty white dress, with her flaming cheeks.

"Do you remember?" Valeria reminded her. "I came the other day to buy flowers for Mrs. Brewster?"

Valeria heard Mrs. Hotchkiss say something, saw

her loom up and blur, and pitched forward across the path.

The next thing she knew there was a coolness on her brow. Mrs. Hotchkiss was saying in the distance, "Poor thing! Out in the sun too long. Can you sit up a little?"

The kind woman who smelled of grass and apples was trying to lift Valeria's head so that she could drink a little water.

The water was deliciously fresh and cool.

"There now. Lie still." She wrung out a rag in a bucket and laid it on Valeria's forehead. "When you feel better I'll help you indoors," the sing-song voice advised. "The sun is so strong, you know. You should not be out in it without a covering."

After a few moments Valeria sat up. "I'm sorry. I'm all right now."

"Did you hurt yourself falling?"

"I don't believe so. How stupid—I never faint."

The wrinkled country woman was surprisingly strong. She helped Valeria up without much difficulty.

"Take my arm now. You can rest inside. I'll make some tea."

Her head had cleared by the time they reached the house. Mrs. Hotchkiss led her into the kitchen which smelled, as she did, of fruit and wild grasses. She helped Valeria to a chair at the kitchen table. Valeria sat there with her head in her hands while Mrs. Hotchkiss busied herself about the stove.

"Are you feeling a little better? And why did you walk so far without young Mr. Brewster?"

Valeria looked up. The moment she always dreaded had come again.

"I don't work for the Brewsters any more. I was wondering if perhaps I could work here. It was so nice the day we came. I know quite a lot about gardening. After the war I grew all our vegetables. I am not afraid of hard work."

Mrs. Hotchkiss nodded, not understanding quite what the poor young thing was saying.

"I can sleep in the barn," Valeria suggested, "until

the cold weather. I don't mind about payment. And I can cook and clean the house."

Mrs. Hotchkiss made a faint clucking sound of amazement. "Oh, my pretty young thing, it is very kind, I'm sure," she said carefully as though addressing someone not quite right in the head. "But you see I do all that myself. There is only myself and Mr. Hotchkiss. Because our son, you see, works on his own farm. He is married, and has three children and so there is only us."

"If you had someone to help, you could grow more," Valeria tried, valiantly battling her old dread of rejection. "I could take the flowers and vegetables to town. You could expand."

Mrs. Hotchkiss did not take kindly to the notion of expansion. She clucked. Surely this poor thing was daft. Being so long in the sun and all.

Valeria made a despairing plunge, "Please let me come here. I have nowhere to go and I cannot get work in town."

"Dear me!' Mrs. Hotchkiss's voice took on a tone of condolence as though she had just been informed of a bereavement. "Well, I must say, it is strange and me thinking you was to marry young Mr. Brewster. You made a nice couple, I was thinking."

The older woman looked down in embarrassment. What could she make of this stranger who came and offered to sleep in the barn? It was all in a way so sad and her not right in the head and what would Mr. Hotchkiss say?

The kettle was hissing. Mrs. Hotchkiss took a long time, as she pondered, to make the tea in the old brown teapot. How could she both help and get rid of this awkward visitor?

She brought Valeria a cup. "There, my dear, you will feel better soon, I'm sure."

She hovered about as Valeria picked up the cup, found it too hot and set it down. "Well, I must get back to my marigolds. You sit there, my dear, and drink your tea until you feel quite right again."

Valeria said nothing. There was nothing left to say.

It had been foolish to come on such a slim chance, on what, she now saw, was no chance at all.

"I am thinking perhaps the priest at your church might help you. They have money, you see, in case of—" Mrs. Hotchkiss hesitated tactfully. "You know what I mean, I'm sure."

"The poor box," Valeria said flatly.

"I would ask him, you see. And there are places that are quite clean. Well . . ." How could she get back to her flowers? She had offered all the help she could. "God bless you, my dear." She faded through the door.

It was peaceful in the little room. A country clock inlaid with mother-of-pearl, probably a relic from the old country, ticked sleepily on the mantel. What more could anyone ask than this? A house of one's own, a garden, things to grow, and peace.

Valeria was grateful for the tea. She must summon up strength for the interminable walk back to town. She took an apple from the bowl on the table and slipped it into her bag, knowing it would be all right to do so, and left.

Mrs. Hotchkiss was once again bent over her work, but was able to watch the strange young lady in white as she made her way through the garden into the lane. Sleep in the barn! My goodness, what *would* Mr. Hotchkiss say?

Valeria concentrated on walking, aware of the road, and of how little distance she covered. She would not waste any energy on thinking.

She passed hay carts returning from the fields creating clouds of dust. Valeria's skirt was long since gray.

At long last she came to Josiah Eaton's. The carriages had gone. The luncheon was over. The place droused in the afternoon heat.

She must learn not to criticize. Josiah Eaton had succeeded where she had failed. He was rich, she was poor. Those were the only standards by which she must judge from now on.

The sun was setting when she reached the Haverfields'. Much as she felt for Ford, she had no desire to venture into that tainted house again.

It came to her that no alternative remained but to ask Sam Garvey for the money he had promised her. Five hundred dollars to get to New York. Five hundred dollars to rest. A breathing space and escape from Arcadia.

As she trudged along Valeria's resolve hardened. The old monster would make more millions out of whatever deal he was planning with Thaddeus Brownlow. The Brewsters would be richer than ever before. Ida would build her opera house. Valeria had earned what to them was a paltry sum and what was to her deliverance. What did she care what any of them thought?

Dusk fell as she struggled down Tremont Avenue. Self-satisfied businessmen on their way home rolled by in their buggies. They would relax in their parlors while their overdressed wives would regale them with the latest gossip. Five hundred dollars would put a thankful distance between herself and those smug parvenus. Her resolution to become more humble and self-effacing had vanished by the time she reached the hill that led down into the two. She hated that sinkhole of commerce and the rage in her heart gave Valeria the courage to keep going. Numbed with fatigue, her legs moved mechanically. Her feet burned as though crushed by some inquisitor's vise.

It was completely dark when she reached Main Street. A sharp pain in her left foot stabbed her. She leaned against a building and discovered a large hole in her shoe. Her stocking was caked with blood. Valeria stuffed a handkerchief into the shoe and forced herself forward. She moved very slowly, placing her feet with a leaden effort one before the other.

At last she recognized the beginnings of Shacktown. There were lights in the tumbledown dwellings. Singing swelled from a saloon. She no longer cared what dirt and refuse she stumbled through.

The lane twisted back on itself and Valeria discovered she had lost all sense of direction.

Suddenly the immense chimneys loomed above her. At their base crouched the house like a black toadstool. There was a glow in the downstairs window.

She reached the iron fence, found the gate, and pushed it open. Her feet found their agonized way up the cobblestone path. She was there. She would not have to walk any farther.

Exhausted, Valeria leaned against the side of the door after pulling the bell. But in the center of her brain a single thought persisted. She must get the money. She no longer cared what she said, what she had to do, how long she was forced to wait. She would not leave without it.

The door opened. A woman with a shawl over her head peered out. At first she saw no one and, thinking it must be some child who had pushed the bell on a dare, was about to close the door when Valeria stepped forward.

"I want to see Mr. Garvey. Will you tell him Valeria Lee is here?"

The woman looked at her, suspicious and affronted. "Who might you be?"

"Never mind who I am. Tell him I have to see him."

"You was the one who worked for Mrs. Brewster, wasn't it?" Tabitha Grey remembered.

"Tell Mr. Garvey I'm waiting," Valeria said with a force that brooked no refusal.

Tabitha slammed the door. Impertinent minx! Giving orders as though she was someone! Turning up in the middle of the night! No wonder Mrs. Brewster had sent her packing!

A few moments later Tabitha grudgingly opened the door again. "You're to come in."

Valeria followed her into a hall so dimly lit that she could hardly see anything. A staircase. A grandfather clock. Everything was coated with dirt and darkness. The house smelled rank as though it were never cleaned.

Tabitha showed her into a large room, the far wall of which was lined with shelves of ledgers, all bound in the same dismal gray. Dark curtains were drawn. Dark walls. Dark paintings. The old tycoon was seated at a big mahogany desk covered with accounts.

Garvey watched Miss Lee as she came in. His face

expressed no interest or recognition. He was crouching there like a great toad, wreathed in cigar smoke.

She heard herself say with a strength that surprised her, "I've come for the money you owe me. You said you would pay me five hundred dollars if I charmed Mr. Brownlow. You appeared to think I succeeded. I would like you to pay me. Now."

Sam nodded. He did not seem surprised. She wondered vaguely if he could have been waiting for her.

"Sit down, Miss Lee."

She went to a wing chair near the fire and sat down. The relief was so immense that nothing else in the world mattered, even the money. She had forgotten what it was like not to be walking, to sit so divinely still.

"You want it in coins or notes?"

"It doesn't matter."

He was beginning to recede from her. She saw Garvey get up, open the panel before a wall safe and take out a canvas bag. He sat down again, loosened the string of the bag, reached in and pulled out a bundle of notes.

"You'd better take it in notes. Five hundred in silver is a lot to carry."

He started to count out the money. There was a heavy, airless silence in the room.

When he had finished, he looked up. Valeria's head, with the becomingly rosy cheeks, had fallen sideways against the side of the chair. She was asleep.

ᙅᙓᙏ CHAPTER TEN ᙭ᙩ

THE YANKEE CAPTAIN WAS LEADING HER down a path overgrown with weeds at Whitebriars into the ruined grape arbor. As he turned to take her in his arms, she saw the terrible sadness in his eyes, the wounds of his spirit, irrevocably damaged by the war. There were points of light in his pupils like distant campfires before a battle that would never be ended for him. She shrank from him and from that sadness as though it would infect her like a disease.

The clock struck and Valeria woke with a start. What time was it?

As her mind cleared, she saw Sam Garvey still sitting at his desk, watching her with the immobility of a Chinese idol. A canopy of thick smoke hung above him. He smiled, in some way softened and humanized.

"You've been asleep three hours."

"I'm sorry," she murmured. "I was so tired."

On a small table beside her were a plate of ham, potato salad, bread and butter, and a bottle of Moselle wine.

Ravenous, she ate in silence. The wine kissed her palate, a kiss of release and reassurance. Valeria remembered: she had the money.

"Where did you go," he asked, "to get so red?"

"The Hotchkiss farm."

"You walked that far?"

"I had a stupid idea she might let me work there."

"On a farm."

"I like to be in the open air."

"You've been looking for work?"

She nodded. "There's nothing for me here. I shall go to New York now."

"Why didn't you come to me before?"

What was the use of explaining that it had been a matter of pride and that she had wanted to reserve her right to despise him?

"Thank you for the supper."

She finished the wine and boldly refilled her glass. She was not fully awake yet, adrift in the vague awareness that she had achieved her aim. Sam Garvey and all he represented and the resentment he had aroused in her were part of a murky chapter that was now over.

"What happened to Hank?" she inquired.

"Back to college. He went on a three-day bender after that night. The police found him and brought him in."

"Poor boy!"

"Did you encourage him?"

"He was so young. I didn't think it was serious."

"It was serious all right. You turned that whole household upside down. Ida split a gut as usual."

"I'm sure she hates me."

"Ida hates most everyone."

"Why? She has everything."

"Not anything she wants." He knocked a long ash reflectively from his cigar. "When you don't work for what you get, nothing adds up to much. Even Thaddeus Brownlow earns his splendor."

An odd word for him to use, she thought. Perhaps he wasn't as illiterate as he appeared.

"Hank is a nice boy. He needs to get away," said Valeria.

"Most people do."

"I suppose you stay because of business."

"I run everything from here."

They were talking with simple directness, without defenses. It was the spell of this strange hour and this strange room and the fact that they were the only two people awake in the silence that blanketed the town. They spoke quietly, but their voices had the clarity of sounds under glass without resonance or echo.

"You should do something for Nancy," Valeria suggested. "She's so unhappy. It's unfair for a girl her age."

"She's Ida's child. I only give them money."

"They're your grandchildren."

"We're not exactly a loving family. You may have noticed."

She looked into the wine, golden with promise. What did she care any more about Sam Garvey or the Brewsters and their harsh, destructive ways? She could buy a new coat and skirt now, a new hat and gloves and shoes. Already Valeria could anticipate the relief of relaxing on the train, watching Arcadia slipping back into the past. How stupid to have endured the last few days, instead of coming to confront him sooner!

"What will you do in New York, Miss Lee?"

"Look for work," she smiled. "Perhaps Mr. Brownlow will show me his Fragonards."

"He'd be glad to, I'm sure. And more besides."

Soothed by the wine, Valeria sat back and observed him. Why hadn't he been like this before, relaxed, ironic, almost likable? She was half tempted to feel that he might not be such a crass old monster after all.

"Have you always lived in this house?"

"Thirty years. I built it."

"Doesn't it depress you, all that dirt and poverty outside?"

"I'm a very hard-hearted man. Haven't you heard?"

"Yes, I have. Still, I should want to clear it away from my sight."

"They're free to get out if they can. I did."

"Poverty doesn't leave much room for freedom, as I've discovered."

"You're not ready to settle for it; that's the difference. You've got your crazy Southern pride."

"I don't see the point in having so much money when you apparently do so little with it. Even your daughter entertains."

"I'd rather keep my money in the bank than sit through one of Ida's dinners."

They both laughed.

"But what *do* you do," she persisted, "when you're not raking in millions?" Valeria glanced 'round. Thirty years in this oppressive room, with the curtains drawn and only the ledgers for company. It seemed a deliberate self-impoverishment that denied, in her eyes, the whole purpose of being rich.

"Maybe I don't know what to do. Ever thought of that?"

It was a strange admission, quite out of keeping with her image of him as a ruthlessly self-sufficient man.

"Don't you ever go away? Haven't you any desire to see the world?"

"Sure. I go away. Like to see where I've been, Miss Lee?"

Garvey got up and opened the glass doors of a bookcase, selected a volume bound in green leather and brought it to her.

"The Old Curiosity Shop," Valeria read out loud.

"I guess I know London as well as Mr. Dickens. I could find my way around there without a guide. And I know Paris, too. I could draw you a map of the sewers. I must have read *Les Misérables* . . . well, at least twenty times."

She was amazed. The binding was one of the most opulent Valeria had ever seen. "I'd no idea—"

"That I read? I read most of the night. When you reach my age, you don't sleep much."

She handed back the book and he replaced it in the bookcase and carefully locked the doors.

It came to her, considering Garvey in his own light and not merely as the instrument of her release from Arcadia, that there must be a good deal more to this rough, irascible old man than anyone imagined. Everything she had heard of him; from Randolph's lurid accounts of his misdeeds, from her own conclusions drawn from her walk through Shacktown, she had not conceived of his long nights spent alone with novels he obviously loved. Yet how was it that at the same time he was immune to pity, that Garvey felt nothing for his family or his workers grubbing for survival in squalor worse than that in which freed Negroes were forced to huddle in Atlanta? The two aspects of his nature didn't mesh.

"But if you enjoy these books so much, why don't you go to Paris and London and see them for yourself?"

"I don't harbor illusions, Miss Lee," he admitted gruffly. "I'm an uncouth, unmannerly old man. If I went to London, who would talk to me? I daresay a few tarts and touts would try to take me for a ride. I know my business and that's it. So I stay here and let Mr. Dickens and Mr. Hugo do the honors. They introduce me to a lot of interesting people and show me a lot of curious things. I consider them my friends."

This unexpected candor for some reason offended Valeria. Iago had stepped out of character and assumed the garb of a penitent, thereby disrupting the appointed outcome of the play.

"You exaggerate, Mr. Garvey. You don't make it easy for people to like you, but you're obviously a person to be reckoned with."

"It's not only Southerners," he said wryly, "that have some pride."

He went back to his desk and lit a fresh cigar.

"You could take Nancy abroad. She's dying to escape from Arcadia."

"She'd die of fright if I even suggested it."

Valeria was confronted by a mystery which, having now settled their accounts, she was disinclined to face. It was too late to discover that Sam Garvey was a human being, bitterly alone and disillusioned. It seemed so much safer to preserve the hypocrisy of disguises than to be lured into sympathizing with someone she had decided, with good reason, to dislike.

"That's the way the world's divided," Garvey was saying, "people who know how to live, like you, and don't have the wherewithal, and people like me who know how to make money, but don't know what to do with it. The rest out there, the flotsam and jetsam, don't know or don't care, and don't amount to anything anyway." He took a long ruminative swig of whiskey. "Take Ida. She'd give anything to have what you've got, your way of behaving and doing things, the way you dress. And you'd like to be rich and you never will be. You don't have it in you to make a cent."

"Not a very encouraging picture, Mr. Garvey."

"We're an unlucky pair, Miss Lee. What we've got ain't no damn good to us." He smiled with benevolent irony. "That's not to say you won't charm some wealthy fellow—into marriage maybe. He'd be getting a good deal in one way, though he'd need a cast-iron patience to put up with your high-handed ways." He chuckled.

"You think I'm a harridan," she said, slightly insulted.

"Let's say I don't think you'll settle down and become a submissive wife."

From habit, he was needling her into a confrontation of wills and temperaments. But where once this habit of caustic challenge had angered her, now, weary and relaxed by wine, she was amused.

"As a matter of fact," Valeria countered, "I don't aspire to much. I thought at the Hotchkiss place I'd be quite content to live on a farm like that, out of the world, at peace . . . and free."

Garvey's sharp blue eyes twinkled with friendly malice. "You'll forgive me, Miss Lee, but I don't see you just spending your days milking cows and your nights stitching potato sacks over the Bible. Any more than I see myself administering to the poor."

"How do you see me?" she demanded. "Ruling some weak-willed business man with a rod of iron?"

"Not exactly. You're no Ida."

She inclined her head. "I suppose I shouldn't thank you as she's your daughter."

"My daughter wasn't so wrong about you. You are a kind of adventuress. I like that. We were all like that in my day. That's missing in Ida and her kids. That's why they won't amount to anything."

Valeria felt that this analysis of her character had gone far enough. "It's late. Or early. I don't know which." She bent down to retrieve her shoes which, in her sleep, she had kicked under the chair. "It's been an odd meeting. All my meetings with you are peculiar. I'm sorry I shan't have the opportunity to know you better."

"If I'm odd enough to make you a proposition," Valeria heard him say as she smoothed out the blood-stained handkerchief over the hole that had chafed her foot, "are you adventurous enough to listen?"

She looked up. "You have a penchant for making me propositions. What is it this time? You want to hire me as your reader?"

"No, it's not a matter of hiring. Rather, you might say, of considering an investment."

She tried to squeeze her foot into a shoe that had become unbearably too small. "You know very well I've nothing to invest."

"I'm not talking about money, at least not yours."

"What, then?" Valeria gritted her teeth and forced her foot into the shoe. The pain was acute.

"Time," he pronounced and blew out a cloud of smoke. "Your time, Miss Lee."

She sank back, defeated. How could she ever manage to walk as far as the boardinghouse? She wanted to leave, but her feet, her whole body, ached. She felt no inclination to pursue this exchange of confidences which had turned, as it always did with him, into some kind of tilting match. Why did Garvey persist in sitting there, eyeing her, and blowing out those interminable clouds of smoke?

He was turning his glass around and around in his hand, as though bringing himself to the point of a decision. Valeria wondered what he had looked like as a young man, before the hardening process of fighting his way to the top had carved his face into such deep lines and angles. Only his eyes had retained their brightness. She detected beneath their shrewdness and occasional malice a gleam. Was it of some lost hope or perjured innocence? Perhaps there remained, even in him, the flicker of an unrealized but never quite relinquished dream.

"You have already paid for my time," Valeria reminded him. "I must take my money and go."

"If I'm so odd," he said abruptly, "you can spare the time to hear just how far my oddness goes. You can still leave for New York if you think your chances there are more auspicious. They may well be."

A wave of fatigue swept through her. She could not summon the strength to resist his evident intention to keep her here.

Garvey was staring at the ceiling, searching for words above the drifting smoke. The gnarled fingers moved along the polished surface of the desk.

He said with slow deliberation, "I'm seventy-three. I've got five or six years more. I shan't last beyond eighty. I asked you once to sell me an evening. You were insulted. What would you say if I asked you to sell me, say—six years? How old are you?"

"Twenty-five," she replied, mystified.

"You'd be, at most, thirty-one by the time I'm done for. Not too old to hide on something better than a farm if that's what you'd still a mind to do."

It did not dawn on her what Sam was suggesting. It had never occurred to her that he could feel any personal interest in anyone, least of all herself. Six years? As his housekeeper, companion, confidante?

"Understand this," he leaned forward and addressed her directly. "I asked Thaddeus Brownlow to dinner because I'm putting through a big deal. It'll take about a year to get it started. The groundwork's already laid. When that's launched, I've a fancy to go away. I'd like, as you said, to see something of the world before it's too late. I'd like to travel. Not a quick trip, running around. I'd like to enjoy things at leisure, things I wouldn't know how to enjoy alone. I had no education, but I'm not dead to appreciation if things are pointed out. I'm not so old up here," Garvey touched his forehead. "And what's here," he indicated his heart, "wouldn't concern you. What I'm offering is a bargain. Strictly that. I don't look for any foolish pretenses or made-up feelings. Nothing personal. I want six years of your time. In return, I'll see that you don't have to worry about money again. You can name any sum you want."

Valeria had no immediate reaction. This proposal, outlined with the dry formality of a board meeting, had no connection with herself at all.

"I'm a rough diamond," he went on. "I don't pretend to be anything else. But this I promise you. I'll keep my word. I want your company, your way of seeing things. In return I'll give you the one thing I've plenty of."

His words fell into the silence of her complete incredulity. She heard herself say with an unreal lightness, "At five hundred an evening, six years would cost you a great deal."

He pointed out in the same flat, deliberate way, as though underlining a clause in an insurance policy, "I'm not asking you to be a kept woman, Miss Lee."

She laughed. It was too absurd. "Why, Mr. Garvey, don't tell me you're proposing—at this hour in the morning and when I'm going away!"

"There are worse things in the world than to be Mrs. Sam Garvey." He grinned. "Not many, maybe, but a few."

She was struck by the farcical aspect of his offer. "When on earth did you come by this strange idea?"

"Oh, I've thought about you. And I watched you when you were sleeping, in that worn out dress and shoes with holes and your scarlet cheeks. I thought, 'What a waste! I could give her everything she needs in a material way. And she could give me, just by being herself, something I've never had.' "

She was floored, but managed to say lamely, "I told Hank when he proposed that he knew nothing about me. What do you know? That I'm a down-at-the-heels adventuress with a bad temper and something called Southern pride? It doesn't strike me as a very sound investment."

"I'm not often wrong about where I put my money."

"If you're looking for a traveling companion," she reasoned, "you should find some beautiful, accommodating creature who would cost you a good deal less."

"Yes, I could do that. And you may find a New York broker who'll set you up in a swank apartment. Or even marry you. He'd want a lot more than I'm asking. This way you'd be independent for life at thirty-one."

It was beyond reason, not conceivably to be considered. "I think you are slightly insane, Mr. Garvey. We have only met four times and each time we've had an argument. I'm sure I should make your life unbearable."

"Maybe. You might make it interesting, too."

She forced her other foot into a torturous shoe. "It's very flattering and I'm flattered, but I can't, for a moment, think you're serious."

"If you'd stop being a Southern belle for a moment," Sam said with a touch of his old asperity, "you'd see, considering what we both are, it's not such a bad idea."

Valeria managed to put both feet to the ground. "What we both are?"

"Two difficult, pig-headed people with more opinions than are good for us. But not above making a sound bargain. It's your time for my money. And no strings attached. Think it over."

She forced herself to stand up. Sharp pains shot through her long legs. "Since you're being so reckless, will you take me home?"

He said gruffly, "I'm not going to wake my man up at this hour."

"You are not only insane, Mr. Garvey, you're ungallant. And where," she asked as an afterthought, "would I live for the year it will take you to launch your deal?"

"Why, here."

"In this house? I'd be ashamed to set foot outside."

"You'd get used to it."

"I couldn't sleep under this roof. No, Mr. Garvey, if you need to be beguiled by female company, you had better look elsewhere."

"You'd have six years of insulting me," he reminded her. "With your disposition I'd say that was a big inducement."

"Yes, I dare to say we'd exchange a few good insults. Well, if you have no conveyance, I guess I shall have to walk."

She hobbled over to the desk and held out her delicate hand for the money.

"Always set on destroying your chances," he said shrewdly as he gave her the bundle of notes. "How many more do you think you'll get?"

"Who knows? I never thought when I came here last night that I'd have such a bizarre proposal."

"No need to be so flip," Garvey said sharply. "I've been as honest as I can."

She leaned on the desk, partly to ease the pain, and looked at him deeply, as though seriously considering his offer for the first time. To Valeria's surprise her heart reassured her. She saw that he meant what he said, that he would keep his word and that, as far as she was concerned, it was safe to trust him.

"I'm very tired," she confessed. "I can't take in what you've said. Probably by the light of day you'll regret every word of it. But I'll think it over."

"Don't think too long. I might take Nancy abroad instead."

"That would be wiser."

He watched her as she limped back, stuffed the bank notes into her purse and picked up her battered straw hat. Despite her recalcitrance, Sam felt only an amused fondness for her; weary, embattled, in her hangdog clothes, with her burning cheeks and disheveled black hair. There was a streak of blind obstinacy in her that would always compel Valeria to miss easy settlements. She would go on fighting long after her last chance had passed her by.

Suddenly, whatever fate presided over her destiny jolted Valeria into an awareness that something extraordinary had happened. Mrs. Sam Garvey? To marry this old millionaire of whom she knew nothing but evil, who represented everything she had most cause to hate, but who had offered her the first concrete solution to her future.

She turned and *saw* him, not as a grim eccentric who had revealed a personal emptiness at the core of his vast financial power, but as a man who had abruptly entered her life. He was *there*. Harsh, forceful, uncompromising, uncomfortably perceptive, but vulnerable in his confessed loneliness and need.

Valeria felt overwhelmingly ashamed for having been so cavalier.

"I'm sorry," she said simply. "I was ungracious and unkind. I'm amazed that you should have thought of me in this way. But I am grateful and I will consider it."

He stood up abruptly.

"Good. Then I'll take you home."

◈ Chapter Eleven ◈

IT WAS already afternoon when Valeria woke. She was at once aware of a sense of immense, beatific relief. She had the money; it was there in her bag on the chest of drawers. So great was the luxury of this knowledge that she allowed herself to sink into it as though into a warm and scented bath.

She had been saved by a miraculous chance. Unaccountably, at the end of that dreadful day, fate had relented. She was free!

Five hundred dollars!

Stretching her aching limbs, Valeria decided that she would stay in bed all day and contemplate her good fortune. There were no shops in Arcadia worth investigating. She would wait until she was in New York and could find some really becoming outfit at one of those smart little couturiers that abounded in big cities. Perhaps Randolph would nobly refuse a share of her fortune. In which case she would have ample time to look around for a position she liked. She might even embark on a career as a dress designer herself. In New York her talents—drawbacks in Arcadia—would prove to be assets. The whole aspect of her future had been changed. Five hundred dollars meant the freedom to wait and consider her next step. It was a blessed renewal of self-confidence and hope.

Examining her aching feet, Valeria saw one had a bad blister where the hole in her shoe had chafed it. Detestable, worn-out objects! She could afford now to throw them away. She carefully anointed her feet with Milk of Cucumber and Almond, a bottle which she had brought from Atlanta. The coolness of this balm was delicious. She bound up her damaged foot with a handkerchief and got back into bed.

How blissful to be able to spend a whole day doing nothing, without any feeling of guilt!

She drifted into a daydream of grateful ease and it was in this semi-somnolent state that, after a while, she remembered Sam Garvey's offer. It belonged in a realm of fantasy along with the terrible scene she had witnessed at Fairlawn. She did not want to spoil her present mood of felicity by dwelling on Ford's misfortune. She would think about that later. Today was for happiness and relaxation.

As for Sam Garvey . . . Had he really asked her to marry him? It seemed impossible that the encounter had ever happened. A strange old man in a tomb-like room talking of Dickens and Victor Hugo and offering her security at the age of thirty-one!

But then Valeria recalled that when he had drawn up in front of the boardinghouse, at whatever unearthly hour it had been, Garvey had cautioned her to think over what he had said. She had offered him her hand and thanked him, her mind intent on the all-important problem of getting upstairs to bed.

Mrs. Sam Garvey? Incredible! Laughable! Outrageous! She could imagine Randolph's horror and Ida's rage. Fate would certainly visit some dire retribution on her, as it had on Ford, if she took such an ill-considered leap from poverty to riches. It was certainly the oddest proposal Valeria had ever had. Touching, too, because Garvey had specified that he wanted nothing except her company and time.

Could he really have meant it? Or had it been a hallucinated impulse due to the untoward circumstances that had brought her there at such an unwonted hour. She bestirred herself to recall the details of that conversation, exactly what he had said and what she had answered, but a veil of unreality had fallen over the whole of that dreadful day.

Valeria pulled herself out of bed and hobbled to the small, cracked mirror over the rickety chest of drawers. Her cheeks were still burned, but luckily her skin was not peeling. She had given it a liberal application of cream before going to bed.

She was twenty-five. What, when she truthfully considered them, *were* her prospects? She had exactly five hundred dollars with which to face the world. Sam Garvey had told her flatly that she did not possess the talent for making money. Without money, what, realistically, were the alternatives? A companion to some crotchety dowager? Another job in another household like the Brewsters' where she might run the gauntlet of another woman's jealousies? Was it likely that in that far more entrenched and stratified society, any bachelor of standing would link his name with a penniless adventuress, if that, indeed, was what she was? Robert E. Lee was not a sufficient recommendation to offset the stigma of being poor. And if no job materialized—what then? A shop assistant, a governess, a seamstress, a translator of French novels? Would New York, in fact, prove to be another larger Arcadia on a larger scale?

Somewhat chastened, Valeria lay down on the bed.

Whatever she might think of Sam Garvey, he had judged her with surprising accuracy. The shrewdness which had been his strongest weapon in years of hard dealing with hard opponents had told him that Valeria Lee was not a woman to woo on any spurious romantic grounds. Perhaps he had sensed what she herself suspected, an ingrained inability to love, not so dissimilar to his own. To be forced, for material gain, to give herself to a man she felt nothing for would have been repellent. But could she gamble on meeting a man she could at least respect, who was well off besides? A sound bargain. What Sam Garvey was willing to pay for was the very quality which had hitherto proved such a drawback; what he considered her style. Valeria supposed that she represented, in his arid life, the same touch of elegance that he found in those richly bound volumes he guarded so carefully behind glass doors.

But then she remembered all that Randolph had told her about Sam Garvey's past. Was he really a criminal? Had he contrived the murder of Josiah

Eaton's father, smashed countless rivals and ruined others? She had the evidence of her own disgust at Shacktown. He had no compunction about exploiting the wretchedness of the men who worked in the mills. As Garvey's wife she would become a party to all that. It would be a total betrayal of everything she believed in. It was impossible to tolerate such evil in return for money.

Dusk fell while she lay there deliberating.

Randolph knocked and came in. "Were you sleeping?"

"No, just resting."

How tired and shabby he looked!

"I was wondering what we could do for dinner. There are some eggs, I think, and the remains of the Italian cheese."

"You can go to the shop and buy anything you please." She smiled lazily. "I would appreciate a bottle of really good wine tonight."

"But, Val—" he protested, "I don't get paid till Friday."

"Look in my bag. You'll find something surprising."

He opened the purse and took out the bundle of notes. She was fondly amused by his amazement.

"Where on earth did you get all this?"

"I went to see Sam Garvey and he paid me the money he owed me. For beguiling Thaddeus Brownlow."

"Sam Garvey—," he gaped. "But Val—!"

"He was extremely nice. Paid up without a murmur and even gave me supper."

"*Sam Garvey?*" he repeated as though she had been consorting with the devil.

She yawned, agreeably self-satisfied. "I don't like to disillusion you, but he's not such a demon as you maintain."

For some reason she felt no inclination to confide in him about Sam Garvey's offer. She had earned the right as a woman to reach her own decision or, at least, to enjoy the pleasures of indecision.

Instead, over a leisurely meal, Valeria told him

about her meeting with Ford, and what had transpired at Fairlawn. "There's no point in supposing," she concluded, "that he can help me in New York. His own situation is too drastic. If I go there, I'll be on my own."

She was testing him. He equivocated. "All the same, my darling sister, don't you think that it's worth a try? There's nothing for you here. If it doesn't work out, you can always come back. I may be established by that time. We can take an apartment and it won't matter whether you find a job or not. You could do dressmaking or give piano lessons like you did in Atlanta. Of course," he added without conviction, "I can't bear to see you go. But I think you owe it to yourself. I'm stuck here for the moment. Of course, if my articles make a stir—"

Oh Randy! Randy! He could not disguise that he really wanted to be free of her so that he could concentrate on work. He had less concern for her than the man he denounced as the arch-example of unconcern. Valeria wondered, with a touch of bitterness, what would have happened to Randy if between them, she and Ford had not nursed and sustained him for so long.

But Randolph manfully refused a share of her capital. "No, Val, you will need every penny. Although the opportunities are greater in New York, so is the cost of living. I can rub along here on what I earn."

It did not appear to trouble him that Valeria would be alone and unprotected in a metropolis where she knew no one. She kissed him good-night. "It's encouraging that you have such confidence in me."

Alone! Her survival, she saw, clearly depended on her own initiative, her own endurance; she could expect nothing from Ford or Randy. Even so, Sam Garvey was too extreme a solution. Better to keep her independence and self-respect. Valeria had the chilling example of what had befallen Ford for having sacrificed himself for money. At least she was better off by five hundred dollars than she had been the day before.

She sat down resolutely on the side of Randolph's bed and composed a letter tactfully thanking Mr. Gar-

vey for his kind and considerate offer. She read it
through and reread it, found it completely false and
tore it up.

It was stifling under the roof. She pushed open the
tiny window and stared out over the wilderness of
roofs. In those drab dwellings countless people like
herself wore out their years in daily toil and daily dep-
rivations. Did they derive any consolation from being
honest and persevering? Six years of compromising
with her principles—or were they really her limitations
—in order to secure, in some corner of the globe, a
sanctuary like Whitebriars where she could live at
peace and cultivate the pleasures which otherwise she
could only know at second hand.

Those poor pensioners of mediocrity would never
be offered the chance which had shot like a star across
her firmament and landed squarely at her feet. Valeria
wondered how much a man with a hundred million
would consider sufficient to insure her security. What
did such uncomputable amounts of money mean in
terms of dollars and cents?

Next morning Valeria concocted a second letter
asking Mr. Garvey to give her time to consider his extraordinary offer. She went down to Randolph's room
and brewed some coffee. Her letter lay on the table
amidst the litter of her brother's data on Sam Garvey's
iniquitous career.

What difference would time make? If she was an
adventuress, didn't it entail risking and daring and
gambling on opportunities? Sam Garvey was offering
her far more than she could ever make herself in six
years, or even in a lifetime, of patient toil.

With all his obvious faults he was not commonplace.
Angered as she might be, she would not be bored. If
Sam Garvey had revealed in one evening aspects of
himself that no one had suspected, might there not be
whole areas of his character to discover and perhaps ,
encourage? She could not imagine what a day-to-day
relationship with such a man would be, but then, could
any woman embarking upon marriage? Love veiled

the perils of familiarity. Could not the prospect of
money do the same?

She tore up her second letter and lay all day on
Randolph's bed in a fever of indecision.

Valeria dreamed that she was in a red damask
drawing room in a New York mansion that somehow
belonged to her. She was admiring herself in a Venetian mirror, gratified by her elegance and by her unusual black lace dress. A peacock-feather fan brushed
across her creamy breast to reveal a necklace of blue-
white opals. No wonder she was the object of so much
controversy. But she was wealthy enough to set a fashion of her own.

She glided across a crimson carpet and came out
onto a landing at the head of a sweeping stairway.
There were tubs of Egyptian lilies and pink azaleas in
the hall. Thaddeus Brownlow had just arrived. A servant was taking his velvet cloak. He came to the foot
of the stairs to greet her as Valeria glided down. She
was conscious of the aura of splendor that surrounded
her. She was serene and magnificently secure.

But when she woke, it was with the vivid sense of
premonition. Had that dream been the voice of destiny, urging her toward a future that now, for the first
time, was within her grasp?

She left a note for Randy, excusing herself from
dinner. Now, more than ever, Valeria needed to be
alone.

Dawn brought her to a decision. It was chance.
Pure chance had thrown a bridge across the quick-
sands of hopeless circumstance. In this harsh world
what else mattered but survival? One paid, in one way
or another, for everything one did. It was not the well
laid plans, the standards painfully adhered to, the
drudgery of virtuous labor that resulted in security and
success. It was an unforeseen encounter, a blind impulse, a word spoken at a certain moment, an old man
in a strange room who had promised to keep his word.

And, in the final count, Valeria was alone and Sam
Garvey was alone and old. Perhaps at this dim hour
between night and morning, he was just as afraid in
his innermost heart as she was.

Perched on her rickety chair, she started to compose the third letter that was to change her life.

An earthquake could not have shaken Arcadia to its foundations more than the news that Sam Garvey was about to marry.

The first tremor was felt when Tabitha Grey skuttled like a groundhog up the hill to The Heights and arrived, breathless, at the Brewsters' door.

She was beside herself with excitement. Shivers of anticipation ran up and down Tabitha's spine at the thought of the shock she was about to administer to Ida. It was an opportunity that came once in a lifetime and she was determined to make the most of it. There was nothing more elevating to the spirit than to be the bearer of ill tidings and these were the worst imaginable. For one splendid moment Tabitha Grey was the most important personage in Arcadia. Ida would faint probably or have hysterics; Tabitha hoped a heart attack might follow. The possibilities of her reactions were wonderfully dreadful. Tabitha adjusted her face and shawl, assumed an expression of the deepest gloom, and rang the brass bell.

Milly, with her cap over one eye, opened the door. "Oh, it's you, Mrs. Grey."

Tabitha announced in the voice of Lazarus, lately risen from the dead, "I must see Mrs. Brewster at once, now. It's a matter of life and death."

"Oh dear! She's in bed, having one of her fits," Milly squeaked.

"I don't care what she's having," Tabitha barked like a drill sergeant. Even if Mrs. Brewster were having paroxysms she must be roused at once. Nothing could deprive Tabitha of her sacred right to administer the lethal blow. "Oh, get out of my way, girl!" She pushed Milly aside, charged in, and beetled upstairs to Ida's bedroom.

She knocked and, without waiting for an answer, went straight in. Ida was lying on her back in bed, snoring. She had consumed a bottle of whiskey the night before and was suffering from what she euphemistically described as one of her migraines.

"Mrs. Brewster, wake up at once. I have news, you see. Important."

Ida continued snoring obliviously.

Tabitha shook her with no result. She shook her until Ida's snores were jolted. Ida stirred.

"What?"

"News!" Tabitha shouted in her ear. Really, it was inconsiderate to be so slow and stupid and to keep her waiting. "News. About your father!"

Ida came to with a start. Was he dead? For one glorious second she thought she was free, of Henry, the house, Arcadia. Paris and the impoverished duke and the carriage covered in coronets flashed through her mind as she struggled into focus.

"Is he—?" she asked, her eyes sharp with hope.

Tabitha launched into her performance. She sank down onto the bed and started to rock to and fro as though at a wake. "It's terrible. Terrible. You won't believe. I can't bring myself to tell you."

Ida glared. What was this stupid woman doing, moaning and rocking about, making her feel seasick. Was her father dead or wasn't he?

"Stop that, Tabitha! What's happened?"

Tabitha peeked at her to see what state Ida was in. She didn't want to miss the onrush of hysterics. "It's so awful. I can't believe it. You could have knocked me down with a feather. I ran all the way." She placed her hand on her side and gasped as though about to succumb to sudden heart failure herself. "Can you imagine—at his age! Oh, the wickedness!"

Any wickedness connected with her father did not rouse Ida in the least. It was enough that he stubbornly remained alive. "Stop that, Tabitha. Stop carrying on. Tell me at once. I'm ill."

That, at least, was encouraging. Tabitha groaned. "I said to myself, Oh poor Mrs. Brewster! That poor woman! To think such a thing could happen! There's only one explanation. He's gone daft."

Ida was now thoroughly put out. "Either you tell me or you can plain get out. I've got a very bad headache." She felt sick to boot.

"Your father—," Tabitha presented the face of an

early Christian martyr about to face the lions, "and that woman—"

"What woman?" Her father had no interest in women.

"That Southern harpy." Tabitha nodded and nodded, bowing her head in shame.

At the mention of Valeria Lee, Ida sat straight up in bed. "What about her?" she almost shouted.

"That harpy and your father—"

Sam Garvey and Valeria Lee? He must be mad. Had Valeria contrived to seduce him as she seduced Hank? That evil, lascivious, unprincipled whore? "Tabitha! Come to the point!"

Tabitha pronounced the fatal words in a voice portending disaster. "They're . . . getting . . . married."

Ida looked at her. It was Tabitha who had gone mad, not her father. "Oh don't talk nonsense!"

Tabitha nodded repeatedly and once again uttered the final word of doom. "Married!"

This was followed by a prolonged wail, then the shawl thrown over her face, leaving a tiny space so that she could see Ida's expression.

There was none.

It was totally impossible.

Her father was seventy-three. He had a perfect right to die and leave her everything. That was expected of him. He had no right whatever to get married. He had no conceivable right even to contemplate marrying that arch Jezebel.

Ida gave Tabitha a savage kick. "Get off the bed! When did you hear this? Who told you?"

"God help us, Mr. Garvey did! God help us, he asked me to be a witness. I said I'd rather die, you see. After all these years. After all I've been to the family. After all I've done for you and what you've done for me. I said, 'I would rather die.' And I meant it. I meant every word. Never, I said. Never!"

She gave another great wail and sank back on the bed out of which Ida was now struggling. For a moment they were both entangled in sheets and blankets. Suddenly the *fact* of what she had been told hit Ida with full force. She fell back against the pillows, her face livid.

"Married!"

She was dressed in a flash, buckling on her stays like armor. She drove a giant hat pin through an artificial seagull, impaling it on the brim of her hat as though skewering Valeria through the heart. Seizing a feather boa, Ida descended the stairs like a thunder cloud. "Haddock, the carriage!" she boomed. "I want it 'round *at once!*"

She was possessed.

She drove downtown like Boadicea facing the Roman legions. She hated to go near Shacktown because it reminded her too forcibly of her beginnings, of all the squalor and poverty that were part of her heritage. Now Ida disregarded it completely. Nothing existed but the iniquity that her father and Valeria were contemplating and which, at all costs, she must prevent.

She marched up the cobbled path and pulled the bell. She pulled it as though springing the trapdoor of a scaffold that would hang them both. There was the porch on which one night, nineteen years before, she had sat with Josiah when that terrible thing had happened. However, it paled to insignificance. Something infinitely worse now threatened her.

At last the door was opened by her father. She thundered in, planted herself in the doorway and confronted him.

"Is it true—?"

"Is what true?" Sam asked calmly, knowing full well that Ida had heard the news.

"That you and that—," she struggled to find an annihilating word, *"creature—"*

He finished for her. "Are getting married? Yes, it's true."

"You—fool!" she exploded. "Don't you know what she is? Don't you know what she did to Hank?"

"I know exactly what she is," he replied quietly. "Why do you think I'm marrying her?"

"It's madness," Ida yelled in his face. "Madness. And it's disgusting."

"You think so? Frankly, Ida, I don't give a damn what you think."

"I won't have that woman in my house."

"You won't have to. Apart from Nancy and your cook there's no one she's hankering to see there."

A hideous suspicion flashed through Ida's mind that Valeria was after Monsieur Emile, that this abominable marriage was part of a larger, darker scheme to deprive her of her social standing, to humiliate her totally before Arcadia.

"I won't allow it. I won't permit you to make a laughing stock of all of us, to drag us through the mud on account of that—that—" There was no word in any language that could possibly sum up her opinion of Valeria Lee.

"We've been dragged through the mud for the last forty years. It never bothered me. Why should it bother you?"

Sam returned to his study and she followed him.

"The whole town will laugh at us. A woman I employed . . . a servant—"

He went to his desk and picked up a half-smoked cigar. "I don't give a shit about Arcadia."

"Don't use language like that to me!"

"You know the meaning of the word, Ida. Though I guess you wouldn't use it since you've become a lady."

"She's nothing!" Ida shouted, disregarding this taunt. "Trash! All the stuff about her being related to General Lee—!"

"I don't care who she's related to. I'm not related to anyone. Are you?"

"You've lost your mind. If you go through with this I'll have you certified."

"No, you won't, Ida. You'll take your allowance and you'll keep your mouth shut. And if I have any trouble from you, I'll leave Valeria the new railroad, lock, stock, and barrel."

Ida reeled. "You wouldn't dare!"

He blew out a coil of foul-smelling smoke. "Look, I don't want trouble. We don't like each other. Let's go our ways. At least you won't need to have me to dinner every other Sunday."

She faced—seen suddenly—a far greater, more disastrous eventuality than the marriage. "You're not going to leave her *money?*"

"She'll be my wife, won't she?"

The smoke of hell blew through Ida's soul, darker, more acrid, more enveloping than the smoke of her father's mills. "Whatever you have belongs to me and the children."

"You're all taken care of. You won't starve."

"It's abominable. That you should part with one cent for that—adventuress—a stranger. Trash!"

"Get out, Ida," her father growled. "And stop calling my wife names."

"Your wife! You senile old fool. Haven't you any regard for us, for your own flesh and blood?"

He looked at her, taking her all in, a blowsy, flamboyant, angry woman in a ridiculous great hat with a bird wobbling on the brim. Sam felt nothing for her but distaste.

"I've done well by you, Ida. You don't have to stay in Arcadia if you don't want to. You're rich. You'll be even wealthier when I die. Why don't you get the hell out, go to Europe, sell that god-awful house? Get something out of life besides feeding a lot of freaks who don't care if you live or die. That's what I plan to do."

"You're leaving?"

"As soon as the railroad's finished. We're going to travel. You and I shan't see much of each other from now on. We can't exactly part as friends. Let's not get in each other's hair, that's all."

Sam stubbed out his cigar as though putting a permanent end to their relationship.

Ida collapsed into a brown leather chair. She was helpless and deflated by the enormity of what he had done to her.

"I can't believe you could have been so taken in. She came here looking for someone, anyone. She tried it with Hank, a boy of eighteen. She doesn't care who it is as long as he gives her money. Oh, I could tell you things! I caught her going through my jewelry. She'd have stolen from me if I hadn't stopped her. She lied and gossiped and intrigued with the other servants. Everything that went on in my house was reported to Josiah. She was planted there by her brother and that terrible Ford Hollister, a man who cheats on his wife with boys from the stockyards. That's the kind of friends she has, depraved, disgusting people. Why do you think she agreed to marry you? Money—yes—but that's not all. Oh no!"

Ida surged over his desk and leaned across it, blasting the words into his face, forcing Sam to listen. "Josiah will know everything that goes on here, all your business affairs, all about the railroad. Every detail of what you're planning. She'll find the combination to your safe sooner or later. There won't be a single fact or figure that won't be in Josiah's hands. He's been out to ruin you for nearly twenty years. You'll see. He'll fight you every inch of the way over the railroad and she'll give him the ammunition."

Ida stood back, seeing that out of the stream of haphazard accusations something had struck home. She had touched on one essential factor in his nature: money. "You—fool!"

She picked up her boa and threw it with a grand, valedictory gesture around her neck.

"I don't care how many women you have. You can have all the women you want if they're still any good to you. But remember I warned you about Valeria Lee. She may be a Southern lady with fine manners, she may play the piano and know how to arrange flowers, but she's in with Josiah Eaton. *Her brother,*" she pointed at him across the room to drive her last point home, "is Josiah's closest friend."

She marched to the door.

"You've always hated me. You think by giving me money that settles everything. It's too late to change that. If you'd ever, for one moment, been anything to me, I might have been a different woman." There was something degrading in Ida's last-ditch honesty. She was not a woman who could afford to reveal herself. Bravado was her greatest strength. "At seventy-three," she sneered, "to pretend that you're anything but a bastard—and I know the meaning of *that* word—who's

broken everyone and smashed everything for money,
it's worse than disgusting . . . it's . . ." she found the
annihilating word, "pathetic!"

After she had gone Sam Garvey sat for a long time
at his desk without lighting a cigar. When Ida's back
was against the wall she could summon a good deal
more force and rudimentary eloquence than her usual
social flummery would allow. She was not altogether a
stupid woman although she led such a stupid life. If
she had married Josiah, Ida might have developed
along other lines. Her whole life, as it had turned out,
was a vulgar and unsatisfying pretense at being something she had no talent for. It was partially his fault,
he knew. He had paid no attention to her as a child.
After his wife had died—he could scarcely remember
that pallid, almost anonymous figure—his only child
had been brought up by strangers. Later on, when he
started to make money, it had been Tabitha. When he
became affluent, he had given Ida a big allowance.
What else had there been to give? It was true that
money had been a plaster that had covered over the
cracks in his lack of family feeling. He had felt nothing
for anyone, really, except Marcus Eaton long ago,
and that had ended in disaster. Had he ever thought of
Ida as he now thought of Valeria, a woman he barely
knew?

So much time had gone by. All those Sunday dinners! Had he ever thought of Hank or Nancy? Sam
had never brought himself to consider that any off-
spring of Ida and Henry Brewster could be worth anything. Where had all the years gone, the nights alone
in this room with Mr. Dickens and Mr. Hugo and the
gray ledgers filling up with facts and figures, debits and
credits, never really honest, never telling the truth of
how rich he was? He was enormously rich and powerful. What did it mean?

And suddenly, out of nowhere, had appeared this
stranger, proud and defensive about her dignity, but
imbued with so much charm and grace, evoking the
image of another world of delicacy and taste and
charm. Was it folly, this sudden desire to protect Valeria Lee from the poverty he knew would tarnish and

erode the luminous quality she had? Was it too late? Had it been too late for more years than he wanted to remember? Too late to suppose that he might change a little? That life itself might offer him something a little softer, a little warmer, after all the harsh battling over money and power, half a century of grasping and amassing and destroying to amass more? At the onset of his old age, Valeria had appeared, resentful and combatative, but admirable in her refusal to capitulate to the terms he was accustomed to demanding; and with her style redolent of civilized and gentle living. Was she the last beguiling vestige of some dream he had once had, imperfectly recalled when it was all too late, a smiling harbinger of death?

Folly? Probably. But perhaps salvation.

Sam must ask her about her brother.

It was for Randolph that Valeria was waiting to impart the shocking, the unimaginable news.

Waiting in his shabby, untidy room, all she could think of were the difficulties, the objections, the righteous indignation, that now faced her. That room was littered with reminders of their life together, of everything she had been brought up to stand for. Valeria felt the fragile thread of her decision slipping from her; she dreaded all the things he was bound to say. And there would be, besides Randy, Ida and then the town and there was Sam Garvey himself in that black house under the chimneys. His reaction to her acceptance had been perfunctory. A terse note to set a date. No ring, no flowers, no encouraging letter. A merger had been concluded.

She felt more abandoned than she had ever been before.

Randolph burst in, elated. She faced him with panic-stricken eyes.

"Val," he announced, "a miracle has happened! The great pornographer has been transformed into the Pascal Lamb. He has accepted everything—with a few minor changes." He flung down his coat and briefcase. "The first article will appear next week, and the second, in which we point the accusing finger directly at your friend, Sam Garvey, the week after. Mr. Eaton has seemingly decided to eat out of my hand." He bent to kiss her soft cheek. "I am not denying a certain element of retribution. Josiah is ashamed on your account and is trying to make amends."

His sister watched him helplessly as the barrier rose between them. Randy poured out two glasses of red wine. "I don't feel so badly about your leaving now because if anything goes wrong, I'll be able to help you. I think my position on *The Courier* is assured."

He raised his glass to her. "I drink to your unsmirchable virtue that drove the lance of repentance through Mr. Eaton's heart. Not the first time, my angel, that you have rescued me."

Never had Randolph's flamboyance seemed more maddening, less opportune.

"Did I not always tell you," he continued, flinging himself into a chair, "that fate would not abandon us? Hail to the great Micawber who rightly held that something is always around the corner! You have your chance to bring New York to its feet and I to become the nemesis of the ungodly rich!"

Valeria was standing there, stricken, unable to speak. In her extremity of nervous tension, she was struck by the ludicrous aspect of the situation and could not restrain herself from laughing hysterically. It was the purest farce to tell her idealistic brother that she was about to marry the target of the articles that he counted on to establish his career.

Randolph was chattering away. She heard nothing and could think of nothing but escape. Something in her expression caused him to break off. "What is it, Val? You look as though you'd seen the proverbial ghost."

"Something . . . *has* happened," she managed to say in the guilty voice of a child caught pilfering. "I don't know how to begin."

She saw a flicker of apprehension in his eyes: that, as usual, she had been the cause of some sort of difficulty that would prevent her leaving. Oh, he so counted on having her safely gone!

"The trouble is that I know in advance everything

you're going to say. Please, Randy, try to understand.
I've gone over it all a hundred times already. Try,
just for once, not to say the obvious things or give me
the obvious advice."

"What on earth has happened?" He was looking at
her in frank dismay.

"I know we have always thought," Valeria approached the shock obliquely, "that there was something commendable in struggling on as best we could,
in fact we've had no choice. But you have talent.
You're a man and can make a career. I can't. I'm not
equipped to do anything but the sort of job I had with
Ida Brewster, and that leads nowhere—as you've seen.
Marriage is unfortunately the only career that's open
to a woman and it's not easy to find anyone when you
have nothing to offer but yourself. I mean anyone
worthwhile. I'm afraid that I m not romantic enough to
want to settle for love in a log cabin, even if I had the
chance which I don't."

She heard her voice struggling on and saw his
mounting concern.

"What are you talking about?" Randy demanded
sternly. "Has someone proposed to you?"

"It's not exactly a proposal," she struggled to ration-
alize in order to deflect his outrage. "It's an arrangement, an agreement, if you like. My companionship in
return for a settlement."

"What?"

"I don't know exactly how much, but it will be
enough. It seemed to me," she sidetracked in desperation, "that if I'm going to work as a companion in
New York—and that's about the best I could hope for
—I might as well do it here . . . for someone who's offered me security." She stumbled. "He's asked me for
six years."

Valeria's voice faded out. She felt suddenly ashamed
to have said so bluntly that she was counting on Sam
Garvey's death at the end of an allotted span. It made
her decision to accept him sound like a deal between
shady politicians, a division of illicit spoils.

"Six years?" Randolph echoed. "Why six years?"

"He's seventy-three and wants to travel. He doesn't

want to be alone." She felt hopelessly guilty, inept and drowning. "He's paid me a great compliment really. There will be nothing between us as man and wife."

Suddenly Valeria saw that her brother had guessed whom she was speaking of. He was staring at her with an incredulity that was turning to a sort of horror.

"Oh Randy," she appealed, "don't hate me and don't judge him. There is another side to him entirely. I've never asked you to do anything important for me before. Please wait and meet him and give us a little time."

She forced herself to go to Randolph and put her arms around him. She laid her head on his shoulder and waited for his response.

There was none.

She was to remember that silence all her life.

They were married at City Hall in an anteroom used for board meetings, with fly-specked engravings on the walls and a large, yellowing photograph of the Garvey Mills over a grate in which no fire was ever lit. Jim Pryor, Garvey's foreman, and Monsieur Emile were witnesses.

Jim Pryor was square, tough and shut tight as a steel safe. Thirty years of working for Sam Garvey had hardened him beyond any reachable resemblance to being human. He was a machine, neither young nor old, dark nor fair. He was hated by the millhands and never smiled. He had long since forgotten, if he had ever known, how to be tired, to relax or to think of anything but his duty to Sam Garvey. They neither liked nor disliked each other. Work was their bond. If Sam Garvey had ordered Pryor to blow up the mills and sell the workers into slavery, he would have done so, promptly and efficiently, and returned to his boss's office to await further instructions.

At Sam Garvey's abrupt decision to get married Jim Pryor had evidenced no reaction. He had been ordered to act as witness. He was there to witness. He shook Valeria's hand as though locking a padlock on the mill gates, as he did every evening at seven o'clock. If he had been asked to describe her afterwards, he could not have done so. She did not work at the mills, and hence, did not concern him.

Monsieur Emile, with a Parisian's instinct for an occasion, was impeccable in a white linen suit and Panama hat. He had brought D'Artagnan along as a festive touch, decked out with a large white bow.

From a personal point of view, his dear Mademoiselle was making a disaster; but Monsieur Garvey was rich, and ladies adjusted rapidly to wealth and arranged their private lives in a satisfactory manner afterwards.

Sam Garvey, wearing the same black suit, the same black boots, and the same black hat in which he was wont to visit Ida for the Sunday lunches, appeared to be in an unusually bad temper. He barely greeted Valeria when she appeared, wearing the white summer dress in which, only a short time before, she had barged into his house and demanded five hundred dollars.

Her heart sank. She was about to be sentenced for the crime of murdering her principles. Valeria was never more grateful for anything in her life than for the sight of the tiny Pomeranian, tethered to a chair, who jumped up and gave her a friendly yap. She picked up the furry mop and hugged it as though saying good-bye to the last vestige of her former life.

The Justice of the Peace was nervous because anything connected with Sam Garvey made the inhabitants of Arcadia nervous. He fumbled with the prayer book, lost the place, and hurried through the formula at breakneck speed.

"Do you, Samuel Garvey, take this woman, Valeria Hortense de la Pagerie" he stumbled over the foreign name, "Lee as your lawful wedded wife?"

Sam grunted.

"Do you, Valeria Hortense de la Pagerie Lee take this man, Samuel Garvey, to be your lawful wedded husband?"

For a wild instant Valeria wanted to shout "no" and flee. She heard herself say, at some great distance, as though in answer to the fatal question of whether she pleaded innocent or guilty, "I do."

Jim Pryor passed the gold band. Sam Garvey fitted it on Valeria's finger as though shutting the door on a kennel in which some unwanted hound was to be kept on sufferance.

Sam didn't kiss her.

The Justice of the Peace was too beside himself with nerves to instruct the terrible man to do so. No one in his right mind would ever think of telling Sam Garvey to kiss anyone.

It was over.

Garvey handed the Justice of the Peace a fifty-dollar bill. He handed Jim Pryor a fifty-dollar bill. He was about to hand the little man in the white suit a fifty-dollar bill, but Valeria tactfully intervened.

She shook Monsieur Emile's hand. *"Je vous remercie d'être venu, Monsieur Emile."*

"Permettez-moi de vous féliciter, Madame. *Je vous souhaite le plus grand bonheur."*

He kissed her graceful hand and smiled knowingly, "And if later you require——" He was offering his unstinting services to the one person who understood that all enduring relationships must be built on a foundation of good cooking. It would require, he feared, a series of *gâteaux royaux* as tall as the Vendôme column to make this union tolerable.

"I'll keep in touch," Valeria said.

It had happened without happening, without its meaning anything. It had not been a ceremony at all. Sam Garvey had married her with the same impersonal dispatch with which he might have signed a new contract for iron ore.

She had no awareness of being married, that she was linked to this gruff old man in any way. Valeria took his arm and they walked together down the passage, as though proceeding from the sentencing to the scaffold. Garvey helped her into the carriage and sat beside her with his hat clamped down over his forehead. He said nothing. He did not take her hand.

They drove back to Shacktown, to the black house on the patch of black ground with the bushes the color of black tea. He unlocked the door and they went inside.

There seemed nothing to say.

She took off her hat with the pale blue ribbon, went to the study's window and looked out.

The smoke from the great chimneys blackened the sky. Across from the iron railings there was a dismal shack beside the gates to the mills where Jim Pryor signed the men in and out each morning and where on Fridays he paid their wages. Below the silence of the house there was the same persistent rumbling, as though tunnels were being bored through the bowels of the earth.

Valeria Garvey felt nothing. She had no sense that the old man who was unlocking a drawer and taking something out and placing it on the desk had any connection to her. But this was, somehow or other, the man she would have to adjust to thinking of as her husband.

"These are for you."

She turned, in a daze of unreality, and saw the red Morocco case. It was this strange Mrs. Sam Garvey who went in her place to pick it up. It was this Mrs. Garvey who had no will or personality or knowledge of herself, an amnesiac who followed instructions, who moved and spoke like a ventriloquist's dummy, who was holding the case and now sat down and opened it.

With this other woman's eyes, Valeria saw the necklace of bluish opals, interspersed with diamonds. A pendant hung from it with one great opal set in diamonds. There were also matching earrings.

She sat and stared.

And from far away there came to her the realization that it had, in fact, all happened. She had crossed the threshold from one life into another and, henceforth and forever, she would be someone else.

Her luminous green eyes clouded. He had remembered.

She said very softly, "Thank you, Sam."

⟡ Chapter Twelve ⟡

SHE WAS MARRIED and she was not married. The man who was now legally her husband and who remained closeted all day in his study, planning and scheming, buying up land that stretched across the state and into the next then into infinity in order to build a railroad, was no more her husband than any stranger in whose house, by freakish circumstances, she might happen to be living. Valeria could not adjust to this relationship; there was no relationship. It was as though the conversation that had taken place one night, in which Sam Garvey had revealed himself, had never happened. It had been, it now seemed to her, a hallucination. Sam had opened the door onto his inner self and closed it again, as tightly as the steel safe concealed behind the wall of ledgers. Had it not been for the fact that she now wore a gold wedding ring and that Arcadia regarded her as the mysterious woman who had captured the town's leading citizen, there was no positive change in her condition. Valeria had moved from the attic room in a boardinghouse to a servant's room in a blackened house in a slum that crouched under the mill chimneys. This man to whom she was now bound for the duration of his life and whom she barely saw was, in the eyes of the world, a multimillionaire. In the eyes of the world she was the rightful sharer of his vast fortune. But she cooked and washed and scrubbed like any of the women who dwelled in Shacktown. In theory she was rich, but in fact she was a pauper. She had been freed from the confinements of poverty, but she was now chained to a daily grind as dispiriting as the worst times in her ruined home after the War.

210

In the mornings the whistle shrilled. Shacktown
stirred from its troubled sleep and Valeria stirred from
hers. The women of Shacktown shuffled into what
passed for kitchens and boiled water on what passed
for stoves. Valeria came downstairs and heated water
for tea, in no way differently from the neighbors. The
mill whistle shrilled again and a crowd of shabby men
assembled at the gates. The wives cleaned up after
their husbands and went to the pumps to draw more
water. Valeria, however, was able to get water from
the tap. Following which she put a bucket on the stove
to fill the tin hip bath. Sam's house was the only one in
the slum that had water and gas laid on. The whistle
shrilled a third time. The gates swung open and the
men struggled in to work. Valeria took Sam his morning tea and a boiled egg; bathed, and emptied the
water down a drain in the pantry. The women of
Shacktown filled their tubs with water and washed
their rags and remnants. Valeria also washed the rags
and remnants of Sam Garvey's life until the suds
turned black.

The house, she discovered, for the most part, had
not been tended to in twenty years. The dirt was ingrained on the floors and had made the cover sheets
in the unused bedrooms filthy. Curtains, as she drew
them, fell apart in a shower of grimy fragments.
When Valeria touched the banisters her white skin was
blackened. If she sat down, her dress was gray when
she got up. And the Turkey carpets had long since lost
the faintest indication of pattern or coloration.

She looked 'round in despair. Where could she begin?

Tabitha Grey had packed her bags and departed before the marriage. Sam Garvey barely noticed her absence. Tabitha had kept her small bedroom relatively
clean; Valeria moved into it. Sam slept in a small room
off his study, as he always had. It contained a
wrought-iron bed, an empty cupboard, a simple chest
of drawers, a bedtable and a lamp. There was a single
pine chair.

The kitchen was tolerable; Valeria cooked. She discovered, wrapped in yellowed newspapers, fine Geor-

gian silver, a tea service, platters, salt and pepper
holders and candlesticks all tarnished from disuse. She
found in a cedar chest in one of the bedrooms a pink
Spode dinner service, still in the wrappings in which it
had first arrived. There too was a linen chest full of
unused linen folded in blue paper and tied with blue
ribbons. A canteen of silverware, black. A cupboard of
glass and crystal, black.

Tabitha and Sam had eaten for twenty years off the
same chipped plates with the same tin hardware and
drunk from the same cheap glasses, no different from
those used by the Shacktown workers.

Valeria's amazement at this prolonged deprivation
or indifference to the amenities turned to a dull anger.
She was confronted with something worse than poverty
or Ida's vulgar ostentation. This was parsimony that
verged on madness.

She was unable to comprehend it.

She started to scrub the dining room on her hands
and knees, but the dirt withstood the new mistress's
efforts with a stubbornness that infuriated her. She
scrubbed in deadly combat. At last the boards appeared. She cleaned and scraped and polished. Gleams
of rich mahogany shone under years of neglect. After
assaulting the curtains, white lace emerged from charcoal suds.

In the evening Valeria brought Sam's dinner to the
study on a tray. She always found him at his desk, poring over maps, wreathed in smoke. A streak of Garvey
territory was extending like a great artery across half
the continent. He was absorbed, obsessed.

"Dinner, Sam."

He grunted.

"Dinner!" she said sharply.

Still no response.

She shrugged and ate. He joined her when the food
was cold.

After two weeks she said to him, "Sam, I cannot live
like this. The whole house is filthy."

"Get someone."

"Where?"

"Ask Tripp."

He refused to be led into conversation. Did he already regret his impulse to protect her, she wondered? Did Sam still want to escape with her finally from this monotony of squalor? Mindlessly she carried out the tray. When Valeria returned with the dessert, he was back at his desk. She felt like sweeping all the maps and papers onto the floor in order to force him to pay attention to her. She opened the bookcase and selected a volume of Dickens that she read in total silence for two hours. The earth rumbled with the heartbeat of the Garvey mills, but Sam only struck a match to light a fresh cigar. Occasionally his pen scratched figures on a sheet of paper. His concentration was total. No other reality existed apart from the plans and figures in his head.

"Time for bed," he yawned. "Here, this is for you." Sam handed her a bankbook as casually as if it were a bill. "Buy what you want," he said. He shuffled papers into neat piles, then snapped the lid of the inkwell shut.

Twenty-five thousand dollars.

More money than Valeria had ever dreamed of. What could she do with it? What could she say?

"Thank you, Sam."

She kissed him good-night. He nodded, seemingly unaware.

Valeria lay in bed for hours listening to the grumbling of the earth, aware that all around this house were disordered alleys in which human beings lived like pigs. She had twenty-five thousand dollars in the midst of a great pigsty.

When the bleak dawn broke, she dreaded looking through the window. She wanted to breathe fresh air, yet something in her close to shame made her shrink from going out, from exposing herself to the sullen stares of the women who hung around the company store.

Sam was already at his desk in an old brown velour dressing gown and carpet slippers when Valeria came downstairs.

"Good morning, Sam."

He mumbled incoherently.

"Did you sleep well?"

There was no answer. He reached mechanically for his tea.

"I want to buy a horse so that I can go riding. I can't spent all day inside this house any more."

Sam glanced up at his new wife as he sucked in his tea. "Ask Tripp." Once a day a laconic Scot appeared at the back door to take her orders. He served as gilly and lived an anonymous existence above the stable.

"Would you like to come for a drive today? It would do you good. It's an age since you've been outside."

"No time."

"May I ask Tripp to take *me* for a drive?" Valeria asked with a flatness bordering on sarcasm.

Her husband nodded. He could not be bothered with trivia in which she now felt herself included.

Turning sharply on her heel, she left the study. Should she take the money he had given her and leave?

A depression as black as the dirt from the mills settled over her. The opals he had given her were in the safe and the bank book was too. She was trapped, far more than on the night when she had come to claim the five hundred dollars. At least that Valeria had in cash. The bills were now in a drawer in her bedroom in the same bag in which she had first stuffed them. A marriage to Sam Garvey, which had cost her Randolph, all for five hundred dollars?

No, she must try to keep her part of the bargain. She must manage somehow until they went away.

Was there any point in cleaning the house, room by room, when they would be leaving in a year? Sam had lived like a hermit in two rooms, eating off broken crockery like any peasant. She would have to survive in the same way.

Tripp jangled the bell for the morning list.

"I want to buy a horse," Valeria said. "Do you know where I could get one—for riding?"

"I hear Mr. Eaton's selling some of his," said Tripp. "I can ask, if you've a mind."

She hesitated. The very thought of possibly meeting

Josiah Eaton again terrified her. Valeria was afraid of his charismatic attraction. And, if she would dare admit it to herself, the newly wed Mrs. Garvey would willingly allow herself to be enfolded in Josiah's strong arms and would respond eagerly to the pressure of his lips. "Ask, but don't say it's for me."

She tidied up the kitchen. There was nowhere in the house she could go to escape. The great chimneys were always there, seen or unseen. The bell of the front door rang. That would be Jim Pryor.

She let him in, shutting off the sight of the bleak, tumbledown shacks across the way. He took off his hat, and nodded before entering the study. It was as if Valeria had admitted a shadow who had crossed the hall and vanished.

She resolved to write to Randolph in an attempt to explain what could not be explained, what he could never fathom. Next, she would contact Ford, but then the futility of writing to either of them overcame her.

Searching for a sanctuary, young Mrs. Garvey went into the parlor. It was a large room with a high ceiling. What color the walls had once been was impossible to judge. The furniture, bought thirty years before when the house was built, had good lines, and was probably either mahogany or fruit wood. The mantel was simple. There were possibilities, if she could find the energy to redo everything. Was there any point? They would go away. But would they ever go? Must she wait here like the trees outside and let the grime settle over her and gradually turn her black and sterile, incapable of any feeling? Would Sam gradually destroy her as he had destroyed Jim Pryor? Everything he came in contact with was distorted, uglified and ruined. Only the ledgers grew in the terrible fecundity of wealth, dead millions that brought slow death. Poor Ida! Poor Hank! Poor Nancy! Sam's millions had touched them with a fatal blight.

Valeria returned to scrubbing in order to relieve her boredom. There was a certain satisfaction in restoring what Sam's factories' chimneys had long debased.

After another week there would be a decent dining room.

Eventually, the furniture shone. The sterling candlesticks stood proudly on the table. The crystal sparkled and the Spode dinner service graced a cloth as white as snow. It was an act of defiance and Valeria was proud of it.

Having changed her dress, carefully set her hair, and rubbed her reddened hands with cucumber and almond cream, Valeria knocked tentatively on the study door.

Sam looked at her through a cloud of smoke.

"Will you open the safe? I would like to wear my opals."

"Here?"

"Yes. I am inviting you to dinner and I want to look my best."

Amused, Garvey opened the safe and handed her the red Morocco case. She put on the earrings and held her necklace around her throat.

"Will you fasten the clasp, please?"

She was deliberately forcing him to consider her. He fumbled awkwardly with the clasp. The great pendant gleamed against the swell of her breast. She kissed him lightly.

"Come along. We're eating in the dining room."

"I eat in here."

"Not any more."

Imperiously Valeria exited with Sam obediently following. He looked 'round the dining room, mildly surprised, and picked up one of the pink Spode plates. "What's this?"

"I found a whole service. Apparently you have never used it."

He looked at the candlesticks, then at the tall, elegant woman with the gleaming jewels. Sam was puzzled at first, but also pleased.

"Will you light the candles?"

She had cooked a careful dinner: *Oeufs Mayonnaise,* Chicken Breasts *Eugénie* with rice and mushrooms, a *mousse au chocolat.* There was white wine in addition to champagne.

"I forgot I had these things. It must have been years ago."

"You have a lot of beautiful objects in this house that are worth preserving."

Sam warmed as the meal progressed. He was returning from a long distance and becoming aware of her and of the room and of the change Valeria had created.

"Why don't you fix up the parlor?"

"I thought of it, but it seemed hardly worthwhile if we're going away."

"Do it anyway. This is not a house for you. Have you got someone to help you?"

"Not yet. I will."

The sardonic twinkle came back into his blue eyes. "I guess I'm a worse obstacle than Ida."

"You're a good deal harder to charm than Thaddeus Brownlow."

"Maybe not." He smiled like a young man.

For the first time since their marriage they liked each other.

"I am going to buy a grand piano. Sometimes in the evenings I'll play for you, Sam. You may find it relaxing and you won't have to make conversation."

"I haven't made conversation in years."

"Since we are practically strangers there should be a lot for us to talk about."

He fingered the stem of his wine glass. "There's not so much you'd like to know about me."

"Are you as terrible as I was told?"

"Worse." He added matter-of-factly, "I'll have the piano shipped in one of my freight cars. Get the best."

He opened the champagne and his bride raised her glass to him. "Shall we make a toast?"

"What to?"

"Perhaps to my finding out that I married you for something other than your money."

He drank, relapsed into silence and said at last, "I can't be any different than I am."

"What are you, Sam?"

"A machine for making money."

"You care for Mr. Dickens and Mr. Hugo; you can care for me," she said boldly.

Sam glanced at her down the long table. He was

embarrassed. His awkwardness, for some reason, touched her.

When the meal was over, he got up to leave the room, remembered, and held the door open for Valeria to pass before him.

In the study she went to the bookcase and opened the glass doors. "Will you read to me?"

"I've work to do," he said gruffly.

"Not tonight."

She took down a volume of *Bleak House* and held it out to him.

He was abruptly annoyed that she was challenging him to interrupt his schedule. She was intruding and she knew it. "I don't read well."

He went past her, disregarding the proffered volume, lit a cigar and returned to his papers.

She made herself comfortable in his chair by the glowing fireplace, opened the novel and started to read aloud, her voice cold, level and determined. He looked up, irritated by her temerity.

After some moments he gave in and listened.

She read till eleven o'clock, her voice gaining color as the narrative unfolded. When she closed the book, his head was resting against the back of his chair. He had forgotten to light a fresh cigar and was staring at the ceiling. He came to a moment later as though waiting for her to continue.

Valeria replaced the volume, then went to him and held out her shapely hand.

He stood up. He had recognized her strength and found that, after all, it did not antagonize him. "It's a grand story. I hadn't heard it like that before."

She kissed Sam on his wrinkled cheek.

"Thank you for a nice evening, Sam."

Valeria was sitting in the parlor the next morning considering what she could do to make it livable when the front door bell sounded. It was Jim Pryor with the morning paper. He gave her a quizzical, suspicious glance and hurried into the study.

A few moments later he returned. "Mr. Garvey wants to see you."

Sam was reading the paper at his desk. She knew at once that he was angry. The omnipotent money-maker had been offended.

"Did your brother write this?" He thrust the paper forward.

She caught Randolph's byline and saw a crude drawing of a man falling into a vat of molten steel. The headline glared, "HORROR AT GARVEY'S MILLS."

"Yes."

"Why didn't you tell me?" he demanded.

"I told you he worked for *The Courier*."

"Did you know about this?"

"It's the first of a series about working conditions in the mills and about you."

He glowered. She took the paper to the fire and started to read. The article was written in Randolph's flamboyant style. It was melodramatic, but it struck home.

"They are holding meetings every other Friday," Jim Pryor was saying. "A lot of men belong."

"I want to see him," Sam announced. "I don't want trouble at the mills right now."

"What good will it do if you see him?" she asked.

"How much does Eaton pay him?"

"I don't know. Not much, I imagine."

"Tell him to come here. I'll make a deal."

Valeria's innate dislike of being given orders prompted her to point out, "He's not doing this just for the money. He believes that things should be changed."

"Whatever he's getting at *The Courier*, I'll pay him double."

"Are these things true?"

Sam Garvey had no intention of discussing the mills or his management of them. It was not her business. He said roughly, "The men are trained to handle the machinery. If they're careless, accidents happen. They happen in any factory."

"It says that these particular accidents were caused by faulty equipment, not by carelessness."

"That's the risk you take if you work at that kind of job," Sam's voice hardened.

She put the paper on the desk before him.

"Randolph won't make a deal," she informed her husband with dangerous calm. "If you don't want trouble you should take measures to see that these accidents don't occur."

For a moment he was flabbergasted by her effrontery. "Don't you understand?" he barked. "Eaton doesn't give a damn about the workers, he's trying to get votes."

"That doesn't alter the facts—if they are true."

"Don't tell me how to run my business!" The muscles of his neck contracted like steel wires. His face reddened. No one dared to challenge him as Valeria was doing now. They confronted each other across the desk: the tall, pale woman with the haughty family nose, looking down at him, her eyes like coldest jade, and the old lion who had ruled his jungle for forty years and whose word was law. "Get your brother here. I want to talk to him."

She had gone too far to back down. "Randy won't listen to me. Even if he left the paper, Eaton will get someone else. He's been gathering this material for weeks."

Sam leaned toward her and said in a whisper of controlled thunder. "Then, God damn it, I'll buy the material. I want him here and I want him here today."

She went, silent and inflexible, to the door.

"Wait!" Sam jumped up and came across the room toward her, his head bent slightly forward in the manner of a bull about to charge.

"Understand this! I'm involved with Thaddeus Brownlow in a deal involving millions. Once that's launched they can print any damn thing they want. These articles can cause me trouble. I want them stopped."

"Why don't you buy *The Courier?*" she said unwisely.

He gaped, speechless, suddenly lost control and shouted, "I've told you what to do. Now go and do it!

You waste a whole evening reading. This is my business!"

"Don't shout at me!" she managed to say in a low voice.

He brandished his arm at her, ordering her away. She saw in that moment the demonic will, amounting to mania, that had been the driving force throughout his life.

"And don't ever question me again!"

Shocked and shaken, Valeria left. She found herself on the stairs, trembling. She went up to her room and locked the door.

She was part of his mania now. She had sold herself to this demon of power and money. She opened the drawer of the dresser to pull out the purse crammed with the bills Sam had given her on the fatal night when, out of exhaustion, she had listened to him. Valeria had been deceived by her despair. A forlorn need to believe that there was some chance of human growth in her outrageous marriage had led her the previous night into a charade as empty as the performance she had witnessed at the theater.

She wanted to weep, but his rage had numbed her.

The earth was thundering beneath her. Valeria held the bag like a drowning person clinging to a spar. She noticed that the lace curtains she had washed only three days before were already turning yellow.

"Mr. Lee's not in. I think he's at his office."

"I'll wait, please."

As Mr. Lee's sister was dressed in the same plain black dress and hat which she had worn on previous visits, the landlady did not associate her with the woman about whom the whole town was talking. The beautiful woman seemed very depressed this morning. Perhaps a family bereavement. The possibility of death aroused her curiosity. She watched Miss Lee go mournfully upstairs.

Despite the usual state of disorder, Randolph's room seemed strangely unfamiliar. Valeria picked up and put away the clothes, made the bed, cleared the remains of breakfast. The table was strewn with papers.

It occurred to her that much of the material Sam wanted to suppress might well be here. A dutiful wife would no doubt simply purloin it and bring it to her husband. But Sam was not her husband. He was a stranger with whom she had made a bargain. Her loyalty to Randolph was part of her deepest being. She was on the point of going through the papers, but then decided that she had no desire to know more of Sam's misdeeds than she already knew.

She lay down on the bed and waited for Randy. She felt as though she had drifted far out to sea, beyond reach of direction or destination.

At lunchtime Valeria heard his footsteps on the stairs. She was panic-stricken. They were no longer brother and sister but antagonists meeting across the chasm caused by her marriage.

He came in. She was standing, as though at bay, in front of the window. Randolph disregarded her silent plea for recognition, for some gesture of forgiveness or compassion, and quietly closed the door.

In this terrible void of being together in roles unrehearsed and unfamiliar, a reversal and denial of everything they had been to each other all their lives, Valeria struggled to find some appropriate words of greeting. He approached the table in a silence that prolonged itself unnaturally, and put down his attaché case. With a sort of forced formality her brother picked up a box of cigarettes, selected one and lit it as though this were part of protocol preceding an interview between litigants in a case for libel.

"I wanted to see you," she said helplessly.

Randolph appeared to have forgotten who she was and, like an actor suddenly bereft of lines, stood there, smoking, not even looking at her, but at the disordered papers on the table.

"Randy . . . please—"

Abruptly he stubbed out his cigarette and addressed the bookshelf on which all the books they had read together were stacked like tiny tombstones commemorating their dead relationship. "What was the point of your coming here?"

Some sense of outrage at his lack of feeling forced Valeria to say, "Don't behave like this. I am still your sister."

"Are you?" he looked at her then. His large eyes, so much like her own, were not shining with mirth and vitality, but were hard with resentment and disapproval.

"You have no right to condemn me. I did what I did for both of us. You haven't met him."

"No, and I've no desire to."

"He's my husband now. You owe me at least that."

"I don't feel," he said deliberately, "that I owe you anything. You did what you did presumably because you lost your head. There's nothing I can do to help you,"—he added like an obituary—"now."

"I'm not asking for help. I want you to meet him, at least, and judge for yourself, not by all that." She indicated the mass of papers. Her common sense warned her that to meet Sam in the mood he had been in that morning would only confirm Randy's worst suspicions. How could she persuade him that there was another Sam Garvey, deeply hidden, seldom visible, that she had seen twice and been prepared to trust?

"Oh Randy, we can't let ourselves be divided. Whatever you did would make no difference to me. You know that. Did you think less of Ford because he married that sick, unfortunate girl?"

"She may be sick and unfortunate; she is not—well —what else can one call him?—a criminal." Suddenly his old self returned. Valeria recognized his anger. "How could you debase yourself by marrying that kind of man for money? I'd have respected you more if you'd let him keep you for a while. At least you could have left him when you'd got enough."

She flinched as though he had struck her. "He's not what you think. He's old and lonely. Sam asked me to stay with him because he wants to travel and see the world. He's been generous to me already. He asked nothing. There's no question of debasement. We're not married in that sense at all."

Randolph looked at her, uncomprehending.

"You don't need to stay here. I can give you enough to go to New York or Europe. Please, Randy, leave this town. You're worth much more than *The Courier*. As it is you're simply a pawn in a battle between two financial giants."

He knew her too well not to detect that she had come there partly from some other motive. "Did he send you to bribe me—to stop me from writing these?"

For the second time in all their years together, the dependence and, on her side, the devotion which had been their mainstay failed.

"He was decent and honorable in not asking me to live with him. He was very honest in what he offered; my time in return for security. I was so tired, mortally tired, of being poor."

Randy sat down at his work table, not wanting to look at her for fear the pain he was causing her would win him over. "If you had just waited! My whole life is changing. Not just these articles. Josiah and I have become good friends. I'm to help him with his campaign. If he's elected I'll go with him to the capital. It was so useless, what you did, and so ill-timed."

"Whatever I did, you have no right to turn against me. We've been through too much together."

He would not move or look at Val. The silence between them became a declaration of his resolve and of the hardening of his heart against her. He had the obstinacy of the weak, the petulance of an abandoned lover.

She steeped back, defeated, looked around for some support and reassurance and, finding none, saw there was nothing for her to do but go.

Valeria had all her life given her utmost love and courage and endurance to this man who had been— far more than a brother—a kind of faith to her. Again, when she needed him most, Randolph had nothing to give her, could not even summon up the strength and decency to offer an armistice, at least.

She went out like a sleepwalker. She was halfway down the steps when he called after her. She turned with a pang of hope that, at the least, he had relented, but Randolph merely leaned over the banister, dangling the bag with the five hundred dollars. "You left this."

He dropped it down to her and Valeria caught it. It was the stone to secure her drowning.

She wandered back to Shacktown, not wanting to return, but not knowing where else to go. She found herself on that ruinous lane that turned back upon itself. It was there that, in her numbed unhappiness, she encountered the blind child again, seemingly standing there where she had left him on that day when she had been gathering material for the article for Josiah Eaton.

He stood there in his rags, staring toward her and not seeing, waiting for some kind of rescue that Valeria Garvey now needed as much as he.

She had forgotten her key and was forced to ring the bell. She dreaded seeing Sam after the scene that morning. He opened the door at last and she went into the hall and passed him near the stairs.

"Please come into the study," he said in his normal voice.

She followed him in and stood near the passageway like a servant awaiting orders. On the desk was the red Morocco case and the bankbook. He sat down in that place from which he ruled his empire like a judge about to pass sentence on some malefactor.

It was the man who had talked to her that night, who had given her the opals and listened to her reading, but it was also Sam Garvey who owned the steel mills and who had felt, in forty years, no regard for the men who worked for him and no remorse when they lost their lives.

"You don't belong here. I was wrong to ask you. These are yours. You're free."

Sam pushed the two objects toward her.

"Are you dismissing me?" Valeria said out of her despair.

"You don't belong in this house. I have no time for what you are. We made a bargain and I release you from it. I'll make a settlement. You won't be in want."

She said in a sort of stupefaction, "What kind of people are we?" Her voice rose with whatever strength she could still summon. "Yes, we made a bargain and I'm ready to abide by it. I'm not ready to be shouted at or given orders like a servant."

"I can't help being what I am. It's too late for me to change."

"It's not too late for you to treat me with some respect. That's all I ask for. No, I won't go. I won't be turned out with a necklace and a bank deposit. I am not that kind of woman."

He managed to control his impatience. "I don't want to fight with you."

"You can fight with me all you want, as long as you recognize that I am not Jim Pryor or any of the men who work for you. You see that?" She pointed to her tapered finger with the wedding band. "That is the contract I made with you. I will stick to it and so will you."

"Why should you go through this?" Sam asked after a moment. "I'll give you what you wanted. You wanted money."

"You'd be astonished if I told you that it wasn't only that. You told me certain things that night and I believed you. Yes, I hate this house. I think the way you live and the way you treat these people who depend on you are iniquitous. I have a right to think you wrong. That has nothing to do with this. I gave my word and I intend to keep it. You said you would keep your word to me."

"I've told you I was wrong," he said in a low voice.

"You're wrong about a great many things. I have been, too. I was wrong about my brother. I went to see him because you drove me to it. He has cut me out of his life because I married you. You owe me, at least, the dignity of standing by me."

He pushed the jewel case toward her as though in answer.

"You can keep those and keep the money you put to my account," she said. "Use them to buy better equipment in your mills. But turn me out of this house because you think you made a mistake? That you will not do." Valeria opened the door. "If I leave, it will be because I wish to and when I'm ready."

She went to her room, changed, went down to the kitchen and cooked the dinner.

She knocked on the study door.

"Dinner, Sam."

He followed her without comment. They ate in silence at the polished table with the gleaming dinnerware. When the meal was over, Valeria went through the door before him, took *Bleak House* from the bookcase, and opened it at the place where she had finished reading the night before.

Sam looked at her with a kind of incredulity in which there was a dawning admiration.

She started to read. He lit a cigar and listened. She read steadily till the mantelpiece clock struck eleven. She replaced the book and went to him and kissed his cheek.

"Good night. And thank you, Sam."

⚜ Chapter Thirteen ⚜

IT WAS AN EXAMPLE of nature imitating art, if *The Courier*'s crude drawing of a man falling into a vat could have been classified as art.

A mill hand named Ben Hallam stumbled and plunged his arm into a vat of molten steel. The arm and shoulder were instantly burned away. The face and chest were splattered with burning fragments which ate through flesh and sinew as though they were lard. He was carried from the mills, pitted and bleeding, like a carcass of a mutilated animal. He regained consciousness for a moment near the gates. His screams, terrifying in their animal agony, rent the air, then, mercifully, he fainted. He died during the night, at home.

In the morning the whistle blew. A crowd of sullen men assembled. A slow resentment burned in these hearts, worn by years of toil and deprivation. Anger renewed their strength.

In the black house near the gates lurked the great beast to whose power and money one of their kind had been sacrificed, as surely as human offerings had been made to the altars of pagan gods. The whistle blew again, and the men straggled in to work. But they walked doggedly like fighters going into battle.

A cloud, not only of smoke and dirt, but of foreboding hung over Shacktown. Like the hush before thunder that precedes a storm, it rivalled the rumbling of the earth that was Sam Garvey's life blood, his very heartbeat. The women of Shacktown carried out their chores, but they were silent. Those who could read pored over Randolph's articles. The second had now appeared. The facts of their own lives appalled them. They saw themselves for the first time as victims of a dire injustice. What had been fatalism, a dull acceptance, stirred. They thought of remedies and revenge.

Sam and Valeria had settled into a routine. They respected an unspoken truce. Sam never referred to his business affairs again. Valeria made no inquiries. She washed and cooked like the women of Shacktown and, in the evenings, she read aloud. Sam's manner was gruff, but his voice was level. Valeria was cool and efficient. She found in the drabness and monotony of her life a certain strength.

One morning, Tripp appeared at the kitchen door with a woman. "This is Mary Doherty, Ma'am. She'd be willing to work for you."

Valeria smiled at the clear-eyed Welsh woman with the Irish name. Ten years before she must have been a country beauty, but her hair was prematurely gray. Tragedy and toil had robbed her of any bloom. Her eyes held a look of constant apprehension.

Mary was the first person in Shacktown to meet the mysterious Mrs. Sam Garvey and was surprised that she was so young and beautiful. And, moreover, kindly. She had imagined some large and overbearing harridan, the sort that suited Sam Garvey's reputation.

"Would you like a cup of coffee?"

Mary could not quite bring herself to answer. She half shook her head and blushed, picking at her plain skirt.

"I'm going to have one, so perhaps you'll join me."

Mary made the same confused movement of her head, half obeisance and half acceptance.

Valeria poured the coffee and sat down, indicating that Mary should also.

"I've only just come to live here," she explained. "This house hasn't been properly cleaned for years. I've been doing what I could, but I would welcome any help you could give me. It's mostly cleaning and washing. The cooking I do myself."

Mary was bewildered. Wasn't Mr. Garvey the richest man in town, as rich as anybody in the whole country? And here was this soft-voiced woman doing the cooking and scrubbing and cleaning like the rest. Perhaps this wasn't really *the* Mrs. Garvey, but some kind of housekeeper or upper servant.

She badly wanted a sip of coffee to steady her nerves, but didn't quite dare to reach for a cup.

"How much time would you be able to give me?"

Mary gulped. Her mouth had gone dry and she found it difficult to speak. She managed to whisper, "Every day, if you like, Ma'am."

"Could you come in the morning and stay till around three? Would that give you enough time to tend to your own home?"

"I have two sons," Mary admitted. "The big one works in the mills. I don't like to leave the other. I do washing, you see, and he has to wait in the street."

"You are welcome to bring him here."

Mary was startled by this idea. "Oh, Ma'am, I wouldn't like."

"Bring him, by all means. Don't your sons go to school?"

"There is no school. My brother teaches what he can."

But Mary Doherty was nervous for some other reason. Her eyes strayed 'round the kitchen, as though she had lost something or was spying something out.

"You haven't drunk your coffee."

Mary managed to pick up the cup, but her hand was trembling.

"Will you come, then?"

Mary nodded and gulped. "I would be glad to, Ma'am."

"How much would you like me to pay you?"

Mary blushed, looked down, plucking at her skirt. "I'm not sure, Ma'am. I will leave that to you."

"Seven dollars a week? Monday to Friday. Is that agreeable?"

Mary's eyes rounded in wonder. "Seven dollars? Oh, my goodness!" It was a fortune, the difference between penury and plenty.

Valeria held out her hand. "Then we can start to-morrow."

Mary wiped her hand on her apron and timidly

touched Valeria's fingers. She was overcome by her own good fortune. As she was leaving she seemed to remember something and cast the same furtive look around the kitchen.

That night at dinner Valeria told Sam that she had found a servant.

"Keep her out of my room and don't discuss my affairs."

"I don't know about your business, so how could I discuss it?"

"There's some trouble at the mills. I don't want what I'm doing talked about."

"Because of the man who was killed?"

"That and your brother's articles."

She said after a moment, "I asked him to leave town that day. I offered him the money to go East or to Europe. But he refused. He and Josiah Eaton have become friends."

Sam looked at her shrewdly. Perhaps Ida had, after all, not been so wrong.

"Weren't they before?"

"No. He just worked for the paper. Randolph plans to help with his campaign."

Sam mopped up the gravy with a circular movement, three times 'round the plate, and then transferred the piece of soggy bread to his mouth. "Is he ambitious?"

"Randolph was very bitter when the War was over. He went into the army at sixteen and was wounded and sent home. One night some of Sherman's men broke into our house and Randolph was shot again in the shoulder. The bullet grazed his lung. He would have died if it hadn't been for the kindness of a Yankee captain."

"You had a bad time of it."

"We tried to stay on, but it was hopeless. The darkies had all fled or moved away. In the end the place was sold to pay the taxes."

"No wonder you hate the North."

"I don't any more. The whole war was madness." It had been the Yankee captain who convinced her. He had given her protection and help to assuage his

own wounded spirit, sickened by slaughter. She had
come to dread the perpetual sadness in his eyes.
"Randy never forgot. He always blamed the Northern
industrialists. Those articles, in a way, are his revenge."

"I guess I'd have felt the same. But Josiah's using
him, as he's using me and the mills, to get himself
elected."

"I think Randolph knows that. But it's an opportunity to express his opinions. I don't fully understand
and I know that it's no use my asking."

"What?"

"Why the men and their families mean so little to
you. There's not even a school to send the children
to."

"I never went to school."

"Perhaps you were too poor, as they are."

"People have to make their own way. There's nothing that forces a man to work for me. I know it's a
dog's life. I worked in the mines ten years."

"It seems . . . shortsighted," she ventured.

"Why?"

"Wouldn't they work more willingly if they were
better off? Everyone has a right to a decent life. It's
supposed to be guaranteed in the Bill of Rights."

"The Bill of Rights never put any money in my
pocket."

"I know," she smiled. "You made everything you
have." Valeria held up her hands to remind him of
the gesture he had once made when telling her the
same thing. "It's a hard philosophy, Sam."

"I'm a hard man."

He was inflexible and uninterested in change. But
he was no longer angered by her mentioning the forbidden subject of his methods of making money.

That night, as she was reading aloud and Sam was
blowing smoke rings at the ceiling, the black doors of
Shacktown opened and tired men came forth, walking
with a new resolve. They trudged down the fetid alleys and converged in twos and threes on the one
saloon that Shacktown boasted. It shrank into the

night that hid the meeting of these tired and angry men.

The only light in the saloon came from a single candle and by it a man was waiting. He had one eye and a face pitted with dirt like everything and everyone that lived in the shadow of Sam Garvey's chimneys. He was a young man of thirty who was no longer young, but was already burdened with the bitter knowledge of a man of eighty.

The men filed in and shuffled into silent groups. They all stared at the lone flame as though it were the last light in the world. The leader was as motionless as a carving, but with the tenseness of a cat about to spring.

At last the door of the saloon was locked and the shutters shut across the windows. The shuffling of the feet ceased and the quiet was as heavy as rising dough.

The man spoke in a low, musical voice so that the men had to strain forward to catch each word. He spoke with the lilting accent of Wales and with the natural eloquence of the Welsh. His passion and conviction found an echo in every heart.

"You all know me, Fletcher Jones. I was born among you and I've worked with you since I was a boy. I've given my life as you have, to the Garvey Mills. I lost my father to the mills, as you have lost fathers and brothers and sons, as we all lost Ben Hallam last week, torn apart like a wild beast and left to die in his agony. Just like we all might die, any day, any week, because the man who owns the mills and grew rich on our labor and sweat and hunger won't spend a penny to protect us and doesn't care if we live or die. There are always others to take our place."

As he spun out the indictment of Sam Garvey and Sam Garvey's greed and brutality, the hearts of the men in that blackened out room hardened with a slow rage. Fletcher Jones was telling them what their lives had told them through the long hours at the mills and the long hours at the tables in what passed for kitchens, and the short hours of restless sleep. All their lives were in the voice of that man with the patch over an empty eye socket. It was as though the steady flame of that single candle and the fervor of that one voice were all that remained to them of worth in the world, their last hope.

Jones spoke of the wages that never paid the rent or the food or provided a doctor if they were sick, or allowed them to rest when they were old. He spoke of the grinding labor they were forced to give in return for living like animals in a rat-infested slum; of the tainted water from the pumps, and the open drains where all the refuse of their slavery was dumped, only to seep back into their drinking and cooking and washing water. Did Sam Garvey care? Were the sewers ever mended? And he spoke of the children that grew up in this filth and squalor and had no books to teach them and no doctor to tend to them and no hope of a better life. They lived like rats and would die like rats and so would their children, and for what? To fill the pockets of one man already bloated with millions, whose money flowed along the lines to the East and piled up in his vaults like a great pyramid. They were nothing more than slaves.

He held up a copy of *The Courier* with Randolph's article and the accompanying drawing. "You all saw this. A hundred men dead in the mills, a hundred men burned in the vats and maimed and butchered. And for what? So that the man with millions can make more millions. And for what? Four hundred dollars. That's what he paid for Ben Hallam's life. That's all his widow has to show for twenty years of labor and want. That's all his children have in place of their father. You see this?" Jones pulled off the patch that covered the empty socket. "You know what the man with the millions paid me for the loss of an eye? Nothing. Not a penny."

There was utter silence. Fletcher Jones dropped the paper on the table and pulled back the patch over his eye.

"Are we going to stand for it? Always? Getting killed and blinded and still getting nothing in compensation? Hasn't the time come to say 'No'? We are free men. And, as free men, hasn't our time come to tell Garvey that we want clean homes and clean water and mended sewers and a school for our children and a doctor for our children and their mothers and for us? Hasn't the time come to demand sound tools to work with and, if there's an accident, decent money for our widows?"

Jones leaned forward and the whisper shot through the room like an arrow of ice into every heart. "Are you going to say 'no,' men?"

A prolonged sigh escaped the crowd, a sigh that came from their souls, worn down by years of weariness and want.

And as the men in the saloon were saying 'No' to Sam Garvey, Valeria finished reading Dickens. Sam Garvey was staring at the ceiling, lost in the tale of Lord and Lady Deadlock and Lawyer Blenkingthorpe and the great house with the battlements.

Sam Garvey's plans, whatever they might be, were advancing, Valeria knew. Men came to the house and were closeted for hours in the study, men with heavy shoulders and rough hands who wore flashy suits and diamond rings. There was also a man who came from Thaddeus Brownlow's bank, in a London suit and a homburg, who carried a large briefcase. He conferred with Sam all afternoon and departed with an air of mystery and satisfaction, as though some great contract had been signed. There was an air of suppressed excitement about Sam. He did not always listen to *Bleak House* with the same absorption and leaned forward in the middle of a chapter to scribble figures on slips of paper and said, when she looked up, "Go on."

Often, Valeria caught him smiling to himself. He was cordial and even got up to refill her glass and inquired if she had ordered the piano and when she was going to start refurbishing the parlor. He paid another twenty-five thousand into her account and told her to order dresses and furs from Chicago, anything she wanted. As far as he was capable of it, Sam Garvey beamed.

Meanwhile Valeria was scrubbing the carpets with Mary Doherty, while the blind boy she had met in the street—Mary's son—sat on a stool in the kitchen and nibbled on cookies Valeria had baked. She had sent him to the doctor who had pronounced it possible that some sight remained in one eye and was giving him treatments. Mary Doherty thought the sky had opened and Valeria was the Queen of Heaven.

Valeria gave her money to buy the children clothes; and the five hundred dollars which she had kept in the bag in her dresser she gave to Mary for the widow of Ben Hallam.

"I don't know, Ma'am," Mary said with tears in her eyes. "I just don't know how it is—you see—" She wanted to say that she did not understand how such a lady with a heart filled with so much kindness could possibly have married Sam Garvey for whom not a person in Shacktown had ever had a good thought or spoken a good word.

Together the women had dragged the Turkey carpets outside and spread them on what had once been grass and scrubbed them until the suds turned black and sluiced them with water. And gradually patterns in rose and blue and crimson emerged. They were fine carpets, finer than Sam Garvey had ever known. Nor —in the past—would he have cared.

People passing in and out of the mill gates never guessed that the woman on her knees in the yard was Sam Garvey's wife. Dirt had become Valeria's enemy. She was determined to conquer it and with her fine white hands in gloves and her glossy dark hair in disarray she felt a triumphant sense of achievement as the lost patterns reappeared.

Valeria found that her attitude toward money was changing. She had fifty thousand dollars in her account, but, contrary to everything she had imagined in her years of struggle and poverty, she was disinclined to spend it on things she had dreamed of, because they now seemed indecent. She heard the whistle shrill and watched from her bedroom window the ragged crowd of men waiting for the gates to open. She heard the whistle blow again and the gates swing back and the men pass through. She knew that it was useless to tell Sam what was in her heart and, increasingly, on her conscience. The evidence was too close, was all around her, was inescapable. Sam had given her money to do with what she wanted. She asked for the bankbook and he opened the safe and gave it to her.

"Sam, am I free to do with this money what I will?"

He glanced at her, hardly listening, and nodded.

"Anything?"

He grinned, knowing that if he set restrictions, she would fight him. "Except give it to the poor."

They were tested antagonists in certain areas; they accepted in their own odd way that their differences were irreconcilable.

"But if I wanted to give it to the poor?"

"You can give it to the devil for all I care."

Valeria was sitting in the kitchen having tea with Mary and her son when she broached the subject that had been on her mind.

The boy's name was Matthew. He had grown used to the presence that gave him sweets and caressed his cheek. His keen perception sought for her. Matthew knew her barely audible tread and her voice. He knew it was different, soft and kind. Already he felt that he knew what she looked like because of the coolness of her hands and a faint perfume that clung to her. There were also her quick movements that were unlike his mother's. She was a ghostly being from another world that he had no need to fear. Valeria placed the spoon in his hand and guided it to the food and what she fed him was delicious and warm. He waited for her and felt protected when she was near.

The doctor had been giving him treatments and the pain behind his eyes was less. Sometimes it seemed to him that he could detect the blurred outline of a shape, the gleam of light on a china plate or some shadowy object. These were his secrets and he dwelled upon them inwardly and waited with the secret anticipation of a child who knows that at Christmas he will receive a present, exciting and mysterious and undisclosed.

"Do you think," Valeria asked, "that it would be a

help if a school were opened for the children of men who work here in the mills?"

"A school, Ma'am?" Mary was now used to the unexpected with her patroness whom she had come to regard as someone almost sacred.

"If books were provided and a teacher?"

Mary gulped, not knowing how to consider such a possibility. "Well, Ma'am, yes, it would. It would be a great thing, but I don't know—" Would the women of Shacktown ever let their children go to a school started by Mrs. Garvey? Would they not all put their heads together and decide it was some kind of trap?

"How many children are there? Roughly?"

"There are so many, Ma'am, it's hard to say."

"Suppose such a school were started. Is there any building where classes could be held?"

Mary thought a moment. "There is a hall where they hold services on Sunday. It's the Lutherans' and it is not used much in the week, you see."

"If there were classes in the daytime for the smaller children, the older ones who work at the mills could come in the evening."

"Who would teach?"

"We should have to find a school teacher. I could certainly teach reading, writing and simple arithmetic."

Mary looked at her in frank alarm. "Oh, I don't know, Ma'am. I don't know if they would like that, seeing that you—well—"

"That I'm married to Mr. Garvey?"

"It might be difficult, you see."

"Where does the Lutheran minister live? Will you take me to see him?"

"I think he lives in town, Ma'am. I can find out." She was doubtful about the project and about Valeria's involvement.

But Valeria had made up her mind. She could not live in Shacktown and passively tolerate the narrowness of Sam's idea of money.

"Let's go and see him now."

Mary was frightened. She did not want to be seen driving through the alleys with Mrs. Garvey. Rumors might circulate that she had joined the enemy. Every

morning she took a roundabout route to the Garveys'
house and every evening she went home by another
way.

And there was something else much on her conscience. Her brother, Fletcher, was the ringleader of
the Workers' Movement. They were holding meetings
and drawing up resolutions and Fletcher was always
asking her what went on in the Garvey household.
She constantly had to put him off. She didn't know
how to explain that Mrs. Garvey was quite different
from anything the people of Shacktown could possibly
have imagined. No one would have believed her.
Everyone would have seen her defense of her employer as a betrayal.

This perturbation of spirit Valeria guessed. She set
Mary's mind at rest. "I'll go and see him myself. Find
out for me where he lives."

The next morning Valeria set out in the carriage
with Tripp. The pastor lived on the far side of town in
a small and lugubrious house beside the church. He
opened the door himself and was much startled when
the tall lady in black with a veiled hat announced herself. "I am Mrs. Garvey. May I see you for a moment?"

Pastor Vanderlip was a small, precise man who
looked as if he had stepped out of the frame of a
daguerreotype and would resume his position on the
wall when his daily round was over. He was dour in
his rectitude. He had never opened a book in his life
except the Bible. The Almighty stood at his side, as
grimly righteous as himself.

He led Valeria into a small room with mud-brown
linoleum on the floor and a mud-brown text over the
mantel. "The Lord thy God is a jealous God."

Valeria explained her purpose and the Pastor listened. If he was capable of it, he was surprised. He
nonetheless recognized the validity of what she was
suggesting. Mrs. Sam Garvey could not be a good
woman. She was the handmaiden of Mammon. Was it
possible that God, in his inexorable justice, deemed it
admissible that good might stem from evil?

"I am greatly concerned that the children are getting

no schooling," Valeria said. "It is not right and it should be remedied. If you would allow the hall to be used for this purpose, I am willing to defray the cost of books and writing materials and a salary for a teacher."

Pastor Vanderlip placed the tips of his fingers together and consulted the Almighty. The Almighty conceded that this sinner had been visited by a higher impulse, but however high the impulse The Almighty was not amenable to His meeting hall's being used for any earthly purpose without remuneration. The Almighty kept strict accounts, not merely of good and evil, but of dollars and cents as well.

Terms were discussed and Valeria agreed to pay the rent.

She visited Arcadia's high school, where Valeria interviewed the principal. Were there teachers available? The principal doubted it. When Valeria offered to make a donation to the school fund, the principal reconsidered. Valeria doubled her offer. Teachers would be found.

She drove to the stationer's and ordered a hundred copybooks, a hundred pens and a hundred inkwells. She also requested textbooks and blackboard and a supply of chalk.

Next, Valeria drove to the doctor's house. The wizened wife whose arthritis was "congenital" barred the door. Here was that fallen woman again who had told lies about wanting to be a cook and working for Mrs. Brewster and who now was passing herself off as Mrs. Garvey. "Mrs. Sam Garvey?" she asked in outraged disbelief.

"Yes, I am Mrs. Garvey."

The doctor's wife stepped back in alarm. Clearly this dreadful person suffered from delusions. She had heard of people who went mad and thought they were Martha Washington or the King of England, and who were shut up in asylums as they deserved to be. She hovered, then shot out, "Wait here!" Quickly, she slipped into her husband's office. He would know how to keep her quiet until the police could be called and the woman taken off.

Dr. Mortlake had long since succumbed to a malady far worse than those of any of his patients. It was a disgust for the human body and all its malfunctionings. He had lanced too many boils, sprayed too many tonsils, swabbed out too many sores. He had examined the old, the shapeless, the malodorous and the afflicted. He loathed the sense of sickness that had pervaded his whole life. The sight of inflamed limbs, swollen joints and infected organs had turned his soul to bile. His eyes were yellow and his fingers stained brown from the cigarettes he smoked through countless examinations. He was the scapegoat for Arcadia's disorders.

The woman who thought she was Mrs. Sam Garvey was admitted to his consultation room and stated her business. He listened listlessly at his desk like a bag of soiled laundry. She wanted a doctor for two nights a week from six to nine to give check-ups and prescriptions to the mill hands and their families. She would pay for all the medicines and she would pay him for his time.

Dr. Mortlake was forced to listen all day to the dismal complaints of his patients and all night to the relentless meandering of his wife. He was inoculated against the plague of the human voice.

She was saying, "Would you be willing to do this? And how much would you charge?"

He roused himself sufficiently to say, "I work from ten to six each day. I have no time."

Valeria was persistent, this woman who purported to be married to Sam Garvey. "What do you earn a week, doctor?"

He shrugged. "Fifty, maybe." It was often less; the poor seldom paid their bills.

"I will pay you that for two evenings a week."

His bleary eyes met hers. "Fifty dollars?"

"It is important to get some kind of clinic started. If you find it too much for you, perhaps later on you could help me to find someone else."

She was opening her purse, taking out crisp green dollars. He saw with the slowest amazement that she had given him a hundred dollars.

Valeria drove on to the printer's. She ordered post-
ers announcing the opening of a free school for children from ages six to twelve and for older boys in the
evenings, with free books and writing materials. Mrs.
Garvey also wanted handbills announcing that a doctor
would be available on Tuesdays and Fridays from six
to nine for free consultations, and that medicines and
treatments would be provided free of charge.

As she climbed back into the carriage Valeria felt
exhilarated. At least she had started something. She
asked Tripp, "Did you find out about the horses Mr.
Eaton is selling off?"

"Yes, Ma'am. They're at Horton's Stables."

"Please take me there."

Valeria no longer felt guilty at buying herself something she could do without. She would escape from
Shacktown on fine afternoons and go for long, solitary
rides into the country.

That night at dinner she saw that Sam was secretly
exultant. His plans had reached the point of consum-
mation.

He said with the smile of a man warmed by his own
achievement, "I want you to buy an outfit, the finest
you've ever had."

"What for?"

"I've a notion for you to open my new railroad.
They'll start laying the rails next month."

☜ CHAPTER FOURTEEN ☞

ROSIE DELMAR WAS LOUNGING in Josiah Eaton's study over *The Courier*. She had changed into a Nile green negligée trimmed with marabou feathers that wafted in suggestive little breaths against her bosom. Her dark red hair was held back by a green velvet ribbon and curls hung in heavy coils about her shoulders. Rosie's eyes with their sapphire gleams offered an abundance of sensual pleasure. What a splendid creature she would have been if it weren't for that loose, guttersnipe mouth, Josiah thought. Poor Rosie!

She held out her glass for more champagne. "You're not very sociable, Jose. What's the matter?"

"I've got a lot on my mind," he said as he refilled her glass. He was thinking of that other woman who had sat in that same chair, so cool and restrained, with her proud little chiseled head, set so elegantly on her neck, her unconscious air of good breeding, the white skin and the large, clouded eyes. If it hadn't been for that damnable picture she might be here now, instead of Rosie. But now she was languishing in Sam Garvey's prison in Shacktown. In the end women were all the same. Queens or whores, they did anything when it came to money.

"What you need is a roll with Rosie." She lay back. Loosening the silk bow of her sheer negligée, she exposed her voluptuous breasts. Rosie was proud of them. She caressed them with deliberate languor and, dipping her thumb and forefinger in her glass, moistened the nipples with champagne.

Josiah had looked forward to a weekend with Rosie, one of those sexual bouts that relieved his tension, but now that she was there, he found that the prospect bored him. He watched her as she let the green silk folds fall back from her Juno-like body and carefully trickled the golden wine down her belly. Drops of champagne sparkled among the burnished curls between her legs.

"You wasn't so nice to Rosie last time, but Rosie forgave you. I've wanted you, Jose. I don't mind telling you, whatever else you don't do, you're the best lover I ever had."

"Not now, Rosie. Later."

Her fingers followed the drops and found the source of her main attraction. "You are a beast! You bring me here all the way from Chicago. You know I'm hot for you and you just sit there tempting me."

The fingers lingered provocatively. Her brilliant eyes glinted beneath half-lowered lids.

"Stop that, Rosie. I'll tell you when I'm ready."

She sat up, offended.

"What did you bring me here for if you don't want to make love?"

"I wanted to find out what your plans are," he lied. "I shan't be seeing you again. As you pointed out on the train, now that I'm going into politics, I'll have to watch my step."

"My plans?" She stood up, taken aback. For the first time in their long relationship her blatant nudity offended him.

"You made it plain you thought I'd treated you badly. I've had it in mind to make amends."

Rosie looked at him in astonishment, hands on hips. "You are an odd one, really. There's no reason why you can't see Rosie. I know how to be discreet." She came over to him with mollified, half-humorous good nature. Her abundant sensuality not infrequently included her heart. "I believe you've fallen for someone. There's nothing that turns a man off more than the love of a virtuous woman." She laughed and ran her hand through his hair. "Oh Jose, you are an old fool!"

He could feel the warmth of her body. Her skin had the richness of ripe fruit. He drew her to him, sliding his hands 'round her waist, under the silk, so that his face was buried between her breasts.

"Never mind about love. A good woman can't give you what I can. We fight when we've done it too much. Six times in one day. I was worn out." She whispered, "Stand up, Josiah."

He did so reluctantly, caught in her experienced erotic snare. She undressed him quickly, dragged his clothes to the floor and lifted his shirt, then ground her hips against his loins. "Take it now, Jose. Now. Be quick."

He had her, forcing her back against the arm of the sofa. It was swift, practiced, immediate, like the rutting of animals.

"Oh, Christ, you drive me crazy!" Rosie cried out.

They came together. He withdrew, resenting her. Josiah went quickly into his bedroom, washed and pulled on his riding clothes.

When he came back, she was stretched out on the sofa, smoking one of his cigars.

"That was a quick one," she eyed him critically. "Where are you off to now?"

"Look here, Rosie, you talked about getting a place of your own in Chicago. I'll finance you if you can manage to keep your mouth shut. What you need is a steady protector, someone who'll support you. It shouldn't be hard. You're the best at what you do."

Rosie watched him. For once her mouth was shut, compressed by an anger her eyes did not conceal.

"I'm sorry you came such a distance. I made a mistake. You're right; I'm not in the mood. So, do you mind catching the evening train?" He laid some money on the table. "Sorry, Rosie."

"I pity the woman who finally marries you," she said with barely concealed venom.

He was glad to get away from her. He went quickly through the office, not pausing to greet the men who were scribbling away at their desks. In passing Randolph, he paused and said, "I'd like to see you about the next article. Come up after dinner if you're not engaged."

"I'll be glad to, Mr. Eaton," Randolph smiled.

Josiah was struck once again by the resemblance to the sister. Something about the shape of the head or the soft Southern drawl perhaps. Poor fellow, he must have suffered a shock when that superfine creature had married the old bastard! Muckraking his brother-in-law! A mad sort of irony! The fact that Sam had married at all was a source of never-ending amazement.

He hurried down to the street.

As Eaton strode along he thought of Sam Garvey. The opportunity he had long waited for was at hand. He had known for some time about the plans for the new railroad. It would be three months at least before the lines being laid in Oregon and those from Arcadia would meet somewhere out there on the prairies. Josiah had received detailed reports from his spies among the engineers and surveyors and knew where the terrain would require blasting and bridging. Three months more or less in which to disrupt Sam Garvey's plans and force him to make a deal.

Garvey had taken care to renew his contract with the existing line of which Josiah was president. It was good for another year, by which time Josiah's line would be virtually out of business and Garvey's in full operation. But there were ways of holding him up, of preventing the steady flow of steel and iron ore. And there were ways of making things increasingly difficult at the mills. Garvey had sunk a large part of his personal fortune into this venture and, even with Thaddeus Brownlow's help, there were limits to the supply of cash, limits to credit. Even Sam Garvey's resources were not infinite; nearly, but not quite.

Fletcher Jones reported regularly to Josiah on the progress of the Workers' Association. Eighty percent of the mill's employees attended the meetings. Josiah had provided funds for a lawyer to draw up a contract which he well knew Sam Garvey would never sign. A showdown might lead to a strike and a strike would slow things down considerably. If necessary he would make available sufficient cash to keep the men out for a time. Otherwise sheer need would force them to capitulate and a valuable chance would be lost.

Meanwhile Josiah was building solid support for himself. The articles in *The Courier* had been well worth it. They were having repercussions and would stir up more, as the revelations became more shocking.

Garvey's sly attempt to offset the anger caused by the latest death of a mill hand was the financing of a school and of free medical care, supposedly under his wife's aegis. But it was nothing more than a bribe. No one in Shacktown should be taken in by it. The facts of minimal wages and nonexistent protection remained unchanged.

He thought of Valeria, as he often did, always amazed at the speed with which she had hooked the old man who was supposedly as heartless as his own steel. How had she done it? She had not struck him at all as the sort of woman capable of such a precipitous seduction. What possible wiles could she have used? Sam Garvey had never been interested in women. All Randolph's research had not unearthed a single rumor about his private life.

It was a mystery, extraordinary, bizarre. That exquisite, sharp-tongued, unyielding young woman and the unyielding, harsh old man. It irked Josiah's vanity that, with all his experience, he had failed to make any impression on her. Evidently Sam's millions had outweighed his abysmal lack of charm.

At the stables he was greeted by Joe Horton, whose face was the color of undercooked beef and who smelled of straw and horse dung.

"I'd like to borrow a horse, Joe. I need some exercise."

"Sure, Mr. Eaton. Take any you like. They'd all be glad of a good ride out."

There was a young gelding Josiah was fond of. It had pained him to part with his horses, but his whole life was moving into another phase.

"Started campaigning yet, Mr. Eaton?" Horton inquired as he lifted down a saddle and harness.

"Getting close, Joe. It needs a lot of planning. There's a lot of territory to cover."

"I'll say. This is a big state."

"Yes, I'll be moving around."

"Say," Horton paused as he flung the saddle onto

the gelding's back, "I forgot; I got news for you. I sold Mimosa."

"You did? Who to?"

"You'll never guess. Mrs. Sam Garvey! Yes, the new one. My, is she a looker! And does she know horses! Went over Mimosa like an expert. Can you imagine?" He leaned against the gelding so that his rank breath struck Josiah's nostrils. "A young, good-looking woman, polite and quick. No foolin' around makin' up her mind. Bought Mimosa in a snap!"

Horton shook his head and started to strap on the saddle.

"I can't figure it out. A real lady, mind you, and that old skinflint! Who'd have thought he'd ever be caught by a woman? But that one, I tell you, she knows her mind. Sharp as a tack. Of course, she done it for the money. What woman wouldn't?" His dissertation on Mrs. Garvey's motives for getting married accompanied Josiah as he led the gelding out of the stall.

As Eaton mounted, the gelding, anticipating an outing, gave him a friendly snuffle and whisked its tail.

"Yep, I tell you she's something. Still in her twenties. A trim figure. Good seat and good hands. Rode off just now. Not many women can sit a horse that well."

"Which way did she go?"

"Didn't say. T'ord The Heights, I reckon."

"How long ago?"

"Half an hour maybe."

Josiah crossed Main Street and took a long hill to The Heights. He looked up at Ida's red brick mansion. Odd that in all these years, living in the same town, he'd never laid eyes on her. Hard to believe he'd been serious about marrying her once, clumsy, awkward Ida! If he'd gotten his hands on the old man's money that way, it would have saved him a lot of trouble. Strange what a lack of sex could do to a woman! Sets up a sort of antagonism they never quite get over. By all accounts Ida was a holy terror. Josiah pitied that worn out stick of a husband he sometimes saw at the bank. All that anger and wasted energy and throwing her weight around could have been curbed and channeled by a good time in bed twice a week. Ida had character and she wasn't stupid. She had a lot of the old man's guts and shrewdness and a lot of his evil temper, too.

It was different with Valeria Garvey. She had, despite her well-trained femininity, a good deal of a man's makeup. Independence. An awkward quality in a woman. She would only give herself when she wanted to. She demanded respect and equality and the right to her own opinions and would never be subdued or blackmailed by sex. But then, Josiah reflected, he'd known too many women like Rosie without any pride or morals, too many whose husbands didn't satisfy them and who looked on a man as a stallion and wanted only one thing from him and cared nothing for what he was.

It was incredible that Valeria Lee had married Sam Garvey. He would have thought her the kind who would starve rather than give in to a man who couldn't possibly attract her. Or was it possible that Sam had understood her in some way that he himself had failed to?

Eaton realized, as he rode down Tremont Avenue, that he had missed the essential quality that a woman could bring to a man's life. He had had too many women and had them too easily. Even when he had been stirred by a woman's beauty or by the indefinable charm that a subtle, well-dressed, clever woman exuded, his affairs had been resolved too quickly and always in the same way. Josiah had never taken the trouble to find out what a woman really was, what she thought or felt, or what her dreams and ambitions were. Sex and money and a crude pride in parading a new conquest! There was a whole area in the relationship between men and women that he knew nothing of.

He had scoffed at love or perhaps had purposely avoided it when it was offered to him. Josiah had never thought he would come to need the dependence and closeness involved in knowing one woman belonged to him and he belonged to her. He was tired of the games, because however he played them, they were always the same. Of all the hundreds of women he had pursued and slept with and paid for there was not one he missed.

The trees along Tremont Avenue were already denuded of leaves and the lawns had yellowed. A few last roses hung on, overblown and faded. There was a breath of ending in the air.

He spurred his horse to a canter and soon was in the country, approaching the Haverfield place. He thought of Ford Hollister and his ill-fated wife. Hollister was not really a man. He had sold himself to money, like his friend Valeria Lee, and paid for it by becoming a male nurse. He was probably one of those half men who preferred other men.

It wasn't new variations of sex Josiah needed. It was that mysterious, indefinable element—love itself.

He passed his own place at a trot. He had been so proud of it when he built it. He really had arrived, he had felt, and was a man of importance, a landowner, a country gentleman. It had lost its appeal of late. All those empty rooms, all that furniture, pictures and silver, symbols of the position he had carved out for himself. Many years of Josiah's life had gone into that house. It stood there, but the years had gone.

He saw Valeria some way ahead, coming idly back at a walk. She was wearing a pearl gray habit and a little matching hat with a white veil. Even at a distance she had a unique distinction.

Eaton spurred his horse to a canter and drew up beside her. She was flushed and lovely and sat Mimosa with a natural ease.

"Good afternoon, Mrs. Garvey."

She glanced at him and urged Mimosa to a trot. Josiah wheeled his horse and rode along beside her.

"Mrs. Garvey, won't you forgive me? I can't do more than apologize."

She looked straight ahead. He noted gold tints in her jade eyes, the set of her firm little jaw. "I would like very much to talk to you. Don't be stubborn." She stared in front of her and then spurred Mimosa to a trot.

"Please?"

He looked very handsome in his buff coat and breeches, strong and male and god-like. It occurred to Valeria that he might be a bridge between herself and Randolph and, dimly, that there might be something she could find out from him that would be of use to Sam. She changed her mind abruptly and reined Mimosa in. Her strangely clouded eyes were cold and forbidding.

"Very well, Mr. Eaton, you may speak to me."

They rode side by side in silence.

"I really have nothing to say," Josiah admitted. "I was ashamed of what happened and I would like you to believe that and not hold it against me."

"I chose not to think of it."

After some moments he said, "I'm glad you bought Mimosa. She's a pretty, spirited thing. A little too light for me."

"She suits me perfectly."

"You ride very well. Few women do."

She inclined her head in acknowledgment of the compliment.

"Where have you been riding?" he asked.

"Along the roads."

"If you'll trust me, I can show you a stretch where you can have a real gallop. Behind my house there's some open country without fences."

She considered this proposal for a moment. "Very well."

He led the way through the gate of his property, up the driveway and around the side of the house. There was a barred gate at the end of his back garden. He dismounted and opened it. "I own all this land, but I don't farm it. I wanted to leave it as it was."

They started to gallop across the turf toward a copse of maples, radiant in the last of their autumn glory. Valeria rode with assurance and he admired the straightness of her back and the lightness with which she held the reins. Mimosa had already accepted her and the mare's nimble hoofs covered the ground with a sense of release and joy.

The attractive couple reined up near the trees. The

warm air had heightened Valeria's color and the exhilaration of the gallop had restored her spirits.

"That was wonderful. Thank you."

They lingered in the dying bloom of the day. The entranced stillness that comes with autumn hung over the trees and the woods behind. The sky was pale gold and the last clouds were streaked with salmon and rose.

"How is Randolph doing?" she asked unexpectedly, without looking at him.

"As it turns out, he's writing the articles himself and doing a good job."

"I wish that he had not written them at all."

"I can understand that."

She playfully touched Mimosa's ear with her crop. "He will not speak to me now. It is a source of great sadness to me."

"He was very much upset by your marriage."

She looked up and away, beyond the turf and the distant house. "It was a strange and sudden thing. Mr. Garvey has been very good to me. I do not care what strangers think, but Randy is my brother. We have always been very close."

Josiah saw with pity and embarrassment that there were tears in her large eyes.

"Is there anything I can do?"

She shook her head, mastered herself, and said in a low voice, "People are not always what they seem. You said that no one's motives are entirely pure. They are not entirely bad either."

He did not know what to say and did not want to offend her by referring to her marrying an old man for his money.

To Valeria it seemed the saddest thing in life was that people should reveal themselves only in unguarded moments as decent and kind and giving. Then when they were in the everyday world, they felt forced to put up defenses, closing over and erasing their true selves from view, much the way a wave washes away footprints on the sand. She had seen into Sam's heart and here she was with his greatest enemy, a man she had despised. For a few moments Josiah Eaton was being civilized and kind. If there were some way that she could get him to see the other side of Sam . . .

"One night at Mrs. Brewster's I met Thaddeus Brownlow. He said the Civil War should never have happened, that in a country this big and rich there was enough for everyone."

Josiah saw what she was getting at and replied, "Perhaps you can persuade Mr. Garvey to believe that."

Suddenly Valeria looked directly at him. "Mr. Garvey made his way at a time when men were not concerned with ethics. But that will change, as the issues that the war was fought over would have changed, without all that bloodshed. Does fighting solve anything?"

"It's man's nature to fight and sometimes he's forced to."

"You mean he wants to. I am tired of brutality and bitterness. It seems to me that any compromise is better."

"If you are trying to reconcile me with your husband, I'm afraid it's a waste of time," he said to her as gently as he could.

After a moment she asked quietly, "But are your motives at their best any better than his at their worst?"

"Perhaps not," Josiah admitted, taken aback by her directness. "We are as we are."

"Men always say that," she said with controlled impatience. "Isn't it simply an excuse for not making the effort to be a little wiser and more tolerant . . . perhaps a little kinder, too?"

"If anyone can convince Sam Garvey of that I'm sure it will be you."

She gave him a level glance. "And who will convince you, Mr. Eaton?"

He shrugged. "I don't know—with my colossal conceit."

They had drawn closer for a few moments, but now their relative positions came between them. Valeria flicked Mimosa with her crop and the little mare started forward.

Josiah rode beside her. She spurred her horse and they galloped into the glowing sunset. Fleetingly, they were both aware of a sense of human completeness, of life as it should be, of a man and woman sharing the freedom and exhilaration of this hour of perfect beauty, in a world without friction and stupid divisiveness.

As they approached the house, they reined in, moved by this stolen exaltation. He said contritely, "Mrs. Garvey, perhaps I shouldn't say this and perhaps, because your husband and I are in different camps, you won't understand, but I wish there were some way that you could consider me your friend."

"I don't see how we can be friends, Mr. Eaton," Valeria answered gravely, "since you and my husband refuse to compromise."

It was the set of that proud little head on her fine neck and a sadness in her clear-cut profile that filled him with a strange kind of tenderness. He realized with a mingled joy and pain that a star had appeared in the empty firmament of his inner being.

She seemed on the point of adding something, of offering some kind of truce, but instead she remained silent.

He wanted to put things right between them, to lay the foundation for another meeting, but she was waiting.

Josiah dismounted at the gate and let her through.

It was evening by the time Valeria reached what she euphemistically called home. As she went up the path the whistle shrilled once again. It was a sound she hated. The gates of the mill swung slowly open to allow Sam Garvey's prisoners a few hours of respite from their grinding labors. In the shacks and alleys of Sam's slum, the dark gathered watchfully and the women waited, eager and on edge, knowing that something was about to happen that would place their lives and their men in jeopardy. The tension in Shacktown increased with each advancing hour.

Valeria found Sam in a mood of scarcely concealed excitement. He was enormously alert. He knew that the men were on the march and that a confrontation was imminent. Like a wary old general on the eve of battle, he was steeling himself for the assault. The lion was ready to fight for his principle of making money on his own terms, regardless of right and wrong.

He had opened a bottle of champagne and greeted her with a sort of husband's jocularity that surprised her.

"What are we celebrating?" she inquired as she took the proffered glass.

"The elegant Mrs. Garvey. That outfit is mighty becoming to you, Ma'am."

"My, we are gallant! What has come over you? You look as though you had just made another million."

"I intend to make many more than one, though I foresee a lot of obstacles, what with the hands and Eaton and a certain scribbler named Randolph Lee."

She remained mystified. "Has something else appeared?"

He nodded. "Did you know that you're married to a murderer, a thief and a man called Nero who must have been a pretty devilish fellow to be compared to me."

"I knew all that beforehand. Randolph was kind enough to point out the highlights of your career."

"One day if I meet your brother," Sam said, lighting a cigar, "I'll tell him the truth—about me and Josiah Eaton and a lot of other men who made fortunes in the last half-century. He'd be mighty surprised to know how his boss put aside enough to buy *The Courier* and most of a railroad and build that big place in the country. Josiah is one of the biggest crooks in the West, but he covers his tracks well. He'll end up as governor, most likely."

She had taken off her hat and was sitting by the fire, sipping her champagne. "Why do you hate each other so?"

"I don't hate Josiah. He obstructs me. He hates me because he spread the story I killed his father. Maybe he really believes it, maybe not. In point of fact Marcus Eaton's death was one of the few foul deeds in Arcadia that I wasn't guilty of."

"Who killed him, then?"

"He was shot by a man whose wife he'd been sleeping with and who he'd infected with a disease. The woman died shortly after. It was rumored she died by her own hand. and the husband shot himself in San Francisco. I helped him escape from jail because I thought he deserved a break. Marcus was a genius in his way. He was my friend and partner until drink and women ruined him. He'd have wrecked me, if I'd have let him." Sam stared at the smoke as it slowly unwound toward the ceiling. "He couldn't handle money. Marcus was a fine man when he was poor, but money was his downfall. You can't tell a man his father was a gin-soaked gambler, riddled with syphilis." He added wryly, "Even I couldn't quite do that."

"Randolph said that half the mills rightly belong to Josiah Eaton."

"Oh sure, they said I robbed his widow and left them in abject poverty. Marcus gambled away his share of the business to a lot of whores and cardsharps. I hocked everything I had, borrowed to the hilt, to buy it back. I'd built it with my guts and I wanted it intact. It took me ten years to pay off Marcus Eaton's folly."

Valeria knew instinctively her husband was telling the truth. It was one of the many revelations of Sam's character that strengthened her innate respect for him, despite their moments of bitter conflict.

"I brought Josiah up, schooled him and trained him for the business. I had no son. He wanted to marry Ida and I thought, 'Why not?' He'd have got the whole thing in the end if he'd played his cards straight. But Josiah inherited a bad streak from his father. He's smart, but he's crooked."

Sam sat brooding for a moment and then looked up and grinned. "I did not aim to tell you about the Eatons. You're the only other person who knows the truth."

"I'm glad you told me, Sam."

"There's a lot I won't tell you. You know enough about me already you don't approve of." He got up suddenly with a conspiratorial gleam in his eye.

"Come, Mrs. Garvey. I got something to show you."
He held up his finger. "And I came by it honestly,
just for once."

He took her arm and led her to the door. It was the
first time he had ever touched her. She felt that in a
few moments their whole relationship had changed.

He led the way across the hall into the parlor where
he turned up one of the gasjets on the wall. "Well,
what do you think?"

In the corner of the room was a rosewood grand
piano.

"I ordered the best. I hope it suits you."

He was as pleased as a child at a Christmas party.
Valeria could find nothing to say because his impulses of generosity were so out of keeping and so
unexpected.

She sat down on the rosewood stool and opened the
lid of the keyboard. Her fingers were stiff from all the
work she had been doing in the house, and she played
cautiously at first.

The music sounded strange in that room where no
music had ever been heard before, a voice from another world of gentleness and beauty.

Sam stood watching her, entranced. A distant dream,
abandoned fifty years before, took shape before his
eyes.

Valeria glanced up and their eyes met and for the
first time a bond between them was acknowledged.

She continued playing until the bell of the front door
jangled. Sam knew that the moment of confrontation
had arrived.

"You stay in here, understand?" he said sternly.
"You don't leave this room until I tell you."

Valeria watched through the window. A starless
night had descended over Shacktown and she discerned
the mass of silent men crowded against the railings.
They were bound in a black silence by determination
and resentment.

Across the street she could make out the pallid
aprons of the women who had straggled out of their

hovels to give their men support. They were there in
little groups, watchful with the rest.

She thought, if Sam loses his temper they could
march in here and kill us. They could burn down the
house and there is nothing we could do.

She felt the same dread that she had endured years
before, through the long nights at Whitebriars when
she had sat alone with Randolph. After he had been
wounded, Valeria would keep the shotgun on the chair
beside her, watching and waiting for the sound of a
footfall on the terrace. Those seemingly never-ending
nights when she had fought against sleep, aware of
every movement in the branches outside, of the furtive
scurrying of animals. Would they come, the ragged
soldiers lusting for money and women? Or the exhausted ones who had escaped from the wilderness of
war and wanted a place to rest and to remember that
they were men who had homes and families and had
once been human and were now degraded, who were
sickened by hatred and bloodshed. Valeria had learned
to know this breed of outcasts. Sometimes they had
slept in the old slave quarters and had stayed and
helped her, mutely ashamed and broken in spirit.
They had stayed for a few days and drifted on.

Now, she watched at the window and her heart
chilled. She prayed that Sam would see reason and not
drive to open violence the men who nursed their
grievances too long. He had given her jewels and
money and a piano. Could he not give them the little
they needed to live like human beings?

Sam was reading the petition Fletcher Jones had
presented. He was barricaded behind his desk and
the deputation of four men and their lawyer waited.
Sam was playing his old game of keeping his adversaries nervous until they wavered and lost their nerve.
But this time these men were prepared to wait, and
however long Sam Garvey studied their petition they
were grimly resolved not to be turned away.

He looked up at last. His face had turned to granite
and his voice was that of a judge about to pass sentence of death.

"Who paid for your lawyer?"

The question was a challenge, the gauntlet thrown down, the declaration of war.

Jones realized that the man with millions who controlled their lives had no intention of giving in and that they must fight him. If need be, to the death. They were no longer the owner and the owned, the driver and the driven, but men fighting over rights.

"Who drew up this petition? You're a lawyer, ain't ya?" Sam addressed one of the four men who was dressed better and stood a little apart from the others. The lawyer shifted uneasily from one foot to the other. "Well?" the harsh voice demanded. "Was it Josiah Eaton? Is he paying you to represent these people?"

Fletcher Jones stepped forward. His one eye glared at Garvey. "We have a right to a lawyer, Mr. Garvey, and who paid him's not your concern. We've come here to demand our rights and that's what we'll discuss. You read our petition. We'll thank you to give us your answer and give it now."

Sam considered him carefully and coldly. "I will repair the sewers and I will meet your demands for compensation in the event of death or maiming. The rest I will not do." He tossed the petition aside on his desk as though it were a trifle not worth considering.

Jones came closer, standing firm and square before Sam. "Mr. Garvey, we're asking for decent wages and decent tools to work with. You have a right to our labor if you pay us. You have not the right to ask us to risk our lives every day because your machinery is old and dangerous. Now, you will treat us fair or we don't work. Ninety percent of the men are behind that petition. They heard it and debated it and agreed to it. Either you give us what we want or we go on strike."

Sam glared back at the one eye that challenged him.

"Strike if you want. It won't do you any good. I can fill your places ten times over. Plenty of men can do your jobs as well as you. If you want to work at the Garvey Mills you work for what I pay. As to my machines, you've been taught to handle them. If accidents occur, it's not my fault. It's a big country; go work elsewhere."

Fletcher Jones leaned over the desk. If ever human wrath could have burned a man alive, as Jim Hallam had been burned, Sam Garvey would have turned to cinders. But he sat there, imperturbable.

"A hundred men dead in your mill," said Jones. "A hundred men with families who were left to starve. You are a man accursed in the eyes of God. But I tell you this, Mr. Garvey: you meet our demands or we'll tear your mills apart and you'll meet a just death. And never would a death be more welcome or more deserved."

"You lay a hand on any of my property and I'll have you put in jail," Sam retorted. "You'll have plenty of time there to make demands. The law won't listen nor will I. Now I've said what I have to say. You can go. And you—" he pointed a murderous finger at Fletcher Jones, "don't show up in the line tomorrow. I'll run my mills without anarchists like you." His voice rose in fury as he addressed the lawyers. "You can tell Josiah Eaton that not all the lawyers in this country will get me to change my mind. Now get out, the lot of you, and take your petition with you."

He snatched up the paper that had been agreed on by three hundred men and hurled it across the room.

"May God punish you for an evil man!" Fletcher Jones shouted in return. "I could kill you with my own bare hands!"

"You show up in the line tomorrow and I'll have you in jail for attempted murder," was Sam's parting imprecation.

"You can buy human lives and kill and steal," Fletcher Jones screamed like a Biblical prophet, "but you cannot silence me!"

"Get out!"

Valeria stood by the window watching the motionless crowd. She heard the men cross the hall, heard the door open and slam and saw the deputation go down the path and open the iron gate. The crowd listened to them for a moment and seemed to sway as though a current had passed through them. They pressed about the four men. The women moved forward and the crowd became one man.

Valeria thought, It's too late. There will be bloodshed now!

When she opened the study door, Sam was sitting slumped at his desk. The muscles of his face had slackened and his mouth had fallen in.

He did not stir as she went to him.

She realized for the first time just how old he was.

CHAPTER FIFTEEN

JONES WAS UP LATE with Josiah debating the best way to force Sam Garvey's hand. Fletcher was dedicated to a cause and was ready to give his life for it. Josiah Eaton, however, was concerned with cornering Sam Garvey in such a way that he would be driven into making a deal over the railroad. Fletcher, in the innocence of his ardor, trusted Josiah. He little realized that the fate of the workers meant as little to Josiah as it did to Sam Garvey. Fletcher Jones was an idealist being slowly squeezed between two stones.

"It seems to me," Josiah said, "that you have no choice at this point."

"A strike is a very hard thing, Mr. Eaton. It would mean great hardship for the men and their families and how long could they stay out with so little money and all?"

The Courier will subsidize relief," Josiah promised, watching Fletcher squirming in a trap like a desperate small animal. "Garvey has a huge investment in the new railroad. He needs to keep the mills running. If he sees that you won't give in, he'll reconsider."

"Mr. Garvey is a very rich man. Even with the mills shut down he can hold out for a long time. The men live on the edge of real need, as it is."

"You have no alternative. He refused to consider the contract. What else can you do?"

Jones stared at the carpet. His wiry body, pulled tight like a knot from years of hard labor and deprivation, was tense with defiance and hatred. And yet he was frightened.

Josiah knew he only needed a little persuasion to

take the great step he was burning to take. "I'll see that nobody starves," he said.

Fletcher took a deep painful breath, as though sucking into his lungs the resolve to face the worst. "Yes, there's a point where you have to fight, whatever happens, whatever it costs. And it will cost plenty. Well," he looked at Josiah with reliance and admiration, "it is a grand thing you are doing, Mr. Eaton. There's not a man in Shacktown will ever forget it."

"I will support you to the hilt, both with the paper and my own money. This concerns more than the Garvey Mills," Josiah said with the expansive authority of a politician. "It concerns every working man in the country. And rest assured, the whole nation will hear of it and wherever there are men working for the wages you get and living under conditions you're forced to live under, you'll find support. Your courage will not go unrewarded, Mr. Jones."

Fletcher stood up. He felt far taller than his five feet four. He felt as though he were standing in the limelight of history and his heart burned with a heroic flame.

"There had to be a turning point one day. You're right, Mr. Eaton, that day has come."

They shook hands and Josiah saw him out.

When he returned, Josiah poured himself a whiskey. He admired Jones as a hunter admires a good rifle. Yes, the day of his reckoning with Sam Garvey was at last at hand.

But sitting alone in that comfortable room with the solid mahogany furniture, he was disturbed to discover that his satisfaction at this long delayed confrontation was marred by an unexpected feeling of guilt. Not because of his own two-faced manueuvers; he accepted them as the familiar rules of the game, but because a new element had entered into his calculations. Now there was something he had not encountered before, which troubled him because it revealed a flaw in the structure of his ambition. A grain of sand was preventing the smooth functioning of his machine. It was incongruous and absurd. But it was there.

Fletcher Jones had his cause. He would win or lose;

that was his risk and his business. But Valeria would be caught in the midst of an ugly battle over power and money and would suffer. For some reason this made him ashamed.

He thought of her galloping over the field on Mimosa. The remembrance of those tears when she spoke of her brother and her futile attempt to reconcile him with her husband cut Josiah sharply. She had spoken with simple conviction of her disgust for battle and bloodshed. Valeria had learned a wisdom that he and Sam Garvey either had not chosen or had not the wits to learn. She had been raised to respect standards of honor and fair play in the more refined but less practical world of the South that he and Sam Garvey had helped to sweep away. They had used their energies and guile to debase the very ideals she clung to. There was no use in pretending that it had been for anything but greed and material gain and the satisfaction of getting the upper hand, in his case for a cold-blooded determination to force an enemy to his knees.

It was annoying and ridiculous that a woman he hardly knew should make him question his motives and the purpose behind his life.

Since she had compromised to the extent of marrying Sam Garvey, she would have to put up with the baseness and brutality of the world he represented. Was it, Josiah asked himself, the only world open to men like them?

For the first time he grudgingly admitted that in the final count he and Sam Garvey were two of a kind.

Why should this woman, after a brief encounter, have made him dissatisfied with power and its attendant subterfuges and countermoves, on which he had now embarked? He was like a general on the eve of battle suddenly unsure of the cause he was fighting for. Valeria had somehow challenged his lifelong conviction that might was right, that the ends always justified the means and that ambition, whatever it entailed, was his main objective.

He did not want to think of her. She was a reprimand and a hindrance.

Tomorrow the strike would begin. Tomorrow he would set in motion not only his long-range plan to force Garvey to capitulate. He would also open the dam of publicity that would carry his name and his program of social reform across the state. Properly aroused, popular enthusiasm would sweep him to the governor's mansion. It needed a clear head, nerve, courage, and a great deal of money, all of which he had.

His confidence returned as he considered the glittering promise that lay ahead.

It was, all the same, a pity that he hadn't met Valeria Lee a couple of years ago.

Next morning Valeria woke to the blowing of the whistle. The sense of dread she had felt the night before remained. It had been with her throughout an uneasy sleep.

She put on her robe and went downstairs. She set the kettle on the stove. In the eerie half-light of early morning a light rain was falling, the first of the coming winter. It washed streaks of dirt from the tumbledown houses, the building behind the gates, and the leafless trees. Everything was dripping with grime, and on the earth that had once been grassy the puddles that formed were pockets of liquid grit.

She was listening for the second blast as though it were the last trump on Judgment Day. Valeria, aware of how long the kettle took to boil, knew that she should be about her usual chores, but instead she stood in the kitchen waiting for the sound she hated most. Would Mary come?"

The kettle hummed and she made the tea. But she could not bring herself to sit down. Leaving the pot on the table, she went into the hall. The house had never been so still or looked so grim. She could hear the cascading rain along the eaves.

Abruptly the second call sounded. She started, frightened, and hurried into the parlor to stand by the window where she had stood the night before.

The men came slowly in twos and threes and soon the usual crowd had assembled before the gates. But there was something different about them today. They seemed more awake and aware. They did not have the lassitude of men who had barely woken and felt no desire to be awake because they faced nothing but the monotony of toil as they always did and were condemned to do.

They were all there, waiting for the third summons and for the gates to open. The whistle sounded as usual and as usual the gates swung slowly back. There lay the way of their fate before them as it always had, day after day, month after month, the way that devoured their hopes and lives.

No one moved.

They stood facing the open way to the mills, to the great chimneys. Not a single man stepped forward. They were frozen where they stood with the rain falling and running off their soiled caps.

It has begun, Valeria thought.

The mills waited and in the hovels and leantos of Shacktown the woman waited; knowing that they might well starve now and that, if need be, they must.

Valeria went to Sam's bedroom and knocked. He was sitting in his worn dressing gown on the side of the bed, expecting his morning tea.

"Something has happened. You'd better come."

He went with her to the window in the parlor and looked at the immobilized crowd.

He said calmly, as though he had already accepted the strike like a bout of bad weather, "They can't hold out for more than a few days. Josiah ain't going to pay the wages of three hundred men. Can I have my tea?"

Valeria knew that it was useless to argue. Sam was wrong and as determined to uphold his position as though he were utterly in the right.

He drank his tea at the desk he always returned to like a king to his throne.

"How will Jim Pryor get in?" she asked. "They are all the way up the street."

"He won't," he said shortly. "We must wait."

This time Sam's usual tactic had been accepted and the workers were prepared to keep him waiting in their turn. He appeared not to be perturbed by the strike at all, as though he had expected it and was inwardly prepared to face it. The facets of Sam's character were as endless as they were contradictory. There was nothing for her to say.

She performed her routine. She dragged the hip bath from the pantry and washed herself. She went upstairs, dressed, came down and cooked Sam's breakfast. And all the time Valeria was aware of the men standing outside. She thought of how wet they must be and cold and weary. But she knew that they were right and had to stand there. Only the old man in the study stood against them with a will as strong as steel.

There was nowhere for her to go.

At noon the wives came with tea and passed among the men. They were drenched by that time, a sorry battalion of the dispossessed.

Valeria felt overburdened by their presence. There was no rumbling in the earth. It was like the silence of a strange death over the house. She brought Sam's lunch on a tray. He was at his desk, imperturbably covering sheets of paper with calculations.

"You'd better leave tonight," he said. "Go and stay at the hotel until it's over."

"I won't."

He glanced up and was about to argue, but he caught that certain look in her green eyes and knew that she had made up her mind. "You know what you're in for?" he asked. "It may take a week."

She wanted to ask him why he was so adamantly set against paying the men the increase they deserved and fixing the machinery that had cost so many lives. It seemed to her the height of irrational obstinacy, especially in view of the way he chose to live which required little more money than the men had themselves. It was this aspect of money as an entity, an abstraction, which Valeria still could not understand. It made no sense to her that Sam had millions stashed away in banks—money that was never put to any use. If he had been wildly extravagant in his tastes, even if he had been a gambler or used his money, as Josiah did, for political ends, there would have been some recognizable motive. But his refusal to meet the demands of the men who made him rich was as absolute as his parsimony. And yet . . . he had been generous to her!

She sat in the kitchen, brooding and on edge, and then went for no reason to sit in the parlor. She had no inclination to play the piano. The only impulse she had was to escape from the house and take a long ride into the country with Mimosa. But she was a prisoner and could not leave. The crowd of sodden men now barred the way.

Valeria forced herself to sew, but she could not concentrate. After making a number of false stitches she had to unpick them. She looked in on Sam. He was sitting in the high-backed chair reading, actually reading.

"Why don't you get on with *Bleak House?*" he asked.

"I can't read." She was drawn back to the window. They were still there.

The day was interminable. Thankfully, at long last, dusk gathered. Thankfully, at long last, the final whistle shrilled.

The crowd stirred, shook itself like a pack of waterlogged dogs and broke up slowly.

"They're going home," she said.

They struggled off, dispirited and numbed. The damp had penetrated their bones. They were freezing and dragged their feet through the mud.

Jim Pryor came only minutes later. If he was capable of reacting to anything, he had to the strike. He hurried into the study and shut the door. Valeria trailed back to the kitchen and prepared Sam's dinner. She knocked gingerly on the study door and found them with their heads bent over the desk.

"I'm going out."

Sam looked up. "Where to?"

"For a ride. Your dinner is in the kitchen. There is enough for two."

Before Sam could ask any questions or make any objections, Valeria had gone. In the stables she

searched for Tripp who had removed himself to whatever strange quarters were above the stalls.

He appeared, half dressed. What did Tripp do all
day and all night up there in the attic? How had Tripp
whiled away the years, unmarried and unknown and
unwanted, except by Sam Garvey on the rare occasions
when he went to town?

"Will you take me to Horton's stables?"

He was half asleep, bothered and confused.

"I am going riding. I want you to come back for
me at ten."

"Riding?"

Who went riding after nightfall in the middle of a
strike?

"Hurry, please."

Sam's horse, that dragged out years as Tripp did in
the dark stable, awaiting the summons that would allow him to trot for an hour or two in the outside
world, now shook himself, whisking imaginary flies
from his hind quarters.

They drove through the twisting alleys to Main
Street and Horton's Stables. Joe Horton was shutting
up for the night and was startled by the appearance of
Mrs. Garvey not even in her smart gray habit or riding
boots, but in an ordinary house dress.

"Will you saddle Mimosa for me, please?"

"You going riding at this hour, Mrs. Garvey?"

Ignoring his question, she moved swiftly past him to
the gelding's stall. The little mare knew her already,
and came forward, her sweet brown eyes full of anticipation and affection. She thrust her head at Valeria
and nuzzled her shoulder.

"I hear there's trouble at the mills, Mrs. Garvey,"
Horton said as he stumped about in the hay.

Valeria couldn't wait to be astride and out of the
stable. She patted Mimosa's head. "Take it easy up
the hill and we'll have a good gallop along Tremont
Avenue."

Mimosa picked up her delicate hoofs and trotted
down Main Street. The horse took the hill leading to
The Heights in her stride. When they reached Tre-

mont Avenue Valeria leaned forward and said to her, "Let's go!"

Mimosa raced along the avenue. The night air, fresh after the rain, blew across Valeria's face and revived her. She kept Mimosa at a gallop until they had passed the houses and were alone in the darkness, then reined her in.

They trotted past the Haverfield place where there was no sign of life and past Josiah Eaton's place that was ablaze with light. He must be entertaining, Valeria thought. Soon they were out in the country, and there was no one but herself, Mimosa and the stars.

The whole of her present life fell away from her like a dream. Her marriage to Sam Garvey seemed like some disjointed phantasmagoria in which she performed with other shadowy characters who appeared and disappeared in different disguises. Nothing was what it seemed. Only one thing had emerged from the bargain she had made with Sam Garvey which still was to her the most extraordinary and illogical event of her life; she cared for him, not as a husband or a fabulously wealthy man, but in some obscure way, as a human being.

It was not love or anything resembling it. It was a strange sort of acceptance and, moreover, a concern. Valeria knew that whatever happened over the strike and however violent her disapproval of his tactics, she could not leave him. It was not that he had given her expensive gifts. In his obstinacy and willfulness, there was a weakness, and he counted on her for something which, in his blind and angry tenacity, he needed. Without even admitting it to himself, he needed *her*.

As she ambled along the road in the soft, damp darkness, it came to her that of all the men she had known or liked or been attracted to or who had wanted her for their own reasons, Sam was the only one who had unaccountably recognized what she felt herself to be. He had not wanted her body or her support or the fulfillment of some absurd longing like young Hank Brewster. He had seen her with nothing —at her worst—and had wanted her because of what she was.

At Whitebriars and in Atlanta, there had been moments of awareness of some other woman, more rounded, more abundantly alive, who she might have become if events had unfolded in a normal way. There had been times when a sudden uplifting of heart, a clarifying of vision, had revealed a heightened reality behind the veil of her life like a lamp turned up in a curtained window. She could not see clearly into the room behind; she could glimpse only a glow of colors and the outlines of objects that evoked an essence of what should have been her home. Such a moment of perception had come to her the night when she had played old songs for Nancy and Hank and had felt the warming security of belonging to a family. And the same fleeting sense of fulfillment had filled her as she galloped over the turf with Josiah Eaton because Valeria had been with a man in the prime of life who in another time might have been her husband, riding in harmony with her toward what could have been their home.

Fate offered these taunting glimpses like the gleams of flame and amber that had lingered in the west as she and Josiah had ridden into the dusk to say goodbye.

Valeria let the reins fall. Mimosa had wandered to the side of the road and was nibbling the wet grasses washed clean by the rain. A watery moon strayed among the clouds.

Unbeckoned, the Yankee Captain loomed before her. In panic when Randy had been wounded, in terror that he might die, she had seized on the Captain's kindness as a God-given panacea. She would have given the earth to save her brother's life; in that nightmare world of ruin he was her one reality. She had succumbed to the Captain's need for tenderness, the reassurance that all semblance of feeling had not been shattered by the war. To lie in his arms in the troubled period had seemed the most blessed relief, a temporary harbor in the midst of that endless storm. It was not passion. There had never been passion between them. It was the hunger to rediscover that they were still human in the midst of such inhumanity. His love making had been like the binding up of wounds.

She could barely remember what he looked like. A tall, nondescript man with lank, blond hair, golden moustache and pale eyes that saw nothing but pain and death and would bear those images in their depths forever. Even the loss of her virginity had seemed to mean little then. Valeria had not wanted to tremble and agonize alone. She had wanted to be certain, when she finally fell into sleep, that someone would watch over Randy. How long had he been there? A week? Ten days? She knew nothing about him except his name, John Richmond of Massachusetts. He had come out of the twilight and returned to the twilight, to what obscure destiny she had never known. She felt only a dim gratitude that he had consoled and sustained her for a while.

There had been too much struggle and uncertainty afterwards to think of love. It had not even been love that she had wanted then, but some recognition of her embattled identity. And that was what Sam, in his own rough way, had given her.

It seemed to Valeria that her life had been a series of stepping stones over a rushing river. Each stone had sunk beneath her just as at this moment the waters were already rising. She must center her mind on the day, less than a year away, when she and Sam could finally leave Arcadia for the ship that would carry them to Europe. The wild sea and the wind would blow all these difficult, unpleasant, unrewarding years away. She must think of London and Paris and the moon-haunted Nile. By that time Randy would have forgiven her, although things between them could never be quite the same.

Meanwhile there was this horrible strike to endure and the building of the railroad. Valeria must find within herself an immense store of patience to see her through.

Mimosa shook her head. What was her mistress doing, lingering here in the darkness? She wanted to gallop back and feel the light, braced body on her back and the steady hands that held the reins so lightly.

As Valeria affectionately patted Mimosa's neck and turned her about, she thought that it was a pity Sam and Josiah Eaton were such enemies and were now embroiled in this senseless conflict. For a few moments Josiah had seemed capable of generous impulses. He had apologized abjectly and offered his friendship and sympathy. After all, he had given her a job and encouraged her when she needed it, whatever his ultimate intentions may have been.

She wondered what would have happened but for that stupid incident over the photograph. She might have gone to work on *The Courier*. She might never have married Sam at all.

Josiah had left Fletcher Jones, grimly satisfied that the wheels were set in motion to destroy Sam Garvey's power. He had kept his word and given Jones money to set up canteens and provide necessities for the workmen's families. Eaton was determined to drag out the strike as long as possible. It would cost him a large sum, but it was worth it because it would help to trumpet his own cause. Tomorrow *The Courier* was coming out with a full-page editorial denouncing Sam Garvey's refusal to come to terms with his workers. Due to his hurt and indignation over his sister's marriage, Randolph Lee's high-flown phrases had reached rhetorical heights of invective which could not fail to arouse response. Josiah, from behind the scenes, was turning the screws tighter on what he hoped would be the coffin of Garvey's pride.

The old tycoon would rue the day when he had ever allowed the strike to happen. And even if he was forced to some kind of compromise, Josiah had a number of other cards up his sleeve. Bridges could be blown up. Rails could be dismantled. It would be a long time before Sam Garvey's iron ore would be rattling along the tracks to the far west and then only when he had surrendered a just share of the profits. Sam's fortune had been built on his father's knowledge. High time he paid back to Marcus Eaton's son a percentage of what was rightfully due.

Randolph was working late in Josiah's study, polishing the editorial he had helped Josiah to concoct with a sort of fanatical dedication. Josiah liked him and felt sorry for him. His sister's marriage had been a shock which had hardened and embittered him.

Looking at that dark head bent over the writing desk, Josiah wondered if he had compunctions about penalizing Valeria in this way. Every accusation leveled at Sam Garvey was a blow at Sam Garvey's wife. Every revelation of Garvey's nefarious past was an added indictment of her mad impulse to sell herself for money. No battle was more bitter than that between two people who had been as close as Randolph and Valeria Lee. In a way, Josiah reflected, it was a microcosm of the Civil War.

"I'm leaving now," Josiah informed him. "I have to get things ready at my country place for the dinner tomorrow night. I have some important men coming, including the editor of the *Chicago Tribune*. It'll be a good chance to let them know exactly what's going on."

Randolph's face was drawn with fatigue. There were purple lines under his eyes. From sleepless nights, Josiah wondered, or unassuageable anger at his sister, or remorse?

"Stay here, if you like," he suggested kindly. "You can use my room. You'll find everything you need."

"Thanks, Mr. Eaton. I may do that. I want to get this absolutely right."

"You're doing very good work and I'm grateful. Apart from the help you're giving me, these articles and editorials will do you a lot of good. I'll be sure to show them to Henderson of the *Tribune*."

"It helps when one believes what one's writing about."

"There's whiskey in the decanter," Josiah reminded him, "or wine in the kitchen if you prefer. Take whatever you want."

He patted Randolph on the shoulder, put on his coat and left.

As he rode along Tremont Avenue Josiah was conscious that the wave of his future was carrying him forward. Everything he had worked for in his life had ultimately come to pass and this combat in which he was now embroiled, whatever the outcome of the strike, could only redound to his credit. It would establish him throughout the state as the champion of the common man. This would, of course, entail a great deal of shrewd diplomacy with the industrialists who would fight as hard as Sam Garvey to insure their right to go on making their present stupendous profits. He must get them to see at the dinner tomorrow that increased wages and improved working conditions were not a threat to industry. The opportunities for continued national growth were tremendous. As industry expanded and employment increased, a complete reassessment of labor relations was bound to follow. Only old-fashioned extremists like Sam Garvey could fail to see that. Thaddeus Brownlow had been perfectly right in telling Valeria Garvey that in a country of such limitless resources, there was plenty to spread around.

Josiah saw the lone figure on horseback as he was nearing the Haverfield estate. He knew her at once by the way she sat the horse, so straight and effortless. As she drew near the whiteness of her face shone in the moonshine like a pearl.

He drew up and raised his lean hand in greeting.

She had been startled by his approach, but then, seeing who it was, reined in.

"Good evening, Mrs. Garvey. I didn't expect to find you out riding at this hour."

"I couldn't get away this afternoon because of the strike."

"Aren't you afraid to be out alone so late?"

"No, it is a great relief." She said suddenly, "Mr. Eaton, isn't there anything you can do? It was so dreadful to see the men standing there all day. Surely with the power you have through the paper—"

"I can only report what's taking place. It's up to your husband to come to terms!"

"The things you've been writing about him, my brother's articles, only make matters worse. They've inflamed the whole situation. I am so mortally afraid there will be bloodshed."

"Don't you think the men have right on their side?"

"Yes, I do and I have told my husband so. If you only could put the facts in a calmer, more dispassionate way. It is bad enough as it is without fanning the unrest."

"The solution is very simple," Josiah said flatly. "Your husband should give the men what they want. He can stop the strike at any moment he chooses."

"That doesn't excuse you," Valeria retorted. "You know very well that you are not supporting the men for their sake, but for your own."

"That isn't entirely true, Mrs. Garvey, though I don't expect you to believe me."

"You *are* running for governor, aren't you?" she challenged. "You don't think prospective voters are naive enough to believe that your present motives are altruistic?"

"We always seem to get back to motives," Josiah said wryly. "We agreed the other day that no one's motives are entirely pure."

"It is always the same thing," she said with a flash of scorn. "People take stands and then refuse to back down. It's the people caught in between who suffer. I admit that my husband is short-sighted. Why can't you admit that you're ambitious?"

"Oh, I never denied that." He smiled, his ivory teeth sparkling.

"I mean to the exclusion of everything else." She looked directly at Josiah. He could not see her strange eyes in the darkness. But the tilt of her head and the sharpness of her voice expressed her disdain. "You sit back and let it happen, no matter who gets hurt. And then you will reap the acclaim of having supported the strikers. Oh, you are all the same!"

She gave Mimosa a prompting kick.

He leaned over and took firm hold of her reins. "I understand only too well the position you're in and how you must feel. You are right to feel so. But surely you must see there's nothing I can do."

There was an angry catch in her throat as Valeria told him, "You could help. You could even go and see Sam to talk things over. This ridiculous feud you have carried on all these years! You are the two most important men in Arcadia and between you, you could certainly do something to stop this stupidity."

"What do you know about our feud?"

"I know that Sam had nothing to do with your father's death as you apparently believe. *If* you really believe it, which I doubt. You fight because you like to, and because it serves your ends though, they aren't worth the amount of unhappiness they cause."

She wrenched the reins from his grasp. She was splendid in her anger. She kicked Mimosa again and the little mare started forward. Josiah wheeled his horse and caught up with her as she started off down the road.

"Mrs. Garvey, I ask you not to judge me because of my position on the strike."

"How else can I judge you?" she flung at him savagely. "Oh, please get out of my way and let me go home."

"I told you that I wanted to be your friend," Josiah reminded her. "I will always be your friend."

But she had spurred Mimosa to a canter and soon vanished into the darkness. He waited there, undecided and dismayed, as the sounds of the horse's hoofs faded.

In the encompassing emptiness of the night, Eaton wondered: if Rosie Delmar could see into him at this moment, would she still say he had no heart?

Dawn found Valeria lying awake in bed, tense and resentful of the coming day. The light came with reluctance, spreading over Shacktown the uneasiness of renewed conflict. In all the hovels and leantos women had risen and were now making breakfast and waiting as Valeria waited. Neither they nor their men had slept. The men had straggled in and sat at rickety tables and their sense of dread had struggled with their resolve. They were like men on the eve of battle, not knowing what the day would bring.

Later when Valeria was in the kitchen Sam came in, wearing his old dressing gown. He also had not slept. Without a greeting, he sat at the table and drank his morning tea.

"Are you determined not to give them what they want?" she asked in a low voice as though the whole of Shacktown were listening.

"If I give in now, they'll end by owning the mills." He repeated doggedly like a child saying the catechism, "No man is forced to work for me."

"It's strange," Valeria dared to say, "that you who were a pioneer in your field can't see into the future."

"What future?" Sam glared at her and she knew that she had reached the danger point.

"The future of this country that has made you rich. You admitted that you had no idea what to do with your money. Isn't the answer there?"

"I didn't make my money to give it away to them."

"They earned it for you."

"What are you?" he demanded. "Some kind of anarchist?"

"We both know what poverty means. I remember, Sam. It seems you don't."

The lines in his face seemed to grow deeper. She poured him a second cup which he took in stormy silence as he retreated to the study.

He was wounded by his wife's lack of support.

The whistle sounded. She started, frightened, and went straight to the window.

It was a heavy, overcast day with rain in the air. A murderous quiet hung over Shacktown. No one and nothing stirred.

It seemed an hour before the next blast. Valeria felt chained to the window, dreading what she knew any moment she would see.

They came slowly, as they did each morning, in twos and threes, doomed but resolute. And gradually, like silt filling up a crater, the crowd formed. They stood before the gates, blocking the street, pressed against the railings, forcing their will against the will of the one man who stood against them.

The battle of endurance had begun.

It had started before the third whistle, before the gates slowly opened. They had been waiting in their sleep. They were waiting for the long hours to pass and for the women to come at noon. They were waiting for the rain to soak them and for dusk that seemed a century away.

The gates slowly opened, but nobody budged.

They'll never give in, Valeria thought.

It was horrible. They had no revolutionary anthem to hearten them, no barricades to man, no weapons to brandish. There was nothing for them to do but stand until Sam weakened. She wondered why they didn't surge forward on some wild impulse, pour into the mills and smash the machines. This was the prolonged funeral of Ben Hallam. They would attend it to the end. They would wait there, figures of glum outrage, until the end.

The sky clouded over threatening a storm.

She could remember the stories Tante Elize had told her about the French Revolution. Her grandfather had been guillotined. To Tante Elize, born in exile, the stories of the Terror had been fresh and real. These men did not know the power of the mob, how it had laid siege to Bastille. The French had stormed the prison, demolishing it stone by stone. They did not know how the mob had rampaged through the city, butchering men and women, piling bodies in the streets, eating the living hearts of those who had not understood in time, as Sam could not understand. Would that terrible passion of revenge suddenly burst like a flame from these grim and stolid men who had no other weapon than this waiting?

Valeria felt trapped and sickened and turned away into the kitchen, grim with the darkening of the sky. The whole house was like a prison in which she and Sam were the only inmates. She was convinced something would happen soon. Their nerve would break. They would tear up the railings and storm the house and kill both of them. What did the lives of two people matter when they had lost so many? They would be right. They would be justified in doing the worst they could.

She went into the hall and, not knowing what else to do, sat on the stairs. Only last evening Valeria had been riding free. A few hours ago she had been thinking of the future in the still country under the moon.

She thought of her effort to start a school and a clinic. What possible good could they do when the men and their families were locked in a battle for their right to live as human beings? Books and pens and medicines could solve nothing. Her own vanity and need had swayed her into thinking that Sam Garvey was capable of feeling, but he was like granite. Valeria saw her husband then as a man of monumental stupidity. Her self-confidence had betrayed her. It was futile to think that he would ever change.

She walked listlessly into the parlor. In the tomb-like atmosphere stood the grand piano. Like the aristocrats who had waited for their names to be called to go to the guillotine, who had played cards and complimented the ladies and talked philosophy because there was nothing else to do but carry on the charade to the end or go insane, she sat down at the keyboard.

What did it matter if the men outside heard her, if the wife of the man with millions had the arrogance and effrontery to play the piano while they waited for the storm to break over their heads? If they heard her and it drove them to madness, it was not her fault. Her only crime was in having married the man they hated. Let them hate her, too.

She played everything she could remember: Mozart, Beethoven, Chopin. Her tapered fingers remembered. The music meant nothing in the airless room in which she could barely make out the furniture. The keyboard glimmered, ghost-like, as though she were playing in some anteroom of hell. Her fingers performed like the mechanical hammers that struck the quarters on the clock.

At noon the storm broke. A long roll of thunder rumbled across Arcadia. Valeria stopped and listened as the air tightened. Lightning flashed, momentarily brightening the room. The thunder was directly overhead. A deafening clap shook the house.

The air was stretched tight as a wire. Nothing breathed. She sat, immobilized, at the piano.

With a dull roar, the rain fell, pounding on the roof. It beat on the hovels and leantos of Shacktown.

It poured down the great impotent chimneys of the mills. It drenched the alleys and turned them into swamps of mud.

She could not bring herself to go to the window. The men were standing there, she knew, like slaves chained in the galleys of the storm.

Suddenly the tension of the morning snapped. She sprang up and ran to the study, bursting in without knocking. "You must do something, Sam. You can't let them stand there in this downpour."

He looked up, expressionless, not even startled by this outburst.

"Do something, Sam. Stop this iniquity." She was at the desk, transfigured by distress. *"What kind of a man are you?"*

He stared at her, his eyes bleary with noncomprehension. "I told you to go away."

"These are men who have worked for you, some of them all their lives. There are boys of twelve and fourteen standing out there. Aren't you ashamed?"

Sam seemed to have lost all interest or comprehension. "I'm not keeping them. They're free to go."

"Talk to them. At least talk to them. They're men. Talk to them as a man."

But he was no longer a man. The mighty Sam Garvey was a machine that had run down. The umbilical cord that bound him to the mills had snapped. They were silent and no longer fed him with their power. Without the deep rumbling in the earth that was his heartbeat, Sam was a lifeless dummy that could only sit there and mouth words and had no volition of its own.

Valeria turned away, defeated, and in a sort of horrified helplessness, leaned her head on the mantelpiece.

He was shuffling his papers.

She said, her voice choking, "You understand nothing." She looked at him, hunched over his desk, the broken down old man shuffling and reshuffling papers. "I thought, whatever you weren't, that you were strong, that you had vision. What are you building a railroad for? What are you going to transport along those hundreds of miles of rails you're laying down? Your mills are idle, your men are drowning. Your railroad will be worth no more than all the rest of your futile money. Shelves of gray ledgers filled with empty words and empty figures. Buy me another piano! Buy Ida another house! That's as far as you can see. It all means nothing."

Sam appeared not to have heard her. His hands stopped drifting among the papers. He was as bankrupt as the mills.

"You read, Sam, you've spent twenty years reading Dickens and Victor Hugo. You respect them. You call their characters your friends. They are great men, great writers, because they have compassion. Laws are being changed because of what Dickens wrote about child labor."

"If I'd had compassion, I'd still be poor. You are living on my lack of compassion. That's what bought you a piano and a set of opals."

"I don't want them, Sam. I want you to do something about the men out there."

"You're a fool. You know nothing about business. Money to you is something you buy schoolbooks and medicine for the poor with. You never made money. You don't know how."

"No, I never made money. But it's because I went without it for so long that I care what happens to those men and their children and the wretched, sordid way they have to live."

"Go and join them, then. It would make a good headline for Josiah. Mrs. Garvey joins the opposition." But he was weary of trying to reason with her. "They won't break me. Let them stand there till they rot."

Sam stood up, his bleary eyes focusing on her. An echo of his old power came back. "I'll tell you something. You talk about compassion, you pride yourself on having higher principles than me. But you married me for money. *My* money that was made out of their sweat, out of what you consider injustice and inhumanity. I make no bones about what I am. Whores are more honest than you. They give service for what they get."

"You think I don't give *service?*" she almost shouted. "I sold you six years of my life—for what? To scrub this house clean of the filth you've lived in, to be ashamed to walk into town because of all that squalor you're too blind to see?"

He made a vague gesture as though the whole subject of their differences was no longer worth debating. "I don't want to fight with you. Just go. Get out and go somewhere that offends you less."

He saw Valeria in the shadowy doorway; wounded, angry, and distraught.

"You want your bank book?" he demanded with the cruelty sharpened by years of striking at the point where his enemies were weakest. "Fifty thousand dollars of my tainted money? That should keep you in compassion for a while."

There was nowhere for Valeria to hide. She sat on the stairs crying because what Sam had told her was the unbearable truth. She felt that the little she had tried to build out of her hopeless marriage had been knocked down and trampled on. After all, Randy and the others, the whole town, were right.

The rain beat on the roof and windows, beat against her humiliation and self-disgust. At last she dragged herself upstairs and lay on her bed. After a time the sound of the rain washed away even her shame. She waited dully for the hours to pass till the dusk would come and she could go.

Someone had nailed a dead rat to the front door. The body swung out and bumped back as Valeria opened and shut the door.

She shuddered and hurried down the path to the iron gate. No time to wait for Tripp to emerge from the cavern over the stable where he had, no doubt, been hiding, as she had hidden in her room and Sam Garvey had hidden behind his desk.

She stumbled and sloshed through the puddles of mud, impeded at every step. Her only thought was to get to Horton's Stables before they closed. To find dear, patient Mimosa waiting and to be away, out of the anger and ugliness of Sam Garvey's world. It seemed that Mimosa was her one remaining friend.

No one paid heed to the woman in charcoal brown, hurrying and slipping along the blacked-out alley. She reached Main Street, mildly surprised to find lights and buildings that had some resemblance to a place where reasonable people lived.

Horton was closing up. He looked at her, disheveled, in her mud-splattered dress and mud-caked shoes. "I didn't expect you, Mrs. Garvey, seeing the weather and all. You taking her out tonight?"

She went past him, intent on the reassurance of the silken head and the patient, lambent eyes.

Mimosa had heard her coming and had thrust her head over the stall. Valeria embraced her. The little mare, knowing her moment of service and liberation had come, nuzzled her mistress's neck.

Horton chattered as he strapped on the saddle. The whole town was in a state over the happenings at the mills. Would the strike be settled? Had she seen the paper? *The Courier* had come out with a blast! "You'd think Mr. Garvey was Satan himself or something. Personally, mind you, I say a man has the right to run his own business as he sees fit."

She was in the saddle and out of the stable and Mimosa was trotting proudly up Main Street.

Horton watched Valeria go. Something mighty strange about Mrs. Sam Garvey taking her horse out after dark. Putting two and two together it was clear there must be some guy on The Heights she'd taken up with. Couldn't blame her exactly, seeing who she was married to. She'd got the money. Like any good looker her age she wanted a good time as well. The idea suddenly struck him that she might be one of Josiah Eaton's women. She must be dead set on him, whoever he was, riding off like that, not even in her habit. She was a deep one, all right! Just think of it— Mrs. Sam Garvey and Josiah Eaton!

What a story! Worth mulling over with the boys at the saloon, considering all that had taken place and

was taking place between those two men who hated
each other worse than poison. Married to one and
bedded by the other! He couldn't wait to discuss
the whole thing over a toddy. Josiah hadn't earned the
reputation of being the hottest stud in town for nothing. It was the best plum of gossip he'd picked in years.

There were lights in Ida's mansion. How simple the
life that Valeria had led there now seemed! Poor
Hank, following her, lovelorn, from room to room.
And she doing Nancy's hair, arranging Ida's dreadful
dinners. Dear Monsieur Emile! She would have welcomed a chat with him, reviewing the gastronomic
delights that only she could appreciate and only he
could cook. She thought of his masterpiece, the *gâteau
royale,* with the shimmering swan. A world of spoiled,
bad-tempered children! And Thaddeus Brownlow, that
unctuous connoisseur with his Fragonards and gems!

When they reached Tremont Avenue Mimosa
needed no encouragement. She broke into a joyous
gallop and Valeria surrendered to the relief of motion
through air freshened by rain.

It was not until they had passed the Haverfield
Place that she asked herself where she was going. She
was not going anywhere. There was nowhere to go.
The fantasies she had had—when was it?—last night?
a week ago?—of London and Paris had been swept
away by the stark realities of the day. Oh, if she could
only ride forever out of her ill-starred life! She was not
one step closer to the security she had dreamed of.
Everything she touched crumbled into disillusionment;
all her impulses and efforts were proved wrong. She
had been infected by the same madness as Ford and
was paying for it in the same way.

It was raining again, but Valeria hardly noticed.
She was alone and miles from home. The rain fell with
a chilling persistence. It was running off Mimosa's
neck. It was drenching her long hair, her cloak, her
dress, soaking through to the core of her body.

Was she crying or was it simply the rain pouring
down her cheeks? It seemed to increase with her desperation. The world, everyone she knew, was insane.
There was no purpose or hope for any of them. The

rain swelled in a few moments to a downpour. It pelted against her face so that she could scarcely see.

Mimosa jogged bravely along, her head bowed into the streaming darkness. Where was she? Lights swam at the end of a driveway. Was that Josiah Eaton's house?

Suddenly she was too tired to go any farther. "I will always be your friend," Josiah had called after her. She had no other friends. Ford and Randolph were lost to her. She could not ride back in this deluge and ask Sam to forgive her. She did not want it nor was she prepared to forgive him. There was no one else in the world to turn to.

She steered Mimosa forward. They plowed up the driveway to the mansion. She slid from the saddle and rang the bell. She had never in her life felt so utterly desolate.

The manservant gaped at this bedraggled apparition.

"Would you tell Mr. Eaton . . ." Valeria hesitated, "that Miss Lee is here."

"Mr. Eaton's busy," the man said suspiciously. "He has guests."

Perhaps she could hide in the stable at least, anything to get out of the torrent. "Just tell him my name, Valeria Lee."

The man hesitated. Some tart wanting refuge or a handout. But one never knew about women with Mr. Eaton. He shut the door firmly in Valeria's distraught face.

It was Josiah himself, resplendent in evening clothes, who a few moments later let her in.

"I'm sorry for appearing like this. I got caught in the downpour."

He did not wait for explanations but led her quickly to a small study off the hall.

"You're soaked!" he exclaimed.

"It doesn't matter. I'd be grateful if I could just wait here till it stops."

He saw at once that her condition was due to something far more than the storm. "What's happened to you?"

"Oh, why ask?" she said bitterly. "It's the strike and Sam and the whole insane mess I am in."

"I have some men here, a political dinner. Look," he came to her with forthright sincerity and took her hand in his strong one, "will you trust me?"

She gave him a little smile. "I'm here."

"Your things must dry properly. Come . . . no one will see you."

He led her to a bedroom on the second floor. Voices could be heard from the dining room as they went upstairs. Otherwise the house was silent. Josiah entered first to turn up the lamps. Valeria's shivering did not go unnoticed. He knelt before the grate and kindled the fire into roaring flames that made highlights dance off his gilded hair.

"Could someone take Mimosa to the stables and rub her down?" she asked, drawing closer to the heat.

"I'll see to it. Have you had dinner?"

She shook her head, covered with dripping ringlets. "Really, it doesn't matter. I'm very thankful to be inside."

"I'll have something sent up. I'll tell the man to knock and leave it outside the door."

Josiah saw Valeria was disturbed to be in a bedroom of a man she had hitherto had no reason to trust. "Don't be alarmed," he assured her. "Not a soul will know you're here."

She was grateful for his simple kindness. "I know that I shouldn't have come. The rain came on so fast."

"Of course you should have come. Get dry and after my guests have gone, I'll take you home."

"You won't forget poor Mimosa," Valeria said as he was leaving.

"She'll be taken care of. Stay near the fire."

Josiah smiled tenderly and left.

There was no turning back now. She had burned her bridges as far as respectable behavior was concerned. She quickly slipped out of her sodden dress and hung it with her cape over two chairs before the bright flames. The cold of the rain still gripped her body. Valeria tiptoed to the door and locked it, then took off the rest of her clothes. Naked, she knelt with luxurious recklessness before the fire.

It was astounding to be in a well-appointed bedroom with all the requisites of civilized living. It was years since she had been in such a room, much less had one to herself.

Try as she might, Valeria could not get warm. She crept nervously into the huge bed. The cool linen sheets sent chills across her skin, so Valeria drew up the silk eiderdown under her chin. Mrs. Sam Garvey hiding in the house of Josiah Eaton! What a topic for town gossip! It would confirm the worst they all thought of her.

"Who cares!" she demanded of the empty room.

It was such a sensuous pleasure to stretch out between such sheets and watch flames dancing in the grate. Everything in the chamber was expensive and comfortable. There were sporting prints on the walls, two Chippendale chests of drawers that perhaps Josiah had bought in England. Her opinion of Eaton was expanding. There was far more to him than she had imagined. She piled up the down-filled pillows behind her head so that she could watch the fire.

The sordid penury of Sam's existence seemed to her more than ever a sort of madness. She had been living in an asylum and this room brought her back into the world of sanity and ease. Valeria consoled herself that after the things they had said to each other, Sam would not care where she was or what she did. Besides, what right did he have to offer objections after what he had called her? She would take him at his word and enjoy in comfort this respite from his cruelty. Never mind who was providing it or what the consequences would be. She was a woman alone and she would take her chances. Valeria had been through too much in the last weeks to care what anyone thought. They would think the worst anyway.

A tentative knock at the door and a man's voice roused her. What had he said? That would be the supper Josiah had promised. She slipped out of bed, unlocked the door and peered out. There was a dinner

tray on a cart. Valeria cautiously reached out a pale
bare arm and drew the food inside.

She would play the whore to the full. She drank the
soup, ate the lamb chops and sipped the Burgundy,
naked in front of the glowing fire, warmed now and
pleasurably relaxed. The world and its enmities and
hypocrisy mattered no more to her. This was her just
reward for the service Sam had denied she had given,
these moments of peace and physical well-being. There
had been few enough of them in her life. Little
Mimosa, too, would be enjoying the comfort of the
stable, munching the sweet-smelling hay.

Valeria climbed lazily back into bed and dozed.
She was safe in a tiny interlude between trouble and
retribution. Oh, they would point their fingers and wag
their stupid, dishonest heads. Sam would thunder and
Randolph had already turned away. But who had ever
given her comfort and rest like this?

She drifted into sleep.

He was knocking quietly. She drew the coverlet up
to her chin and calmly said, "Come in."

She thought that he was truly a handsome specimen.
His tuxedo gave him a sort of grandeur. He was perfectly cut out to be a politician. She could see him addressing the state senate or opening a gubernatorial
ball. Valeria had a sudden vision of herself as the mistress of such a man in a New York or Paris apartment,
living in secluded luxury and receiving visits from her
protector. How quickly she could forget the morals and
conventions of her upbringing which in the end had
given her so little!

"How are you feeling?" he inquired.

"You have been very kind. I hope I have not caused
you a great deal of embarrassment."

"None whatever. No one knows you are here."

"I was wrong in thinking that we could not be
friends," Valeria admitted. "You have been a real
friend tonight and I am grateful."

"You've been having a bad time, I'm afraid." Josiah
felt her clothes where they had been draped. "Almost
dry." He put more logs on the fire.

Without warning an urgency coursed through her

body, to have him not as Josiah Eaton, but as a man. She wanted a man who could make her feel like a woman, relieved of pride and anger and disappointment. He was standing before the fire. She admired his broad shoulders, the strong back and narrow hips.

"When you're ready," Josiah said without turning, "I'll take you back."

Josiah walked to the door. The moment is passing, she thought. We shall be forced to become ourselves again, no longer two people without names in a cozy room shut away from the world.

He looked at her, with her tumbled jet-colored hair against the pillows. She was smiling, womanly and appealing, as he had never seen her before.

"May I talk to you or would that annoy you?"

"Oh, I am past being annoyed," Valeria said.

He returned to sit by the fire, carefully keeping distance between them because of the temptation her beauty awakened in him. After a long silence, he asked, "What are you going to do?"

"There's nothing I can do. The strike will be settled, one way or the other. It is all senseless and wicked to me."

"We live in a senseless and wicked world."

"Isn't it the world you like?" Valeria asked without rancor. "You helped to make it."

Josiah looked away from her. The light of the flames touched his golden hair with copper. There was a sadness and dignity about him as he said, "I've wanted lately to live in another world."

She said, as though speaking her thoughts aloud in a way that under normal circumstances would have been impossible, "It's the same for all of us really. We're forced to behave in ways we don't really want. I've been forced into being someone I never meant to be. Nothing about my life has been what I wanted."

"What sort of woman would you like to be?"

"A woman in a room like this, not forced to strike attitudes, with someone I respected and belonged to."

"Have you never loved anyone?"

"No."

A forlorn admission, Josiah thought, but probably

true of most people if they had the courage to admit it. It was certainly true of him.

After a pause he asked, as though he had known her all his life and had a perfect right to ask such a question, "Why did you marry him?"

"I saw another side of him one night and I thought perhaps . . . Women always think they can bring out the better side of men; it is part of our conceit. I thought that money could solve everything. It solves nothing by itself; I see that now."

"It hasn't taken you long to learn." He stared into the fire. *"We* fight to achieve something. Ambition keeps us going—that's our vanity. But it isn't enough. We need exactly the same things women do."

"You lead a full life. Aren't you satisfied?"

"Lately . . . I don't know. I guess I'm tired of going it alone."

A different silence fell. An unspoken question hung between them, tempting and tentative. They each wanted the other to know that this moment was in some way different from similar moments in the past. Their sudden need for each other was more subtle and true and delicate than it would have been under other circumstances and with other people.

If I went to her now, Josiah thought, she would feel I was taking her out of commonplace desire.

She was thinking, If I asked him to come to me now, he would think I was offering myself like all the other women he has known.

Their hesitation prolonged itself into a tension of apprehension. For the first time with a woman Josiah felt awkward and inadequate because of the special regard he had for Valeria.

She had no means of telling him that she wanted him without lowering herself in his eyes.

"Things don't turn out right for any of us," he said at last.

I have not the courage. Neither has he, she thought.

The moment was passing. They were losing this chance, secret and opportune, that might never come again.

Josiah sighed heavily, facing the ebony-haired

woman he wanted so much. "I wish I could tell you
what I feel."

And suddenly, as though in a dream, she raised her
graceful arms to him. The movement caused the coverlet to fall back, revealing her full breasts tinted the
color of honey in the glowing light. Josiah went to her
and lay slowly down beside Valeria, embracing
her eager body. They were together. Wonder lifted
them out of themselves into a new identity; not separate as they had been, but as one.

After several minutes, Josiah reluctantly left her to
undress. Valeria smiled as she watched. His clothes
had suggested an athletic build that was now confirmed. Her eyes drifted lovingly across his broad back
and shoulders, noticing every sculpted muscle that reflected earlier years of hard physical work and continued exercise. Josiah's chest of silver and blond hairs
tapered gradually to his narrow hips and firm torso.
When he turned and came toward her, Valeria felt as
though, in some classical myth, she were about to surrender to a god.

Josiah slid his hand up Valeria's smooth arm and
softly kissed the curve of her throat, breathing in her
sweet, natural smell. Then he drew slightly away to
gaze into her gold-flecked, green eyes. She looked
longingly at this man she had tried so hard to hate,
and she could no longer deny the immediate attraction
she had first had for him. Tracing the chiseled line of
Josiah's profile with her tapered fingers, she tenderly brushed back burnished strands from his forehead, then caressed his eyelids.

Josiah pulled Valeria closer so he could nuzzle the
pearled lobes of her small ears. The pace of desire
quickened between them as he moved his hands beneath her back, over her flat stomach, and up to the
curve of her rounded breasts, delighting in each lovely
contour. With the tip of his tongue he licked her erect
nipples, then covered first one, then the other fully
with his moist mouth. Valeria took joy in the wonderful
nudeness of her body against his bare skin. She felt
the length of his male body against hers and his taut
member against her thigh. They were a man and a

woman without names or histories who, in the intensity of this closeness, belonged nowhere but together.

Heeding Valeria's short, rapid breaths, he kissed the length of her abdomen. Josiah rubbed his fingertips rhythmically back and forth through her black, curly triangle, increasing the pressure as her moans grew more ardent. With his other hand he spread apart her long legs that were entangled with his own. As he entered her, Valeria arched her back. Her hips rose and fell with growing earnestness as Josiah thrust, withdrew, and penetrated ever deeper. Hot waves of release flowed through her whole being until she surrendered willingly to his urgings.

Afterwards, she lay in Josiah's strong arms wanting to keep him within her, in a drifting, emptying peace. He did not move or withdraw, but held her as a ship is lulled in harbor. She wanted to lie with him thus forever, never to stir again or separate or remember.

He was leaving her, ebbing away. The void was filled, satisfied by the tenderness; and they spoke to each other without words.

He was smoothing her silky hair, touching her forehead and eyelids with his lips as she had done earlier. "Stay with me," Josiah whispered. "I'll look after you."

Valeria did not want to speak or to remember who she was. Words would be a betrayal of this stillness that lulled her like some strange and wonderful narcotic.

He kissed the sweetness of her mouth. "Will you stay?"

She did not want to think of her life or the woman she would have to become again. In this blessed silence of anonymity she lay with him at rest.

Josiah moved slightly against her and she felt the strength and gentleness of his manhood stir again. And she received it because it was silent and secret and what it gave her was beyond words and without identity. She was shaken by its force. The walls of her body shuddered and her innermost self gave way like a wall of sand before the sea.

She was shaken by the thrusts of his body, grown

suddenly great like the body of a titan, yet the pain filled her with burning joy. She moaned and her fingers clung to his wet back. The movement of his buttocks was like a pounding of a hammer. A spasm of death shot through her. She thrust against him in this iron embrace that was stronger than her life. Tightly as he held her, she felt herself falling away, moaning. And they were still.

They lay in the darkness and the sense of being separate slowly returned to her. "Will you stay with me?" he asked again.

Valeria heard herself answer in the alien voice of her former self, "No. You must take me back."

Josiah was no longer the man who had made her one with him. He too was remembering, rebecoming the man he had been before.

She knew that he was leaving her for the other world they were both forced to live in. The love they had created in paradise was drifting away. Josiah was moving about the room, picking up his clothes. The door closed behind him. He was gone like the Yankee captain into the twilight.

Valeria was alone.

After a while her brain cleared. She got out of the bed that was no longer a sanctuary and washed briskly from an available water jug. Her clothes were still damp but she put them on and swung the cloak over her shoulders. They no longer seemed to belong to Valeria. She stared into the dying fire contemplating the change in herself.

He knocked and she went out and quickly followed Josiah down the stairs without even glancing at him. He opened the front door and she climbed into the trap. He got in beside Valeria and wordlessly shook the reins. The horse started down the driveway. It occurred to her to ask what had happened to Mimosa, but she had no voice yet for words.

The rain had stopped.

She was numb with a sort of impersonal misery. She felt no kinship or sympathy for the man who sat beside her, who had been her lover and could not possibly be the same Josiah Eaton whom she had formerly disliked.

Tenderly, he took her slender hand, thinking that her silence was one of sadness at leaving him. Her hand lay lifeless in his reassuring one. After they had reached Tremont Avenue and he had felt no responding pressure, he released her hand and she withdrew it to her lap.

They passed along Main Street and into Shacktown. Cardboard buildings in a deserted cardboard town, more dismal than the night that promised no respite from the battle that would begin again next day.

He drew up before the Garvey house, forbidding, against the half-light of the waning moon. Josiah got out and helped her down.

Valeria would have left him without a word because of this slow bleeding of her heart, but he detained her. "Remember if you need me I am always here."

She nodded. A stranger held open the gate and watched her as she went up the stone path.

She went inside the hated house like a prisoner returning to face her doom.

❦ Chapter Sixteen ❦

The early train blew its whistle the next day, bringing the lonely message of the prairies and the greeting of the distant city. It roared through the stockyards and drew up with great hissing steam at Arcadia's railroad station.

All the doors of the train burst open like steel traps and released a herd of surly men with bloated and battered faces and scarred fists. They were lower than men, without the dignity of beasts.

And out of the steaming conglomeration of brutal riffraff Jim Pryor emerged in his black suit, with his face that bore no expression, and with one intent; to carry out Sam Garvey's orders.

He raised his arm and led the herd of bruisers and degraded outcasts through the station yard into the slum of matchstick houses. The mob of hired bullies disrupted the dreary silence like a stampede of cattle.

Justin McGiver, the chief of police, crawled out of bed with the youth whose body was pallid as lard. Scratching his thighs, he ambled to the window of the bare little outer room that was as clean as it was poverty-stricken and peered through the tattered blind.

He watched the shabby gang tramping down the street. "Sam Garvey's moving to a showdown. There'll be bloodshed this morning," McGiver said to an empty room.

He went back into the bedroom, pulled on his pants and said to the youth who was lying motionless in bed, watching him, "You make one move and you'll get it. Remember that."

"You haven't paid me," the youth responded in his hollow voice.

McGiver fished in his pockets, took out some coins and flung them on the bed. The youth threw back the covers and scrambled to retrieve the money. McGiver struck him hard across the buttocks. His hand left a mark on the white skin.

Hell, he thought, there's time yet to deal with Sam Garvey's men.

He grabbed the youth by the legs and dragged him to the edge of the bed. The youth clutched the money in his fist. He whimpered as McGiver fumbled and prodded and finally thrust into him, and was quieted by a blow across the back of the head.

The chief of police took his pleasure and finished dressing and left. The youth lay on the bed and counted out sixty-five cents.

He remained motionless as the rumble of the stampede faded into town. Ford Hollister had been much kinder to him than McGiver. He would have to spend all day lurking 'round the stockyards in order to make up what he owed in rent. The men would abuse him, and knock him about and kick him as he groveled for the few coins they threw on the ground. If there were only some way to sell the knowledge of all the humiliation he had stored up in his body, he would do it gladly out of revenge.

Randolph encountered the horde on his way to work. He saw at once where they were heading and raced to the paper's office and through the private door, up the stairs to Josiah's suite.

Frantically, he banged on the door. After some moments Josiah appeared, tying up the heavy cord of his burgundy dressing gown.

"There's a crowd of roughs on their way to the mills. Garvey must have hired them to break up the strike."

"Get down there and get your sister out! Take her to your place or bring her here. I'll get McGiver."

Josiah hurriedly dressed and ran down into the street to the police station. A sleepy sergeant was making coffee on a kerosene stove.

"Where's McGiver?"

"Hasn't come in yet, Mr. Eaton."

"Go find him. There's going to be a riot at the mills. Get every man you can lay your hands on and get down there." As he sped out Josiah shouted over his shoulder, "Tell him not to waste a minute and tell him I said so."

As he ran to Horton's Stables he was thinking of Valeria, marooned.

The mill hands were standing in their terrible patience like markers in a graveyard, as they had stood for the last two days before the open gates. They blocked the lane that passed for a street, a solid barricade of bodies welded by dull resolve.

Their wives heard the onrush and knew the waiting was over. It was war and they must fight to defend their own. The women snatched up skillets, brooms, knives, any possible weapons, and ran through the back alleys, transformed into furies who would kill to defend their sons and husbands.

Jim Pryor turned the corner of the lane and the horde behind him came into view. The men who formed the barricade saw them and tensed. Every hand in the crowd clenched into a fist.

Pryor led the hired strikebreakers down the narrow street and held up his arm. The mob stopped. He shouted, "Clear the way!"

The gulf between the two groups was wide and fatal. It seemed to be a void into which, if a muscle moved, the whole town, the mills, and every man now confronting his enemy would crash headlong into oblivion.

"Break it up!" Jim Pryor yelled. His voice sounded as far away and ineffectual as the cry of a distant bird. "We're coming through!"

Suddenly into that chasm of silence, as though materialized by a bolt of unseen lightning a stout woman in an apron appeared. She was there, out of nowhere. Before anyone could grasp her presence, she ran a few steps toward Pryor and struck an iron skillet across the side of his head. He staggered. Her arm swung again and the heavy pan struck him down.

It was the signal.

The barricade broke ranks and the marauders broke ranks, converging and erupting into a ferment of battle. Men lurched and struck and fell and were trampled on and struggled up and hurled themselves into the fray. Men hurtled and meshed and tangled. Bones cracked and blood flowed. A knife flashed. A man cried out and fell against the railings and the woman who had wielded the knife was thrown down in turn.

Valeria heard the din and ran downstairs to the parlor. Sam was already standing at the window. She saw the turmoil in the lane outside and she saw with horror the expression on Sam's face. It was gray with satisfaction. He was transfigured by lust for the violence that his obstinacy had unleashed.

She heard a pounding on the far window and screamed, "They're breaking in!" In a flash of incredulity she saw that it was Randolph. He signaled to Valeria to raise the sash.

Before she could speak, Randolph grabbed her arm. "You've got to get out of here!"

"Who are you?" Sam demanded, swinging around.

"It's my brother!"

Sam waved a manic arm. "Take her to the stable garret."

As brother and sister turned to escape, a man on horseback flashed past the front windows. Josiah had charged through a rift in the fighting and vaulted the iron railing. He was pounding on the front door.

Randolph ran into the hall. Josiah came in. He was *there,* confronting Sam. In his strength and wholesomeness, he was a beacon of sanity in the midst of chaos.

"You've got to stop them! Get out there and let them see you. You are the only one who can call a halt," he shouted in the voice of a general commanding an insane monarch to come to his senses.

The grim satisfaction drained from Sam's face. "You tell me to stop them," he roared. *"You tell me!* You and your God-damned paper, you and your God-damned lies!"

He struck Josiah on the neck.

"Pull yourself together. People are being killed. Jim

Pryor's dead," Josiah said calmly, holding Sam in a firm grip.

Sam wrenched free and swung insanely. He hit Josiah on the side of the jaw. His fury strangled his power of speech.

He's gone mad, Valeria thought. "Listen to him, Sam!" She ran forward. "Randy, stop them!"

As Randolph stepped forward to pull away the mad old bull, Sam gave a rasping yell. His head lurched forward and then jerked back. He fell through Randolph's arms and slid between the two men to the floor.

He was unconscious for a moment, but he was not dead.

Unable to breathe, he retched to suck in air, clutching at his chest. His body convulsed. Sam was breathing in short rasping spasms.

The group was locked in a drama that deprived them of any awareness of what was happening. Glass splintered behind them and sprayed into the room.

"Carry him to the bedroom. Off the study," Valeria ordered.

They lifted the old tyrant who was gasping in agony. His mouth opened and shut, unable to swallow air.

Randolph and Josiah carried him into the little room smelling of age. Valeria grabbed pillows and stuffed them behind Sam's head. "Not flat. He must sit up."

She darted to the bookcase in the study and opened the lower doors where he kept the liquor. Mercifully, there was brandy. She ran back to the bedroom and forced Sam's head up against her breast and pushed the throat of the bottle against his lips. The brandy poured over his mouth and down his chin like a discharge of discolored blood. His teeth were clenched. She said sharply, "Open your mouth, Sam." The mouth sagged and some brandy passed between the blue lips.

She looked up at Josiah. "Can you get Dr. Mortlake?"

Valeria was asking the impossible. What chance

was there of bringing a doctor through the bedlam that reigned outside?

"We can't leave you. He must take his chances."

She was aware of Randolph beside her and, as she forced the bottle against Sam's lips, heard herself ask, "How did you get through?"

He moved and she saw his coat was torn. There was blood on one of his trouser legs.

"Are you hurt?"

"I'm all right." Randy touched her shoulder lovingly.

Josiah disappeared.

Sharp whistles were heard above the din, then shots.

"That must be McGiver with the police," Randolph said.

Suddenly Valeria could no longer understand what was going on. She was solely intent on forcing brandy down Sam's throat. His chest was soaked and her skirt was sticky with brown stains.

Randolph had shut and locked the door and was standing against the small window, opaque with accumulated grime. "Is there a gun in the house?" he asked.

"I don't know."

Meanwhile Josiah had remounted his horse and was shouting to McGiver and the mounted men to force their way through the turmoil. They edged forward, swinging truncheons, firing into the air. Horses screamed and reared. But the battle was waning. Josiah steered his frightened horse that side-stepped and whinnied toward the gate. He yelled, "Stop the fighting! Garvey will sign your agreement. He'll give you what you ask."

No one heard him. As the mounted police pushed forward, the fighting ebbed. The strength drained out of the crowd of enraged combatants like air from a pierced balloon. Men collapsed against the railings or against the walls of the shacks opposite. They were bleeding and battered and exhausted, no longer able to swing their cut fists or see through the blood that blinded them. They crumpled with throbbing heads and aching limbs. But they knew one thing and it was enough; the assault on the men who worked in the mills had failed.

"Find Fletcher Jones! Your agreement will be signed. You've won!" Josiah was shouting.

Out of the disordered mass, the man with one eye emerged and managed to make his way to the iron gate. His face was bleeding from a gash that had cracked his cheekbone. He staggered like a drunkard and fell against the gate.

"Get the agreement," Josiah said from the height of his frightened and swerving horse. "You shall have it signed by morning."

McGiver and the police were rounding up Sam Garvey's hired band. The workers were straggling away, dragging their mates who could no longer stand. Jim Pryor was carried off by the police with the side of his head bashed in like a melon and his jaw shattered. But he was breathing. The woman who had used her kitchen knife was borne, bruised and bleeding, to her hovel while the man she had stabbed lay dead in his own blood.

Josiah rode back into town to fetch Dr. Mortlake who would be kept busy far into the night.

Randolph judged from the sudden silence that the storm had ended. He went to Valeria who had propped Sam up against the pillows.

"It seems to be over. I think it's our turn for a brandy."

They found themselves in the study each holding a glass. She could not yet fully realize that Randolph was there, that he had come to her and that, once again, they were together.

When Josiah finally returned with the doctor, Valeria was sitting in the wing chair by the fire. Randolph was at Garvey's desk reading his notes and looking through his maps. It seemed no longer to matter that Sam was building a railroad or what his intentions were or even what had happened during the last few days.

Valeria went with Dr. Mortlake into the bedroom. The lugubrious man of medicine who detested the human body examined Sam, propped up like a broken dummy. At last he pronounced, "He's had a serious attack. He'll need complete rest for some weeks. You must give him laudanum."

Dr. Mortlake departed to do the duty he detested. Valeria went to Josiah and simply leaned against him. He was somehow or other, it seemed, the man who had saved their lives.

"I've arranged with McGiver to keep the men on duty in front of the house till the agreement's signed. He must do it before morning." Josiah laid the document on the desk.

He brushed Valeria's soft cheek with the back of his fingers. "I'll come back later."

It seemed impossible that only a few hours before she had lain in this man's arms. She felt ashamed that she had shown so little feeling for him afterwards. She went with him into the hall.

"If he still won't sign, you must leave here. Randolph can bring you to my place or you can go with him."

"What will they do if he refuses?"

"Kill him most likely. I can't say I'd blame them." She stood there, helpless and desolate.

Josiah said to her gently, "You owe him no further loyalty. You must see that."

"But it was true," Valeria protested weakly. "You did start it and I warned you this would happen."

"I guess," he admitted, "that we are both to blame."

He kissed her tenderly and went out.

She leaned against the door in utter weariness. The grim old house was still as death. She felt that she must do something, must occupy herself, in however meaningless a way. She went into the kitchen and prepared dinner for herself and Randolph, surprised that she could still remember which pans to use.

Later, when Valeria looked in on Sam, she found he was sleeping despite the irregular, feeble gasps.

There he was propped up against the pillows, an amazing shrunken old body retaining such will to live yet another day to inflict his anger and venomous disregard for suffering, just to get his way.

At present there was not much she could do for

Sam, so Valeria rejoined her brother. It was not that the rift between her and Randolph had been mended. They were together because they had always been together in times of crisis. It was a bond, not so much of kinship, as of shared experience.

Neither of them felt the desire to talk. During her excavations of Sam Garvey's mysterious possessions, Valeria had found in a drawer a pack of cards. They were old and soiled, relics of a time when he played poker with business associates. She handed Randolph the cards and they sat at the desk playing double solitaire, noting their losses and gains as if money was at stake.

She had no idea what time it was when she sat back, spent. "I must sleep. I'm dead."

"I'll wait up."

"No. I'll sleep here."

It occurred to her that Randolph would be surprised at the contents of the bookcase. She opened the glass doors. "You can read if you like."

He looked over the books, his fingers touching with admiration the beautiful, gold-tooled bindings. "I'd no idea he was literary." Randolph began to read.

She sank into the chair by the fire and fell into a deep sleep.

Once during the night Valeria woke. Randy was reading. She went in to Sam and roused him for his laudanum drops. The tired, listless blue eyes watched her as she moved about the room.

Valeria wondered anxiously if Sam would sign the agreement. Would he still hold out? And if he did, where would she go?

In the half-light of dawn, she woke again. Randolph was asleep with his head on his outstretched arms.

She picked up the document and went into the bedroom and to give Sam more laudanum. He was awake, his eyes shifting to avoid her, not meeting hers as she bent over him.

"Here's the agreement. They want you to sign by morning." Valeria noted a stiffening of Sam's jaw as she laid the paper on the bed table.

She went to the kitchen and, like all the women of

Shacktown, put water on the stove and made the first breakfast after the battle that was not yet solved.

She found in this interim, between twilight and full morning, a calm and impersonal resolve.

When dawn had broken and the gray light of an overcast sky filtered into the grim old house, she went back into Sam's bedroom and sat down.

He was awake and watching her. She could not tell what thoughts were passing through his head or what he felt about her.

"You must sign the agreement or I shall leave you. Tabitha Grey or someone else will have to come and look after you. I cannot stand any more," Valeria said clearly and precisely.

Sam's jaw was set, his teeth clenched. Breath wheezed fitfully in his nostrils.

"Very well. Then I must ask you to give me the combination of the safe. I will take what is mine and go."

She stood up and looked down at her husband. She felt neither dislike nor pity. His inflexible will no longer concerned her. She found a pencil in the drawer of the bed table and held out the scrap of paper on which Dr. Mortlake had written Sam's prescription.

After a long moment he took the paper and scribbled something. It was a set of figures. She went into the study where Randolph was stretching.

"There's coffee in the kitchen," Valeria told him.

He yawned and straggled out. She pulled back the shelf of ledgers that concealed the safe and turned the lock back and forth. The safe opened. There, at the side of the canvas bags filled with money in coins and notes, lay the red case that contained her opals and the bank book.

Hearing a hoarse exhalation of breath that was neither a word nor a cry, Valeria fled to Sam's room.

He had turned sideways against the pillows with his head averted from her in shame.

Sam Garvey had signed the agreement. It was there, the wavery but distinct signature at the foot of the list of demands made by the men.

He could not bear for her to see him at this moment of his worst defeat. Valeria, touched by a pity stronger than her immediate relief, bent and kissed his cheek. Sam could not bring himself to look at her because she would see in his eyes that what he had done was the denial of everything he stood for and that his innermost pride was debased by this public admission of weakness. He had fought to the last and lost.

When Josiah came, strong and dependable and real as the new day, she went to him gladly. "He has signed."

"He did this for you," he said with a sort of sad reluctance, as though admitting that there existed, after all, a bond between Sam Garvey and his wife. "He would have done it for no one else."

They were conscious that what had happened between them and had seemed the choice of two free people had been, in fact, an adulterous act.

"I want to come with you," she said. "I want to bring it to them myself." She took from the safe one of the canvas bags and shut the safe. Turning to Randolph, she said, "Please stay till I come back."

It was still early as they set out to find Fletcher Jones's house.

Mary threw up her hands, "Oh, Ma'am, it's you! I am glad! I've been that worried. Oh, God be praised, you're safe!"

The man with the patch over one eye stood up as the tall, bedraggled, white-faced woman stepped into the dingy room with Josiah Eaton. Matthew knew at once it was the beautiful woman who gave him her concern and kindness.

Valeria touched the boy's face tenderly. "I didn't know you were related," she said to Mary. "Is this your husband?"

Mary was crying. "No, my brother. Oh Ma'am, I wanted to come to you. I wanted to all along. But I couldn't, you see, I couldn't."

Valeria hugged her. "It's all over now."

Holding out the agreement to Jones, she said, "He accepted your demands. I'm sorry it was not done sooner."

Fletcher stared at the paper and the signature as though he could not believe that it was real. It was a victory without joy. They were all too tired for elation. "He's only signed in pencil. Will it be legal, Mr. Eaton?"

"It can be properly drawn up," Josiah assured him. "Mr. Garvey will keep his word."

Valeria took the notes from under her cloak and put them on the table. "You can use this money for the men who were hurt and for anything else they need."

Fletcher saw that this weary, compassionate woman, who was by some tangle of mischances Garvey's wife, had suffered with them and been unable to do anything to help. He nodded. "I will see that it's fairly used."

Dimly, now that the tempest had subsided, Valeria realized that life must go on. They would all somehow pick up the broken pieces and resume the daily struggle. "Later on, when things have quieted down, I want you to see that the school is opened and that the children and the older boys who work in the mills attend it. Dr. Mortlake will be there two evenings a week as arranged. Please see that the families go to him and get help when they are ill."

"I'll talk to them," Josiah offered.

Fletcher nodded. "I will try to do what I can."

"And later on," Valeria managed to focus her burned-out brain, "there may be other things we can do. One evening perhaps you'll let me come here and we can talk it over."

"We can form a committee," Josiah backed her up. "It's time that some effort was made."

Valeria turned to Mary, "Will you come back tomorrow or will that be difficult for you now?"

Mary was drying her eyes on her apron. "Oh, no, Ma'am, I will come. Indeed I will."

There was nothing more to do there. Valeria kissed Matthew good-bye. "And you come with your mother. I have missed you."

He clung to her. "Will there be cookies like before?"

"Yes, I will bake you the kind you like."

They said their farewells like people parting after a funeral.

Together they went back through the squalid byways.

"I hope," Josiah said, "that you really will let me help you with the work you want to do."

"What you can do to help you must do for them, not me."

When they reached the house Josiah held back with his hand on the iron gate.

"When may I see you?"

Out of the depth of her weariness she looked at him levelly with her large jade eyes, "We cannot meet again. You must know that."

"I won't accept that. You can't cope with everything alone."

"Randy will help me now. And there's Mary. I can manage."

"I can't leave you like this."

"It is quite impossible," Valeria said firmly. "What happened was out of context. You have your life and I must go on with mine."

"Valeria—"

"Please," she said with a touch of despair, "don't make things more difficult. I am grateful—truly. But it is over. Now," she waited for him to lift his hand, "let me go in."

She had turned her head away, her face drawn and pale. Josiah saw that this was not the moment to argue.

"I will always be here," he said helplessly.

Unexpectedly, as though wanting to make amends, as though trying to tell him something for which there were no words, Valeria cupped his large hand with her smaller one against her face, kissing Josiah's palm. Then she quickly went up the path.

He knew as he watched her go that it was not over and could never be. There was an unbreakable bond between them, however long they might be divided.

An hour later the whistle shrilled as it always did. At the second call the men assembled with bandaged knuckles and patches over cuts, bruised and limping. When the gates opened, they straightened up and walked through. But now they walked with a new pride.

Valeria heard the whistle as she stepped out of the tin hip bath. She stood arrested with a towel draped around her. She was waiting for the familiar rumbling in the earth and when it came, a short time later, she thought, It has all started again, perhaps a little better than before.

Sam Garvey heard the deep reverberation that was his heartbeat. He listened and smiled to himself.

CHAPTER SEVENTEEN

A GREAT CHANGE HAD COME over Ida Brewster. Her energies were now absorbed by something far more important than her social obligations. She no longer dreamed of impoverished noblemen and coronets on her carriage, nor did she derive pleasure from flaunting her wealth in order to intimidate her rivals. The dinners she still occasionally gave had another purpose. She endured the sly digs and innuendos of Mrs. Shawcross and Mrs. Bancroft because in the course of conversation she picked up snippets of gossip that she could later incorporate into the great patchwork quilt of scandal she was stitching together. She was a detective carefully amassing a web of evidence that would finally enmesh and convict a felon. The absorbing interest that had taken precedence over every other consideration and activity was her hatred for Valeria Lee.

There was an element of dedicated passion in her determination to smash this woman who had assumed in Ida's mind the symbolic proportions of evil. Ida lay in her great French bed, under the dimpled bottoms of the angels and the cascades of lace, thinking of Valeria and how she could ruin her and drive her into the outermost abyss of shame.

It was not so much that Valeria had had the audacity to marry her father. Ida cared nothing about him. It was not even, though she would never have admitted it, that as his wife, Valeria had usurped the right to inherit part of the Garvey millions. Ida knew there would be plenty of money when the old man died. It was more closely allied to the fact that Valeria had dared to go her own way in total disregard of *the* Mrs. Brewster, had left without collecting her pay, had driven weak-witted Hank into a bout of hysterical drinking and finally, with that cool, self-centered ease which had so infuriated Ida, had twisted that old wretch into making her his wife. *His wife!* It was Valeria's high-handed independence which gnawed at Ida's vitals. In that declared battle of personalities Valeria had ignored all the rules; without even a fight, without even allowing Ida the satisfaction of insulting her, she had simply gone her way.

In Ida's mind, Valeria Lee and Josiah Eaton had merged into a great monster that consistently defied her efforts to be a woman of importance in her own right. There had never been a time when Ida had created an image that had entirely convinced anyone and—what was more galling—had never even convinced herself. It was some indefinable quality missing from her own makeup that both Valeria and Josiah possessed. She hated to be thought inferior and she hated these two because that was what, for all her pride and anger, they made her feel. Ida wanted to trample them underfoot and rise from their abasement and know that her power and importance were unassailably her own.

Tabitha Grey had been busy on her behalf. Tabitha had many contacts in Shacktown and reported regularly on events involving Sam Garvey and that terrible woman. Valeria had been sticking her nose into a variety of unlikely corners and bending her energies to create a variety of unlikely changes that had all the women of Shacktown in a state of perturbation. Her audacity and intemperance knew no bounds. The women of Shacktown simply could not grasp what her intentions were or what was the motive behind them. Tabitha reported with outrage that they had resented her efforts to start a school and had refused to allow their children to attend it. They bitterly objected to her arbitrary ways and her condescension and had gathered up the books and inkpots, the blackboard and the supply of chalk, and flung them over the fence of Sam Garvey's house. They had put up with enough from Sam Garvey over the years and were not proposing to have their noses rubbed in the mud of his wife's determination to educate their children. They could do it themselves if they considered their children needed educating, which was doubtful in Tabitha's opinion. They were not going to accept a few patronizing sops flung at them by the wife of the man with millions. Not after years of penury and ramshackle homes and stinking drains. And what had that terrible woman done? It was unthinkable! She had ordered more books and inkpots and had stationed herself in the Lutheran hall and conducted a class for the smaller children herself. A few of the weaker souls who had no decent pride had grudgingly let their children attend and the poor mites who knew no better had come to accept and even to like her. It was inconceivable and it was wicked.

As for that miserable old Dr. Mortlake! He had been bribed and cajoled and browbeaten into giving his services, Tabitha was sure. At first the women of Shacktown had been convinced, as far as Tabitha could tell, that this was another dirty trick and that the medicines were surely poison. It was simply a lowdown hoax concocted by Sam Garvey's wife to reduce them all to rubbish. Well, they had fought him and won over the contract; they would fight him and win over the medicines. Hooting with scorn, they had emptied them down the open drains. But Dr. Mortlake had persisted and that terrible woman had persisted, and Tabitha had observed that some of those poor, dimwitted creatures had brought their children and he had treated them. By the merest accident the children had been cured.

That horrid woman was causing more controversy and trouble in Shacktown than Sam Garvey had stirred up in all the years he had owned the mills.

"And there's to be a library and a laying-in room—*free*. As though any decent soul can't have her baby in her own home without any interference!" Tabitha ranted. To crown it all, Valeria, in her insolence and audacity, had officially opened the new railroad, dressed like a queen and dripping with furs. She had cut a ribbon and broken a bottle of champagne on the first line and a lot of low devils, hired by Sam Garvey for the occasion, had cheered. They had actually *cheered* that brazen hussy who was not only no better than she ought to be but, in Tabitha's opinion, a whole lot worse.

Of course, Mr. Garvey was ill and was completely in Valeria's power. It was shocking to think of the old man, who might have his faults, as they all knew, but who was a person of great importance, was practically a prisoner of an ambitious, ruthless, power-hungry woman who could force him to agree to anything because he could hardly move.

People in Arcadia were getting used to the sight of Mrs. Sam Garvey riding about in her pearl gray habit on that horse she had bought from Josiah Eaton who, as the whole town knew, was her husband's deadliest enemy. And that was the most interesting and scandalous part of the whole business. There was a connection there. There must be. And not just on account of the horse, Tabitha was sure.

Wasn't it strange that after the strike, the attitude of *The Courier* had changed so suddenly about Mr. Garvey? Wasn't it more than odd that the paper had started *praising* Mrs. Garvey's antics in Shacktown? Of course, her activities all fitted in with Josiah Eaton's trumpeted support of the working man: getting their wages upped and improving them out of their wits and so on. But even though he was rushing about the state making speeches and promises and causing a lot of trouble that no decent hard-working person approved of, wasn't it altogether the strangest thing that Josiah Eaton should be on a committee along with that rabble-rouser Fletcher Jones, that half-witted Pastor Vanderlip and Mrs. Garvey's brother, when the sole purpose of the committee was to put Mrs. Garvey's self-styled reforms in motion? And not only did Mrs. Garvey's brother work on *The Courier,* but he was also traveling around with Josiah Eaton and helping with his campaign. They were thick as thieves. Mr. Eaton had attended meetings in Shacktown and had given money and was raising funds for those hare-brained schemes of *hers.* They were all in it together and Tabitha was sure it certainly wasn't for love of Mr. Garvey.

Joe Horton had let it be known that Mrs. Garvey had gone riding *late at night* and *alone* when the strike was on. She had ridden off by herself into the country and returned at very odd hours and not just for the good of her health, you could be sure. It was scandalous what was going on behind the scenes, what these people who thought themselves so high and mighty were involved in. Tabitha was shocked. It was wicked.

And now, at last, Tabitha's very worst suspicion had been confirmed. She could not wait to impart her newest and most terrible news to her friend and protectress, Mrs. Brewster. She scuttled up the long hill to The Heights in her slate-gray coat with her slate-gray moleskin tippet and her slate-gray eyes gleaming. She was agog with the juiciest morsel of gossip that had ever come her way. It was thrilling to be in a position to shock and delight Mrs. Ida Brewster who had suffered so badly at the hands of the worst female creature that had ever set foot in Arcadia.

Ever since the great change had come over Ida's life and she had devised her master plan, she had taken to coming downstairs at noon and spending all day in her dressing gown with her hair unbraided and no rings on, walking up and down that dried-blood-bath nightmare of a parlor and cogitating and scheming about her great idea. Ida no longer cared how dirty the house might become or how perfunctory were the meals that Monsieur Emile might serve. She ate whatever was on her plate and did not even care whether Henry Brewster was there or not. She scarcely saw Nancy who preferred to eat in her room, in the self-enforced cell she shared with Jane Eyre and Mr. Rochester and other dear and romantic souls. Ida no longer cared where her daughter ate. Henry might droop in his corner reading the want ads, or sneak out to visit Helen Tennant. She no longer cared about him either. Ida was completely dedicated to her great scheme for reducing her two deadly rivals to dust and ashes.

Tabitha Grey scuttled into the parlor and plopped down breathless on a chair.

"Oh, my dear," she gasped, "I have so much to tell. I hardly know where to begin or whether I even ought to, because of the shock it will cause." She waved her liver-spotted hand before her face as though to check the rush of scandal on her tongue. "You will not believe, but it's as you and I always surmised and it proves everything. It's as clear as day. She is far, far worse than we gave her credit for. I said to myself as I came up the hill, 'Should I tell poor Mrs. Brewster who had suffered enough as it is?' Oh my dear, it's a heavy burden on me to bring you such news, to be sure."

Ida was used to these tedious preliminaries and cut her short. "I'm not in the mood for talk, Tabitha. Tell me why you've come and be quick about it."

"My dear, my dear Mrs. Brewster," Tabitha marshaled her forces for the kill, "I have a good friend, Mrs. Nobby Pincraft. And Mrs. Pincraft—God bless her, she's a good God-fearing soul—has a brother-in-law, William Pincraft who, for want of a better job, God help him, works for Josiah Eaton. Oh, he could tell you a lot that goes on in that house! Well, William Pincraft informed Mrs. Nobby only the other evening —he comes down to see her from time to time because she's a widow and he's a dutiful Christian— that . . . on a certain night—during the big strike— a certain person appeared. It was raining and she was on horseback—Mr. Eaton had guests . . . Well, she rang the bell, bold as brass, and as good as ordered him to tell Mr. Eaton that she was there."

Ida was all attention. She loomed over Tabitha. "Go on. Go on!"

"Well, he wasn't sure, you see; there was guests. But she said, and he remembered distinctly, 'I am Valeria Lee. He's expecting me.' As though she'd been used to going there often at all hours as we both surmised. So he went to the dining room and whispered to Mr. Eaton who got right up in the middle of dinner and went out and let her in. He took her into the study and she was soaking wet. And later—" But it was too much for Tabitha. She didn't want to spoil the whole story by telling it all at once. She leaned back, fanning herself as though for want of air.

Ida hated these false theatrics. She wanted to kick Tabitha, but she resisted and said harshly, "Will you get on!"

Tabitha got her second wind and steadied herself like an actress nearing her greatest scene. "He took her up to a bedroom and William Pincraft was told to take up a tray of food and a bottle of wine. Can you imagine? To the bedroom! He knocked on the door and as he was about to leave he saw her reach out and take the tray in." Tabitha's voice sank to a whisper of horrified delight. "She had nothing on, Mrs. Brewster. Not a stitch, you see."

Mrs. Brewster was standing there, but something was going wrong. She was not reacting as Tabitha had anticipated. She was not gloating or angry or outraged, as she usually would have been. Ida was strangely still.

"And after the men had gone," Tabitha continued in a small, mean, secretive voice, "Mr. Eaton went up and stayed with her—in the bedroom alone—for a long time. It was three o'clock, can you imagine, when he went to the stables and put the pony in the trap and drove her home. William Pincraft," her voice was so low that Ida could barely hear her, "says that her own horse, Mimosa, the one she bought from Mr. Eaton and which William Pincraft knew, stayed in the stables all night. Mr. Eaton himself took her back to Horton's Stables."

But why was Mrs. Brewster just standing there? Why had the color drained out of her face? She was turning the color of putty.

"It's all clear, isn't it now? It all adds up. That's why the paper changed its tune about Mr. Garvey. That's why Mr. Eaton's on her committee, why he talked to the men and got them to take her medicines and read her books. They've been carrying on all this time. If you ask me," Tabitha fired her culminating shot, "she was his mistress *before* she married. It's as wicked as anything in the Bible, isn't it? Mr. Eaton of all peo-

ple! After all he'd done to Mr. Garvey and him being
behind the strike as everyone knew! Oh, they concocted the whole thing together. It's as clear as day."

Ida backed away from this voice that hammered
relentlessly at her. With an odd, dead look on her
face she sat down and sagged like a great bundle of
washing.

Tabitha got up and went over to make quite sure
what was happening. "Are you all right, my dear?"
she asked, thinking that perhaps Mrs. Brewster had
been taken with a sudden faintness.

"Give me my bag. It's there," Ida said indistinctly.

She motioned vaguely toward a table and Tabitha
brought the bag. Mrs. Brewster fumbled in it and
pulled out some money and handed it to Tabitha. "Go
ask in the kitchen if you want something."

"Mrs. Brewster dear—" Tabitha began, curious to
see what had unexpectedly caused this change.

Ida's brows contracted in a sort of spasm. She managed to say, "Go away."

It was very strange and it was annoying because it
deprived Tabitha of her right to conduct an involved
post-mortem on the information she had bought. She
went in puzzlement and pique to the door. "If I hear
anything more . . ."

Her friend and protectress had evidently no desire
to listen any more.

Ida sat there stunned, and for the first time the
enormity of what Valeria had done to her exceeded her
capacity for hatred. Valeria had seduced her son, her
father and now the man she had hated and loved for
nineteen years. Valeria had robbed her of everything
that through her own folly she had lost.

Ida got up and fumbled behind the edition of
Washington Irving. She fished out the whiskey and
drank straight from the bottle, without even bothering
to lock her door.

The obscenity of Valeria's conquests was so colossal, so unmitigated that it robbed Ida of any reaction
but shock.

As always when she thought of Josiah, a wave of
the old despair welled up in her, washing up the hor-

rifying awareness of her own gross and unwanted body. She was condemned to live forever in this carapace of unwanted flesh.

Drinking steadily, Ida tried to banish the memory of Josiah on the porch of the old house long ago and the thought of that tall, graceful creature who had so easily beguiled him.

It was worse than death, this knowledge that there could never be any escape from what she was.

When Henry Brewster slunk into the room with the evening *Courier,* he found her sitting there glassy-eyed on the sofa. There was something frightening and repellent about her immobility.

He hovered briefly and then carefully crept out.

She sat there in a stupor. Gradually, like some object submerged in the depths of a stagnant pond, there rose to the surface of her mind the conviction of exactly what she must do.

⚔ Chapter Eighteen ⚔

Josiah Eaton was making the discovery that true love was painful. It was not much consolation to know that Valeria lived in the same town when he could not see her. And there was no joy at all in discovering that she intended to fulfill her duties to her husband and was not amenable to extramarital meetings, however romantic. For once, he had met a woman whose resistance was stronger than his desire.

He had thought he wanted love as a panacea for what he had come to feel was the emptiness of his life. But now that this disturbance of his senses and willpower and peace of mind had come over him like an infection to which he had hitherto been immune, Josiah was at a loss to know how to deal with it. He both wanted to love Valeria and, in saner moments, did not want to because it interfered with his political plans and absorbed too much of his mental energy at a time when he could ill afford it.

He had attended the meetings of the Workers' Committee in the hope of seeing her. Valeria was not present. He had written to her with suggestions as to how her reforms could be implemented. She had turned the letters over to Fletcher Jones. Josiah had written asking her to meet him out riding on the road near the Hotchkiss farm. The letters remained unanswered. He had caught glimpses of her riding down Main Street and had missed her by half an hour at Horton's Stables. These frustrations had driven him to moods of desperation where he had been on the point of recklessly going to Sam Garvey's house and confronting her. But Rosie Delmar had been right in warning him that since he had embarked on his campaign and was surrounded by people who would be only too happy to disgrace him, he was forced to watch his step.

Often in the middle of a dinner or a meeting or at his office, when he was trying to compose his thoughts before making a political speech, Josiah would think of her. Valeria was there in his mind when he needed to concentrate, to be fully cognizant of what he must try to say. She would sit up in bed and hold out her lovely arms to him and the covers would fall back from her swelling breasts and Josiah would savor again that moment when he had so smoothly entered her. What had been the special magic of that embrace that made it so different from all the others? He had known many more beautiful women, more experienced, more ready to satisfy his whims. She had done no more than give herself simply and fully. Yet he had known such peace as Valeria lay comfortably in his arms, as though after a lifetime of wandering he had at last come home.

He was ashamed that he lacked the willpower to overcome this need to think of her, to torment himself with the remembered sweetness of their union. How had it happened, when he had always been able to dismiss any woman he slept with, even those who had intrigued him and whom he had desired? Why was it that something about this one woman haunted him like an intangible perfume that would not fade? He was mystified by what his common sense told him was sentimentality, and yet astounded that at his age he was capable of a sustained emotion that had hitherto been quite alien to his nature. And Valeria had put him at a grave disadvantage. How could he fight Sam Garvey over his railroad without causing her added pain?

When he balanced what was at stake in money and satisfaction against his loyalty to a woman, he could not understand how he had reached the point of even considering one at the expense of the other. He argued back and forth as he rode in his private railroad car on his journeys about the state in search of support. How could he have set up such a choice—this woman, against the chance of forcing to his knees the man he had hated and despised for the greater part of his life? It was the final outrage for Sam Garvey to have married the one woman capable of disrupting Josiah's normal functioning. It was the one trump card which, in their protracted vendetta, he would not have dreamed the old bastard could ever play. What stood between him and the final reckoning was a woman he had slept with once and who had kissed his hand at the gate to that filthy house she was condemned to live in. It was Sam Garvey's slyest trick.

In his efforts to rid himself of Valeria's recurrent image, Josiah tried to convince himself that her appearance that night had perhaps not been accidental, that she had been sent there on Garvey's orders, that she had, in fact, very subtly seduced him in order to weaken his support of the strike. She had made a tentative effort to get him to stop the articles at their previous meeting on horseback. Perhaps she was no more than a cold-hearted intriguer who had used her charms on behalf of the man who gave her money. Had he fallen for her charms like an inexperienced boy? It had worked, he considered ruefully, because he had called off the articles and had commented favorably in the paper on her charitable activities. Had it been all along simply the tactics of a clever woman out to get her way?

But could Valeria have dissimulated so expertly when she was in his arms, when she had moaned in passion and held him in her and lain so still? She had said nothing on the long drive home. Perhaps a woman with that degree of objective guile could pretend to anything, like an actress playing one of a variety of roles. Why, then, had she so simply and humbly kissed his hand?

Josiah sighed and looked at his watch. Half an hour wasted! He had not written his speech. It was a sorry state for a man to be in, especially at this all-important juncture in his life.

Josiah had taken Randolph with him on his campaign tour. He had grown fond of him and he was a link with Valeria. Sometimes when he glanced at that dark head, bent over a writing pad as he reworked some speech, Josiah would look for that resemblance to the sister, not so much in feature, but in a certain distinctive charm. He had several times, without seeming to open the subject, asked Randolph oblique questions about their upbringing in order to hear him speak of Valeria as she had been in those early years. Then, abruptly, he would resent Randolph and want to send him away because he was a reminder of this woman who troubled him and whom he wanted to banish from his mind.

Randolph was aware that something was troubling his employer who was now his friend. He could not fathom why Josiah was occasionally short with him, and absent-minded; or why he sat staring through the window of the private car at the countryside he obviously did not see. The campaign was going well. People were beginning to feel there was something a mite different about the new candidate for governor. He seemed a touch less of a politician and more a man. He was less bland and declamatory and less obviously self-seeking. There was a certain warmth—even a sincerity—about Josiah which most of these citified men who were out to wheedle votes and advance themselves and get rich didn't have. Josiah was not aware that neither his resonant voice nor his expansive charm nor the plausibility of his promises were winning him support, but rather a shift in his personality that made him a little more human, a little closer, a little more real. When he stood on the platform of the train and addressed a crowd at a wayside station, these rough, suspicious, cynical country folk felt that although his campaign promises would probably not be kept, maybe he would at least make an effort to keep them because he seemed just a degree more dependable, even a degree more honest.

Eaton stood there, a commanding figure with his handsome golden looks, and promised these hard-working people a better deal and better representation. Although they did not believe him, they were prepared to like him and to think that maybe for once it was worth a try.

The train would start and Josiah would wave and

the country folk would cheer. Josiah would go back to his private car and wonder if they had believed a word. Then he would wonder whether it mattered as much as he previously had thought it did.

There were so many things that he should be planning aside from the campaign. There was his scheme for disrupting the building of Sam Garvey's railroad. He should be making connections with certain men who controlled certain gangs who knew how to blow up bridges and pull up rails. And again, when he thought of it, the whole thing bored him. He had unloaded his shares in the existing line some time before, and financially stood to lose little when Garvey's Midwestern and Pacific started rolling.

What was happening to him?

Often, he would decide to turn in early, telling himself that tomorrow he would get a fresh start and concentrate on what was important. He would put this romantic nonsense out of mind. His career and power were what his life was actually about.

He would climb into bed in some strange hotel, in some one-horse town, lost in that penetrating silence of the prairies and he would thankfully turn down the lamp. He must sleep and wake refreshed tomorrow and be ready to begin.

But he did not sleep. The treadmill of his thoughts would start spinning again. What *was* his life actually about? He had passed thirty-seven alone and all of his ambitions did not compensate for this feeling of incompleteness. How wonderful it would be if he could marry Valeria! What an asset she would be to a politician, with her grace and savoir-faire and her instinct for manipulating men. Oh yes, she had that, sure enough. She had fatally manipulated him!

It was the worst mischance, Josiah would think as he tossed and turned, that Sam Garvey hadn't succumbed to that heart attack. How simple things might have been!

Why couldn't he sleep?

He would turn up the lamp, light a cigar, glance through the local paper and find himself staring at the fly-spotted wallpaper. Why wasn't Valeria there?

To console himself he would write her letters, sometimes allowing his thoughts to flow over six or seven pages. The phrases of love he used seemed flat, commonplace and inadequate. But he labored over them, seeking some deeper, more truthful expression of what always remained in some mocking and maddening way inexpressible.

Sometimes dawn would find him still writing. Josiah would seal the envelope, dissatisfied, and address it, but later in the day when Randolph would collect the letters he had to mail, he would withhold Valeria's. He was reluctant to part with it because this declaration of love was too much a part of himself and was, in some way, a link to her. And at last, when he forced himself to slip it into a mailbox, he had a sudden fear that he had said too much or said it ill and that she would take offense at such frank avowals and persistence. In his mind he would follow the letter on its cross-country journey; time its arrival in Arcadia; time its delivery; imagine her receiving it, opening it, reading it; and wonder if she would be pleased or angered.

Josiah's letters were a source of constant apprehension to Valeria. She dreaded the sight of one of them in the wire postbox.

She had been grateful for his first short note offering advice on how her work in Shacktown could be carried forward. She was grateful for his efforts to get the women to send their children to the school and avail themselves of Dr. Mortlake's visits. But when he asked her directly to meet him on horseback by the Hotchkiss farm, she was disturbed. She had no intention of meeting him again.

She was determined to put that incident out of mind, to concentrate on her duties to Sam who needed her constant care, and on the lessons she gave to the small children at the Lutheran Hall.

They had gotten through the strike and everything pertaining to it was over. She wanted to obliterate from her mind those turbulent and nerve-racking days. Partially from a sense of guilt, she was assiduous in her attention to Sam, anticipating his every need as he passed through the various slow phases of his convalescence. He started to eat again and then to sit on the side of his bed before taking a few faltering steps, leaning heavily on her arm. Eventually with a cane in his other hand, he made the laborious journey across the study to his desk. Valeria was always at his side.

She cooked delicacies to tempt him, read to him in the evenings, was always on hand with his drops at the appointed times. No professional nurse could have been more constant or efficient. She wanted to fill her days with these duties so that her mind would not drift back to that night when she had unaccountably surrendered to her husband's enemy. She did not want to recall that particular joy and peace she had experienced in his arms. It had happened, but it would never, Valeria was adamant, happen again.

She was apprehensive that she would meet Josiah when she drove into town on some errand. When she went to the stables to collect Mimosa, Joe Horton, with sly intent, would drop hints as to the hour when Josiah went riding.

"Mr. Eaton takes the same horse every afternoon and rides out to his country place. Don't seem to be using the place much unless he has special guests, but probably you have passed him on the way, Mrs. Garvey, because you go in the same direction." He would grin knowingly.

These innuendos annoyed Valeria. She sent Tripp to bring Mimosa to Sam's stable where she could take her out unobserved. She began to leave town by another route, past the railroad station and over the tracks, down an uninteresting road that led through flat pasture land but usually had the advantage of being deserted.

The effort not to think of Josiah brought him constantly to mind. She would catch herself remembering the copper gleam of the firelight on his hair and his sadness when he admitted that he had wanted lately to live in a different world.

She was immensely relieved when she heard from Randolph that they were leaving on another tour and would be gone some weeks. Arcadia was no longer a threat to Valeria and she rode on her errands and walked to the Lutheran Hall with a renewed sense of safety and freedom. She even rode one day along Tremont Avenue past the Haverfields', past Josiah's without a qualm. He had gone and would now recede from her mind like the Yankee captain. In only a few more months she and Sam would have left Arcadia and time, like a healing wave, would wash away those fatal footsteps in the sand.

But then the letters started dropping into the mailbox. They lay in wait for her like conspirators. Valeria opened the first and read two pages. She was startled and then shaken. Folding the pages firmly back, she replaced them in the envelope and stuffed the letter into the kitchen stove. He had spoken of love; he had said he loved her. If there was one added complication to her life that she did not want, it was anything pertaining to romance. It had no place whatever in her carefully ordered curriculum. Her days were planned and she carried them out accordingly. She had raised the drawbridge and refused to consider that she was under siege.

The letters came, some bulkier than others, with various postmarks. She dreaded the sight of that level, conventional, copybook handwriting which erupted into such wild and unconventional words. These letters, only partially read, followed the first one into the stove. She resented the mail and pounced on it, looking through Sam's voluminous stack in order to extract her own indictment, that reminder of an act of surrender which the sight of one of those long blue envelopes revived.

It was crass, uncivilized and, after two weeks and six letters, cruel. She could defend herself by avoiding him when he was there by riding along a road he did not frequent, by shutting her mind against the thought of him, but against his letters she was helpless. They simply came.

She debated whether she should write and tell him to desist and searched her mind for words strong enough to make her intentions irrevocably plain. But Josiah was moving from town to town and no letter of hers would ever reach him.

It was brutal to inflict this anxiety and to rekindle constantly her sense of guilt.

She thrust the seventh letter into the stove.

She needed some fresh activity, something to absorb her surplus energy, so that her mind would not wander to that firelit room and a man with whom, in another forbidden life, she had known such rapture. She must be occupied every hour of the day so that at night she would fall exhausted into sleep and not lie there dreaming of things that could never be.

Valeria would get into bed, lower the lamp and try to compose herself. But as she turned over she would feel him beside her, an almost palpable presence.

ℰ✗ CHAPTER NINETEEN ✗ℰ

A SHORT MAN with a clipped moustache and shining pince nez, and dressed in a brown suit and a small round hat, was lurking around the stockyard as night was falling. He was so insignificant that he was immediately noticeable. The youth with the face like lard observed him. He was hiding between two freight cars in the hope of catching one of the men on their way home.

What was that neat little man doing there? Was he with the police, or was he an inspector from the railroad making some kind of a report? If McGiver had sent him he had to watch out because with McGiver anything could happen. He wasn't afraid of McGiver's sending him to jail. He was afraid of being knifed or shot down near the tracks. They would find his body next day and who would care?

He hung back and watched. The devious man had stepped forward into the light of a gas lantern. He was fumbling in his pocket and taking out money. Odd! He was letting the coins fall from one hand to the other. Deliberately. One by one. The youth could catch the tiny, distinct sound as the coins clinked together.

Was it a trap? Were there other men waiting behind him in the darkness? They could kill him easy as winking and throw him down on the rails and a train would cut him to pieces. Who would know it wasn't suicide—or care?

The youth was fascinated and frightened by the ominous little man dropping the coins to show someone or other that he had money. Was it a signal? Could that neat city man with the round black hat be looking for a renter? It didn't seem likely. Not the type. But then you could never be quite sure.

The youth was cold with fear. There was no one around tonight. The stockyards were silent as a grave. So silent that that man could whip out a knife and stab him without making a sound. Even if he yelled for help who would come? No one cared if he lived or died.

He was hypnotized as a rabbit is held by the magic of a snake. He needed money. He owed back rent and he needed cash for food. All day he had had nothing to eat but the remains of a greasy stew. He would have to resort to sleeping in the yards soon. All he now had were a bed and the sheets and the silk comforter Ford Hollister had given him. Ford had been the one person in his whole life who had treated him decently. Just his luck that Ford had gone away!

The little man was whistling clearly but softly like a a bird in a bush. What was he doing now? He had put the silver back in his pocket and taken out a billfold and was counting. He had stepped right under the lantern so that the green bills could be easily seen. He must be crazy to flash money around like that. Likely as not one of the stockyard men might see him and make off with all that money. How much could there be? Fives, maybe tens. Fifty dollars at least. Crazy!

The light from the lantern glinted on the stranger's glasses. McGiver must be trying to snare him. He was clammy with fear.

His heart stopped. The little man had stepped forward. He was walking, step by step, soundless as a mole in his neat, polished boots. He was walking toward him, taking his time, straight toward that passage between the cars where the youth was hiding.

The reflection in the glasses was cut off abruptly by the shadow of the cars. He stood a few feet away, stock still, and then turned and spoke into the darkness in which the youth was cowering.

"I want to talk to you. No need to be afraid."

The youth shrank back. His blood had turned to ice cold sweat.

"You can earn some money. I want to talk to you.

That's all. I will pay you for information. There's nothing to fear."

The boy gulped, unable to speak.

"I want to ask you some questions and I'll pay you well. Perhaps a lot if you can tell me what I want to know."

It was a nightmare. It was horrible. What was he talking about?

"Take me to where you live. We can talk there. Come along." The short man said it as though speaking to a child—quite kindly.

He turned and walked back. The youth managed to get his breath. His whole body sagged with relief. Money? For answering questions?

He peered 'round the side of the freight car. There was the man back where he had been under the lantern. Suddenly at the risk of his life the youth ran down the passage between the cars. He caught a glimpse of the shiny glasses on the little man's nose and stopped dead.

The man nodded. He turned in the direction of town.

The youth was horribly drawn to follow like a stray dog used to punishment but lured irresistibly by a bone.

The little man preceded him past the wall of the station building into the street with the straggling matchbox houses. He walked neatly and unassumingly, as though it were the most normal thing in the world.

The stranger walked along one side of the street and the youth followed. The man stopped and the youth stopped. The man turned and waited.

The youth hesitated. He felt sure now that this person who was willing to pay for information had not been sent by McGiver. McGiver didn't need information. He knew all he had to know. And he was not from the railroad. Why would the railroad people pay him anything? He knew the man in the round black hat was not from Arcadia at all.

His mind was working again. What information could he possibly have that was worth paying for? About the men who rented him? Not men from the stockyards. Who would care about them? Ford Hollister maybe or McGiver or one of the others? Blackmail? Maybe. He had to be careful, though. Once he had squealed they would know and kill him—whoever had sent that man with money to spend. If he could get the money and split out of town on the early train . . .

It was worth risking—just.

He went cautiously up the side of the street to the house.

He reached the house and waited. The man stepped quietly across the street. He was so unflustered that he was certainly not a renter. They were always furtive and glanced up and down and sidled in as though they were trying to make themselves invisible. This man was perfectly visible and evidently intended to remain so.

The youth slipped inside and the man stepped after him into the passage and carefully shut the door.

The youth waited for the unexpected move, the flash of a knife in the darkness or the sudden threat.

Nothing happened.

He turned up the lamp.

There was the stranger, waiting, neat and insignificant and calm.

The boy backed off to the mantel in which no fire had ever been lit.

The man sat down. He did not take off his hat, but instead produced a notebook and a pencil out of his coat pocket.

He said in a precise voice without any inflection, "I am a detective. I work for an agency. I have been instructed to ask you some questions. My client will pay a high fee if you are able to answer. I know your name and what you do."

The youth's fear had passed to mystification.

"You have lived here since September a year ago. You see a number of men. Sometimes in the stockyards, sometimes here. It's about the men you bring here that I want to ask you."

"Why?" The youth's eyes were wide with amazement.

"That doesn't concern you. I am instructed to pay

you from a hundred to five hundred dollars, depending on how much you tell me."

The youth's senses reeled. Five hundred! He couldn't have heard that right. It was more than he had ever dreamed of. Almost nobody in the world had five hundred dollars all at one time.

"There's no risk to yourself. This is strictly confidential." The light shone on his glasses and concealed his eyes. "You have nothing whatever to fear."

Suddenly the youth believed him, though he had no comprehension of what was happening.

The man pointed his pencil as though it were a miniature cannon about to fire at his notebook. "Do you know the names of the men you bring here?"

"Some."

"Who are they?"

"How do I know you're not from the police?"

The man took out his wallet and extracted a card which he presented to the youth: The Blanchard Agency, 25 Walnut Street, Chicago. The youth nodded impressed, appeased.

"Now. Can you give me their names?"

"How do I know you'll pay me?"

The little man pursed his lips under his bristly moustache. He took out his wallet and placed a hundred dollar bill on the rickety little table, the only piece of furniture in the room.

The youth eyed the money covetously. He was salivating, desperately eager. He realized that the little man meant business and that his offer of money and secrecy was not a hoax.

"McGiver," he said boldly. "He's the chief of police."

The detective wrote. "You're sure?"

The youth nodded.

"How often does he come here?"

"Once a month, maybe. Sometimes more."

"How long does he stay?"

"Hour or two. If he's drunk, all night."

"What does he do?" The man elucidated, "What does he do with you?"

"You want to know—*that?*"

"If you want the full amount you must tell me everything."

The youth squirmed. But he remembered. It was a chance to pay back for a lot of blows and for money flung crassly on the bed.

"Well, he has me—knocks me about. He likes to draw blood and when he hits me he likes to have me then. He drinks and throws up—other things."

"What other things?"

"I don't want to say. He gets drunk and acts like a pig."

The little man was writing in his notebook.

"Sometimes," the youth said sadly, "it takes me a whole day to clean up the mess he makes."

"Who else?"

The youth squirmed and shifted. "Men from the yards. Mostly they don't come here. The foreman, Mike. Don't know his last name. He has fights with his wife and gets mad and works it out on me, I guess. He broke my finger once, twisted it till I thought it would break right off. He had his hand over my mouth so I couldn't scream. He liked that, I think. Said he'd break my neck if I said anything."

The pencil stopped with a neat full stop.

"Does the name Ford Hollister mean anything to you?"

The youth froze. In the chilly silence, he struggled with himself.

"Do you know the name?"

The youth hesitated between desire for the money and harming his only friend. He shook his head.

"You're sure?"

The youth nodded.

The little man took out his wallet and placed another hundred dollar bill on top of the first.

"Do you know Josiah Eaton?"

The youth's eyes were glued in despair to the money that could take him out of that room, out of the town, away.

"Josiah Eaton," the detective repeated. "You want the rest of the money, don't you?"

The youth felt he was drowning and had nothing to

cling to. The detective had been hired to dig up dirt. If Jodie didn't name another important person, the detective might not be satisfied, might not pay him the money. "Yes," he whispered. "I know him."

"He comes here?"

"Yes."

"What does he look like? Can you describe him?"

"He's tall. Fair hair. A big man. He owns the paper." He had seen Josiah Eaton riding down to the yards to confer with Mike, the foreman. He had something to do with the railroad, too. Handsome, he thought. And rich.

"How often does he come here?"

"Now and then."

"Have you ever been to his place?"

"No."

"What does he like to do?"

"You mean . . . the same."

"What precisely?"

The youth was scared. It was different telling the truth about McGiver whom he hated. But five hundred dollars meant a new life. It was the only big change he had ever had.

He drew in a deep breath and plunged ahead. The man from the agency wanted details. He'd give him five hundred dollars worth of details.

"He likes me to play with him and he likes to do other things. He does about everything."

He was shaking.

The pencil inexorably moved across the page as the descriptions got progressively more graphic.

The youth was sweating.

"I want every detail," the man insisted.

Suddenly the youth jumped up. His face was distorted with fear and disgust. "I've told you enough. I won't say any more. Give me the money and let me go."

"I told you it was confidential. I must know everything."

The youth moved like a trapped animal up and down the cage of his room and spewed out the details of his miserable and squalid life. Most were real, some were imaginary, but every word sprang from the pit of his misery and shame.

"Are you always alone with him? Are there others?"

The youth was within arms' reach of the two one hundred dollar bills.

"Yes. Others. Sometimes three or four. I went to his house once and there was a lot of men who was staying there."

"His house in the country?"

"Yes. He took me there in a hack. There were six or seven—including McGiver. They all got naked and they was drunk." The youth broke off with a wail of hopeless disgust at himself. "Oh, it doesn't matter! It doesn't matter!"

He broke down.

At last the detective saw there was no point in questioning him further. The youth was sobbing in a corner with his fists stuffed into his eyes. He took the other three bills from his wallet and placed them neatly on the table, vanishing into the night.

CHAPTER TWENTY

As THE WEEKS PASSED Indian summer settled over Arcadia. Sam Garvey recovered slowly. He was frail and walked with shuffling steps. He knew that physically he would never be the same.

But there were compensations and he found to his surprise that they made up to a degree for his defeat over the strike. Sam had made the discovery that to give in did not necessarily result in a sense of failure and self-abasement; that there was a strange relief in relinquishing a battle and even a reestablishment of strength in another way. That new strength was unfailingly supplied to him by Valeria. He had come to rely on her for everything and he secretly admitted that although her activities in Shacktown were short-sighted and ill-advised and would result in nothing but her being exploited by a lot of worthless people, there was a short-term value in her endeavors. The mills were running smoothly. The faulty machinery had been replaced. The drains had been repaired and no longer regurgitated to the same degree. The smooth conduct of work at the mill resulted from these improvements. It could not be ascribed to Valeria's opening a school and providing a doctor and planning to build a library, all of which he thought ridiculous and wasteful; but he admitted grudgingly that the temporary results were useful. She had bribed the women who had in turn influenced the men. It was an aspect of feminine illogic which he was willing to accept as a temporary measure at this time when he needed a general amnesty because the railroad was under way.

What puzzled Sam a good deal more was the change

in Josiah Eaton's public attitude as it was expressed
in the editorials of *The Courier*. The inflammatory
articles had ceased and Valeria's charities had been
commended. Josiah was even on some sort of committee to help the workers to improve themselves. One
could of course put that down to Josiah's need to curry
favor with the voters, though here too Valeria perhaps had brought to bear some kind of subtle pressure
through her brother. It was certain that Josiah had not
suddenly reversed the tactics of twenty years and been
smitten by remorse for having caused his heart attack.
It might all be due to the effect that Valeria seemed
to have on people, directly or indirectly; she had a
highly developed sense of diplomacy that had its effect
behind the scenes.

Valeria was a mysterious marvel and he would often
watch her as she moved about the house, ministering
to his needs, and wonder if there were indeed another
aspect of life which he had never experienced, except
indirectly through novels. Even they could not ap-
proximate the extraordinary quality that Valeria had.
She belonged to a world of different standards. He
readily admitted that considering the condition he was
in, he was fortunate to have this extraordinary and
selfless being there to mitigate the difficulties of what
some instinct warned him might be the final phase.
She was an idealist, Sam knew, with a strong sense
of duty and with odd and impractical ideas about
sharing money. Of course, it was not money that she
would ever have known how to make herself. She was,
in some way, above that. It was *his* money, amassed
by means she disapproved of. He was astonished that
Valeria should put some of it to ends that were to
him a total waste. Curiously enough, he did not mind
how she chose to waste it because she had earned
the right to her eccentricities by nursing him and,
so to say, nursing the general situation with such unstinting care.

Sometimes in the evening when he sat in the parlor
Valeria had refurbished since the strike, listening to
the curious, soothing sounds that came from the piano,
he wondered if he had come to love her as great

authors wrote of love. He knew nothing about love or
if it had anything to do with this sense of admiration
and dependence. It made him vaguely uncomfortable
and he preferred not to dwell on it. But he was grateful that it was there.

The parlor was unrecognizable. It astonished Sam.
Valeria had bought bolts of lilac linen and had taped
them to the walls with the help of Mary and a step-
ladder. She had covered the chairs in yellow velvet
and used printed chintz in green and lilac for the sofa
and the curtains. A multitude of plants arrived by
freight car, including a mimosa in a tub. The room
looked like some strange kind of female conservatory.
But for some reason he could not pinpoint, Sam Garvey
enjoyed it. It was light and strange and restful; it was
typical of Valeria.

Brass bands, which occasionally blared through the
town, annoyed him so; Sam had rarely listened to music
before. At first the things she played had seemed a
jumble of sounds and discords, but gradually he had
come to distinguish certain pieces. And if he sat
back in his yellow chair and didn't think about it,
these curious repetitions of notes eased him. He did
not attempt to understand them and they had no
value except that she played them and everything
about Valeria had come to have a special significance
for him.

Sam would observe her, as she sat at the piano in
the soft lamplight, her long glossy hair falling loosely
about her shoulders, wearing one of her colored
dresses, and a sense of the inner meaning of life would
come to him like a distant, beguiling echo. Was this
what he had been missing for most of his life?

Valeria had a note from Randolph announcing his
return from the campaign tour. A tentative bridge had
been built between them during the last days of the
strike and it seemed foolish not to resume relations,
although they could never quite be what they had been
before. She decided to ask him to dinner and broached
the subject to Sam.

"Sure. Let him come and see the worst man in Ohio for himself."

Valeria was not without apprehension about this meeting. She trusted Randolph's discretion not to mention the one name that could not be voiced in Sam Garvey's house.

Nonetheless, when he arrived bearing a bunch of golden chrysanthemums, she said quickly in the hall, "Don't discuss anything controversial. He's not up to it yet."

"Oh," Randolph said blandly, "you mean the great pornographer? I am not quite that gauche, Val."

Sam Garvey eyed this raven-haired troublemaker and did his best to scowl.

"You caused me a lot of trouble with your articles," he growled. "If it hadn't been for you and your damned paper that strike wouldn't have happened."

"I venture to say," Randolph replied, "that it would have happened anyway. At the most my articles may have accelerated it a little."

"I can tell you one thing," Sam Garvey said. "You don't know a damned thing about business. Neither of you does. You give away your profits to the people who work for you, you end up as poor as they are. If you Southerners had had any enterprise you wouldn't have lost the War."

"You are right there," Randolph agreed. "Like you, we were behind the times."

Sam grunted.

"Well, that's passed," Valeria intervened. "We are in a period of reconstruction."

The two adversaries eyed each other from opposite ends of a historical perspective.

At dinner Randolph, not to be denied the chance of demonstrating the fallaciousness of Sam's whole scheme of things, expounded the new theories of Karl Marx, an exiled German living in London, whose new book *Capital* he had been studying. The theories were revolutionary in concept. But Randolph was convinced that once they were grasped and digested, they were the inevitable answer to the unchecked growth of industry at the expense of labor.

He spoke with his customary vigor, outlining the principles of Marxism and adding his own explanatory comments. Sam listened with ill-concealed impatience, as though Randolph were some half-baked student reciting jibberish he had learned at school. But he was forced to admire Randolph's command of the language which reminded him of Marcus Eaton who had talked in the same lucid way in their early prospecting days.

"The ultimate fact," Randolph concluded, "is that one either adapts to history or succumbs to it."

"Well, I don't aim to succumb," Sam assured him tartly. "You should try going to work, and I don't mean jotting down words on paper. And when you've made your first million then come and tell me your views on capital and labor. I'll listen with more attention."

The argument continued. They were an ill-matched pair, Valeria thought, waiting for the moment when she would have to interrupt. But by the end of dinner, Randolph had conceded that whatever else he was or wasn't, the old tyrant was a decided character. He was salty, shrewd and, in his own adamantly unrepentant way, uncommon. In comparison to Josiah Eaton, who was himself a cut above the average, this wounded old lion had a knotty and seasoned wickedness which Randolph found intriguing. Sam, in turn, was more entertained than angered by this impetuous theorist who talked so glibly and knew so little about the tactics of making money. In his view his own immense fortune settled the outcome of that discussion.

"Seems to me," he said wryly, as Valeria came 'round to help him up, "that I've landed in a nest of anarchists."

"I might say my sister is a female Daniel in the lion's den," Randolph replied with a good-natured laugh.

"Your sister got a few bad scratches," Sam conceded as he struggled up. "Was Daniel the guy who pulled a thorn out of the lion's paw?"

There was a twinkle in his eye as he took Valeria's arm.

Nancy came, bundled in her winter coat trimmed with a white rabbit collar. She flew into Valeria's arms.

"Oh Miss Lee, I just had to come. I couldn't wait a minute longer. I just *had* to see you."

Valeria kissed and hugged her.

"Do you think grandpapa will *kill* me?" Nancy asked as she unbuttoned her heavy coat. "Things are so *awful* at home. It's worse than being in prison. Mother has gone quite mad and doesn't even *dress*. And *never* goes out and the meals are terrible. And Father eats at the club. I don't know *what's* going on."

"What news do you have of your brother?"

"None, he never writes. He's not coming home for Christmas." She looked down at the floor. "He loved you. He really did. Much more than any of us knew."

Valeria led her into the parlor.

"Sam, here's Nancy."

Nancy hung back, fearful of meeting her grandfather who had, somehow or other, performed the unbelievable feat of marrying her only and most beloved friend.

"Well, Nancy," Sam endeavored to look a trifle less like an ogre than usual, "so you've come to see your new grandmother."

"Oh my!" Nancy sank against Valeria who put an arm around her in support, "I just can't imagine Miss Lee as a grandmother. I mean she just *isn't*. You couldn't be *anybody's* grandmother, much less *mine*."

Randolph dropped by after work. A coterie was forming in the black house under the chimneys. It was Valeria's entourage. Sitting in the plush yellow chair watching them as they sipped their sherry, Sam listened as they exchanged their own special pleasantries. He lost track of what they were saying, but their agreeable voices threaded back and forth, spinning a pattern of words with the incomprehensible charm that had ensnared Thaddeus Brownlow. He found that he was quite willing to be ensnared himself.

Squatting on a little stool before the fire, Nancy was gazing enraptured at Miss Lee's brother. She thought him the handsomest man she had ever seen, with the classic profile and the *terribly* romantic lock of hair that kept falling over his brow and the wonderful, *expressive* voice saying such clever, sophisticated things. He was right out of a novel. She could not resist imagining herself as a heroine suffering so bravely for the *beau capitaine*. Or perhaps Rapunzel letting down her long golden locks from a tower, so that Randolph, a prince in disguise, could climb up and rescue her, curl by curl. If only he would suddenly go quite blind so that she could *dedicate* herself to nursing him in some ruined château in France!

Nancy swooned deliciously inside and her joy was complete when Valeria brought her a glass of sherry and said, "I think Nancy is old enough to join us."

Never before had the room in that house known such mellowness. It was all Valeria's doing, Sam thought, but then everything she did was unlike anything that anyone had ever done before.

In the mornings he was at his desk and the rough-looking men in flashy suits and diamond rings would come to report on the progress of the railroad. The maps would be spread out and pens would point and the red lines would be traced from one state at one end and from another distant state at the other. The two lines were growing closer, creeping across valleys and rivers and tunneling through hills across the endless land.

Only one thing disturbed Sam Garvey. As the days stretched into weeks and the two red lines were approaching their meeting place, a gnawing suspicion nudged and needled his peace of mind. It was all too easy. It was going too well. The shipments of steel and ore were making their scheduled way to Chicago along Josiah's line. It was only a matter of weeks before the new railroad would be completed. Not a single disruptive incident had occurred.

Why had Josiah Eaton made no move?

Out of the blue, one afternoon Valeria received a visit from Ford Hollister whom both she and Randolph had assumed had long since returned to New York.

He appeared, suave and debonaire but with an unhealthy pallor. He was bearing an oil painting in a gilt frame.

"Allow me to be the last to congratulate you," he said with affected irony as he kissed her lightly. "I feel very remiss in not having called on you sooner or even written, but I've been completely cut off from the world for the reasons you know."

"I had no idea you were still here. Randy is always asking if I have heard from you. How is Althea?"

"Much, much better. Almost herself again. She has been asking for you."

There was something forced and artificial in his manner which Valeria found disconcerting.

"I have brought you a wedding present," he announced. "Something for the lady who has everything or could have," he glanced 'round the hall, "if she wasn't for some reason living here. My, my!" he touched her cheek, "such momentous changes! I can hardly believe what has happened to my chillun. You are now the queen of Arcadia and Randy the *éminence grise* of our future governor. I am dying to know how it all happened."

His manner was as artificial as a courtesan's. There was none of his old wry humor left.

"Come and meet Sam," Valeria suggested, "and bring the picture. I need something nice to hang in the living room."

"Yes, I can imagine," he said archly as they crossed the hall.

He paused in the parlor doorway. "I can see you have been at work. Definitely a Valeria room."

Sam who was ensconced in his favorite chair looked 'round, at once suspicious of this visitor.

"This is Ford Hollister—my husband," Valeria introduced them. "You remember my telling you; Ford and I grew up together in Atlanta."

"Mr. Garvey!" Ford shook the rough, gnarled hand. "I won't say that I've heard so much about you. In Arcadia one hears of no one else, except your daughter, of course!"

Sam scowled. He had no patience with dandified men and was embarrassed by them.

It was dreadful, Valeria thought. What had happened to Ford? He was like an actor performing in some highly stylized play. His face, under the malicious smiles and smirks, had no expression of any kind.

"Ford has brought us a picture as a wedding present," Valeria said to cover her embarrassment. "Ford is a talented painter. He used to do portraits and very good they were."

"That was in my antebellum days when Southerners had time for such trifles." He turned the painting 'round for them to see. "I expect you'll recognize it," he said to Valeria. "It's a copy I made in Venice on my honeymoon."

Sam was shocked by this portrayal of a naked woman, apparently floating in the sky, with a shower of gold coins falling into her lap.

"It's lovely, Ford. Titian, isn't it? I am delighted. We'll hang it here."

"What is that woman doing?" Sam demanded as though catching someone in a shameful act.

"It's Danaë and the shower of gold. Do you know the legend?" Ford asked with deliberate condescension. "She was the daughter of a king who had been told by an oracle that his grandson would murder him. As Danaë was his only child, he shut her up in a tower of bronze, guarded by savage dogs. Zeus, the father of the gods, fell in love with her and managed to seduce her by turning himself into a shower of gold. Ladies, I understand, favor that kind of metamorphosis."

"Some gentlemen, too," Valeria reminded him.

They both laughed for no reason that Sam could understand. To appear what he hoped was proper for Valeria's sake, he said, "You did that? It's a good picture, I guess. One can see what it represents though I don't much care for the subject matter."

"Ah, you're not classically inclined."

"You're mistaken, Ford. Sam has a whole library of classics. He's far better read than you or I."

Gratified by her defense of him, Sam suggested on an impulse, "Why don't you paint Valeria? I'd like a picture to hang over the mantel. I can't see any more what that damned thing is." He indicated a landscape that had long since receded into obscurity under a layer of factory grime.

"I'd be delighted. Would you permit me, Mrs. Garvey?"

Valeria did not wlecome the idea. Ford's manner was so strained and unnatural. As he turned his face to the light, she perceived a thin coat of flesh-colored paint under his eyes.

"Mind you, I'd want her with her clothes on," Sam insisted. "You could paint her in her riding habit. She looks good in that. I'll pay you the going rate."

"I wouldn't think of it, Mr. Garvey. You must allow me to give it to you as a present. What do you say, Valeria? Besides, it would give Althea so much pleasure to see you."

"Couldn't you paint me here?" Valeria asked doubtfully.

"The music room at Fairlawn has a perfect north light. You can combine your sessions with me with your afternoon rides. You go riding out our way, I believe."

How did he know that? And what was he getting at? Valeria asked herself quickly. There was something sly and conspiratorial under Ford's waspish manner.

"We could drive out together, Sam, if you'd like," she suggested. "It would do you good to get out sometimes."

"I have too much to do, my dear."

Valeria reluctantly agreed.

As they were going back across the hall, Ford said in a theatrical whisper, "He's an authentic tycoon I can see. Quite in the grand manner."

He bundled himself into his fox-lined coat and drew the collar up around his chin. He was a man playing a woman's part.

"Well, my dearest Val, I can't wait to hear the whole astonishing story."

But as he opened the door, the mask fell from him

for a moment and she saw in his eyes an unhappiness, bordering on despair.

"We never guessed what would happen to us, did we?" he asked looking down the path toward the waiting buggy. "How's dear Randy?"

"He's well and busy," she said, touched by an old pity.

"Does he like Josiah?" he asked, bringing himself to look at her.

"Yes, he seems to. I don't see him often. We had a falling out after I married Sam."

He kissed her abruptly and said, "Please come. You don't know what it will do for both of us."

She watched as he went down the path. He had loved them and stood by them and however much she disliked going to that home she could not, out of a sad gratitude for the past, desert him.

It was a clear cold day when she set out for Fairlawn. Valeria had not ridden this way for some time, but since Josiah's letters had ceased she was less apprehensive about meeting him. He had at last understood her silence, she presumed, and had accepted the fact that she had lowered the curtain for good on their brief liaison.

She rode up the hill to The Heights without as much as a glance at Ida's mansion and cantered along Tremont Avenue. The sky was gray with a promise of snow. Mimosa was delighted to please her mistress, exhilarated by the air and the exercise.

Valeria turned down the driveway of the Haverfield estate. The sycamores, denuded of leaves, had a stark and funereal look. The mansion, with most of its shutters closed, had a deserted air.

She rang the bell. The door was opened by the Italian, insolently good-looking and peremptory.

"Could you have my horse taken to the stables, please?" she asked.

"I will attend to it. Come this way."

He led her to a room which she had not seen before. It had a high, half-moon window where an easel had been set up with a canvas in readiness. Ford rose to greet her.

"So glad you came," he kissed her.

Ford led her over to Althea who was lying on a chaise longue with a fur rug over her legs. Althea's face was stark with a curious, strained rigidity, but her great eyes lit up with pathetic pleasure as Valeria took her hand.

"I'm so pleased to see you, Althea," she said gently.

Althea seemed to find difficulty in speaking, as though the words stuck in her throat. She clung to Valeria's hand and then suddenly said, "Yes, I've asked Ford often. He said you were busy and couldn't come."

"My husband has been ill," she explained. "I wasn't able to leave him, but he is better now."

"Oh, then you will come often?" Althea asked. "I want you to play for me . . . I remember how well you perform."

"Of course, I will," Valeria touched her shoulder. "Would you like me to play something now before Ford starts painting?"

"Please, please do!" Althea exclaimed like a child. "I am better now, too. We . . . shan't be going away —not till spring. It's so lonely here."

The great desolate frightened eyes followed Valeria as she went to the piano.

"I remember what it was you liked."

"The barcarolle!" Althea clasped her hands as though Valeria were giving her the rarest gift in the world.

Valeria took in the room as she ran her deft fingers over the keys. She felt an overwhelming pity for the gaunt woman seemingly paralyzed on the sofa, and for Ford standing before the fireplace. He seemed without color or entity like some mechanical fixture that was part of the furnishings. They were a doomed couple, she thought, prisoners of a doomed marriage.

Althea seemed quite transported by the music. "Oh, that was lovely! It was quite—transcendent! Oh please, you must play some more."

"After tea," Ford said out of his gray anonymity. "I don't want to miss the light."

"How would you like me?" Valeria asked. "Standing or sitting?"

"Will it tire you to stand? I'd like it to be full length and that habit shows off your elegant figure."

"Oh yes, she is elegant!" Althea exclaimed. "You have such remarkable coloring and how wise of you to wear gray. My mother wears gray, but it doesn't become her. You have such beautiful eyes. I never saw anyone with such eyes, so lushly green like jade. I have a beautiful jade ring. I must give it to you. Ford," she suddenly twisted herself around, "Please get my ring. I want to give it to Valeria."

Suddenly this piece of jewelry was of the utmost importance to her. Valeria bent and kissed her. "You mustn't, Althea dear."

"Oh, but I want you to have it. It will be perfect for you. Ford—!"

"I'll fetch it later, Althea," Ford said warningly. "Now relax, my dear, the light is not very good today."

Althea sighed. She was greatly hurt and frustrated by his refusal to fetch the ring.

Valeria took up her position in the window across part of which Ford had drawn a dark gray velvet curtain.

"It will be a study in grays, subtle tonalities as befits the subject." He started to sketch out Valeria's outline on the canvas.

Althea had sunk into a mood of despondency. A silence of quiet concentration enfolded Ford and Valeria.

Suddenly Althea, as though feeling it incumbent upon her to make conversation, said in a loud voice, "Do you read Greek, Valeria? I've been reading Sappho. I mean I read her all the time. It is so tantalizing that the poems are just fragments. Sometimes I feel that I almost know what's missing. They are so lovely and the translations are so bad. I sometimes think I'd like to translate them again myself. Do you think I could?"

"Why don't you?" Valeria suggested. "If you feel them so deeply, I'm sure you would do them well."

"You hear, Ford? You hear? Valeria thinks I could translate Sappho. Greek is such a wonderful language, It's so vivid and delicate and yet strong. English is heavy and blurred. Perhaps I will try. Yes, I'll try."

She relapsed into silence. Valeria, sunk into her own abstracted thoughts, was hardly aware that Josiah Eaton had entered the room.

"Hello, Josiah," Ford said, putting down his charcoal. "How nice of you to stop by."

"I hope I'm not intruding."

They were shaking hands. He was bending to shake Althea's hand. They were talking. Valeria had frozen and was aware of these sounds and movements at a distance. He was there. He was in the room.

"You know Mrs. Garvey, don't you?"

He was coming toward her. She stared fixedly in front of her. She could feel the weight of his presence.

"How are you, Mrs. Garvey?"

She glanced briefly at him and away. She inclined her head without answering. Why was he staring at her in such an obvious way?

Fortunately, as though instinctively averting a crisis, Althea asked shrilly, "Have you come to tea? Ford, ring for tea. It is so nice when people drop in for tea, almost like being in New York."

Valeria was rooted to the floor. Her gaze was fixed at a windowpane across which a spray of ivy had wandered. She could see exactly the chiseled outlines of the leaves.

Josiah, defeated, had turned away. "I'm afraid I'm interrupting."

"No, sit down. I just want to continue until the light goes."

Ford resumed his sketching. Josiah was sitting down somewhere out of her sight but she could feel his gaze upon her. Why couldn't she get control of herself? Why couldn't she stop staring at the spray of ivy?

Althea exclaimed, "Isn't Valeria beautiful in that habit? It will make a beautiful portrait. Ford is doing it all in grays."

Why, Valeria thought, as a sort of panic seized her, couldn't that idiotic woman shut her mouth? She wanted to move and could not. She fought the hot flush that she felt rising to her cheeks. Was he really there? Or was it a hallucination? She did not want to confront him in flesh and blood.

He sat still, his handsome frame at ease in the gilt French chair.

"How is your campaign going?" Ford inquired.

"Well, I think." His voice sounded deeper than she remembered.

"I was forgetting," Ford went on, "Randy Lee's working for you. What does he do, ward off the importunate females?"

"He helps me to write my speeches. And—" his voice fell away, "other things."

"I'm sure you will make an excellent governor. Though it's a mystery to me why anyone goes into politics. Have you set your sights on the White House? That is the next step, isn't it?"

"Oh," Josiah laughed, "I'm not looking that far ahead."

"How exciting!" Althea put in. "To become President. I can't say I care for President Grant. He's so stolid and pompous. I can't think of any president I've liked. Lincoln tried to be so homespun and authentic."

"He was a fine man in his way," Josiah said.

Valeria was immensely relieved that at this juncture the Italian brought in tea. He set the tray down with the silver tea things on a table near Althea.

Althea twisted herself 'round in her awkward way. "Valeria, will you pour out tea? I can't lift that teapot lying down. It's so heavy. I'm not in favor of teapots," she laughed. "I like the Russian way. A samovar. You just turn a little tap."

Valeria heard herself say in a remarkably cool and distant voice, "I'm afraid I can't stay for tea. I have to get home. My husband doesn't like to be left this long."

Althea let out a wail, "Oh, don't go. It's not late. Valeria, please! I want you to play for me again."

Valeria came to her and said firmly, "Next time, Althea. I simply must go. Sam will be needing me." Forcing herself to look past Josiah toward Ford, she asked, "Will you send your man to bring Mimosa?"

Ford was aware of the tension that had arisen. He looked at Josiah who was looking at Valeria in a wounded, bewildered way. "Yes, of course."

"Good-bye, Althea," Valeria kissed her. "It was lovely to see you."

"You will come again. Soon again." Althea clung to her hand. "I want to give you the ring."

"Soon. But you mustn't give me the ring. Wear it and then you will think of me."

"Oh, but I do think of you. Often." The plaintive voice followed Valeria as she crossed the room. Ford was holding the door. She was thankful to find herself in the hall.

"Is something wrong, dear?" Ford inquired.

She said sharply in a low voice, "You did not tell me he was coming. You know very well I cannot meet him because of my husband."

"I'd forgotten. It's all so complicated—what with Randy writing those articles."

"Ford, don't play these sorts of games with me."

"What games?" he asked with an unconvincing innocence. "He drops by sometimes. He lives just down the road."

She was angry now. As Valeria pulled on her kid gloves and picked up her crop from the hall table, she said, "If you want to paint me, you must do it at my house. I cannot come here again."

"Don't you think," Ford suggested as she stood aside for him to open the door, "that you're being a trifle dramatic? Josiah hasn't insulted you."

"I think you did this on purpose because you like to create situations. It amuses you, but it doesn't amuse me."

"It doesn't amuse me to see you behaving like an indignant schoolgirl," Ford said tartly.

She went past him and stood outside. It was true. She had behaved absurdly. She had betrayed herself and embarrassed them. She turned swiftly to apologize, but Ford had already closed the door.

She stood there in the biting air, at odds with herself, impatiently tapping her riding boots with her crop.

She heard the door open again and knew that it was Josiah standing behind her.

"I'm sorry if I offended you," he said in a low voice in which she could detect his pain. "It was not Hollister's fault. I didn't know you were here."

She was staring at the ground. Her cheeks were burning. "It doesn't matter."

"I think you know that you could have answered one of my letters."

"I never read your letters!" she flared up, moving away.

"They were not easy for me to write. It wouldn't have hurt you to have read them," he said after a moment.

"I told you once before and I meant it; there can be nothing more between us. You should have taken me at my word."

"Yes, I should have. It would have been the right thing to do. But I couldn't."

Valeria could feel his eyes on her neck. Why, she wondered in despair, didn't the Italian bring Mimosa around?

"Is it really impossible to meet? Just to go for a ride together?"

She turned sharply. She saw that her attitude had stricken him. "You know very well what would happen. You're running for governor. If anyone saw you with me . . ."

"We could ride behind my house. The place is empty." Receiving nothing in response but her harsh impatience, Josiah nonetheless added, "You could at least have come to the meetings. I only went because of you."

His hangdog persistence, so out of keeping with everything he was, annoyed her more than anything about this hopeless, inopportune meeting.

"It seems impossible to get you to see—"

At this point the Italian appeared with Mimosa.

She mounted quickly and turned Mimosa toward the drive.

He came to her side and said doggedly, "Don't be like this, Valeria. It is hurting both of us."

"It is not hurting me in the least," she said between her teeth.

He put his hand on the reins as he had done once before. "You must see me. We must talk. It can't go on like this."

Suddenly Valeria's patience snapped. In a flash of wild exasperation, she raised her arm and struck him with her crop. The blow fell on his shoulders, grazing his cheek.

"For God's sake, *let me alone!*"

She spurred Mimosa savagely and cantered off.

In utter dejection Josiah watched her go.

The Italian had been observing this scene through a crack in the front door. As Ford came up behind him he said slyly, "He loves her, that Mr. Eaton, and she loves him."

They watched Josiah as he walked away, head down, with his long and loose-limbed stride.

"How could you tell?"

"She hit him. Her eyes flash. Oh yes, she love him that Mrs. Garvey."

Ford turned the Italian's head toward him. "Like this, you mean?" He kissed him hard on the mouth. His hand moved down the muscled back to the sturdy buttocks.

The Italian allowed himself to be kissed and fondled. When Ford released him, he ran a contemptuous finger under one of Ford's eyes.

"You are painted up like a whore."

ℰ𝔛 CHAPTER TWENTY-ONE 𝔛ℰ

HELEN TENNANT WAS GETTING very bored and impatient with Henry Brewster.

He had finally handed over the money to buy the yards of pink material with flowers to make the curtains. By dint of weeks of her wheedling and pouting and dropping hints, he had stretched a point and given her enough to buy some more material to cover the sofa and the chairs. But these innovations only pointed up how threadbare the carpet was. Henry balked at a new rug. The flat still looked dingy because it was dingy and Arcadia was dingy and so was Henry and so, she was beginning to feel, was she.

Part of the problem was that Donovan had left to find a better job in a large slaughterhouse elsewhere and she missed not so much him, because he was a great unwholesome clod, but rather the one thing he had to offer, that splendid appendage which had filled her with so much satisfaction. After Donovan's bull-like assaults which had stretched her to absolute delight, Henry's insipid fumblings amounted to no more than perfunctory intrusions. They not only disappointed her physically, but left her mentally frustrated. However she looked at it and whatever allowances she tried to make, after Donovan, Henry Brewster was a letdown.

She was bored with her life in Arcadia and was day by day, night by night, waiting around for Henry, determined to get out of it. Time was passing. She was not getting any younger or prettier. There were distinct saggings and bulgings and floppings in places difficult to disguise. She tinted her hair and pulled in her stays till she was breathless, but it was no use pretending. If she didn't get to Chicago soon, it would be unlikely that Helen would catch an established gentleman who could support her in the style which she now, with a touch of desperation, craved.

Henry would rock by the window staring into the empty street and Helen would sit on her newly upholstered sofa refurbishing one of her blouses that was past repair. He was occupied with his thoughts about the singular behavior of the killer whale he was married to and Helen was occupied by unkind thoughts about her protector who was as stingy with money as he was with details. "You don't tell me anything," she complained as usual. "You go on saying she's behaving strangely, but you don't tell me how."

Henry Brewster tilted back the rocker and gazed at the ceiling. "Ever since the old man married, she's been cranky and she's getting crankier. She's up to something and whatever it is, it ain't good."

"Up to what?" Helen demanded.

"Can't say precisely. It's to do with the railroad. She's spending money."

"Buying shares, you mean?" Helen ventured shrewdly.

"Maybe. She's taken all her cash out of the bank and she's hocked most of her jewels. Now, they were the only things that meant anything to her. She loves those gems more than she loves the children."

"That's not saying much," Helen pointed out. "She doesn't seem to care a rap for Nancy, and Hank's not even coming home for Christmas."

"Those gems meant a lot to her and they were worth a lot."

"How much did she raise on them?"

"Plenty. She doesn't wear a single one of her diamond rings. Not one."

He started rocking again.

"And her social life. You know how she talked about her social life. Her dinners and meetings and building an opera house. Never mentions them. She hasn't had a dinner in weeks now. You know something?" He fixed Helen with a jaundiced stare. "We had beef hash for dinner—*twice*—last night and the night before. Hash, mind you! With a French cook. Now that's not like Ida." He rocked in perplexity. "It's not like Ida the least bit. She's plotting something."

Helen examined her blouse. It was a wretched old thing and she could only wear it around the house. If only Henry would stop blabbing on about awful Ida and give her some money for clothes! She needed a new outfit. Several! A long way she'd get if she showed up in Chicago looking like a rag doll from a rummage sale!

"What's happening with the new railroad?" she asked. "When do they plan to open it?"

Henry shrugged. "Soon, I guess. There's talk it's the biggest deal the old man's ever pulled off. It'll make him a multimillionaire ten times over."

"It's about time you stood up for your rights," Helen said firmly. "All that money in the family and you just struggle along at the bank and go home and eat beef hash. You've got no pride, Henry, that's your trouble, and no ambition. If I'd married into a family with all that money and about to get a whole lot more, I'd have seen I was taken care of. I'd demand my share. You're her husband. You're the father of her children. What she has belongs to you, her gems belong to you, even the house belongs to you—in a court of law—if you'd stand up for yourself." She sighed. "You're dumb, Henry."

He didn't refute this opinion.

"Your children will inherit everything, won't they? If Ida dropped dead, they'd get everything. And what would you get, eh? Damn nothing, as far as I can see."

"I'd get something," Henry opined without conviction.

Helen perched herself on Henry's knee and they rocked uncomfortably together. "We could have such a nice time, Henry," she said in a little girl voice, twirling one of Henry's locks around her finger. "We could go to Chicago, New York, *and even* Europe. You never go anywhere or do anything and it's because you don't *ask*." She laid her cheek against his and cooed, "Why don't you ask, Henry? Ask Ida for a nice lump sum and let's dress up and go somewhere and have *fun*."

The prospect of having fun did not fire Henry with much enthusiasm.

Helen said mournfully, "You just don't try, Henry. You don't try for me. You don't care about poor little old Helen one tiny bit."

Helen weighed more than was conducive to caring for anything much, least of all having fun. Her fingers fumbled coyly between the buttons of his shirt and sidled 'round under his vest to tweak his nipple.

"We could have fun, Henry. Lots and lots of fun, if you'd only get hold of a nice fat chunk of money."

She pinched his nipple hard and he flinched. Their heads bumped.

"Don't do that!"

Helen, affronted by his lack of response to her seductive foreplay, climbed off Henry's knee.

"I don't know why I waste time on you. You're no damn good." Her fleshy bosom rose in righteous aggrievedness. "You're no good and no fun and you don't try." She thought of Donovan's splendid appendage and flung at him, "And you're no damn good in bed!"

She flounced out into the kitchen.

Henry rocked. Ask Ida for money! From that monolith who barely noted his existence? He remembered with dull horror the nights after their marriage when Ida had lain there beside him waiting for him to do his duty. She had lain there in such a monumental, angry silence that he had been too abashed to perform. He had tried surreptitiously to achieve an erection. "Stop that, Henry!" she had commanded. From that moment Henry had started drooping. Everything about Ida made him weak. He was too far sunk in moribund uselessness to find the courage to confront her about anything, least of all money. She might give him something one day but only, he surmised, to get rid of him. The alternative was Helen with her ceaseless questioning and complaints and stupid little advances that failed to arouse him. Pinching his nipple! That had hurt. And it was vaguely indecent. There was a lot about Helen he found indecent. Why was he rocking there? He sympathized with the emptiness of the street because he felt equally empty and useless and deserted.

He sat motionless and stared. For once, surprisingly, something occurred to him. If he could find out exactly what Ida was up to . . . why she had taken all her ready cash from the bank and hocked her gems . . . perhaps there might be some way not yet apparent to him that he might get something out of her.

Ida Brewster was busy. When she had to, she could summon up the same degree of concentration as her father. He was totally absorbed in the building of his railroad and she was totally absorbed in getting control of it. This was her great scheme and her obsession. She wanted to get control so that she would be in a position to dictate terms and her terms would be annihilating as far as Valeria Lee was concerned. If her father refused, she had a trump card of unparalleled vindictiveness up her sleeve and she intended to play it if she had to, at exactly the right moment. It was the one thing she knew that would force her father's hand. He had capitulated over the strike, but that was nothing to the degree of abasement she had in store. Like a gambler staking his total fortune on the turn of a card, with her instinct for taking calculated risks, inherited from the man with millions who had taken a good many prodigious risks himself, Ida was prepared to stake everything to gain this triumph. It would establish her once and for all as the ruling force in the Garvey family, the sole and rightful heir to the Garvey millions. And in some deeper sense which she did not consciously acknowledge, it would relieve her of the sense of inferiority that had dogged her all through life.

She sat in her dressing gown at her desk in the study, as Sam Garvey sat at his desk. And as he daily traced in red ink the two lines that were drawing closer and closer, so Ida drafted cables to brokerage firms in New York, Boston and Chicago and bought more and more shares just as fast and as often as they became avail-

—

able. Bartlett, the coachman, was constantly driving up
and down the long hill from The Heights to the office
of the telegraph company. The wires sizzled with Ida's
orders. She kept a book of figures, as her father kept
his books, and her desk became a wild disorder of
scraps of paper covered with calculations. Ida was not
the daughter of Sam Garvey for nothing.

It was a long time since "the" Mrs. Brewster had
needed money, but now she needed a great deal and
she needed it fast. She had pawned her jewels and she
had raised, without Henry's knowing, a mortgage on
her property, but it was not enough. She needed a
very big sum, something in the nature of two million
dollars. There was only one asset remaining to her,
but it was the most valuable one she possessed. She
was the daughter of a man known throughout the
country as a steel and iron-ore king. The mills testified
to his power and financial worth and the shipments
that rumbled along the tracks to Chicago were collateral for almost any figure she cared to name. She
was his only child and her children were still minors.
Henry was practically nonexistent. When her father
did his paternal duty and kicked the bucket, she stood
to be one of the richest women in America. But her
father had not died and had acquired a second wife.

Ida paced around her study and paced around her
parlor that was now covered with a film of dust because she had no interest in giving orders to the servants
and the servants, according to their nature, did no work
they were not told to do. Ida sat down and cogitated
then went upstairs. She had prospects that were potentially prodigious, but she needed proof.

Sometimes when the hypertension induced by her
scheming became unbearable, she would drink to calm
her nerves and the terrible temptation would seize her
to read that statement which she already knew by
heart.

In the bottom drawer of her sadly depleted jewel
case was the signed statement of the detective concerning the revolting practices indulged in by Josiah
Eaton and his friend McGiver. It lay there like a
scorpion waiting to administer a fatal sting.

There, lying in a pale blue envelope that was so deceptively innocent, were the pages, so neatly written, so precise and so explicit, that could ruin Josiah Eaton and ruin him for good. When she held the report in her hands, she had the grimly pleasurable sensation of weighing Josiah's life. The power of destruction which she could now wield over him almost equaled the sexual fulfillment he might have given her. And she was justified in having bribed the dreadful youth to make his confession and justified in having paid the detective so exorbitant a fee because Josiah's crimes were so horrendous and depraved.

She would swallow a gulp of whiskey and lie down on the bed and open the envelope. She was like an addict indulging in some unmentionable vice. She would reread the detective's statement and her head would fill with obscene images.

Whiskey and more whiskey until her inflamed, unbalanced mind reeled into burning sleep.

She would drag herself up next morning, pull on her dressing gown and, with trembling legs, support herself on the stair rail. She would stumble, step by leaden step, downstairs. "Coffee!" she would shout and Milly would come clattering down from the floor above with her hair in a tangle and no apron. Ida would find herself, dazed and shaken, at her desk. As she drank cup after cup of steaming coffee, her head would clear and she would return to her calculations and draft more cables.

She decided that there was only one way to get the money she needed to complete her plan. For the first time since her marriage she needed Henry.

Ida bathed and dressed and did her hair and went downstairs and waited. She was formidably composed, as though she were waiting to receive guests for one of her *important* dinners.

Henry slunk in with the evening *Courier*.

"Good evening, Henry."

"Evening," he replied, surprised by this cordial greeting.

"Did you have a good day at the bank, dear?"

Henry was unnerved by this inquiry. "Same as usual."

"You look tired, Henry. Sit down."

Henry sat.

Ida rose, a juggernaut of solicitude. "Would you like a drink, Henry?"

"Well . . . I guess . . ." Henry was now frankly frightened.

"I have been thinking, Henry; it is a long time since you had a holiday," Ida said with a purr like a Bengal tiger trying to pass itself off as a tabby cat.

"A holiday?"

"Yes," Ida said, "you should take a little trip somewhere. You could take the waters. Saratoga. Why don't you go, Henry?"

Haddock appeared. Since the great change in Ida's way of life, this representative of superior serfdom had submerged himself in the Brewsters' cellar. He was working his way through the Burgundys and was approaching the champagnes.

"Bring Mr. Brewster a whiskey and soda," Ida commanded.

"Yes, madam," Haddock agreed.

Ida returned to her chair and sat very upright and imposing.

"You should take a holiday. I'm sure Mr. McGraw will agree you richly deserve it."

Henry knew with dread that Ida was leading up to something and that whatever it was, it was bound to be something he didn't want to do.

Ida proceeded with this terrible cordiality that made Henry feel as though he were being bound hand and foot to a stake. "There's something I want to ask you, Henry. You remember when my father made his will? Who actually witnessed it?"

"McGraw, I think."

"Only McGraw?"

"I guess someone else at the bank." —

"You couldn't, of course, because you are a legatee," she pointed out.

"Well, I don't know that I am. But I am a member

of the family," Henry asserted his right to this doubtful privilege.

"I'm sure my father has left you *something*," Ida allowed, as if to say every dog was entitled to a bone. "Where is the will kept, Henry?"

"In your father's safe deposit box," he replied, surprised.

"And he has the key, of course."

"Well, yes."

Ida pondered this self-evident fact.

"And who else," she inquired at last, "might have a key?"

"The bank. There's a master key."

"Who at the bank?"

"It's locked in the main safe."

"And who has the key to the main safe?"

"The bank."

"Don't go on saying 'the bank', Henry," Ida said impatiently. "*Who* at the bank?"

"McGraw, I guess."

Ida thought and then asked in the smallest voice of which she was capable and which sounded as incongruous as the peep of a penny whistle emerging from a trombone, "Do you?"

Henry gaped, "Me?"

"You're a partner. Could you get the key to the main safe and open my father's deposit box?"

Henry stammered, "Why?"

She fired her broadside, "I want my father's will for a week. And I want you to get it for me."

Into the chasm of shock that yawned before Henry Brewster entered Haddock with a whiskey and soda unsteadily balanced on a tray. Henry reached for the glass but his nerve failed. Ida knew that he was cowed, that he was helpless and that he would shortly, after the expected number of feeble objections, do what she wanted.

"Put the drink down, Haddock."

Haddock managed to distinguish the table from the pattern on the carpet and placed the glass on it. He walked with superb equilibrium to the door and passed through it into the dim beyond.

Ida looked at her husband as she might have looked at a worm she was about to crush.

"I want the will, Henry. And when you've got it for me you can go on a holiday."

At that moment, in the depths of his debasement, Henry Brewster's long since crushed sense of self-preservation stirred. The specter of Helen Tennant rose like a ghost from his subconscious. She had sat on his knee and tweaked his nipple and mentioned a lump sum. It had never occurred to Henry that the occasion might arise when he could extract anything from the titanic adversary to whom he was, by some quirk of destiny, married.

But it seemed to him, as he teetered on the brink of succumbing as usual to Ida's superior strength, that such an occasion had arrived.

In his colorless voice he asked, "What is it worth to you?"

Ida was not sure she had heard right. "Worth?"

Henry nodded, staring at the carpet which had turned into a pond of uncertainty.

"Worth in money."

"That is not your business," Ida retorted. "What I choose to do with the will is my concern, not yours."

Henry just managed to keep afloat long enough to mutter, "I mean for me."

Ida was thunderstruck. Was Henry daring to question her, to make objections, to obstruct?

"I don't understand you. I've said you could have a holiday."

It was too late to turn back. Henry managed to look at her and she saw with amazement and indignation that despite his consummate weakness, Henry was resisting.

"Suppose I don't want——"

"Want what?" she asked fiercely.

"A holiday."

"Of course you want a holiday," she swept this objection aside. "I will give you enough to take a holiday in Saratoga. What else could you possibly want?"

Henry sank, as it were, for the third time, and in

his drowning stupor his whole life passed before him. He was altogether astonished to hear himself say in quite a distinct voice:

"A lump sum."

Two days later Ida Brewster, wrapped like a mummy in an immense fur coat, and crowned by a huge black hat with a raven skewered to its brim, departed on the morning train for Chicago.

She traveled in state in her father's private car.

CHAPTER TWENTY-TWO

NANCY SAT on her little stool in the lilac room gazing raptly at Randolph. She was hopelessly in love. Of course she was far too timid to say anything. Words would have spoiled the sheer perfection of their relationship. He would smile at her vaguely sometimes, scarcely aware of her existence. She would gather his smiles like the rarest of flowers and press them in her memory book. Unlike most romantics she had found that the reality far exceeded her expectations.

Ford was adding a few touches to the almost finished portrait. It was a distinguished likeness. He had caught the imperious tilt of Valeria's nose and the enigmatic gaze of her misty green eyes. The grays and mauves of the background and a touch of light green on a Chinese vase created an impression of elegance and distinction.

Valeria had come to terms with her old friend. He had agreed to continue the painting at Sam's house. despite Sam's continual interruptions and suggestions. She, in turn, whenever she learned through Randolph that Josiah was out of town, would ride out to Fairlawn and spend an hour or two with Althea, playing for her and listening to her translations of Sappho. She was impressed by Althea's skill, by her feeling for words and by the genuine beauty of the lyrics she had built around the Greek fragments. In an odd way she had grown fond of this highly intelligent and unfortunate young woman who clung to her company and was so eager for her praise. Only the presence of the Italian servant disturbed her. She knew that Althea disliked him and was perhaps afraid of him and that some faintly sinister involvement existed between the three.

Ford had been more like his old self during their sittings. Being with Randy again restored his good humor, and his waspish wit was no longer marred by malice. His love for Randy, she saw, was the one pure emotion of his life.

Sam had gone a long way in his new role as an art patron. He had had his chair moved so that he could watch the proceedings from stage to stage. The construction of a portrait was as mysterious to him as the music Valeria played.

"I want to see her hands," he had insisted as Ford labored over the luminous pallor of Valeria's face. "And don't make her shorter than she is. I don't care how big it is. You can add on another foot if need be."

"You are not permitted to comment, Mr. Garvey," Ford had warned him. "You may watch, but you may not comment."

"Why the hell not? I'm paying for this thing."

"I told you when I agreed to paint Valeria, this portrait is a gift."

"I don't want gifts," Sam had retorted. "I want a portrait that's like a photograph, not like that damned naked woman floating around in space."

"You will not get a photograph," Ford had told him. "You will get a portrait of Valeria's soul."

"What do you know about her soul?" the prospective art collector demanded.

"Oh, you will see. Be patient."

Sam grunted, unappeased. "I want something that looks like her. God damn, I should know what my own wife looks like." It was the first time he had ever referred to Valeria as his wife.

She smiled across at him. "Hush, Sam, Ford knows what I look like, though his vision of me may be different from yours."

"A person looks like he looks," Sam thumped the floor with his stick, thoroughly put out by this artistic double-talk.

But as the sittings proceeded he gradually became

silent, watching the emergence of the familiar figure on the canvas with mystified concentration.

On that particular evening he was not watching Ford, nor was he listening to the music. He was troubled. He could not rid himself of a gnawing apprehension that something about the way things were going was very wrong. Something underhanded was moving like a dark amphibian through the unnaturally calm waters toward his flagship. The railroad was almost finished. Nothing to disrupt its completion had occurred.

He had all along accepted the inevitable. Josiah Eaton would, in some way, retaliate. But Josiah appeared to be exclusively concerned with his campaign. He was traveling about the state making speeches and getting himself known and winning adherents. Sometimes he took Randolph with him on short journeys, more often he went alone. It was unusual for Josiah Eaton to be alone. He had always thrived on company. Like all people endowed with charm, he needed to win admirers just as a peacock, by its nature, spreads its tail. But now he saw no one except on business, and that mostly political. He was selling his country place. He lived in bachelor seclusion above *The Courier*. He traveled into small towns and smaller hamlets, to remote farming communities. He talked and listened and seemed genuinely concerned and sincerely eager to fulfill his promises and obligations.

Sam Garvey could not understand it.

Nothing in his long life had come easily. There had never been a deal made or a step taken or a plan proposed that had not entailed a struggle. Sam enjoyed a fight. It was test of skill, ingenuity and endurance. Josiah's silence and his apparent indifference to the completion of the railroad irked him, troubled him and rankled him to a deep suspicion.

He missed Jim Pryor who was still in the hospital nursing his broken jaw. His jaw had mended, though he salivated from the corner of his mouth. His head had mended, though he suffered from blinding headaches. Valeria had insisted that Sam pay all his medical expenses. It was another of her charitable whims.

He could have discussed things with Pryor who could have put out feelers and found out what Josiah was really up to. His enmity with Josiah had long since become a component of his life. He relied on it and without it he felt in some way unsteady and bereft.

The new foreman, Murdock, was a stranger who had been hired from another mill. He was burly and forthright and had opinions which Sam disliked. He was on good terms with the men, which Sam disliked even more. Everything was changing. Sometimes he had the disagreeable sensation that his whole life was slipping away and that he was stranded in an ebbing tide.

Then one evening, Nancy appeared with a suitcase and asked if she might stay because she was afraid of being alone in her mother's mansion. Sam did not think it strange that Ida should have gone on a visit to Chicago or that Henry should have gone on a holiday to Saratoga. What either of them did was no concern of his. He had no reason to connect Ida's abrupt departure with the railroad. He had allotted her and the children shares because whatever rifts might have occurred within the family, the Garvey enterprises were still a family affair.

The men in flashy suits and Mr. Brownlow's impeccable representative came to report. And all the reports were good. Just because they were so persistently and unnaturally good Sam Garvey was worried and unable to sleep at night.

Cascades of liquid notes ran from Valeria's fingers. She looked very beautiful, Sam thought, in a deep purple dress, cut very severely as all her dresses were, with the opals gleaming about her throat. When she bent forward to strike a chord, the pendant swung from her bosom like a small moon. It was still an amazement to Sam that this rarefied creature should have come into his life.

The bell of the front door jangled.

"Randolph, see who that is, would you?" Valeria asked.

He went out, Nancy's eyes following him. No other man walked with such easy grace or carried his head with such nobility. She heard his voice in the hall and then he came back and said, "There's someone to see you, Mr. Garvey. A woman."

Sam Garvey turned in his yellow chair. No woman came calling on him. No woman ever had.

"Who is she?"

"She says she has something important to tell you." Randolph came to the old man as though to help him up. "Her name is Helen Tennant."

When Sam hobbled out of the lilac-decorated parlor, he peered at the dumpy, florid creature in the hall. She was poorly dressed and had a moth-eaten red fox stole around her shoulders. Her frizzy hair straggled out from under a hat that looked like some kind of abandoned pancake with a tattered crepe fringe. She was obviously nervous, confronted by the sinister old tycoon about whom she had heard so many alarming tales.

"What's this?" Sam growled. "You've got something to tell me?"

"Yes, Mr. Garvey," Helen trembled. "It's something you ought to know."

"Who are you?" he demanded, unimpressed.

Helen's mouth had gone dry, but she summoned sufficient courage to confess. "I'm a friend of Henry Brewster."

Sam grunted. He was surprised that Henry had it in him to have a friend, even such a commonplace, run-down frump as this. Though, God knows, any man married to Ida needed someone.

"Come in here." He nodded toward the study and made his way dragging his feet.

The lamps were lit and a cheerful fire was burning. Going from one place to another bothered him now. The distance seemed so great. He advanced across the expanse of carpet and was relieved by the proximity of his desk. He always felt much safer behind it.

Helen followed him in and stood uncertainly by the doorway. As Sam sat down, Helen caught a glimpse of a tall, purple vision at the threshold.

"Are you all right, Sam?" the woman asked.

"I want a cigar," the old man announced.

"Now, Sam, the doctor said—" The vision glided across the room with a soft rush of trailing skirts.

"Damn the doctor. I haven't had one all day."

Valeria took a box from a drawer, selected a cigar, took off the band, and handed it to her husband. She swept over to the marble mantel, barely glancing at Helen who had begun to feel decidedly meager and second-rate. Mrs. Sam Garvey, the fabled Valeria of Henry's stories, held a spill to the fire and returned to the desk, guarding the flame with her hand. She lit her husband's cigar. All very wifely and gracious, Helen thought.

Sam bit off the tip of the cigar and spat. It landed with experienced accuracy in the bowl of a brass spittoon.

How stately, really magnificent, she was! Helen could well see that it would be no trouble for such an imperious woman to wrap all these half-baked men around her finger. But then she was still young and had fine clothes. Those jewels!

With a cool inclination of her head, Valeria paused long enough to murmur, "Excuse me," and went out.

Ensconced behind his battlement, Sam blew out a slow and threatening cloud of smoke.

"Well?"

From the drab exile in which the unmonied are forced to dwell, Helen managed to say, "It's—er— like this." Suddenly, confronted by this legendary monster, she could not muster her thoughts to explain just how it was. She was in a tenuous position because she had come for money. It was a sort of blackmail at which she was not experienced. It had seemed easy in the safety of her dingy flat, fired by Henry Brewster's betrayal, but now, facing the great Sam Garvey across such an expanse of carpet, and pinioned by the steely glint in his small blue eyes, she stammered and her resolve ebbed.

"It's like this," she repeated, in a minor key. Not knowing how else to express herself, Helen resorted to tears.

It was good to cry at this moment, she felt, fumbling

for a handkerchief and holding it against her mouth and giving sympathetic little sniffles. She hoped that she was giving the impression of a woman in great distress, someone who had been shamefully treated and who was in need of help.

"You've got information? Something you picked up from Henry Brewster? Well, let's hear it."

Helen glanced up, so Sam Garvey could see there were genuine tears running out of her eyes. "Henry made promises and he hasn't kept them. I've been true and loyal to Henry. He's gone away and thrown me over—without a word. And it hurts. Very much." She gave a great gulp and sobbed. "He's gone to Saratoga. He promised to take me and he didn't. I've given up the best years of my life to Henry. Oh, I guess you think I'm a wicked, sinful woman, but it isn't my fault that he and his wife don't get on. I sacrificed myself because I love him. He's been the only man in my life and I believed he would be true to me and good to me in return for all I've done. I gave him everything and in the end it has all been for nothing."

Sam found it difficult to listen to this drivel. Why any woman should have any regard for Henry Brewster he could not imagine. She was a tart, that was obvious. Henry had grown tired of her and she had come to get her revenge. That he could understand. The principle of revenge was to him quite valid.

"What are you after? I haven't got all night."

Helen drew in a long painful breath. She was a wronged woman and she had a right to get something out of this rich, horrible family.

"Henry promised me," she said more boldly, "a thousand dollars. I've taken very little from him because I loved him. Now he's gone away and he gave me nothing. I think it's the least I deserve after all I've been through."

"Why the hell should I give you a thousand dollars?"

"Because I can tell you something you don't know. They've been plotting against you, Henry and his wife. They've committed a criminal act. I know about it because he told me. Not in so many words, not all at once. I've put it together, bit by bit."

"What sort of a crime?"

Helen hesitated. Should she demand the money first or should she tell him first? If she told him, would he turn her out without giving her anything?

"He stole your will from the bank and his wife took it to Chicago. He was in a terrible state about it—all aquiver. He came to see me and drank a whole bottle of red wine. He's scared stiff someone will find out. That's why he's gone to Saratoga. He's going to stay there till it all blows over and he can put it back."

"My will?" Sam leaned forward and glared at her, his attention aroused.

"His wife has gone to borrow money—against what she'll inherit when you're dead."

Sam Garvey considered this. At the back of his mind a suspicion nudged him. His apprehensions had been justified, but he had been waiting for developments from the wrong quarter.

"Why?"

Helen sensed immediately that she had a momentary advantage.

"Do I get my thousand dollars?"

"Yes, yes, to hell with that. Tell me what else you know."

She stood up swaying her hips, and adjusted the pathetic fur. "I'd like to see the color of your money, Mr. Garvey," she said brazenly. "I've been put off with enough promises from your family."

"Henry Brewster is not my family!"

"Well, it's your family that's been plotting against you. It's your daughter, Ida, who put him up to it."

"God damn your hide!"

Victory steadied Helen. She found she was not as frightened of the old wretch as she had been before.

"Give me my money first!"

Sam muttered some dreadful imprecation, raised himself, pulled back the panel of ledgers and opened the safe. He took out one of the canvas bags and un-. tied it, fishing out a bundle of notes. Helen gasped. There must be thousands! He counted out ten one hundred dollar bills, drew the bag's string tight and closed the safe.

"You'll get it when I know the rest."

At the sight of those ten crisp notes, Helen's determination returned in a rush.

She approached the desk and declared like someone making a deposition in court, "Ida's buying up shares of your railroad. She's been doing it for months. That's why she wants the money. She's hocked her jewels and mortgaged the house and taken every cent she had out of the bank. She's aiming to get control."

"Of my railroad?" Sam was incredulous. Ida in control? It was absurd.

"And I can tell you why," Helen delivered her *coup de grace*. "Because she hates your wife."

Sam Garvey sat perfectly still. Absurd as were the accusations of Henry's mistress he could see that in the illogical world of women, they made some sense. Ida had hated Valeria from the start. Vindictiveness, he supposed, in a woman's mind could be carried to the point of mania. It half came to him that the lengths to which Ida was going paralleled those to which he had gone in his fight against the strike. Yes, it was possible, even among men, even between himself and Josiah. Their feud had lasted for twenty years.

Ida and Valeria! After all, there were motives as powerful as money.

He sat back and blew out an immense cloud of smoke. It hung like a thundercloud over his head.

Ida! It was not, of course, only Valeria. It was her own sterile life, her loss of Josiah, her loveless marriage, her struggle to become the most important woman in Arcadia. Ida had always lived off hatred of one kind or another.

"And now," Helen said with a toss of her head, her mission miraculously accomplished, and with the full satisfaction of the future odium she had brought down on Henry, "I'll thank you for my money."

Sam had altogether forgotten about Henry's whore. Helen waited a moment and then hurried to the desk and snatched up the money. She clutched it firmly in her hand. Escape—clothes—Chicago—an established gentleman.

It was some time before Sam noticed Helen had gone.

He got up slowly, grasping his cane, and made his way across the interminable length of Turkey carpet, slowly across the hall and slowly into Valeria's lilac enclave. The group was talking quietly but stopped as he entered.

Valeria saw at once that something momentous had occurred.

Sam focused on Nancy who was sitting on her usual little stool before the fire.

"When is your mother coming back from Chicago?"

"The day after tomorrow, I believe."

This was not the time, Valeria knew, to ask Sam anything.

Even the others could tell that the old man was in a towering rage.

Sam said nothing for two days. He abandoned the parlor for his study. When Valeria came to tell him that the portrait was finished and ready to be hung, Sam nodded and said, "Good." He made no effort to move.

Valeria bundled Nancy home the day before Ida was due to return. The girl was terribly frightened of her mother's finding out in whose house she had been staying.

In the hall Nancy nestled up to her most beloved friend and whispered, "Can I confess something?"

Valeria kissed her, "Is it fearfully important?"

"It's the most important thing that has ever happened to me." Nancy hid her face against Valeria's shoulder. "It's changed my whole life. It's everything I ever dreamed of."

"Mercy!" Valeria hugged her. "Whatever can it be?"

Nancy broke away and kissed her three times in succession.

"I'm in love. It's so wonderful, so unbelievable, in love! And it's forever."

She flew through the door like a bird. As she ran down the path to the gate, she turned to call out, "Randolph!"

She was laughing as she got into the carriage and drove away.

Valeria closed the door. Poor Nancy! She might as well love Randy "forever" as anyone. The "forever" of youth was so quickly over. That painful euphoria struck like an arrow, but the wound so quickly healed.

Now that Josiah was mostly away, she had entered an interlude of comparative peace that she could tolerate and even, to some extent, enjoy. In the mornings she would bring Sam's breakfast to the study and, having seen that he had all he needed, would put on her old black coat and skirt and make her way through the alleys of Shacktown to the school.

It was true the women of Shacktown did not like her. They never would because she was rich and was a symbol of the authority they hated. Nor did they accept her as in a certain sense they accepted Sam Garvey who was a necessary evil, part of their lives like poverty and hard work and dirt and growing old. All that they accepted as their fate. But Mrs. Garvey was an enigma. The best they could think of her was that she had some sort of conscience and that she was trying to offset her guilt by doing what she considered good. Of course, it was not good because she was doing it for herself and not for them. They might as well take whatever she offered because it was there. If she wanted to come in the mornings and teach the children to read and write, that was her business. She was ashamed as she should be. The most they would do for her was to allow her to feel less ashamed if she were able to.

They watched her as she made her way through the muddy alleys. They did not smile when she smiled. And when they brought the children to the school and Mrs. Garvey greeted them, they did not respond. Let her spend her money if it made her feel better. She had millions. She was a fraud, and they had no intention of being patronized by her.

The children were different, however. Going to

school was a change and an adventure which brought a touch of excitement into their drab little lives. Mrs. Garvey was a wonder and a mystery who brought them cookies and bags of fruit. She was kind and patient as they struggled to learn their alphabet and stretched their minds to comprehend numbers.

Going to school was fun. And Mrs. Garvey was funny. They liked her and they trusted her to surprise them, and day after day she did.

The children pained Valeria because they were pinched and eager and had so much wasted energy. She knew that the women resented her. Seeing how darned and tattered the children's clothes were, she bought supplies of sweaters and pants and sturdy little dresses for the girls. It was no use, she soon discovered, giving them directly to the children who needed them most. Instead she would leave them on the teacher's desk and in the morning they would be gone. The children did not wear these new clothes to school. Their mothers would not give Mrs. Garvey that satisfaction. But ambiguous and difficult as her position in Shacktown was, Valeria persisted. A chore had been added to the drab routine of the Shacktown women. After they had got their men off to work, they got the children off to school.

Valeria ordered three hundred books from a sale in Chicago and they arrived in boxes and were stacked in a small vestry at the side of the hall. Shelves were made, and with Mary's help the books were unpacked. They were second-hand books on a variety of subjects. There were novels by great authors and histories of America. Gradually the inhabitants of Shacktown became aware that, oddly enough, they were citizens of America. Sometimes in the evenings, when Dr. Mortlake was giving his consultations and handing out prescriptions, his patients would sidle into the schoolroom to stare. It took several weeks before any of the books were taken down. The people of Shacktown handled them as though they contained dangerous temptations and only told of things they had no use for. But during the course of the winter, it sometimes happened that a family would gather around the table with a certain guilty awe. Whoever could read among them would open one of these mysterious and forbidden volumes and announce, as though they were about to enter into traffic with the Devil, "Chapter One."

Her experience with the school caused Valeria to deliberate a good deal on the subject of finances. She had endeavored to read the book by the exiled German that Randolph had lent her. But it seemed all too complicated and too far removed from the realities that concerned her. She was not interested in theories, but in practicalities. She had herself for too long sought to make money in various unsuccessful ways, but now that she had it, she realized that her old evaluation of money was too simplistic. One thing had become evident to her: money must move, it must turn into things, it must be put to use. The fortune Sam Garvey had on deposit in banks and hidden in the safe was like spoiled food. It turned bad and corrupt and spawned maggots that ate into people's minds and distorted their natural functions. It turned into greed and meanness and a lust for power and waste. She did not consider that the little she was doing in Shacktown came under the heading of charity. She disliked charity. Her work was simply common sense.

At noon she would go back and prepare Sam's lunch and in the afternoon came the time that she considered hers. She had earned the right to a few hours of freedom. Tripp would take her to Horton's Stables where Mimosa had been returned after the strike, and she would ride off into the country. The release of trotting along country roads erased the problems of Sam and money and Shacktown. Valeria relished the open land in those still, crisp days of the long winter.

During Josiah's absences the denizens of The Heights grew accustomed to the sight of Mrs. Sam Garvey, that awful adventuress, riding down the avenue. Mrs. Shawcross and Mrs. Bancroft often interrupted an exchange of gossip to watch her through lace curtains. Mrs. Garvey was of course quite unacceptable by any standards of polite society. She rode alone which was bad enough. But also no decent, churchgoing Christian would disport herself in public in that outrageous habit, topped, if you please, by that audacious little hat with a veil. Mrs. Sam Garvey had joined the hierarchy of the scandalous, and reigned supreme equaled only by Josiah Eaton. They were the king and queen of the unpardonable, both altogether too wicked and too interesting to be permitted within the pale.

Valeria was, in general, calmer, or perhaps more resigned. The date of departure from Arcadia seemed definitely closer. Paris and Rome and London were no longer the shimmering towers of a mirage, but places she and Sam would actually visit. She could look forward to years filled with compensations.

Her relationship with Sam had stabilized to a degree she would never have thought possible. She continued in her duties to him, not because she was compelled to, but because she wanted to. His need for her, in a man of his strength and obstinacy, touched her. It was a protective fondness because he was old and failing and because little by little, she knew that his world was ebbing away from him.

Sometimes, passing Josiah's place, now boarded up, she would allow herself to remember the night she had stayed there and the brief rapture of those embraces. She no longer fought to eradicate them from her memory. They were there as the Yankee captain was still there, two episodes which had happened to someone else.

But there was sadness when she thought of him, not only because of the anger and pain of their last meeting, but also because her youth was passing. Next year she would be twenty-six. It was strange that although she had lived her life without love, all those years of poverty and solitary struggle had apparently not robbed her of her capacity to give herself to a man. Valeria had given herself to Josiah freely, as though she were in the habit of taking lovers. She evidently had in her nature this capacity for physical surrender, separate from her mind with its overcritical, overobjective faculties. That sensual alter ego Josiah had awakened remained hidden, but like Ford's talent for painting, it endured.

Yes, she could look forward to a life filled with beautiful rewards. She could buy exquisite clothes and stay at the best hotels and collect opals, if she'd a mind to. She could enrich her mind with the wonders of art that Europe offered. There would be magical moments, she was sure; Sorrento and the Pyramids and the shining peaks of the Dolomites. From all these sights and experiences she would compose her life. And there was Nancy whose future she could influence for the better and there was Randolph to encourage. There were many positive and worthwhile things.

But in her afternoons of riding, as she looked across the bare fields touched with frost, or at the pale, cloudless sky in the perfect stillness of winter, she thought that all those brief hours with Josiah had given her was the realization that she was alone.

She faced that unappeased hunger from which love alone could free her. She must learn to live without it because she could not face deception. Six years, Sam had said in the beginning. Independence at thirty-one. By then she would have gotten used to an empty heart. She would enjoy and experience many things, but never that soaring joy and peace and fulfillment which she had known in Josiah's arms.

One day, with a start of panic, she saw him in the distance. He must have come back sooner than expected. She saw him galloping toward her and caught sight of the glint of sunlight on his yellow hair. Possessed by terror, she spurred Mimosa down the lane that led to the Hotchkiss farm and up a bank into the orchards where the branches of the pear trees hid her.

Her heart was beating wildly as she heard him thunder by.

For a single moment she was on the point of casting her resolutions to the winds and dashing after him. She wanted to be in his arms and safe. To know that nothing else mattered, that no duty or loyalty or obligation had the power to rob her of such happiness.

But in a sickness of self-denial, her will held her, frozen and shaken, where she was.

CHAPTER TWENTY-THREE

SAM GARVEY, silent and determined, drank his coffee and sent for Tripp. He made his way down the path and climbed into the carriage. His black hat was set well down on his head and the heavy Malacca cane was grasped firmly in his gnarled hand.

Sam Garvey was bent on vengeance. The fact that Mrs. Henry Brewster happened to be his daughter was of no account whatever. She had crossed him. She would be punished.

The carriage rumbled through Arcadia. It rambled slowly up the long hill to The Heights while Sam Garvey ruminated on his daughter's sin, more heinous than any other.

He climbed out of the carriage and stomped up the steps, one by one, to Ida's brick monstrosity. Tripp followed and rang the bell.

After a lengthy pause Haddock opened. He was aghast at what the aftermath of a night of heavy drinking could do to affront his nerves. Haddock had reached the champagnes and his mornings were unfortunate. He stared at this apparition risen from the hell of delirium tremens and clung to the knob for support.

"Where's Mrs. Brewster?"

"In the s-s-s-s-study, sir, I think."

Sam passed him and made his inexorable way across the hall to open the study door.

Ida was revealed at her desk amidst a drift of papers, in her dressing gown and her hair in disorder.

"Good morning, Ida."

Ida's heart shrank.

Sam planted himself on a French chair of doubtful

provenance and regarded this lowly reptile that had dared to assert its will. He considered her for several moments in stormy deliberation.

Ida knew this terrible gambit. Her turn had come.

"I want my will," her father said at last. "Get it. Now."

Ida rummaged amongst the clutter until she found the will. Rising like a battleship, she brought it to him.

"Henry will be fired from the bank. You know that."

Ida knew. She knew that somehow the tyrant had found out everything. It didn't matter how. The inescapable fact confronted her. He knew and he was forcing her to meet him for the duel which, ever since she had embarked on her perilous conspiracy, she had known would be inevitable. He had decreed the time and the place contrary to her intentions, but she was not prepared to give him the satisfaction of firing the first shot. Ida was confident of her weapons. She returned to her desk. It had come sooner than she expected. Let it come.

The old man came straight to the point. It was his habit to knock his adversary out in the first round whenever possible. "How many shares do you own in my railroad?"

"Fifty-two percent," she informed him. "The shares you allotted me and the children were the deciding factor."

"How did you pay for them?"

"I pawned my jewels, mortgaged this house. I had money in the bank."

"And the rest you borrowed on my will?"

Ida turned brick red. But at this moment, when she and her father faced each other in mortal combat, she was formidable in her own right.

"I shall change my will. You know that."

"You can if you want," she countered, "though it's hardly in your interest now."

"What do you know of my interests?"

"I control them. You mortgaged the mills to put up the twenty million against Thaddeus Brownlow's loan."

They were speaking very clearly. They had not

raised their voices. In this struggle over money and power it was essential that both state the facts of their case as concisely as possible. The Garveys were well versed in the rules of this particular game.

"You think you've cornered me?" Sam asked with the amiability of a crocodile.

"Enough to state my terms."

"You have *terms?*"

"Yes." Ida stared without flinching. "I wouldn't have done all this if I hadn't."

"And what . . . are they?"

Ida was steadying her nerves. Weeks of frenzied planning, of sleepless nights, of taking appalling risks, all the alarms and excursions that preceded the dread moment when the ultimatum is delivered were focused in this moment. Her madness shrank to the head of a pin.

She announced in pear shaped tones, "I want you to divorce that woman and I want a guarantee that you won't leave her any money."

She had declared war. There was no longer any possibility of retreat or compromise. She was daring to face her father for the first time in her life from what she had convinced herself was a superior position.

Her demands were so outrageous that even Sam Garvey was momentarily thunderstruck. "Divorce—?" he asked, inopportunely. "Why?"

"Because," Ida said between clenched teeth, "I won't accept her."

"You—won't—accept?"

"It's a disgrace to have her in the family. The whole town knows she's Josiah Eaton's mistress. Everyone knows but you." She saw that she had shocked him and swept forward to press her point. "She rides out there in broad daylight—every afternoon. She even stayed there one night during the strike. The servants saw her. Josiah stayed with her in one of the bedrooms till three o'clock."

The old man's face was turning gray, as though the strength of his anger was draining from him.

"You care for nothing but business," she continued.

"It's all you ever cared about. It doesn't occur to you what I have to suffer from this scandal."

Sam stared at her with a sort of senile incredulity.

"There's a group of depraved people who meet at Josiah's house. I shan't name the others, though I know who they are. I have statements to prove it. It's a club and they meet for all sorts of debased activities. That woman is one of them. In fact she's the only woman!"

It flashed through Ida's mind that if she continued forcefully enough, he might have another heart attack and die right there. Then the whole problem would be solved.

"We stand for something in this town," she hammered on. "It's because of the mills that it's here at all. I have my position to keep up and so do you. And there are the children to consider. As it is, I can hardly show myself. Everyone hints and smirks. You never go out or see anyone. She's hypnotized you. I'm doing this as much for your sake as for mine, to protect you—"

Sam smacked his hand on the arm of the chair. "That's enough!"

Had she gone too far? Had she said too much too soon? But she still held her trump card, the one wild card in the pack that would force his hand.

Sam breathed slowly and deeply. He was making a superhuman effort to keep control. He said very quietly, "You'll regret this, Ida. You'll regret this till the day you die."

That implacable threat, uttered so quietly, struck fear into her heart, the old fear she had always had of him. She backtracked, trying to keep her voice level, so that he would not see that he still held power over her. "I am not saying that I would not be ready to make a deal."

"Oh," he replied with the same deadly quietness. "You'd make a deal?"

"If you'll divorce that woman for the sake of the family, I'm willing to sell you all my shares. Then you'd own the railroad, lock, stock, and barrel. And I'm not saying you shouldn't. It *is* yours. It was *your* idea. Of course," she added hurriedly, "I'd need a guarantee that you'd continue to pay my allowance and that everything would be left to me and the children. Otherwise," her voice arched into an artificial tremble that barely concealed her mounting panic, "I might be forced to do the one thing I don't want to do."

Sam got up. Was he going to strike her? He was gripping the Malacca cane so tightly that his knuckles stood out like scars.

"And what's that, Ida?"

"This has cost me everything—trying to save the family from disgrace." Ida managed to say in the same hysterical falsetto, "I might be forced to sell out —to someone else—if you won't listen to reason, if I'm pushed too far."

Sam Garvey knew exactly whom she meant. There was no need for her to specify the name.

It was the moment of triumph she had longed for. It was to have made up for everything she had suffered at his hands, for her miserable childhood treatment and neglect, for all the petty humiliations inflicted at the Sunday luncheons. But now that she had hurled her thunderbolt, the dread he had always inspired, her subservience to his authority, the power of his money which had ruled her life, robbed her of the expected satisfaction. She had struck back at the image of her father, but Sam Garvey remained standing grimly in front of her, unscathed.

"Let me tell you something," he was saying, "since you're so intent on telling *me* how my wife spends her afternoons. She went to Josiah's during the strike because I sent her there. She and her brother know Josiah. My wife worked for him after she walked out on you. I sent her to persuade him to lay off the mills till the strike was settled. If you read *The Courier* you may have noticed the articles against me stopped."

"A likely story!" Ida sneered. "One of the servants saw her come out of the bedroom naked and take in a tray of food."

"Servants see and repeat a lot of foul garbage. And you repeat and believe a lot of it," Sam informed his daughter. He took a step toward her and struck the floor with his cane to insure her complete attention. "My wife rides down Tremont Avenue because she likes to ride. She goes with my full knowledge and consent. We made a bargain and she has stuck to her side of it and I will stick to mine."

"She married you for money. She's deceived you like she deceives everyone, all down the line."

"If she married me for money I shall leave her money. A great deal of money, Ida. As to your shares —you keep 'em. I'll show you how much they'll end up being worth."

Ida looked very large and dreadful and menacing with her red face and red, disordered hair, and the wild look of panic she could not conceal.

"It's your choice between Josiah and me," she flung at him, fighting to retain some sense of the victory he was wresting from her. "If you choose him no doubt you can keep that woman," she heaved up her shoulders in theatrical contempt, "if you're still mad enough and sick enough to want her, now that you know the truth."

For a moment Sam felt a dizzying constriction in his chest and the onrush of strangling pain, but he resisted and it receded. Ice flowed back into his veins.

"I'll smash you, Ida, as I've smashed a good few others in my time. You made a mistake in thinking you could better me."

Shortly afterwards an accident occurred on the railroad line of which Josiah Eaton was still director.

An engine at the head of a long line of freight cars, chugging its way across the prairies in the vast still night of winter, lurched off the rails onto open ground, roared up a bank and, with a thundering crash, exploded in a volcano of flame and steam, rolling over like an immense iron dinosaur, burning and hissing, its wheels spinning insanely. The cars behind crashed and churned in a screaming melee, reared onto each other and overturned, horribly entangled like discarded toys in a giant's playground. The driver was crushed under a wreckage of splintered steel. His mate extricated himself from this inferno, with broken bones and one side of his face burned off, and wandered, dazed, like a sleepwalker, along the rails to find the cause of this catastrophe.

There were no rails.

News filtered back to Arcadia and the town's pundits were agog. It was obvious what had happened. Josiah Eaton had bided his time and, when his rival was least expecting it, had struck.

The crumpled mass of wrecked freight cars lay in the wilderness while snow fell and blanketed the industrial carnage. Soon all that remained was a shapeless mound. A shipment worth many thousands of dollars was rendered valueless by the impersonal winter weather.

Another train left Arcadia for the site of the disaster. The cars still on the tracks were re-shackled and towed back like wounded veterans.

It would take weeks before fresh rails were laid, *if* they were laid, *if* Josiah Eaton chose to lay them.

Meanwhile Sam Garvey was stymied. There was no way to deliver his shipments to Chicago until the repairs were made, and made they were not likely to be, in the town's opinion, until Josiah Eaton and Sam Garvey made a deal.

"A bad move," Mr. Shawcross, the lawyer, opined over a whiskey at the club. "Not good publicity for Josiah when he's trying to convince folks he'll make an honest governor. I thought he'd outgrown such foolishness, but old feuds die hard, I guess."

The accident was reported in *The Courier*. An act of sabotage committed by unseen hands and for purposes unknown.

Not a single person in Arcadia doubted what the purpose was or doubted who had directed the unseen hands. The body of the driver, or such parts of it as were recoverable from the wreckage, was brought home and solemnly interred. Pastor Vanderlip delivered a eulogy, thunderous with Biblical anathemas pertaining to the Golden Calf and the wrath of Jehovah soon to descend upon those who worshiped money above the Ten Commandments; first among which was "Thou shalt not kill" and second among which was "Thou shalt not covet thy neighbor's wife, nor his ox nor his ass." Nor his railroad, the assembled parishioners understood, righteously feeling for once that their poverty was praiseworthy. Some highly moral citizen lugged a ladder to the offices of *The Courier* during the early hours, daubed out the word "Governor" on Josiah's banner, and substituted the word "Jail." Arcadia nodded in approval. The ghost of the driver sat on the steps of *The Courier* and wrung its remaining hand. It was seen by several inebriates staggering homewards who promptly swore off liquor and, shivering with terror, determined to mend their ways. Sam Garvey certainly deserved no sympathy, but Josiah Eaton was the target of Arcadia's righteous indignation. When he rode down Main Street in his buff coat and breeches with the winter sunshine gleaming on his golden hair, he received stern looks and a few open insults. A snot-nosed boy, eager for the approbation of his elders, flung a pebble. It struck Josiah's horse on the flank, but otherwise did no damage. The child had his head patted by a baker who had observed this incident, and who gave the child the further accolade of a jam-filled doughnut. The town enjoyed the opportunity to assert its Christian conscience.

Arcadia was still humming and buzzing and moralizing over Josiah's wickedness when it was racked by further news. A bridge on the incomplete Mid-Western and Pacific was blown up—dynamited to smithereens in the dead of night, leaving a tangle of rails and beams gaping over a frozen river.

The town rose to the excitement of the now declared battle between Arcadia's two leading citizens. Once again it divided itself, for sporting purposes, into two camps. Bets were laid and odds given as to which of the titans would gain the upper hand and how soon and on what terms a truce would be signed. It was obvious that Josiah Eaton was maneuvering for a share of the new railroad to offset the losses inflicted on the old. Sam Garvey was not noted for making deals favorable to his opponents. But how long, the town debated, could he hold out with one line out of commission and the other not completed? The population relished the suspense and forgave the two protagonists their shortcomings because they were providing a welcome relief from the daily monotony. This tug-of-war brought a little spice into lives worn bare by the servitude of survival.

The Courier duly reported this second act of senseless destruction, committed, again, for an unknown reason and by unknown hands. Josiah Eaton announced that repairs to the old line were being rushed through. A crew had been sent to the disaster site and new rails were being hammered into line. Why had Josiah gone to all the trouble of spiriting away the rails in the first place, people wondered, only to replace them in such haste? Because, it was pointed out, Eaton was torn between his enmity for Sam Garvey and his ambition to be elected governor. He had given Garvey a taste of what he was capable of and now he was giving the voters a chance to admire his willingness to redress wrongs, even his own, which was a lot for a politician. What he took away with one hand, he thought it expedient to give back with the other.

It was the old game of piracy and politics which Arcadia thoroughly enjoyed.

As the rumors circulated and spread like ripples on a lake, the more serious voters reconsidered the encouragement and confidence they had invested in the prospective governor. They had unwisely hoped that the old days when warlords fought over the resources of the United States were over and that a better-regulated and more decent era might begin. They shook their heads. Not much, after all, was likely to change as long as men were so greedy and ambitious and so forgetful of the ideals on which America had been founded. What did men like Garvey and Eaton stand for? Profits and power. It had not taken long for their great country to become as corrupt as any other, as rapacious as the old lion of England from whose dominion they had with such a flourish of idealistic trumpets announced their independence. Idealism faded as fast as the flowers of spring.

Josiah was mystified by these accidents that were so patently not accidental. In the light of his forbearance he could not understand why Sam Garvey should jeopardize his enviable position. Unless there were other manipulators. It was possible, and yet somehow in this instance it seemed unlikely. Thaddeus Brownlow was not reputed to indulge in sabotage in order to extract higher rates for the money he loaned. His terms were drastically demanding, but he was more honest than most. Were there other shadowy figures behind the scenes, hatching plots to get a slice of Garvey's future profits?

Josiah was well aware these incidents damaged his prestige. He had worked hard and was winning an enthusiastic following and the elections were approaching. Could it be some deep-lying scheme to undermine his chances? He could not believe that Garvey who had no interest in politics except as a means for bribery when he needed some advantage or concession would have gone to such lengths when he had so much of his own at stake. Josiah offered five thousand dollars through the paper for any information concerning the theft and removal of the rails which had resulted in the accident.

Arcadia sniggered. That reward was not likely to be claimed!

Josiah was inextricably linked to his own past. Because he had been a party to such cabals before, it was hard to convince anyone he was innocent of these current crimes. How could he explain his growing distaste for all these machinations that now seemed unworthy of the position he hoped to occupy? How could he hope to explain the mystery of this change of heart inspired by the high regard in which he held a woman, when everyone well knew what his attitude to women had been all through his notoriously promiscuous life? The world judged one by one's record, not by what one wanted to become.

Valeria had, in turn, accepted the fact that Josiah had finally revealed his natural colors.

It was Randolph who said to her one evening when they were sitting over coffee, "I don't believe Josiah had anything to do with it."

"He must have," Valeria protested. "Who else could it have been?"

"As the wife of a tycoon, Val, it must have been born down on you that big business is not conducted according to rules of chivalry. It could have been anyone connected with the railroad industry, any one of a hundred men who don't care to see your husband get any wealthier."

In her heart she hoped this might be true, but her reason warned her it was unlikely.

The only two people in Arcadia who were fully aware of what was going on were Sam Garvey and his daughter.

As Ida paced her parlor she was tormented by apprehension as to what her father would do next. On paper she controlled the new railroad, but she did not control her father, as she had intended.

She owned the shares, she kept reassuring herself. She was disastrously in debt with looming payments on the vast amounts she had borrowed; payments on her jewels and on the house and to certain gentlemen in Chicago who had been willing to advance Ida the amount she needed at exorbitant rates of interest and who would descend in a whirlwind of high-pitched accusations if they discovered that her father's will was no longer valid as collateral. It could mean ruin. Public abuse. Jail. She had not, in the first flush of fanatical determination, fully considered these ghastly eventualities. They loomed ominously about her now.

But the fact could not be altered that she was potentially richer than she had ever been, and in her own right for the first time. The shares were her arsenal, her property; they assured her a position of supremacy. Why, then, did her father fail to acknowledge it, fail to acknowledge her at all? He had made no move to implement her terms. He had not to her knowledge taken a single step to divest himself of that whore of Babylon he persisted in considering his wife. He too had vast commitments, vaster by far than hers. He too had payments to meet. How much longer could he dig into hidden capital to meet them when Josiah's railroad was out of commission and the new one was held up by the destruction of a bridge that might take weeks to rebuild? Was the whole structure of Garvey Enterprises about to break asunder and catapult them all into disaster? Had it all been her doing?

Drink did not calm this agony of uncertainty in which she passed her days. She drank and slept and woke to face the same ungovernable tension. She had fits of absent-mindedness when she could not remember what day it was, or what had started her on this colossal misadventure, or what her life had been like before her hatred of Valeria Lee had taken hold. She had fired Haddock whose drunkenness reminded her too powerfully of her own. Monsieur Emile had given notice that he would be leaving her household soon. Sometimes there was no dinner at all and she was forced to make her way down to the kitchen and eat scraps from the pantry, stale bread and the remains of last week's meals. She was living through an unendurable imprisonment in her own fortress, waiting hour by hour for the reassurance that she was triumphant. It did not come.

Sam Garvey had shut himself up in his study. He was unapproachable. The accord between himself and Valeria was apparently forgotten or in abeyance. He barely greeted her, ate on a tray and nodded to her like a servant when she removed it. She had never seen him so adamantly silent. But she was aware, when she moved about the room putting things in order, that he was watching her. She caught glances of suspicion, even of contempt. Several times she tried to draw him into conversation, but he only grunted and returned to his calculations.

He no longer joined the coterie in the lilac room. When Ford or Randolph called in the evenings, and occasionally Nancy escaping from the nightmare of her mother's red brick mausoleum in order to gaze at Randolph and dream about her desperate romance, they spoke in low voices as though the house were being watched. They felt obscurely guilty for being in each other's company. They were conscious of Sam's brooding in his study and of an indefinable feeling of disaster.

Valeria was subjected to blacker looks than usual from the women who surrendered their children to the school. Arcadia and Shacktown were aware that the man with millions was engaged in some deadly struggle over the railroad and assumed that Valeria was party to his schemes.

Only Mimosa greeted her with the same warm affection, nuzzling her shoulder and happily whisking her tail. But Valeria now disliked to ride down Main Street. She had become, she felt, a disagreeably controversial figure. This sense of being watched and criticized and scorned did not leave her until she had passed the station and was out free along the unfrequented road.

In this prolonged lull before the final battle, Sam Garvey was grimly waiting.

And Ida too grimly waited, though with less steely composure than her father.

There were strange and ominous developments.

The patch of missing rails on Josiah's line was speedily repaired, but no shipments were forthcoming from Sam Garvey's mills. Smoke poured from the chimneys as it always had and the earth rumbled in testimony that the mills were operating. But the steel and ore piled up at the mills and at the stockyards. The trains no longer chugged across the lonely, snowbound prairies.

Mr. Brownlow's representative made a sudden appearance in his expensive London suit, with his expensive homburg, and bearing his expensive briefcase. He remained closeted for a long time in Sam Garvey's study. Valeria, sewing in the exile of the parlor, wondered what they were discussing and why they took so long. And why, above all, had Sam banished her from his counsels as though she had committed some deadly sin?

It occurred to her that perhaps through the gossip

of servants, repeated along the grapevine of The
Heights below-stairs, Sam had learned of the night she
had spent at Josiah's. Was that the cause of the bitter,
searching glances she sometimes caught? He had not
technically the right to jealousy since their marriage
had been strictly one of companionship. Was it that
he was wounded more deeply than she might have
guessed because for the first time in his life he had
accepted a woman as worthy of admiration and discovered that she was fallible like the rest? Or was her
infidelity compounded by the fact that she had betrayed his trust with the man who was now trying, as
she believed, to disrupt his greatest scheme?

At last Mr. Brownlow's representative emerged, tight-
lipped and scandalized. Sam Garvey had announced
that he was unable to meet the payments on the
Brownlow loan. He had asked for an extension. Sam
Garvey was, he had made shockingly clear, in financial
straits. He admitted he had misrepresented his position.
The Garvey empire was in jeopardy and the fabled
supply of cash was running low.

Mr. Brownlow's representative carried this news
back to New York and a conference was held in the
sumptuous offices of Brownlow's Wall Street bank.
Thaddeus Brownlow, in his greatcoat with the sable
collar and with his great ruby ring gleaming, debated
the likelihood of Sam Garvey's being in such difficulties
as he pretended. Thaddeus Brownlow was well versed
in the tactics of tycoons. In these poker games involving millions, a great many extra aces made their
appearance at critical moments. He was convinced
that Garvey was concealing his full quota. He declined
to extend the dates of payment. Let Garvey look up
his sleeves and shake out his trouser cuffs and perform those useful sleight-of-hand feats. He had doubtless mislaid a few million somewhere. Let him reexam-
ine his accounts.

Nonetheless, from these conferences held in complete secrecy with partners and directors of the highest
integrity, little leaks and whispers found their way
through the brokerage houses to the exchange. The
Mid-Western and Pacific was soon rumored to be in

trouble. Old Sam Garvey had overextended himself and could not finish the building, could not make the repairs, could not meet the payments on the loan, could barely keep the steel mills open. The man, who had always kept his vast financial dealings in his head, had miscalculated by several million. This new undertaking had proved too much for him at his time of life. Sam Garvey on the best authority, not to be repeated, mind you, was pretty well washed up.

The shares in the Mid-Western and Pacific began to fall.

Ida received this disagreeable news from her New York brokers. Pacing up and down the parlor which had shrunk to the claustrophobic confines of a cell, she heard the letter drop through the mail slot in the front door. She hurried to tear it open. She suffered an inner landslide which laid bare a cave of panic. She knew with a dreadful certainty that she had underestimated her father's resourcefulness and the lengths to which he would go to enforce his will.

Her fifty-two percent of the shares in an unfinished railroad were now worth considerably less than she had paid for them, but her financial obligations remained as staggering as before. She found her way back to the parlor and sank onto the sofa. In a flash of objectivity, she was overcome by the stupidity of her hatred for Valeria, for her father and for Josiah, the absolute folly of her obsession with proving herself more powerful than they. If the shares continued to fall she would lose everything. Even if she sold the house and all her furniture and silver, she could not meet the payments on her jewels and on the Chicago loan for more than a few months. How could she ever have so deceived herself? It had all seemed so clear and now nothing was. Even her own motives were confused by the paramount threat of ruin. She owned the shares; she controlled the railroad. But there was no railroad. Her father was determined that there should be no railroad until the shares fell farther and still farther. And then, even if she had to, how could she dispose of them? There was still the blue envelope lurking in her empty jewel case. There was still Josiah.

She thought with a sudden wild regret that caused a cold sweat to break out all over her of the life she had led before she embarked on this insane intrigue. She had been *the* Mrs. Brewster. She had entertained the great. She had enjoyed the respect and envy of her rivals on The Heights. Above all, she had been safe.

Her whole existence, that she had turned to such splendid account with her dinners and committees, her sterling candlesticks and trays, her English butler and French chef, had been derailed by the appearance of Valeria Lee. Yes, Valeria had sabotaged her and she felt herself crashing and hurtling toward a defeat more terrible and total than anything she could have imagined possible.

A few months. But in a few months anything might happen. Her father might see reason and give in. Could that consummate bitch be worth such sacrifice? Surely, surely if she could just hold out she might still beat him at this deadly game.

She must wait. It was Monday. She must last out six more days. He had given in over the strike. When his back had been against the wall, he had finally given in. If she had to sell everything, she would. She hated the house anyway. She hated the whole town. Let Arcadia wait. Let her father wait. And let that devious whore wait and know that her days were numbered.

Ida had never in her life felt so horribly alone.

Even Henry would have been some consolation. But he was still hiding at Saratoga. What had Henry to come back for? Her father had had him fired from the bank. Henry had extracted a sizable sum from her in return for purloining her father's will. Henry could rest easy at Saratoga and take the waters to calm his nerves. There were no soothing waters to calm her nerves. There was no fat allowance paid quarterly into her account. Her father had stopped that. She had to face the totality of combat by herself.

She drank till noon. Where was Nancy? Locked in her room as usual. Cowering in her room. Nancy's evident terror of Ida maddened her. After all, Nancy was her daughter. She owed her something. She owed her obedience and concern when her mother needed her. Nancy was weak and stupid and frightened of everything. For once Nancy could do her duty. She had given Nancy everything. She wanted Nancy now.

Dazed and sickened she dragged herself into the hall to the foot of the staircase. She no longer had the strength to haul herself upstairs.

"Nancy!" she called. Her voice was too blurred to carry. "Nancy!"

Nancy wouldn't come. Nancy hated her. This hatred that bound them all, every member of the family, one to another, was like some infectious, disfiguring disease.

She fell on her knees at the foot of the stairs in the dusty hall with only the tilting suit of armor for company. Her great bulk lay supine.

She no longer cared.

By the end of the week the shares had fallen farther. Just before Christmas Sam Garvey closed the mills.

CHAPTER TWENTY-FOUR

THE FIRST WHISTLE did not sound that morning, nor the second. From the long habit which had become instinct, the men assembled before the gates to find them closed. There was a notice fixed to the gates and the men pressed forward to read it. There was a buzzing of confusion. Until further notice, the mills were closed.

The men murmured and churned about, not understanding what had happened. Where was Mr. Murdock? They knocked on the door of Mr. Murdock's office beside the gates, but Mr. Murdock was not in his office. Something had happened to him and something, they grasped in slow consternation, was happening to them.

Valeria had grown so used to the routine of the morning that she had not been aware the whistles hadn't shrilled as usual. She had gotten up and performed her duties as usual without realizing something was amiss. But gradually she sensed that this morning was different from others. She glanced out the window and saw the crowd.

She made tea and took Sam's tray to the study. He was already at his desk.

"Why have the gates not opened?"

"Because I closed them," he said curtly. She put the tray down before him and he reached for his cup.

"Why?"

"Because I ordered it."

"Sam, what has happened? What has gone wrong?"

He sipped his morning drink and without looking at her said, "It does not concern you."

He had lowered the invisible curtain behind which

he was unreachable. She went to the window and looked out. The men were hanging about and talking among themselves. It reminded her of the strike.

"Are the mills to be kept shut?"

"Don't ask me questions. It's a matter of business. Go on with what you're doing."

She stood there, dumbfounded. He had decided to be unapproachable. She went back to the kitchen, mystified.

Mary came, removing the shawl from her head. Her eyes were as big as saucers. "Oh, Ma'am, whatever is it? The men can't get to work."

"I know. Mr. Garvey says it is a matter of business. Beyond that I know no more than you."

"Oh, Ma'am, they are terribly bewildered. If the mills are closed what is to happen then? And it is Christmas, you see, and the money is needed."

She sat down in great distress. Valeria poured her a cup of tea, but Mary sat staring at it, unable to gather her thoughts because everything was disrupted. She was filled with apprehension.

"I don't like to bother you, Ma'am, because it is not your doing, I know, but did Mr. Garvey say—"

"He said nothing, Mary, and I know nothing. We must just get on with what we have to do."

The closing of the mills fell like doomsday upon Shacktown when, after months of skimping and saving, of going without and making do, of scraping the very bottom off every pan, of patching clothes that were past patching, of sitting in cold kitchens and sleeping in cold beds, the men and women of Shacktown were looking forward to a little meager cheer. Even the anger of the strike could not exceed the fury of disappointment and resentment that burned in the hearts of every man, woman and child in Sam Garvey's slum.

When Valeria appeared to take her morning class at the school, she found herself surrounded by a horde of harpies, ready to tear her limb from limb. Even the children stared at her in accusing disbelief. There would be no penny toys or paper hangings or crusts of fresh bread with beef drippings. All the fires

of Shacktown had been put out and all the small and
sorry hopes that flickered in the hearts of the children
had been doused. The harpies hurled questions at her.
Why had the mills been closed? When would they be
reopened? Would the men be paid while they were
not working? What in damnation was the bastard up
to? Having a game with them, was he? Because they
had rubbed his nose in the dirt over the strike? Taking
his revenge on them? And in the meanest, most con-
temptible fashion any man on earth could take?

Valeria saw their problem as clearly as they did
and was as outraged in her heart as they were over
Sam's inhuman action, whatever the mystery or the
necessity behind it. She extricated herself from the
horde and went straight home, into the house and into
the study. She shut the door firmly behind her. Sam
looked up through the usual cloud of smoke that was
as much a part of him as the white hair on his head.
He recognized by the tilt of the family nose that she
had come for an explanation.

"Sam, I must talk to you. You have appeared not
to want to talk to me for some time. I know that
you have had problems with the railroad and I have
tried not to intrude. But I can't be shut out any longer.
I must know why you've closed the mills and why
you've chosen this moment to do it."

"I told you, it's a matter of business. I don't want to
discuss it further."

"But Sam, this is the one time of year that they
all look forward to. You can't deprive them of their
right to some kind of Christmas."

"Go buy them puddings if you feel so badly. You've
spent enough on books and notebooks and Dr. Mortlake. You want them to have a good Christmas, go buy
them Christmas."

"Why are you behaving like this? Why are you
angry with me?"

"I'm not angry. I've closed the mills because I find
it convenient to do so at this time."

Valeria took a deep breath. She knew all the storm
signals and knew that he was only moments away
from an outburst.

"If it's a matter of money," she said, "you are welcome to have back all you gave me. I have spent about three thousand dollars. Please take the rest."

"I don't want your money," Sam said, looking away as though he were both embarrassed and yet suspicious of her. "This involves a very large sum. What you have would be a drop in the bucket."

"Well, it is there if you need it," she offered. After a moment she added, "I'm sorry, Sam. I thought that we had reached an understanding. All of a sudden, you have changed."

He made no comment.

"Has someone been saying things about me?" she asked gently. "I'm sure lots of people do. People in small towns always gossip. Is that it?" There was no answer. "Is it because I go riding alone? They think it's—unconventional?" Still there was no answer. "Do they think I am keeping assignations in the country? It has crossed my mind. You know it isn't true."

He refused to look at her. "I've tried to do what you expected of me. I have been happy doing it. I thought we were over the bad times." There was total silence. "I see that you don't trust me after all."

Sam was embarrassed and he was pained. He wanted to say something to Valeria, but did not know how. He did not believe the evil that Ida had spoken of her, but such rumors must have some foundation. He did not want to refer to it in case she should lie to him. It was acutely distasteful to him that she might, for his sake, to spare his feelings, be forced to lie.

He wanted to ask her what her relations with Josiah Eaton were, but he could not bring himself to do so because even if it were true that she had spent the night in his house, he did not want to know it.

He glanced up and saw her looking at him with sadness and disbelief and remembered all that she had done for him.

"I can't explain about the mills right now. It won't last long. I am doing it to force someone's hand because—" He broke off. How could he explain about Ida's machinations and their motive?

Sam could not pay the workers now because it was essential for the town and Ida to think he was broke.

"You can do whatever you think best about Christmas—for the men, I mean. I'll reimburse you later."

"Thank you, Sam."

Valeria went with Mary to her house and sat down across from Fletcher Jones. The man with one eye had come to accept her as a decent woman who could not do all she wanted because of the obligations of her marriage. But he respected her, in spite of not understanding how a woman of her caliber could possibly have sold out to such a mean-spirited despot as Sam Garvey.

"I want you to help me," Valeria said. "I want you to tell me exactly what it would cost to pay the men their wages while the mills are closed. If I am able to do it for two weeks I will. But I want your word that my name will not be mentioned. You can say it was some anonymous well-wisher. Anything you like."

Jones nodded, not believing that she was willing to do this out of her own funds. "It would run into a big sum," he warned.

"I will do it if I can. And I would like there to be a Christmas party for the children at the Hall. Will you help me with that? There should be a proper tree and presents and things to eat. They deserve it and they should have it."

"You are a generous woman, Mrs. Garvey."

"It isn't that." She tried to explain what could not be explained. "I do not understand about business and I know that my husband would not have done this if it could have been avoided. There has been trouble over the new railroad."

"I have read of it. But why, in the name of God, did he not talk to the men? Why did he not try to explain?"

"Mr. Garvey has been ill. He is not strong. He has had a lot on his mind lately." She said suddenly, "It's no use supposing he will ever understand you or that you will understand him. We must simply do what we can."

"It is you I don't understand, Mrs. Garvey," Fletcher Jones said frankly.

"Your loyalties are simple," she replied. "Mine are less so."

Large snowflakes fell on Christmas Eve blanketing the town. Arcadia seemed to recover a lost innocence. People trudged through the pure, lovely drifts and their souls were touched by wonder and their vanished faith was partially restored.

Home-made wreaths hung from doors, candles shone in windows, and waifs, muffled up to the ears, caroled the songs of the season from other countries and other times. People who had not bothered to greet each other for the last twelve months smiled and wished each other well.

Josiah Eaton watched the snow falling outside the window of his apartment over *The Courier*. He had received a number of invitations and had refused them all. He had seen all the people and shaken all the hands that he felt inclined to for some time to come. The elections would be in January and by the end of the month he would know in what shape his future would be cast. He felt alone, but he did not want anyone's company. Watching the soft and silent crystals covering the scars and blemishes of the street, Josiah decided that this would be his last Christmas in Arcadia. Whatever the outcome of the elections he would leave this town for good. His life here was over.

He had built up the crackling fire and poured himself a drink and was thankful for the quietness that the snow had brought.

What would Valeria be doing this Christmas? Randolph, Josiah knew, had been invited there for dinner. The pain of his separation from Valeria remained. She was an exceptional woman, and while her loyalty to Sam Garvey seemed to him altogether exaggerated, he had come to understand that she was determined to stand by it for no other reason than that Sam was her husband and she owed her allegiance to the legal status of being his wife.

What Garvey was up to Josiah could not fathom because he did not share the town's opinion that Sam was broke. He knew that the accident on his line and the blowing up of the bridge were linked to the rapid fall in the Mid-Western and Pacific shares, but why should Sam deliberately endanger what must be a vast investment?

It was all a deliberate manipulation, designed for his own reasons and for his own ultimate profit, that was certain. The old fox was playing some very devious game.

Strangely, he found that he was no longer as concerned as he had been with what Sam Garvey did or didn't do. In some way, Josiah had outgrown that enmity, as he had outgrown Arcadia and *The Courier* and his country house. It was all too parochial and the outcome was no longer sufficiently rewarding to him personally to expend the time he had contemplated on forcing the old scoundrel to make a deal. He now had other concerns of greater importance. A whole new future was on the verge of opening up if the elections turned out in his favor. Moreover, as a result of getting to know the state and its people and their problems, he had resolved to be as good a governor as he could be. He didn't want only the glory and power that went with the position. It would also be a great test of his vision and administrative skill. And there was a new temptation to which, to his own amusement and surprise, he found himself not unsusceptible. The lure of honesty might prove as compelling as the lure of self-indulgence. He had never before considered things except in terms of profit and pleasure. Josiah wondered if the experience of being honest might be as unusual as the night he had spent with Valeria.

It must be the good influence of Christmas, he concluded, and the moral resolutions it supposedly engenders. Experience in politics would no doubt prove to him that whatever one's good intentions and lofty aspirations, expedience and dishonesty were the needed weapons for survival. Still, it was agreeable to consider the alternative.

A knock on the outer door revealed the scruffy

office boy with a note that had just been delivered. "Urgent," the boy insisted and received a fifty cent piece for his pains.

The handwriting was large and irregular as though penned in a violent hurry.

The note began without any form of address.

> I must see you. *It is urgent. It concerns a matter of great importance to you and your political career*. I have matters to discuss with you alone. Do not fail me. You will regret it. It can give you everything you have wanted or destroy everything you are.

He turned the page and read the signature with astonishment. *Ida Brewster*. Underneath and underlined with three heavy strokes that had nearly torn through the paper. *Come at once*.

He had not spoken to Ida in nineteen years and had never before received any written communication from her. The melodramatic tone of this appeal, half threats, half desperation, made him think that it must be a hoax. Some friend who had known of their old acquaintance was playing a Yuletide prank.

And yet the note compelled attention. Josiah read it through again and decided that it was genuine. It must be connected, in some way, with the closing of the mills and the disruption of the new railroad. Perhaps it was true that Sam Garvey had run out of money and Ida was proposing—but what could Ida possibly propose to him?

He debated if he should answer the note or merely go to see her as she asked. It was the possible connection between the Garveys and the election that disturbed him. Neither Ida nor her father had any interest in politics, except when they needed to pay off public officials. Still . . .

. . . *a matter of great importance to you and your political career*.

He decided that he would go to see her, and set out through the snow up the long hill to The Heights. Seen through a softening veil of snowflakes Ida's mansion had a certain gloomy grandeur. There were no lights on in the front of the house, no Christmas wreath on the door.

He rang the bell and waited. He waited a long time and concluded that the Brewsters must have gone out to some festive gathering. Josiah was just about to leave when the door opened, and he dimly discerned against the blackness of the hall a large figure which he assumed, without recognizing her, to be Ida.

They peered at each other through the falling snow. "Ida?"

"Come in." Her voice sounded strange and muffled.

The figure retreated into the darkness. The hall was pitch black and he waited there for some light to indicate the way. A door opened at some distance and he saw Ida passing through into a lamplit room. He noticed that the back of her green evening dress was unfastened and that there was something glittering in her hair.

He followed her across the room and into a study with a large French desk strewn with papers. For a moment he couldn't find Ida and then saw that she had stationed herself in a corner that was deep in shadow. He was aware of her large presence, but could only dimly make out her face. It gave Josiah an uncomfortable and eerie feeling to confront a person he could not see.

"You sent me a note saying that you had something to discuss."

There was no answer from the effigy in the shadows.

"Why do you want to see me, Ida?"

She seemed to project a watchful silence that was threatening and yet full of uncertainty and fear. She was like a cornered animal, trapped by a hunter, preparing to defend herself and repel any move that was made against her.

He waited, increasingly uneasy at her prolonged silence.

He moved toward her into the center of the room and heard the creak of her chair as Ida pressed herself back against the wall.

"What is the matter, Ida? You asked to see me.

What is it you have to say?" Josiah asked with a touch of impatience.

He could hear her heavy breathing, and as his eyes adjusted to the dark he could make out her large, flaccid face and unnaturally distended eyes that seemed to be shifting between him and the desk as though she had some weapon hidden there and was trying to judge the distance between herself and it.

"Look, it's Christmas Eve and I have friends to see," he said sharply.

Suddenly she got up and moved along the wall, staying in self-protection among the shadows and avoiding the pool of yellow light cast by the lamp on the carpet.

"Yes," the muffled voice admitted, "I had to see you. It's for your sake as well as mine. I know certain things. I don't want to mention them—unless I have to. I know how important it is for you—being elected. What you do is not my concern." Abruptly the dam was broken. Ida's resistance gave way and she talked rapidly with mounting incoherence.

"I've been going through a very dreadful time. It's my father. He's gone mad. He's in the power of that woman. He has done terrible things to me—because she made him. He's taken everything from me and my children. We have nothing. We're beggars. Beggars."

She was moving back and forth like some wild animal, avoiding the lamplight. He could see her hands clasping and unclasping and the jewel in her hair glinting in the gloom.

"I have only one thing left. One thing. And she wants that, too. She wants to ruin me and my children. She wants to put us on the streets—with nothing."

Josiah heard her take a deep, rasping breath.

"I have shares. I own fifty-two percent of the new railroad. Totally. In my name. My father's doing everything he can to force me to sell out. He arranged the accident with the train and blowing up the bridge. I know what's been going on. He shut the mills and pretended he couldn't pay Thaddeus Brownlow's loan. Everyone thinks he's run out of money. He wants them to think that because he wants my shares. She's threatened to leave him unless he owns everything outright. I tried to save him. I staked everything to save the family. I stand to lose everything I have. All I have now is the shares. He won't finish the railroad until he gets them. I don't know how long he can hold out. I can't—much longer. I have no one to turn to. They've all deserted me." Ida stopped pacing then and said in a loud voice, "It's what you've always wanted. Ever since you were a boy. To get the better of Sam Garvey. Well, I don't care any more. You can fight it out between you. You're men. You're used to fighting. I can't go on any more. I can't keep up the payments. They'll eat up everything I have."

Ida came forward, clumsy and gross in her distress, and Josiah saw her, a big-boned, haggard, ugly, desperate woman in a dull green evening dress with a Christmas tinsel ornament pinned to her loosely coiled hair. She seemed quite demented, in a state of wild disorder. He was aware of an unpleasant odor—rank —that comes with fear.

"I've got to sell. I can't hold out. It's not just money." All the breath went out of her and she managed, as though at the end of her physical and mental rope, "I can't wait any more. He's ruthless, ruthless! Between them they want to kill me. I must end it before I go mad or die."

She lurched into the full glare of the lamp. He could barely recognize her.

Ida clasped and unclasped her hands. "Please— help me. I can't go on."

She was suddenly stricken with shame because she saw his expression of shock and of disgust and turned to lean on the mantelpiece to hide her face.

He was torn between revulsion and a sort of horrified pity.

"What is it you want me to do?"

She said with her face averted and her great bulk trembling, "Buy the shares. They're worth less than half of what I paid. It's what you've always wanted. I—just—want—peace."

Josiah did not have time in the midst of this nightmare interview to consider this opportunity and what it might mean to him or the position that the owner-ship of the controlling interest in Sam Garvey's rail-road would place him in.

"If you know your father is only playing a game, you should hold out. He has to come through. He's got to finish the railroad. He must have huge commit-ments."

"He raised twenty million on the mills. Yes, he'll come through. He'll have to—in the end."

Her resistance to his seeing her in her present state abruptly deserted her. She lurched away from the mantel and sank into a chair. Without any effort to hide her abject defeat, Ida said, "I just can't go on. I didn't realize what a hold she has over him. She won't let him give in and she hates me!" Ida threw back her head. "You were all taken in by her. You should know. She sleeps with you. She's the lowest—the vilest. You should know."

She gave an hysterical, unreal laugh and her head rolled from one side to the other.

"She slept with my son, my father, and with you," Ida spat out as though her mouth were filled with poison. "That—whore!"

She was breathing rapidly and her eyes were rolling from side to side like marbles because she could not bring herself to look at him. "You and she—and the others—that filthy boy!"

Josiah wanted to get out of the room, away from the stench of lunacy that she exuded.

"Ida, you're ill," he said firmly. "You should see a doctor and go to bed, you're not in any condition to decide what you ought to do about your shares. Be-sides I have other commitments now. I'm not in any position to enter into large financial deals. What you say about Mrs. Garvey is quite untrue."

Ida gave a caricature of her famous smile. "Don't lie, Josiah. She spent the night with you during the strike." She leaned forward, glaring. "I know. I know all about you. Everything. I have that boy's statement, signed and sealed."

"What boy?" he asked, shocked that she somehow knew about Valeria's nocturnal visit.

She sneered with elaborate contempt, "Jodie Packer. Jo-die Pack-er." She pursed up her mouth as though she were about to spit at him. "You disgust me. All of you. You and McGiver and Mrs. Samuel Garvey. Filth."

He turned to leave. Ida was totally insane.

As Josiah reached the door, she shouted, "You want me to publish that boy's statement? It was taken down by a detective from the Blanchard Agency, twenty-five Walnut Street, Chicago. You think you can get away with anything. You think," her voice rose, "that you can do anything you want because you've got McGiver in your pocket. You paid his gambling debts and he looks the other way. He's part of your disgusting games. You and he and Jo-die Pack-er. It's all there. Every revolting detail." Ida heaved herself up and came toward him. "If I publish that statement, it'll ruin you. Once and for all." Her large, dreadful, bloodshot eyes burned with a fury of destruction. "I think, Josiah, that you'll buy my shares. You'll buy them because you've got no choice."

She swerved away to her desk and opened a drawer and took out a sheaf of papers tied at one corner by a blood red string. "Read that and tell me you can't make a commitment. Read it. The very thought of what you do makes me vomit."

Josiah went back to her with the singular calm of a sane man dealing with a lunatic, took the sheaf of papers, and stood in the middle of the room reading. She was leaning on the desk with her head hanging forward, crying. She sat down, collapsing, spent, on the gilt chair. With her big, flaccid arms hanging loose, she was crying with broken gulps and sobs, the tears running out of her eyes.

He read to the end without comment while she sat there crying. He placed the sheaf of papers on the desk.

His voice sounded unnaturally calm. "Do you really believe this?" Josiah asked as though appealing to whatever dim residue of reason Ida might still possess. "You know perfectly well it isn't true. I never heard of Jodie Packer. Whatever else I may be I'm certainly no sodomist."

She was whimpering and sobbing, her whole body shaken. She shook her head. "It's the end of all of us. Me—you—Sam Garvey." She added weakly, as though she no longer had any strength left to battle or accuse, "It was all wrong—from the start—all that's happened."

Ida leaned on the desk and sobbed. The long weeks of tension and waiting, of endless tormenting doubts and wild hopes, all broke on her. There was nothing left but this meaningless release in tears.

Josiah saw that the statement he had just read, in the hands of this woman who had reached such a pitch of desperation that she no longer had any grasp on reality, might well ruin him if she showed it to almost anyone. Any of his opponents would seize on it. The question of whether it were true or not would be of little consequence. The very hint of unnatural vice would finish him. His past with its flaunted excesses would rise to corroborate every detail. The whole town believed he was responsible for the derailment of the train. They would be only too ready to believe the worst.

"Ida, pull yourself together. Where is the actual statement?" he said more cautiously.

"Upstairs," she sobbed into her hands.

"The whole thing is a total fabrication. I suppose you bribed this Packer to say these things."

"I don't know. I don't know," Ida wailed.

"Is this the only copy you have?"

She nodded. "I don't know if it's true. It doesn't matter." She looked up, her eyes streaming. "I'm so tired, Josiah. I don't know if it's true. I thought it was that other man—Ford Hollister, but he said, he swore —he signed it." She suddenly begged him, "Can't you help me? You can have that—" she pushed the tied papers toward him. "You can have it if you buy the shares."

He was sickened by the sight of her and turned to the fireplace, thinking in what way he could most speedily free himself from the trap she had set for him.

"How much do you want?"

She rummaged blindly among the papers strewn about her desk. "I had this statement yesterday—from New York—what they're worth now. I want two hundred thousand more than the market value."

He took the broker's report and read it. It was still a very large sum, far more than he could lay hands on without selling *The Courier* and his house. That would take time. He had securities, but to raise that amount . . .

"How soon do you want the money?"

"By New Year's. Not later. I can't hold out."

She was exhausted, too drained even to go on sobbing. She sat there, a shapeless bulk at the desk, desolate and pleading.

"What guarantee do I have that you haven't made other copies of that rubbish?"

"There aren't any more. Only this."

An idea came to Josiah of how he might, at one stroke, settle the whole matter and extricate himself from Ida and her threat to his career.

"Will you be here tomorrow?"

Ida nodded, her great bloodshot eyes upon him.

"I will see what I can do." He reached for the detective's statement, but quick as a snake, her hand was on it.

"After," she said.

"I'm doing this not because there's an iota of truth in it, but because there are a good many people who don't care about the truth. Any lies are good enough for them. They seem to be good enough for you."

"You'd deny it anyway. You'd have to. But a signed statement is good enough. It doesn't matter in the end what's true and what isn't. Perhaps no one knows. Perhaps none of us really knows."

She stood up quite calmly and announced, with a grotesque reversal of her gracious manner as a hostess, "You'll find the money."

He left her then, let himself out of the darkened madhouse and found himself in the clean and soothing snow. All the way down the hill into Arcadia he

debated the best way of silencing Ida Brewster. She
was no less dangerous because she and her accusations were insane. He knew without question, in her
present state she was capable of anything. That horrendous statement, even with the deletions that any
newspaper would be forced to make, was dynamite to
the fuse of public scandal. It would blast his chances
of election. He would be forced at the best to leave
the country and live like other moral lepers in Florence
or Algiers in that shady half-world of assumed names
and ruined reputations. As far as Josiah was able to
consider Ida with any degree of objectivity, he could
see from her totally distorted point of view that she
might consider herself justified. It was a long-delayed
and bitterly debated revenge. But there was not only
himself to consider; there was Valeria. Ida must have
found out about that visit through one of his servants.
Who had let her in that night? William Pincraft, was it?
Servants always gossip and gossip always spread. He
had never bothered about gossip before. If it were
true that McGiver consorted with this Jodie Packer
and if that—through Ida's madness—became known
. . . She had thrown a net of scandal over them all.

There was one possible way out, Josiah thought. It
was a long shot, but in this emergency it was worth
trying.

Then it occurred to him that if he bought the shares,
if he raised that amount of money against securities, he
would finally have gotten the better of Sam Garvey. He
would have that fatal statement and control the new
railroad at the same time. Instead of ruining him, Ida
would have handed him on a platter the ultimate objective of years of planning, years of hating the man
who had robbed him of his inheritance. Josiah had
never truly believed that Sam had been guilty of his
father's death. His own researching, done years later,
had led him to discover many things about his father
which he had not been willing to admit. Ida was right
in saying that it mattered very little what was true or
false. People believed what served their purposes and
passions. Valeria had said to him that if people on
both sides had compromised, had stood by common

sense instead of hatred, all the bloodshed and bitterness of the War could have been avoided. He had intrigued for so long against Sam Garvey, justifying his maneuvers by supporting the popular notion about his father's death, that the plotting and planning had become a crusade in itself regardless of what had caused it. It was this animal inconsistency in man, these drives against reason in favor of the bestial release of greed and hatred, that turned human society into a jungle. Ida was a terrible example of a woman who had become animalized by a lack of tempering reason. She had loved no one except—perhaps long ago, before he had understood such things—himself.

Josiah had crossed Main Street, strangely transformed into a fairytale thoroughfare of golden lamps and dancing snowflakes. He made his way down a side street toward the little slum that surrounded the railroad yards.

He walked slowly, peering at the numbers of the wretched dwellings. Had McGiver, in this same dead of night, made his way down here to a sickening rendezvous with this young male whore? It was possible. One knew nothing of what went on when the blinds were drawn on other people's lives. Any one of a dozen incidents in his own sexual saga, if publicized, would have ruined him. And yet they were things that everyone did, at some time or other. Josiah felt a sudden and profound gratitude to Valeria for having given him a love that transcended his own base nature. Perhaps the secret to Jodie Packer lay in Ford Hollister whose masculine attributes he had always doubted.

Few of these ramshackle houses seemed to have numbers. There were no street lamps and Josiah slipped and stumbled, striking matches. Twenty-one. Nothing for three doors. A chalk-smudged twenty-six? This house, then, two stories with a light upstairs, must be twenty-seven.

He knocked on the door.

A window was wrenched up and a woman's rasping voice called down into the white oblivion, "Who's there?"

"Jodie Packer?" Josiah called up as the flakes swirled on his face.

"Gone," the voice called down. "Left town and good riddance."

The window shut with a muffled rattle.

"Gone!" Josiah yelled into the deserted street. No hope, then, of forcing a retraction from Jodie Packer.

Randolph was startled to see Josiah whose hat and shoulders were white with snow.

"What on earth are you doing here?" It was the one house where Josiah Eaton was most unlikely to call.

"Is Sam Garvey in?"

"Yes. He's in the study."

"I'd like to see him."

Josiah stamped a small avalanche of snow from his coat, brushed his shoulders and shook out his hat. As he stepped into the hallway he could hear what he guessed must be Valeria playing.

"I certainly didn't imagine the Christmas spirit would extend to seeing you here," Randolph said.

"It's not the Christmas spirit, Randy. Business as usual." He shook Randy's hand. He had come to regard this loyal enthusiast as his only personal friend. "Give my greetings to your sister," he added, as he made his way to find Sam. Randy was watching him, perturbed. Had he guessed, Josiah wondered, on those journeys about the state, how many of his moods and spells of abstraction had been caused by his attachment to Valeria?

As he knocked on the study door, he caught sight across the hall of a long portrait of her in her gray riding habit. He had a sudden longing to see her, but the gruff voice summoned him.

"Come."

The old man was sitting at his desk and looked up with surprise as Josiah came in and shut the door behind him. A familiar scowl drew down the bushy, iron gray eyebrows.

"Don't be put out," Josiah greeted him. "I haven't come to wish you the compliments of the season."

"Didn't think you would," Sam growled.

"I have just seen your daughter. I thought it would be a good idea if we had a little talk about what she said."

A flicker of interest sparked in the sharp blue eyes. "Since when are you on speaking terms with Ida?"

"I'm not. She sent me a note. I may as well tell you straight, Ida is out of her head."

He drew up a chair and sat down. Sam was watching Josiah, all attention and sly shrewdness.

"I won't beat about the bush. Ida offered me her stock in your railroad. It seems that by putting up everything she's got she now owns fifty-two percent." He paused to observe Sam's reaction. The blue eyes were half closed, very bright and steady.

She wants the curret market price, plus two hundred thousand. It's a great deal of money—even at the price you've forced them down to. Oh, she knows about that. Ida's mad, but she's no fool."

Sam waited. The cigar shifted slowly from one side of his mouth to the other.

"I could raise that amount. Not at once. It would take negotiation. I don't know," he continued levelly, "whether you'd prefer *me* to own the controlling stock or Ida. I told her to hold out. I can't believe you've gone this far just to let the whole thing slide. And I don't believe you can't lay your hands on enough cash to finish building—as you've put about. A lot of people would love to think you're ruined. But I'll pay you a compliment since it's Christmas. I never underestimated you. Evidently Ida has." He offered Sam a sugar-coated pill, "She's ready to throw in her hand."

Sam took his well-chewed cigar from his mouth and carefully deposited a small column of ash in a brass ashtray.

"You may find this hard to believe," Josiah went on in the same steady tone, "but I've finally had enough of this town. I'm thinking of clearing out."

"Think you'll be elected?" Sam inquired.

"I think I stand a chance."

Sam accorded this information a doubtful "Humph!"

"I'm thinking of putting *The Courier* up for sale and

closing up my country home. If I'm elected my interests will lie elsewhere."

Sam evinced no concern for Josiah's plans. He was waiting for the proposition.

"As I say, I can raise the money. The point is that I'm not sure I want to. I know that once the railroad gets rolling it would make me very rich. It would make you very rich indeed if you owned the controlling stock. Not that you need money. You live so simply. But you're fond of money, aren't you, Sam?"

"Very," Sam admitted, waiting.

"It's a big sum, but nothing to what those shares will be worth later on. You planned the Mid-Western well. You'll get a lot of business along that line. Added to which, and I'm sure you've thought of it, the present line will be hard hit. I sold out a year ago, so I don't stand to lose, except my director's salary. But it could be bought up, once you get started, for a fraction of what it's worth today. I guess you're planning to repair the bridge and open the mills as soon as you get the shares?"

Sam disregarded this question. "She offered them to you," he pointed out.

"Yes. She offered them to me." Josiah had concluded the preliminaries.

They both took a break to observe each other. They shifted their positions and noted the ticking of the clock and the cheerful crackle of the fire.

"So why have you come to me?" Sam inquired. "You say you can pay Ida's price. It's the chance you've waited for."

"I know. It's the chance I've waited for. The question is I'm not sure it's the chance right now I want to take."

"Better make up your mind. Ida's liable to sell."

"She won't sell out to you, that's certain. She'd rather die and have the shares buried with her. It's a pity to be losing so much money, Sam—with the mills idle. I understand you put them up as collateral with Brownlow. Something like twenty million, Ida said."

"Maybe," Sam conceded, chewing on his cigar.

"Suppose I buy the shares at Ida's price. I pay her an extra two hundred thousand. How would you like to buy them back from me with another hundred grand thrown in?"

Sam's eyebrows rose slightly. "Why should I? I'll buy them on the market when Ida sells and she will soon enough. I won't have to pay either of you a cent."

"That's true. But if I close with Ida you won't get that chance. I'm in a position to hold out. I can hold out a long time, Sam, until you and the mills go bust."

"If I go bust there'll be no railroad," Sam said grimly. "It's a lot of money for you to ante up just to prove a point."

"Wouldn't be the first time a railroad's been reorganized when the original owners run out of dough. I might take it over myself with Brownlow's help. I'm not exactly inexperienced, you know."

Sam very carefully shifted some papers on his desk. He moved one batch to the right and shifted his inkwell just a fraction to the left.

"I'll give you fifty grand."

"No, Sam, a hundred. It's a nice round figure. Little enough when you consider what I'd make if I keep the shares."

"Keep 'em," Sam snapped. "I can hold out as long as you."

"With the mills closed? You're not the only one who knows how to pull up a stretch of line. It could take a long, *long* time to repair them another time."

Sam smiled unexpectedly. "I made a mistake when I put you in the accounts department."

"Look, Sam," Josiah admitted, "I've got other fish to fry. Give me a hundred grand and take the Goddamned shares and let's call it quits."

Sam considered him, this tall, golden-haired, urbane, successful man who was about to be elected governor. He was not convinced that there was not some other motive behind Josiah's comparatively mild proposal. Had it to do with Valeria? Had there, after all, been some element of truth in Ida's accusations? Josiah was not a man to make altruistic gestures over business. Who ever did? To throw up a fortune for a sum that would not affect his financial position much, one way or the other! But many strange things had been happening lately. There was a whole world of ambiguous gestures and attitudes which made no sense to him. They were as strange as Valeria's paying out a lump sum to cover the men's wages during the Christmas layoff. He had assumed that Josiah belonged to his own world, with its own cut and dried rules, where no one gave anything for nothing and yielded nothing without a knock-down, drag-out fight. Valeria's principles and loyalties he could accept, along with her sentimentality about the poor, as part of her peculiar, unrealistic nature. But Josiah was nothing if not a realist. Was it because he himself was tired and no longer had the same grasp of things?

"How would you think of arranging it?" he asked.

"McGraw would hold the full amount in escrow. When I close with Ida, he can transfer Ida's share to her account and the hundred grand to mine. I'll hand the shares over to McGraw. You trust him, don't you?"

Sam nodded.

A dead silence fell. The deal was made.

Josiah rose and stretched.

"An odd kind of Christmas present for both of us."

Sam stubbed out his cigar.

"So you think you'll be elected. I dare say you will be. It's a profitable business—politics."

"You know something, Sam? I'm struggling with a new temptation, almost as great as making money. I've a notion to be an honest governor."

"You'll never make it."

"Good luck with the railroad," Josiah said from the door. "It rounds out your career quite nicely."

A long look passed between them.

As Josiah was putting on his greatcoat in the hall, and feeling a sense of something achieved and a great weight lifted, the door of the parlor opened and Valeria came out.

She stopped in the doorway. She had never seen

him look more handsome. But there was a new air about him that far exceeded good looks. Humanity and generosity of spirit enhanced his whole bearing. It is useless for me to pretend any more, she thought. She no longer had the desire to fight against the feeling she had for him.

He was, in turn, dazzled to see the woman whose image he had carried with him on his journies and which had haunted his days and nights. Her beauty was touched by a fine sadness, but her exquisite grace as she came toward him seemed to Josiah like that of no other woman on earth.

"Happy Christmas, Valeria." He held out his strong hand.

"And to you, Josiah." Their hands, as they joined, sealed an appeasement and a reconciliation. She lowered her head slightly and said in a low voice, "I'm sorry." And raising her lovely, troubled green eyes, she said, "You understand now, don't you?"

"Yes. Do you?"

She nodded slowly and withdrew her delicate hand.

"I hope this will be a good year for you. You are sure to be elected and that is what you want and what you deserve."

"It is not all I want, but it must do."

"We have to settle for what we have."

He kissed her gently on the cheek.

"Much happiness, my dear."

They both knew that ultimate happiness could not be theirs, but they were now able to accept this. Their doubts and torments and regrets vanished to be replaced by the stoic knowledge of their regard for each other which would endure.

She heard the study door open and Sam's shuffling steps. "Good-bye, Josiah," she said quickly and turned away.

Saddened and grateful, he went out into the snow.

From those few words a new stage in their relationship had started, something that they could both respect and cherish. And from that meeting, the long feud between Sam Garvey and Josiah Eaton ended.

There was no need to erect a commemorative tablet with a suitable inscription and R.I.P. engraved upon it.

They simply passed out of each other's lives.

⚔ Chapter Twenty-five ⚔

Thaddeus Brownlow had been justified in thinking that Sam Garvey had a number of extra aces up his sleeve. Once the deal with Josiah Eaton was concluded and Ida's shares were safely in his hands he produced these aces with surprising speed.

The mills reopened on the second day of January. What he had taken away for Christmas he gave back for the New Year. Repairs on the blown up bridge were hurriedly completed. Once again the shipments of steel and iron ore rumbled across the prairies to Chicago. A number of imposing gentlemen came and went from the Garvey stronghold. Meetings were held and administrative posts allotted; directors were voted in and minutes taken. Not one of these fortunate functionaries was allowed to forget that these formalities were just formalities and that Sam Garvey had every intention of running the whole show himself.

Large sums of money appeared by magic from mysterious accounts where they had been quietly proliferating under aliases. Thaddeus Brownlow's payments were made on time. Jim Pryor emerged from the hospital with a large red bandana pressed to the side of his mouth to stem the flow of saliva and a dark green visor to protect his eyes from any glare. Once again he took orders and carried out orders. Mr. Murdock received a raise. An amount equal to the sum that Mrs. Sam Garvey had paid out for the workers' salaries was restored to her account. She also received a stole of superb Russian sable, and a large bracelet set with the finest opals.

Arcadia congratulated itself that the town's lead-

ing citizen had proved himself worthy of distinction.
Gentlemen at the club, swilling their whiskey, admitted that the wiley old bastard had a deal more
spit and vinegar left in him than they'd expected.
They laughed at the way he had taken them all in.

The only person whom Sam's burst of magnanimity
and munificence did not include was Ida. The quarterly allowance did not fatten her emaciated account.
As far as Sam Garvey was concerned, Ida Brewster
had ceased to exist. She had paid the price for thinking
herself the equal to her sire. She had fought and lost.
Sam extended no commiseration to the vanquished.

In New York the impeccable directors of Brownlow's bank debated these events and a spate of impeccable rumors found their way to the brokerage
houses along Wall Street. The shares in the Mid-
Western and Pacific dutifully rose. Not that this was of
much advantage to investors, as the bulk of those once
again valuable certificates was held by one man. From
being a mere millionaire, Sam Garvey was now on his
way to joining the hierarchy of financial titans known
as the Midas Club, which included Thaddeus Brownlow, William K. Vanderbilt and the ubiquitous, some
said iniquitous, Jay Gould who at that time was busy
trying to corner the entire gold reserves of the United
States. The fortunes of these giants might be, to a large
extent, on paper, in promissory notes, in loans, in credit
or in the opportunities for bluff and blackmail that their
reputations afforded; but imaginary or not, they were
mightily impressive. From starting with a pair of no
good deuces Sam Garvey had surpassed himself and
won that round with a royal flush.

The other topics of conjecture that occupied the
town's interest and fluttered at the tea tables on The
Heights were the *For Sale* notice on Josiah Eaton's
country property, and the more controversial issue that
crept along the grapevine to *The Courier* offices and
shuttled back and forth between the desks: was *The
Courier* itself up for grabs? Those always weary and
always persevering pen pushers who struggled week
after week to get their newspaper out on time now
nervously wondered how long they would hold their

jobs in the event that their boss abandoned them for
the highest desk job in the state.

It was pretty self-assured, some people decided, to
sell up in preparation for a move to the capital before
the returns were even in. Maybe Josiah had inside information. Maybe sympathetic hands would count the
votes. Or Josiah, from being too damn sure of himself,
was in for a big surprise.

Due to this general resurgence of activity, Valeria
was unable to find an auspicious moment to broach
the subject that was uppermost in her mind, namely
when it might be feasible for Mr. and Mrs. Sam Garvey to leave Arcadia. Although only six months had
gone by since her marriage, it seemed possible, now
that his main objective had been reached, that Sam
might agree to embark on their great voyage of discovery a little sooner. Spring would be ideal. Spring in
England was legendary. Between the downpours, daf-
fodils gilded the parks of stately manor houses,
bluebells carpeted the woods, and primroses peeped,
pert and innocent, from every hedgerow. The long
drawn out winter, with its unbearable tensions and
confrontations, had worn down her resistance. The
routine of the black house that she detested depleted
her energy, and even her afternoon rides with Mimosa
failed to still the insistent urging of her heart to be
en route.

It was not only on her own account that she was so
eager to get away.

Although Sam had revealed nothing of the drama
which had resulted in the acquisition of the shares,
or of the roles which Josiah and Ida had played in it,
Valeria was aware, having grown familiar with every
nuance of his moods and humors, that the mysterious
tug-of-war had taken a greater toll on him than he
would ever have admitted or perhaps even known.

For the most part, Sam was in excellent spirits and
was even, when he remembered, attentive to her, but
his bursts of intense concentration were followed by
lapses of depletion. He was at his desk at the same
time every morning, but she observed that it caused
him an extra effort to assemble the details that must be

attended to. The discipline of a lifetime had not deserted him, but his general capacity for work was less.

Valeria still read to him in the evenings and he would often come for half an hour to hear her play, but he drowsed and dropped off and lost the thread in the middle of a sentence. He forgot things and counted on her to remind him and, indeed, appeared to have accepted as permament their roles of nurse and semiinvalid.

Sometimes, when she came in to announce dinner, she would find Sam still working at his papers, but his face would be gray with fatigue. He ate little, drank his usual quota of whiskeys, smoked incessantly, but he was grateful, when the clock struck eleven, for the relief of sleep.

To the world, to his subordinates, he was the same gruff and tireless figure of authority, demanding the utmost in service and obedience, but to Valeria he was increasingly a worn old man.

It no longer surprised her that Sam's welfare had come to be as important to her as her own.

As Ida's name was never mentioned, it was from Nancy that Valeria learned of *the* Mrs. Brewster's decline into what the frightened girl could only describe as madness. Nancy's reports of her mother's unspeakable condition and behavior, her prolonged drinking bouts and outbursts of hysteria, the sudden sale of all the silver spirited away by unknown buyers to Chicago, alarmed Valeria. Nancy begged to be allowed to come and live with her. Anything, but *anything,* to escape from that loathsome mansion, never cleaned and never visited, through which Ida roamed at all hours, talking to herself, crying out and falling drunk on carpets. These frightening reports prompted Valeria to broach the subject of sending Nancy to a finishing school.

"If she stays in such an atmosphere with no one to talk to and her mother in this condition, I'm afraid she'll become ill with nerves."

"Do whatever you think best," was all Sam would volunteer.

"Shouldn't *something* be done about your daughter?

She seems to be quite irrational. Why should she suddenly be selling off her things?"

But the steel curtain had descended. Ida's condition meant no more to Sam than a name written in chalk and wiped clean from a blackboard at the end of class.

The perils of Nancy's life at home were further stressed by Monsieur Emile who paid an unexpected call one afternoon, natty in his winter suiting, and shielding D'Artagnan with a white silk umbrella.

Valeria was delighted to see him.

She led him into the lilac enclave, brought him a glass of sherry, and D'Artagnan a ginger cookie. The little man, whose natural tact and born civility made him at ease in any surroundings, complimented his dear Mademoiselle on the transformation of her parlor.

"Even if I did not know you lived here I would recognize your touch. Such charm and originality! Ah, Mademoiselle Valeria, if I may be permitted still to call you that, I often think of the dinners on which we collaborated. They are among the brightest souvenirs of my career."

"How have you been, Monsieur Emile?"

"Mademoiselle!" The little hands rose and fell in a Gallic gesture of fatality. "It is no longer possible for me to remain *chez* Madame Brewster. I tolerated Madame Brewster because, as you know, I have long had the intention of returning to Paris and my service with her would have made this possible."

Valeria knew how this perfectionist had suffered from Ida's culinary vulgarities. They had left a permanent scar on his sensibilities. But she saw that it was not of such matters that he had come to speak.

"I do not wish you to think that I am a bearer of evil tidings, but I am forced to say that Madame Brewster's behavior is no longer tolerable. Something very serious has happened. It is not for me to invade the family privacy. It is of Miss Nancy that I think. It is on her behalf and yours and to bid my dear Mademoiselle *adieu* that I give myself the pleasure of calling on you."

"You're leaving then?"

"I go to New York where I must work for perhaps a year before I have made sufficient economies to return to Paris."

"Are you still thinking of opening a restaurant?"

"That is my dream, but like many dreams it may be hard to realize."

Valeria was so charmed to see her old friend, her only solace in many unhappy hours, that she asked, "If you won't think it an intrusion, how much would you need to start a restaurant without spending a year beforehand in New York?"

"That would depend," Monsieur Emile said seriously, "on the location. Perfection would be in the vicinity of the Rond Point, but there, alas, I fear, the rents are high."

"Tell me about it."

"It is close to the Champs Elysées and the new boulevards, to the Place Louis Quatorze, now renamed the Place de la Concorde. Many large hotels are there, along the Rue St. Honoré. It is a quarter where important people live. One could gather a distinguished clientele."

"Would you consider allowing me to invest in such an enterprise?" Valeria asked fondly. "I have no doubt whatever that it would be a great success."

Monsieur Emile's eyes opened wide. "My dear Madame Garvey, I could not consider a financial transaction between friends, if I may presume to call you that. On the other hand—ah, if you and I could embark on a joint venture. With your taste, your sense of style . . . !"

"Very well, if you prefer, we can go into partnership."

Monsieur Emile sat bolt upright. "Can you be serious?" he cried. "It would be paradise!"

"Tell me how much you need and I will arrange it. I think it is foolish for you to waste time in New York where they will not appreciate your talents."

Monsieur Emile was quite overcome, not merely at this promise of financial aid, but at such a tribute to his art.

"I shall call it Chez Valerie or, with your permission, *tout simplement,* Valeria. I can see it . . . an awning of light green and lilac, like this room—the interior in lilac and *jaune citron* with linen as white as snow. A spring garden. Restful to the eye and lightly stimulating to the appetite. Oh, Mademoiselle, what joy! I have no words to express myself."

After this moving interlude, he returned to the subject of his visit.

"I tell you frankly I fear for Miss Nancy and for you. Madame Brewster is no longer in possession of her senses. There is an atmosphere of violence. I can only express it so. Madame Brewster is working herself into a state where she will precipitate *an act.* Miss Nancy sees a terrible person, terrible because she is as bad as she is stupid. And Miss Tabitha. Together they concoct things of great wickedness. Miss Nancy should not stay in that house alone."

"I don't think," Valeria demurred, "however sick she may be, that Mrs. Brewster would resort to violence."

"Do not underestimate these people," Monsieur Emile said in a low voice, as though they were isolated in the midst of the wilder tribes of Central Africa. *"Se sont des sauvages,* Mademoiselle."

After a while he rose to go.

At the door he bowed and kissed her hand. He opened the silk umbrella over D'Artagnan and surveyed the gloomy street. *"Quel sale endroit!* Ah, for you to live here dear Mademoiselle, *franchement, c'est completement fou."*

Prompted by Monsieur Emile's dire predictions, Valeria wrote a note to Nancy telling her to pack an overnight case and come to stay with her and Sam. She posted it on her way to Horton's Stables.

She could not bring herself to believe she was in actual danger. Ida might be mentally ill, might be devoured by irrational hatreds, but it seemed beyond credibility that she would instigate a crime. Monsieur Emile had been raised in the tradition of *crimes passionées.* French ladies frequently shot their lovers in fits of jealousy and French patriots, between impassioned speeches, flung bombs at royalty like bouquets.

It was part of the Gallic temperament. Only war or struggles over business roused the stolid Anglo-Saxons to such excesses. And yet her own experiences during the Aftermath at Whitebriars . . . But she put such disturbing memories out of mind.

It was a strange day without color. A white sky met a white earth. Houses and trees stood out like etchings. The incline to The Heights was slippery where the snow had hardened. Valeria dismounted and led Mimosa for fear the little mare might slip and hurt herself. Mimosa gave her a look of mild reproach at this unnecessary precaution. She knew herself to be quite capable of carrying her mistress over any terrain, however hazardous.

The Brewster mansion looked unusually grim. The red brick had darkened, as though sullenly resentful of the drifts of snow that had piled up along the terrace. The entrance was practically impassable. Perhaps Monsieur Emile was right. It looked like a house where murder might be committed.

She remounted on Tremont Avenue. It was too icy to gallop, but Mimosa trotted briskly. Valeria could not shake off her malaise. Was it the day and all this dead and glaring whiteness? Trees stood over her like pallbearers. Every house had the closed solemnity of a funeral home. Crows rose, cawing, from high branches and circled against the stark pallor like specks of coal.

Even the countryside did not refresh her. The fields were scarred with black stooks that stuck out from the snow like warning relics of a holocaust. She shivered. Should she turn back?

Fairlawn stood with a mournful, deserted air at the end of its leafless avenue. She was on the point of turning in and spending an hour with Althea but for some reason she was not in the mood to cope with Althea's peculiar intensity or Ford's abstracted efforts at cordiality.

Josiah's place was boarded up. Two covered wagons were stationed in the driveway. Men were moving out furniture. She had come to think of Josiah with a sad acceptance as part of her past. There had been too many impediments between them and their paths were carrying them farther apart. She wondered if she would ever see him again.

There was no use in dwelling on what might have been if circumstances had been different. Their hearts might have proposed, but fate had disposed of that brief involvement.

A little farther on another sign announced that the Hotchkiss farm was for sale. Valeria reined Mimosa in. How still the orchards were! It seemed impossible that these skeletal trees had once been heavy with fruit. She wondered what had happened to the apple-cheeked woman who had been so bewildered by her plea for work and had made her a kindly cup of tea. Had she died during this winter that seemed longer than any other?

She turned Mimosa up the path that led to the farmhouse. Here the secretive enchantment of the snow still lingered. Trees glittered, their smaller branches encased in ice. Tufts of snow lay cupped like nests between the twigs. Like arctic Spanish moss the icicles dripped, glistening, where later the leaves would be. Not a bird hopped over the blanketed earth. The farm was listening.

As she approached the house, Valeria heard the sound of an axe. Someone was chopping wood. The house looked smaller, shrunken without the clematis and climbing roses, no more than brown vines still clinging to the walls.

The axe blows stopped and a man came around the side of the house, mopping his face. He stopped, amazed at the sight of the ghostly gray figure waiting there on a phantom horse, as though materialized out of the snow itself.

He came toward her, mopping his neck slowly, suspicious and on guard. He was a broad burly fellow in his thirties with a bull-like throat and small, unsmiling eyes.

"I see that your place is up for sale," Valeria said. Her voice sounded cold and clear.

"Yup!" What was that to her, this grand strange

woman with the haughty look and skin as white as the sky? He mistrusted her on sight.

"What has happened to Mrs. Hotchkiss?"

"Dead. Afore Christmas. I'm her son."

"I am sorry to hear that. She was a kind, good woman."

"Been here afore?"

"Twice. We talked."

It was sad. The simple and steadfast spirit of the farm had deserted it. She thought of the woman bent over her runner beans, and of all the flowers they had picked that day. Mrs. Hotchkiss had understood her beans and marigolds and that was a worthwhile knowledge in this world of half-truths, compromises and contrivances.

It occurred to Valeria that this would be a good place for Mary to bring up her sons. She could take the elder boy out of the mills and Matthew would grow strong in the clean air with the scents and sounds of the country to supplement his lack of sight. It would also be a good place to leave Mimosa when she went away. And perhaps there might come a time when she would need to sit by that stream to restore her spirits, pick fruit and ruminate in the quiet kitchen, alone with a ticking clock. That old and cherished dream of peace, put away like a wedding dress in a camphor chest, prompted her to say, "How much are you asking for it?"

Mrs. Hotchkiss's son peered up at her. What business was it of hers how much he hoped to get?

"Three thousand."

"What does that include?"

"Orchards. Two of pears. Two of apples. One of cherries. Land 'round the house up to the trees and a ten-acre field behind."

"I will buy it," she said calmly. "I have always liked this place and I will see that it's kept up."

His jaw dropped at the off-handed way she agreed.

"If you'll go to the National Security Bank and ask for Mr. McGraw, he'll give you the money and draw up the bill of sale. I am Mrs. Sam Garvey. Just ask for Mr. McGraw."

Mrs. Garvey? The wife of the man who owned the mills? Hotchkiss was thunderstruck.

Valeria leaned down and offered him her hand.

The farmer wiped his big paw on his hip and took the slim gloved hand in his.

"Good-bye."

It had happened in a moment. He stood with his mouth open, watching her as she rode down the lane, very straight and slender and imperious, a grand pale lady who seemed to fade into the pallor of the sky.

As she passed through the orchards, Valeria wondered why, each time she got rid of some of Sam's money, she felt relief. It seemed to restore her link with the human race and assuage her conscience which had never condoned her motive for getting married. She had wanted money so long, and often so desperately, but in her heart it repelled her because she knew from what toil and deprivation it had been wrung. She could not reconcile herself to the hypocrisy of being rich. She was, Valeria supposed, a greater hypocrite than Sam because she was aware of the human issues behind his wealth—issues that had never troubled him. Each of these gestures was a moral lie. The right of indifference was one of the main advantages of money, but no free schools or libraries, no gifts to friends disguised as investments could mitigate the fact that she had entered the world of the secure and damned.

As she trotted down the road, she noticed the man in the field. She thought absently that he was a farmer out shooting crows. But he turned as Valeria approached and she glimpsed, with a start of fear, the red woolen scarf tied across the lower part of his face and the sinister cap pulled down to the level of his eyes.

As she spurred Mimosa to a canter and sped past, she caught the glint of a raised rifle.

A shot cracked.

Mimosa screamed and reared and, in a flash of telescoped insanity, plunged into a gallop. Despite the scalding pain in her flank, the mare was possessed by a single instinct: to carry her mistress out of danger.

A second shot smacked past. Valeria threw herself across Mimosa's neck.

Moments later, as they sped through terror, a third shot exploded in the snow ahead.

Mimosa raced, blood pouring from her flank. She would never stop until she fell.

As they reached Josiah's place, Valeria caught sight of the covered wagons before the house and reined the straining, agonized animal in. She pulled her into the drive, but at the gate, Mimosa's front legs gave way. Valeria jumped from the saddle as Mimosa fell on her knees and, whinneying pitifully, rolled over on her side.

Horrified, Valeria knelt beside her. The little mare's mouth was dripping foam. Valeria wiped it away, tore off her jacket and stuffed it under Mimosa's head.

She ran up the driveway, calling. She hoped in her desperation that by some miracle Josiah might be there.

She accosted two men who were carrying out a chest of drawers.

"Is Mr. Eaton here?"

"No," one of the men grunted. "Ain't showed up."

"I need help. My horse has been wounded. Can you find me some blankets and a horse so that I can ride into town?"

The men heaved the chest of drawers into the wagon and turned to stare at the tall, distracted woman without a coat or hat.

"Please—can you help me? My horse is lying there by the gate."

If Valeria had asked them to pull the moon out of the sky and pack it onto the wagon, they could not have been more idiotically bereft.

"Don't stand there!" Valeria could have struck them. "There must be blankets in the house or the stables. I am a friend of Mr. Eaton's."

One of the men, mopping his neck in a leisurely way, said, "Well, I guess—I'll see."

"Shot? Why'd they shoot a horse?" the other queried.

Valeria cut him short. "Please bring the blankets—there by the gate."

She ran back. Mimosa struggled to rise, but fell again. Kneeling beside her, Valeria gathered handfuls of snow and packed them over the wound.

The second man sauntered after her. He stood looking down at her as she cradled Mimosa's head in her lap.

"Reckon you'll have to shoot her," he said.

"Oh, go away!" Valeria shot a glance of pure rage at this dolt. "Of course, I won't shoot her."

"Back leg, ain't it? Not likely she'll walk again."

It dawned on his slow brain that he should do something. "There's a horse box in the stables. Reckon we might get her in."

"Then go and get it, and for God's sake, hurry."

The man, aggrieved by her anger, turned away.

It was bitterly cold and a sudden terror seized Valeria that the man with the gun might appear out of this white silence and shoot her as she sat there, alone and unprotected.

She heard a horse's hooves and the rattle of harness approaching. Moments later, miraculously incarnated for this emergency, Josiah turned his buggy off the road and stopped with a jolt by the gate.

"Valeria!"

He was beside her, blessedly real and strong and reassuring.

"What's happened to you?"

"Someone shot at me and hit Mimosa. Please help me. One of your men has gone for a horsebox from the stables."

At once he took command.

"Come. Get up; you can't stay there. I'll see to it." He was lifting her up, he was helping her into the buggy. She was dazed and dizzy.

"Please help Mimosa. She saved my life."

"You stay in the house. I'll attend to everything," Josiah told her with calm authority.

How thankful she was for him! He was so sane and sure of himself and of what needed to be done. She was shivering and looked back at the stricken animal, lying so helpless in the snow. "We must get Dr. Mort-lake. He can extract the bullet. I must save her."

He drove to the house in protective silence and led Valeria in.

She found herself in the little study into which he had once before brought her. There were dust sheets over the furniture and packing cases waiting to be nailed shut.

"You are to stay here, Valeria. I'll tell the men what to do."

"Thank God you came. I was terrified. It was so unexpected."

"You're not hurt?" he asked anxiously.

"No. Mimosa galloped so fast. I don't know how she did it."

"Sit down, darling." He wrapped his arms 'round her and patted her shoulder. "I'll tell the men what to do."

He left her and Valeria sank into the chair. She heard him giving orders outside. But she could not wait there, useless and helpless. She hurried to the door.

"Hitch the box onto the back of the buggy," Josiah was saying. The men obeyed without a murmur. Suddenly there was bustle and efficiency. He signaled to her to go back inside. "Don't wait there. You'll catch cold."

But she watched as Josiah drove back to the gates with the men running after. She watched as they roused the prostrate horse and pushed and shunted and cajoled her into the box.

Josiah turned the buggy and drove back to the house. He shouted, "Please go in." But she followed the buggy 'round the side of the house to the stables.

Here, under Josiah's instructions, with much effort and confusion, Mimosa was eased and dragged and shifted into a stall. She collapsed on the straw. Valeria pushed her way past the men and knelt beside her. The poor creature's eyes were glazed and bloodshot, but she acknowledged Valeria's presence by trying to nuzzle her hand.

"Take the buggy to Dr. Mortlake's and bring him

back as fast as you can," Josiah ordered. "Tell him it's imperative, that it's for Mrs. Garvey."

The buggy clattered away. The stall smelled rankly of horse sweat.

Josiah bent over her. "Please come indoors. She will be better off if you leave her. Let her rest if she can."

Valeria allowed herself to be led away. She realized how cold she was and how exhausted.

"Is there anyone who could make something hot to drink?"

"Yes, if you promise to stay in the house."

In the study he made a fire. She watched Josiah, so broad-backed and sound and capable. His good male hands never fumbled.

He drew up a chair for her. He was full of gentleness and concern. It was an immense relief, a sort of luxury, to be helped and protected by a man. With Randolph and Sam, the responsibility for help and protection had always been hers.

"Now, tell me what happened."

"I'd been to the Hotchkiss farm. There was a man in a field. I thought he was a farmer out hunting. He deliberately fired at either me or Mimosa. It couldn't have been an accident. He shot three times."

"Did you see what he looked like?"

"No. He had a muffler over his face. Oh, Josiah, it was so incredible. It happened in a few minutes. I still can't believe it. If Mimosa hadn't galloped so hard . . ." She shuddered. "But why? Why should anyone want to kill me?" As she said it Monsieur Emile's warning sprang to mind.

"Do you often come riding this way?" Josiah was shocked and angry for her sake.

"I used to—every afternoon." She did not want to confess that she took the station road whenever he was in town. Her fear of meeting him seemed so wrong now and absurd. "Sometimes I go another way."

"Who knows you use this road?"

"Joe Horton, perhaps. The Hollisters. I sometimes drop in to see Althea." She swept back her long black hair which had come undone. "It may be an insane coincidence but Ida Brewster's chef, Monsieur Emile, came to see me yesterday."

Josiah was instantly alert, watching her intently. "What did he say?"

"He was worried about Nancy, Ida's daughter. He said that Ida had gone completely mad. It all sounded too dreadful and unreal. She has always hated me. But it couldn't be—even Ida—and why?"

"I would not put it past her," Josiah said grimly. He thought for a moment. "There's not much we can do. Whoever he was, whoever sent him—if he was sent for that purpose—he'd be far away by now." He exclaimed with a sudden passion, "You should never, never have come to this town."

Valeria said in a low voice, "It's because I married her father. She thinks I am after the money." She leaned back and closed her eyes with a deep sigh. "And I was in a way—not her money—only what he promised me. Besides, it has all changed since then."

"Ida's so consumed by ambition and jealousy and frustration, she's capable of anything. You know the whole drama over the shares?"

"No. Sam never discusses business with me and I don't ask. What shares?"

He was about to tell about the events of Christmas Eve and then decided not to. He did not want her to know about his making money out of that deal or about Jamie Packer's spurious confession.

"Well, it's no matter now. Thank God you're safe!"

He thought that she looked more lovely sitting there with her head back, the long curve of her throat and her long tumbled hair, than he had ever seen her. White, stricken and despairing. He longed to take her in his arms and console and protect her.

"I'll make some tea."

As she sat there perfectly still with her eyes closed, the fear and distress eased out of her. She was thankful to be with Josiah, thankful that she was no longer afraid to admit that she cared for him. It came to her that perhaps in the whole world he was, except for Sam, her only friend.

He brought in the tea on a kitchen tray, a small brown pot and two cups, and sugar on a saucer.

"There's no milk, I'm afraid. The good things are packed away."

She sat up and opened her large eyes. "You're really moving? Where will you live?"

"It depends on the outcome of the elections."

"How good do you think your chances are?"

"I can't tell at this point," he said, pouring the tea. "I seem to have met every single person living in Ohio, addressed every organization and made more darn speeches than anyone has ever made before. And I'm not through yet, I'm afraid."

"You're going away again?"

"A week in Cleveland and a few other cities." He handed her the cup. "Sugar?"

"Two, please."

It was almost peaceful, almost domestic, being together in the dismantled house before the fire.

"How much longer are you going to live in that house? It's the last place for you to be."

'We're leaving for Europe soon. Once the railroad's officially open."

He looked up quickly, pained. "Europe?" So far away!

"That was part of the bargain Sam made with me. He wanted to see the world before he was too old and he wanted someone to go with him." For some reason, she felt the need to explain her marriage, to justify it and her attitude toward Sam. "No one understands why I married him. I was penniless and Sam can sometimes be very kind. He's never traveled and he thought that if he went alone no one would talk to him. It's sad that a man who's achieved so much in his way has so little confidence. He has never known how to love at all." She smiled sadly and stirred her drink. "My strange marriage has turned into an even stranger friendship. You may not believe it—after the way I behaved—but I am devoted to him. Perhaps because he so trusts and depends on me."

He said quietly, "I can believe that—of you."

"We had many fights in the beginning," Valeria admitted ruefully. "He can be cruel and neither of us has the best of tempers." She glanced at Josiah with a tender smile. "As you know."

"It must have been a difficult adjustment. No one could believe that Sam would ever marry. He's never shown the least interest in women."

"He's been a very lonely man."

They were talking now as they had once talked before, like old friends, with a simple honesty. It brought back to both of them that other firelit room, and that night together shut away from the world.

"I did not behave very well to you," she said slowly. "I had made a precarious balance in my life and when you appeared it was shaken."

Josiah wanted her then as he had wanted her on that other occasion. He wanted to take her in his arms and make love to her, not so much from desire, but as a reaffirmation of what he felt for her and as a consolation for all the weeks and months of their separation.

"I have never stopped thinking of you. I guess you knew that."

"Yes, I guess I knew," Valeria said softly.

She put down her cup and went to him. Josiah put his arm about her small waist, resting his head against her breasts. They stayed thus in silence for a long moment.

"I'm so sorry, Josiah," she whispered.

Valeria wanted him to know that she regretted they could not be together. She regretted the love that might have been theirs but had been denied them. She had had no choice but to stand by her word.

He kissed her hand.

She disengaged herself. Dusk was falling.

"I hope Dr. Mortlake comes soon. Sam will think I've been kidnapped."

"He's lucky you haven't been," Josiah said with a warm smile.

"I would like to go back to Mimosa, please."

"I left your coat in the buggy. I'll bring a rug."

He went with her to the stables and lit a lantern and brought water for Mimosa. Valeria sat in the straw.

Mimosa was aware of her. Her great brown eyes rolled pitifully and she bared her teeth in pain.

Valeria fell asleep with her hand on Mimosa's neck while Josiah stood guard.

It was unbearable to him that this woman he loved had been in danger. He would gladly have killed anyone who tried to harm her. Far worse, in a little while he would lose her, this time perhaps for good.

It was past eight when Dr. Mortlake deposited Valeria at the house under the chimney. He bade her a somber good night.

He had failed to extract the bullet from Mimosa's flank and had pronounced her incurably disabled. Valeria had refused to have her shot. Mortlake had administered his usual cure-all, a large dose of laudanum, and had gloomily pronounced that there was not much hope for the animal. But then, according to Dr. Mortlake, there was not much hope for anything on this ungodly earth.

Sam greeted his wife with a mixture of anger and consternation. "Where in Hades have you been?"

Blue with cold, she presented a sorry sight in her filthy habit, streaked with blood and dirt, without her smart little homburg.

Weary as she was Valeria told him all that had happened, not omitting the kindness and help that Josiah Eaton had given her. With all the confusion of her meeting with Josiah and her concern over Mimosa, she had not fully grasped that someone had tried to kill her.

Sam refused to believe it. "Crap!" he retorted. "No one would dare. People may hate me; they've no reason to hate you. It couldn't have happened—not like that!"

"Whatever it was, it was no accident. He fired three times."

A blow at Valeria struck at the very foundation of Sam's life. He was shaken. To hide his agitation, he made her recount the whole incident again.

"Some crackpot! It couldn't have been planned. This town's full of madmen, granted. At the most . . ."

he didn't want to consider it. "It could only have been someone who had it in for me."

Valeria did not bring up the question of Ida's complicity. She was too tired to go into it.

"Perhaps he didn't mean to shoot me. Perhaps he thought I'd be thrown and injured. It may have been just a warning, but whatever it was, Sam, I can't stay here."

The silence of monumental rage which she knew so well was Sam's only comment. He poured her a glass of whiskey and averted his eyes as his wife began to cry from sheer nervous exhaustion.

She wept openly and reached for his hand. It was one of the few moments where there had been any physical contact between them. It embarrassed him acutely.

"I can't stay here, whatever was behind it. If you can't leave yet, I'll take Nancy to New York and wait for you there."

He went back to his desk. Sam wished she would stop crying; it unnerved him.

Valeria was crying for Mimosa who had saved her life, for Ida's senseless hatred, for the loss of Josiah, for all the sadness and ugliness that filled their lives.

"Yes, we must go. You're right. I've been too busy," he said at last. He shifted some papers on his desk. "There was one last thing I'd wanted you to do for me, but I won't press you now."

She dried her eyes. "What was it, Sam?"

"I planned to take one trip the length of the new railroad—just there and back." He added tentatively, "We could have traveled in my private car."

She saw how important this was for him and at once consented. "Of course, you must do that. I should enjoy it, too. Can we take Nancy?"

"Yes, bring her," Sam gratefully assented. "And you can start making the arrangements—I mean for leaving here."

It was upon him. He could no longer delay it or avoid it, the dread eventuality he owed her. But it had come too late. Sam had known without facing it or daring to mention it to her; the time for that voyage of discovery had passed him by. Valeria had become the main prop and mainstay of the borrowed life which had followed on his heart attack. He could not break his promise or deprive her of the reward she had so dutifully earned.

This attempt on her life, if it had been that, had shattered the frail security she had made possible. Valeria had enabled him to marshal his remaining strength to push his last great project through. She was his will and his endurance and he could not carry on without her. For the first time Sam felt helpless. He did not know how to retaliate, whom to accuse, what steps to take. If it were Ida she would have covered her traces and if it were not, on whom could he vent his fury among that host of possible enemies who might have struck at him through her? It was as though some phantom hand had reached through the curtain of the dead to smash his final stronghold. He cursed himself: he was old, his resistance was running low and he no longer knew how to defend her.

Sam sank back, very gray and drained and shrunken. If only this had happened ten years ago!

Two nights later another incident occurred which, had it been generally known, would have split The Heights in two.

That it remained more or less a secret was due to an unexpected change of heart in Mrs. Nathanial Shaw-cross who discovered in herself a capacity for that rarest of all virtues, silence.

She was returning from a musicale at the McGraws, where their niece, Lavinia Babette, had obliged with Scottish airs rendered in a shrill and unreliable soprano, with harp accompaniment, followed by a reel that shook the chandeliers. As their carriage turned into the driveway, Mrs. Shawcross spied something protruding from a clump of rhododendrons. It looked uncannily like a human leg, moreover a naked human leg unattached, it appeared, to a human body.

"Look!" Mrs. Shawcross exclaimed. "What's that?"

Mr. Shawcross stopped the carriage and descended to investigate. He approached the rhododendrons and

saw, with a shock of horror, that the leg was, in fact,
attached to an all too naked female body and that
this scandalously large and outrageously nude form
was that of Ida Brewster who had apparently fallen
into the rhododendrons and was bleeding profusely.

Mr. Shawcross hailed his driver. He shouted to his
wife, "Stay where you are!" But Mrs. Shawcross was
not to be deprived of such a horrifying discovery. She
saw what the two men saw and screamed, "It's Ida!
My God, she's dead!"

But Ida was not dead. She stirred at that moment
and a fresh gush of blood issued from between her
legs.

For a moment all three were turned to stone. It was
bad enough that Ida Brewster had fallen into their
garden, bad enough that she was stark naked and
bleeding, but in addition to all that, she was alive and
must be tended to and must be removed somewhere.
And where else but into their house? It was a catastrophe that made even Mr. Shawcross, that hard and
wiley lawyer, immune to pity, shrink into indecision.

Mrs. Shawcross was the first to regain her reason.
"Lift her," she ordered. "Carry her inside."

The two men struggled to extricate Ida from the
bushes. It was no mean task, for Ida was a mountain
of all too solid flesh, and in her condition—both limp
and supine—she was practically immovable. She kept
moaning and her head lolled from one side to the
other, and the blood flowed from where it should not
have flowed in a seemingly inexhaustible flood. The
sight of *the* Mrs. Brewster naked was in itself enough
to make a strong man faint; but she was half dead and
bleeding besides, and it was more nauseating than
anything any of them had ever seen.

They contrived to drag her into the house. They
lugged her like some beached marine monster up the
steps into the hall where it flashed through Mrs. Shawcross's mind that the dark, glutinous blood would ruin
her Turkey carpet. She yelled at the perspiring gilly,
"Get a blanket!" Mr. Shawcross, gasping for breath,
yelled back, "We can't leave her here!" There was a
moment of consternation. "Carry her upstairs. Wait!"

Mrs. Shawcross screamed and, darting into the dining room, brought back a lace tablecloth.

She flung the cloth over Ida before they carried her upstairs into the spare bedroom. Ida was moaning and her arms flailed and fell about. Her eyes opened and stared blankly.

"Get Dr. Mortlake. Hurry!"

The maid vanished with relief.

"Get a basin of cold water and some towels," Mrs. Shawcross thrust her husband through the door. Her patchwork quilt was already ruined. The dark stain had spread across the tablecloth and was now spreading across the bed. It was the most terrible sight Mrs. Shawcross had ever seen. She had seen a good few terrible sights in her youth and those years in the rough and tumble West came to her rescue now. She kept her head.

Her husband returned with the basin and the towels.

"Leave me," his wife ordered. She whipped the lace from Ida and, plunging a towel in water, wrung it out and pressed it between Ida's legs. She remained at Ida's side for the next hour, changing the blood-soaked towels and replacing them with fresh ones, pouring the bloodied water into a chamber pot and fetching fresh water. It was incredible that any human being could bleed so much.

It was close to midnight when Dr. Mortlake, roused from his mournful slumbers to confront the endless spectacle of human sickness and human degradation, arrived with his black bag and his usual dour expression.

He examined the source of Ida's wound. Probing carefully, he extracted a pair of scissors.

There was not much that he could do. It was the most bizarre attempt at suicide he had ever encountered in his long career.

"She's lost a bucket of blood."

"Is she mad? She must be."

Dr. Mortlake shrugged as he washed his hands. "Let her sleep. We'll know more later."

Mad? He had long since come to the conclusion that sanity was as rare a condition as good health. What he had been forced to see, what aid he had been forced to give, merely confirmed his profound disgust for the human race. They were all mad, in one way or another. If the human race had indeed been made in the image of God, as the Bible stated, then God was not anyone he wanted to believe in, and if, as he preferred to think, there was no God, the prospect for the human race was even more hopeless than he deemed it. Lunatics and vultures, with the possible exception of Mrs. Sam Garvey who he was prepared to admit might be a lunatic of a slightly higher order.

Mrs. Shawcross sat down in her now contaminated room and regarded the sleeping woman she had known so long. She knew that she was face to face with human tragedy at its starkest and, however distasteful, its most pitiful. For once, she had no desire to recount the details of this terrible incident to Mrs. Bancroft or Mrs. McGraw or any of the other ladies of her acquaintance. There were things too terrible to speak of, and the debacle which had engulfed Ida Brewster was one of them.

She was shocked into an awareness that this woman she had always disliked because of her arrogance and ostentation had suffered in a way that did not permit questioning or condemnation. Whatever grievous sins Ida had committed, she had paid for them with an agony of spirit and mind that had driven her to the ultimate of retribution. She had tried to kill herself. It made Mrs. Shawcross feel strangely humble and dutiful. It decided her, there and then and without equivocation, on nursing that broken soul to the utmost of her ability, and for as long as it was needed.

In this crisis of enlightenment, Mrs. Shawcross saw with blinding certainty that what lay in the spare bed was the glaring truth of what lay behind the facades and pretensions of more people she had known and scorned and envied than she cared to think of. What lay behind the sham of human existence was just this naked suffering. There was nothing to do but acknowledge it, respect it, and ease it as best one could.

She closed the door softly and went downstairs. Mr. Shawcross, still very shaken, was sitting in the parlor with a glass of whiskey. Mrs. Shawcross went to him and placed her hand on his shoulder. "Nat, we must keep her here and we must not tell anyone. It's not our concern what drove her to it. It must have been a very dreadful thing."

A crowd had assembled at the new and incomplete railroad station to witness the departure of Sam Garvey, his wife and granddaughter on the first journey of the Mid-Western and Pacific Railroad.

A brass band had been mustered and blared forth a noisy hallelujah. Arcadia's mayor presented Mrs. Garvey with a bouquet consisting of ferns and red roses, and made a speech that no one heard because a number of the town's more stalwart citizens broke into cheering and waving small flags. Sam's past misdemeanors were forgotten in the general jubilation over his latest achievement.

Arcadia was now linked to the Far West and California and from the Far West and California new prosperity would pour into everyone's capacious pockets. It was a great age with unparalleled opportunities and the iron monster churned out steam, hungry to devour the miles that separated Arcadia from its distant neighbors.

The old man, around whose ambitions Arcadia had grown, climbed slowly onto the observation car and turned to acknowledge the greetings and good wishes of all those people who had hated him so long. Mrs. Garvey and his granddaughter smiled and waved. Everyone was gratified. Another cheer went up. A whistle blew. The engine emitted a roar of steam. A great new railroad was under way.

Sam's parlor car was luxurious. It was a triumph of convenience and bad taste. It comprised a drawing room in red plush with armchairs, sofa, velvet curtains, inlaid mahogany walls, and even a small organ with which to while away the tedious hours in transit. In addition there was a large bedroom with a brass bedstead, two smaller bedrooms, a bathroom with gold-plated fittings, a kitchen with an icebox, and a dining room in purple plush with a mahogany table and six chairs with seats embroidered in lavender petit point. There were brass spittoons, cut crystal vases filled with flowers, and an observation deck with rattan chairs and a telescope. Nancy was enchanted. It was a dollhouse on wheels. She would have liked to live in it permanently with Randolph.

Sam's day of glory was completed by the appearance of Monsieur Emile who, attired in a faultless tunic, served champagne. Valeria had persuaded him to join them on this voyage across the tycoon's dominions.

Sam raised his glass to Valeria. "To you, my dear, and many happy journeys. And to you, Nancy. Glad to have you with us."

Nancy was awed by her grandfather's benevolence.

Shortly thereafter they were summoned to the dining room where Monsieur Emile produced a delicate *Tortue Claire*, a perfectly cooked pheasant with, as a special concession to his benefactress, English bread sauce. It was, though he was too loyal to admit it, Madame Garvey's only lapse.

A chocolate bombe, bearing a tiny train in spun sugar, completed this exquisitely restrained repast.

They repaired to the drawing room where Valeria and Nancy played duets on the organ and Nancy summoned up sufficient courage to sing "O, for the Wings of a Dove!" Sam sat by the window beaming on these two who had come to constitute something he had never had, or even contemplated ever wanting, a family.

When later Monsieur Emile appeared with whiskey for Mr. Garvey and madeira for the ladies, Valeria broke into *"Partant pour L'Algérie"* and then, more appropriately, *"Paris, Paris, je t'aime."* Carried away by the occasion, Monsieur Emile forgot his usual decorum and performed a deft quadrille while D'Artagnan, who was shocked by this behavior, ran barking to and fro between his master's feet.

Sam laughed. He had rarely in his life succumbed to happiness. It was somewhat, he discovered, like getting drunk. He felt that at last his life had come full circle.

At eleven they retired. Valeria kissed her husband at his door. He undressed slowly and climbed into the big brass bed. It was the first time in thirty years that he had slept in anything but his narrow cot. He lay there listening to the clickety-clacking of the rails. Eternity was passing beneath him, but he found that it no longer troubled him.

So much experience, so many incidents and battles, so many failures and hard-won triumphs, were rattling away into the past. It seemed to him that the best thing that had ever happened to him had been his impulse to marry Valeria. He was quite willing to spend whatever time remained traveling about with her, in peace and comfort, from one place to another, over the rim of the known world.

For Nancy it was the beginning of a new life. Free of her mother's nightmare presence, she stretched out luxuriously, lulled by the rhythm of the train. She saw herself, hand in hand with Randolph, crossing a great moor clouded in mist. Out of the drifting wraiths, a ruined castle loomed. She could see the moonlight slanting in ghostly rays through the gutted windows. He pushed back the great wheezing door into a vast stone chamber and led her up a winding stair to the bedroom which, alone of the derelict pile, was unimpaired. There was a four-poster bed with a damask canopy and tufts of ostrich feathers at the corners. She lay there in a pink lace nightgown, watching the dancing flames in the great fireplace casting gleams and shadows across the walls. He came toward her with his wild black hair and brilliant eyes, filled with desire and tenderness!

But it was not polite to let her imagination go any farther. She turned down the lamp and composed herself for sleep.

Valeria, too, listened to the chatter of the rails.

Ever since the attempt on her life or, as she preferred to think of it, the warning to leave town, she had entered a realm of fantasy in which she carried out her daily duties, looked after Sam, encouraged Nancy, consulted guide books, made lists of hotels, wrote to reserve suites, and prepared for the journey she no longer truly believed would happen. She no longer stopped to consider the validity of what she did. And behind these amorphous activities she felt a dull ache, a slow malaise of the soul which she lacked the energy or even the desire to banish: the need to be with Josiah. Even though she knew in her reasonable mind that it was as futile as a desire to see Whitebriars again or Tante Elize or anything else, now vanished, which she had loved, still it was there; she carried it within her. It was the invisible cross she bore; a stigma of the heart.

She thought of him often. Josiah's image appeared and faded and reappeared again. Her heart evoked him in the firelight, in the lantern of the stable when she was visiting Mimosa, in some shifting shadow on the snow, in Randolph who had been with him and carried a reflection of his presence. Her brother became a medium through whom she communicated with her dead.

She fell to daydreaming of what this voyage might have been if it had been with Josiah instead of Sam. She saw herself with Josiah in London, in Paris, in luxuriant nights along the Nile. It was not so much a yearning for the physical delight he had once given her, but for the abundance of his male strength which had made her feel in her inmost self what it meant to be a woman so protected by being loved and a woman capable, in a way she had never been before, of loving. Valeria was emotionally too depleted to rebuke herself for this imagined infidelity. It could not happen in life; she allowed it to happen in her dreams. It was her secret indulgence. She became as miserly of these memories as Sam had been of money.

She lay in her narrow bed on that fictitious journey through the night and conjured up that forbidden journey with Josiah which would have been the fulfillment of everything which her strange and difficult destiny had, as though by design, denied her. She thought of him, golden haired, his gray-blue eyes steady and sad and constant with the love he felt for her. How had this impossible attachment happened out of a few brief meetings that were receding farther and farther from her? Her mind flew back like some bird on a last migration which had lost its way to the sunbaked architraves of that longed-for temple in the south. It wheeled in the darkness and fell, despairing, into sleep.

All the next day they trundled across the endless expanses still carpeted with snow. The train would draw up with a great sigh of steam in the middle of nowhere. Groups of people would be waiting to see for themselves the phenomenon that was joining them to the rest of the universe. Quiet people with a lost look in their eyes who had forgotten that there existed beyond the wilderness towns full of streets and buildings, bustle and events. They stared in mute disbelief at these denizens of the inhabited world, sometimes handing up a basket of eggs or some jars of preserves or a loaf of newly baked bread, as though to remind these privileged, almost supernatural beings that they, too, existed and would like not to be forgotten as they had been for so long.

Herds of buffalo thundered in flight from this iron-clad hunter. Indians swarmed out of nowhere and rode alongside with war whoops and threatening rifles and fell back before the enemy they knew was the herald of their decline.

The infinity of the land cast a spell and they began to feel, as they sat staring through the windows, that it was too immense ever to be crossed or conquered. They could make no progress; the sense of motion was an illusion.

In the strange hypnosis cast by these snow-covered territories, marked on maps but without identity, Sam Garvey's mind drifted back to his beginnings. Things he had forgotten for fifty years returned like shadows wheeling across the snow. It was a chronicle as involved and varied, as crammed with characters and incidents, as the novels of Mr. Dickens that he knew by heart and identified with because they contained so many elements and people similar to those in his own life.

He was not really talking to Valeria and Nancy but to his alter ego who was taking leave of him. They listened as though Sam were reading aloud as he had listened, on so many evenings, to Valeria recounting the stories of Lord and Lady Deadlock and Martin Chuzzlewit. This was Sam Garvey's story which he had spun out of experience and accidents and twists of fate, but which he felt in some way no longer belonged to him.

"I grew up in Philadelphia in the slums. My mother was a washerwoman and my father was a drunkard. He had something to do with horses, an ostler maybe; he disappeared early on. A big man, I recall, who knocked my mother about. I had an older brother and a sister, my mother washed all day in the room we lived in. It was always full of steam and smelt of soap and the wet clothes that were strung out on lines to dry, inside in the winter. Wherever we slept or sat they dripped on us. We lived in a pile of washing that was never done.

"My brother Jack was a thief and he taught me how to be one too. When I was six I was apprenticed to a man who trained kids like us to be pickpockets like Fagin in *Oliver Twist*. He used to hang around bars and hotels and sometimes the theaters and we'd swipe anything we could. We were sharp little devils and fast as rats. I was a runt and this man whose name was McGuiness taught me to climb through windows. I could wriggle through anything without making a sound. Once I got inside I would creep around and hand things through to McGuiness. Candlesticks and bits of silver and sometimes boots and coats; they were expensive then. I didn't get much money, but I was quick and I had a trade and whatever I kept I hid. I don't recall ever having much to eat. After a while Jack and I stopped going home. We used to sleep in abandoned buildings and sometimes in McGuiness's cellar. We were close, Jack and me, and he used to fight off anyone who tried to filch what we'd put aside. We got along somehow. It was rough in the winters because we had no shoes. We used to bind up our feet with rags and put newspapers inside our vests and pants. They weren't clothes; rags, but they covered us. McGuiness did well out of us. He didn't treat us so bad, but kept the goods and kept the money. Fifty cents for us was a good day.

"We'd stake out a house where the people had gone away. There was a grand sort of house, down by the river. I don't remember just what went wrong, but McGuiness and Jack were nabbed. I was inside and I hid and the cops didn't find me. I was so small I could crawl in anywhere. When I got out I was alone. I had nowhere to go. I hadn't seen my mother and sister in some time and didn't much care to, so I set out and walked to Pittsburgh. I had ten dollars I'd saved. I wouldn't take rides from farmers with carts. I was afraid they'd rob me. It was bitter cold that winter and it took me a long time. My feet bled so bad I finally spent a dollar and bought a pair of beat-up shoes. They were my prize possession. Those shoes got me to Pittsburgh.

"I was nine then—thereabouts. Well, I went back to my old trade and then I got a legitimate job sweeping out a bar. I did odd jobs for the man who owned the place and when it closed up, in the early hours, I used to sweep out the whole place and scrub the bar and the tables. I was in a good way because I had a place to sleep. I used to curl up under the bar. It was the first dry place I'd ever slept in. I felt I was getting on.

"I heard a lot of talk among the men who hung around that place. Big things were happening out west. Men were setting out to make fortunes. It seemed a place with a lot of opportunities if you had the guts to get there. So I set out. I was what Mr. Dickens would call a regular toff. I had a coat and shoes and I had a cardboard box with other important things. Can't recall now just what was in that box, it was a shoe box, I reckon, but it made me feel mighty important. I protected it with my life.

"I would get from one place to the next somehow, always moving westward. Some folks were kind and gave me a meal now and then and I did odd jobs. I didn't always repay those folks like I should have. I filched what I could and sold what I filched at the next stop and I saved those pennies. It was my fortune. It was the beginning of Sam Garvey. I was determined, somehow or other, to get rich. I had no idea how I was going to do it. I couldn't read or write. But I had a goal. I wanted money and I didn't care how I got it.

"A lot of time went by. I wasn't getting anywhere because I didn't know anything, only what I heard. When I was fourteen I got a job in a mine. It was murderous work, down there in the dark. I hauled the trollies with the coal. Fourteen hours a day for seventy cents. And out of that seventy cents, I saved a quarter. Later I became a miner earning ten dollars a week. I worked ten years in the mines. There seemed to be no way out. I taught myself to read and I borrowed or stole anything written about prospecting. Everyone was prospecting then. It was a disease like consumption, and once you'd got it, it generally killed you. A few struck it rich. Not many. And those who did mostly drank it or gambled it away. I never drank. I never went with women.

"One night I was going home from work. I had a room at the top of a house owned by an invalid woman and her daughter. I paid two dollars and fifty cents a week. It was a lot of money, but I needed a place where I could read.

"That night I saw a man being beaten up by some roughs outside a saloon. People were always fighting and shooting it up in them days. I don't know what made me, but I stopped to watch. They knocked him out cold and he fell into the gutter. It crossed my mind that he might have something on him that I could steal. When you earn ten bucks a week for ten years you're not averse to getting hold of a little money by some other means. Besides it was the way I'd kept myself when growing up.

"What I found in that man's pocket wasn't money. It was something much more valuable. It was a book. In a foreign language. I learned afterwards it was Latin. I'd never heard of Latin, but it meant this man was educated. He was different. A gentleman. Know what I mean? His hands weren't rough like mine. He had a refined sort of face. I had what I guess was a flash of inspiration. I knew that man could teach me something. Instinct, I guess."

Sam smiled at Valeria. The same instinct, he wanted to convey, that had told him the night she had fallen asleep in the study chair that it would be a good thing for him to marry her.

"I helped him up and took him back to my place. That was Marcus Eaton. We became partners. He was a geologist, it turned out. He'd been to Harvard where young Hank goes. He spoke differently than anyone I'd ever known. He knew just about everything. He knew the language—like Randolph. He was the first friend I'd ever had. Well, maybe not a friend. I knew that Marcus Eaton had the key to what I'd been looking for.

"I'd saved quite a bit of money over the years. My shoe box had become a black tin box with a key. I quit my job and Marcus and me went into partnership. He knew all about soils and deposits. For a long time we just struggled. Nothing happened. My savings were going down the drain. We just couldn't hit on the right place. Well, it wasn't long before we'd reached the point where we had nothing but a tent and a frypan and precious little to cook in it. But I knew Marcus would do it one day and one day, by God, he did.

"I had no money to stake a claim and although you could just mark off a piece of land, you needed papers to prove that it was yours and you needed money to get going. I'd seen it happen too often where some poor beggar would find a deposit and take in a partner to develop it and pretty soon the partner'd taken over and the guy who'd made the strike was back where he started—broke. I was determined that wouldn't happen to me and Marcus.

"I went back to town and took that room at the top of the same house where I'd lived before. The woman who owned it had something wrong with her legs or thought she had. She had to stay lying down. Her daughter ran things. A big, scrawny girl who never said much and didn't take to people and had no friends either. She worked all day keeping the place clean and read the Bible most of the night. Men paid her no heed and she paid no heed to them. I set out to court her. It took me two months, at the end of which I married her. It was by means of that house that I raised the money to legalize our claim. And that's how the whole thing started."

He was smiling, seeing not the reflections in the window or the dim shapes that sped past outside as night was falling. He saw Marcus Eaton and himself and those days of struggle and triumph and the excitement and suspense. The figure of the gaunt creature he had married did not return from oblivion to share in this retrospect. She was beyond resurrection.

"I was right about Marcus. He was a genius in his way. Weak, but a genius. I mortgaged that house to the hilt and I staked out a lot of land and I had all the papers safe and locked up in my tin box. It turned out we'd struck the biggest deposit of iron ore in the state, one of the biggest in the world, I guess. In two years we were rich."

He chuckled.

"I think, looking back," he went on after a long pause in which he tried to define the mystery of Marcus Eaton, "that it wasn't his fault he couldn't take it. He'd been through hard times and he'd been brought up gently. Unlike me. Once the money started rolling in, Marcus went to pieces. He wanted the things he'd done without. Clothes and a decent place to live and the company of women. He loved women."

Nancy and Valeria were watching him as he watched night falling, blotting out the wilderness, as time had blotted out the traces of his past. Maybe Marcus wasn't so wrong, Sam was thinking. Marcus had known how to live, how to enjoy things. It hadn't been all vanity and loose morals. In his own case he hadn't allowed himself enough leeway. He'd narrowed things down instead of letting them expand. Why had he turned his back on experiences that might have widened his horizon? Everything had shrunk to that house and that room and those ledgers, and only books to remind him that he was still alive. What had he been afraid of? Marcus and Valeria had known something he had never allowed himself to learn. He needed another twenty years to reap the harvest of all that he had sown.

He looked around. Nancy was staring at him in open wonderment. She had been at a play; she had shared in a revelation. She had discovered that her grandfather was not just a dreaded symbol of authority, an unapproachable titan who had no relation to ordinary life.

What could he read in Valeria's silence? She was sitting very composed and still with the lamplight haloing her fine head with its fine-boned features, but her green eyes held some expression he had not seen before. Not sadness or disapproval, something deeper, more enigmatic and yet softer. Pity, maybe, or maybe a sort of love.

"Well," the old man concluded, "you know the rest."

They sat in silence for a while as the train gently jostled onward.

Toward twilight of the following day the landscape changed. There were woods and hills and farms and signs that men had been taming the land and bending it to their uses. A town appeared. It seemed incredible that at the other end of nowhere there were church steeples and streets with trees and buildings three stories high and a river with two fine bridges.

The train drew up in what would be a fair-sized station when it was finished. There was a concourse of people waiting who broke into cheers and waved handkerchiefs. There was a banner across the front of the scaffolding. "Welcome to Sam Garvey and the Mid-Western and Pacific."

The mayor presented Mrs. Garvey with another bouquet and announced that a civic reception would be held and a carriage would be sent to collect the guests of honor.

People climbed on board and swarmed through the parlor and exclaimed at the furnishings. The crush became unbearable and Valeria saw Sam was beginning to look gray. She did her best, with gracious smiles, to encourage these enthusiasts to leave. But they were excited with the glory of enterprise and were not to be persuaded. They were determined to celebrate this victory of technology that now linked them to the East as Arcadia had celebrated its union with the West. The United States was drawing together into a great conglomerate that would soon be spurring quantities of goods and profits in both directions.

It was a long time before they pushed their way out with their praises and promises and good wishes, with their eyes lit and their hearts aglow.

Sam sank into his chair by the window. He looked very frail and spent.

Valeria drew down the blind. "Are you all right?" she asked.

"I think," he said meekly, "that I'll skip the dinner. If you don't object, I'd like to go to bed."

The carriage appeared and Valeria sent her regrets. Mr. Garvey was very tired. He had not been well and needed rest, but he sent his warmest thanks and all possible good wishes. At long last, exhausted themselves, Valeria and Nancy were alone.

All that night people came to examine the train and climbed up and down the steps of the observation car and peered in at the windows. They walked 'round the train and examined it from every angle. Valeria and Nancy, as they ate their dinner behind drawn drapes, could hear their comments and exclamations. There was something touching in their gladness and in their faith that this mechanical invention would somehow change their lives.

They started back next morning. Sam stayed in bed till noon. They were rattling across the wilderness when he came into the parlor and returned to his chair. He was deeply gratified, but he was tired.

He ate little of Monsieur Emile's delicate concoctions, but he was cordial to Nancy and frequently glanced at Valeria as though to reassure himself that she was there. He liked her to sit across from him so that he could observe her obliquely. She was content to read aloud or simply to sit and watch the interminable miles slip by.

He appeared not to be interested any more in what

passed the window and paid scant attention to the great vultures that soared over the passing train. He said unexpectedly, "Did you bring your opals? I like to see you in them."

She had brought her deep purple gown, and that evening she wore it with the opal necklace and the earrings and the ornate bracelet. He nodded. He was proud of her. She looked very regal and distinguished. "We must find a ring to go with the rest."

"You know I never wear rings, Sam." She smiled. "These are quite enough."

After dinner he asked her to play. In Valeria's opinion the organ was an instrument that belonged exclusively in church, but to please him, she played as softly as she could. He drowsed with a smile on his lips, a worn old man in a red plush chair with a rug over his knees.

The journey back seemed endless. The enchantment and novelty were gone. The incessant jolting and rattling and the quivering of the crystal vases frayed Valeria's nerves. They became aware that this was a confined and unnatural way of traveling and longed to be stationary, on solid ground.

For the first time since she had come there, Valeria was relieved to see Arcadia, relieved to see Tripp and relieved to help Sam from the observation car into the carriage.

There seemed to be some celebration going on. A band was playing along Main Street and there was cheering.

"What's happening in town?" she asked.

"Everyone's turned out," Tripp told them. "Mr. Eaton's been elected."

Her heart lifted with gladness. She was happy that he would be happy, and felt a vicarious fulfillment because Josiah would now, although divided from her, be fulfilled.

Valeria was glad to see the great chimney belching smoke, and to guide Sam into the house she no longer hated. He walked with her slowly into the study and sat down behind his desk. He reached for a cigar and lit it. He was home.

He did not fall asleep as she thought he would but seemed quite alert and made inquiries about their journey. They were to stay for two weeks at the Fifth Avenue Hotel and then embark on the maiden voyage of the Empress of India for England. They would drive by slow stages up to London. She had reserved a suite at Brown's Hotel.

He approved. Valeria had arranged everything with her usual care.

"I'll show you London," he said. "I can show you where the Deadlocks lived in Portman Square and where Oliver Twist worked at Wapping and the law courts where Miss Fleet ran about with her deeds and papers. And, we must find the alley where Sidney Carton and Lucy heard the footsteps that brought the Revolution back into their lives. It's all there, you know."

Monsieur Emile had cooked an exemplary dinner. As Nancy had excused herself, they ate alone at the shining table with the candles casting a soft glow on Valeria's ebony hair which she had taken to wearing piled up in casual folds and curls that set off her long, proud neck.

Sam ate well and raised his glass to her.

"Thank you, my dear. You have made it all very pleasant. Very pleasant for me, indeed."

She came to his side and helped him up and, arm in arm, they crossed the hall into the parlor where a fire was burning.

Sam stationed himself in the yellow chair where he could admire her and also, from time to time, glance up at Ford Hollister's portrait. "It doesn't do you justice, but it's nice. I'll have another done in London. Will you play, Valeria?"

It was agreeable to hear the light clear notes of the Bechstein after the wheezing, asthmatic tones of the organ. She played Schumann's *Arabesque* because it seemed an appropriate choice to close that long and tiring day. It drew in the night and erased the sight of those stark expanses that remained imprinted on the brain.

Valeria thought, as she looked across at him, that of

all the people she had known in her life, she had finally come to know Sam Garvey best. She knew him and understood him and accepted him with all his complexities, foibles, obstinacy and in his strange generosity to her. She could see, watching Sam as she played, the small boy without shoes trudging to Pittsburgh with his cardboard box stuffed with the proceeds of small thefts and painful savings. After all, the risk she had taken had not been wasted. Her instinct had not been wrong.

He was listening to the notes that fell from her fingers like drops of water in a way that he had not listened to them before. It seemed to him that these sounds, so clear and so persuasive, contained in some hidden way the answer to his life. He must try to follow them more closely in order to guess their meaning. They were like the book in a foreign language that he had found in Marcus Eaton's pocket. They were the language he had never had time to learn. The notes, rising and falling like bells, rippling in small cascades, resounded in his head, drawing him away. He must follow them to find out what it was, all along, that he had missed. What it was that, in his other self, he had been searching for. It had not been money, after all, but something different, more mysterious, more benign. The notes were leading him into a realm of mystery where he would find the answer and come to terms, at last, with the question of what he was. There was time enough, for these notes were time itself, just as the promise and the dream were beyond, in a world of transfigured light.

When she paused, Valeria saw that he was sleeping. She went to draw the rug over his knees and realized that his silence was deeper than sleep.

Chapter Twenty-six

Ever since the election Josiah Eaton had been surrounded by a cloud of horseflies. They buzzed at breakfast, swarmed at luncheon, deafened him with a concerted roar at dinner. The entourage blew into his suite at the Columbus hotel, with briefcases jammed with plans and projects. People cornered him in lobbies, entryways, and passages and made themselves known and offered congratulations. They ingratiated themselves with an eye to future employment and emoluments. Women hummed 'round him, simpering and smiling, stinging him all over with invitations both intimate and public. Experienced souls gave advice and warnings and made discreet offers of future services. Men dropped hints and winked and nudged him and ever so slyly indicated their willingness to participate in various enterprises of a more or less questionable nature. These horseflies rose in a dense and raucous swirl as he descended the staircase of the hotel and broke into a storm of clapping and applause. Josiah had been greeted and backslapped and handshaken and shouted at and addressed until all these enthusiastic and anxious and avaricious people became like one vast vociferous insect that would not desist for a single moment of the night or day.

Cheers rang through the lobby as the new governor, looking superbly handsome and important, descended into the humming, drumming, surging, pressing, exulting swarm of his constituents.

Josiah was well aware that at all these celebrations, a group of sardonic gentlemen remained at a distance and did not participate in any demonstrations. They puffed their fat cigars and expectorated seriously into large spittoons and made a few laconic comments

461

which did not commit them to anything because they had no need. They ran the state and one governor was to them little different from another. They had every intention of manipulating Josiah and expected him, out of respect for their power and substance, to allow them to do so. But Josiah was determined not to be as amenable as they expected. They exchanged greetings across the hubbub. These grave gentlemen regarded him as a puppet and he regarded them as obstructions. But all the compromises and arrangements and "understandings" that would constitute his relations with these commercial cabalists would come later when the serious business of administration got under way.

Ladies with bountiful bosoms and imposing pompadours swirled through the lobby and eyed the new governor and thought what a very great pity it was that a man so handsome and successful should not be further enhanced by a wife of equal qualities and distinction. Each of these ladies considered herself eminently worthy of this position and struggled to display herself to the fullest advantage in order to captivate this noteworthy victim of involuntary bachelorhood. Their eyes flashed, their cleavages heaved, and their deft and acquisitive fingers flourished fans and kerchiefs.

Josiah was deafened by the din of applause. As he made his way with difficulty toward the main entrance, he caught sight of Randolph, on the fringes of the crowd, waving a newpaper. He was trying to force a way through this throng of admiring pesterers.

Randy was excusing himself right and left, elbowing and nudging his way toward Josiah. At last, in this press and pressure of people, they met and Randolph thrust the paper into Josiah's hand. It bore across the front page, like a declaration of international war, the headline:

SAM GARVEY DEAD.

As he stared at the paper, Josiah's heart leapt to his throat. With a wild jubilation that exceeded even the joy at his election, he thought, Oh God, she's free!

The culminating event of that winter which had kept Arcadia agog and which was to go down in the town's memory as a winter unlike all others, was the burning of Fairlawn and the discovery of a charred body in the gutted shell.

The unsavory triangle that locked together Ford, Althea and the Italian servant had reached a pitch of repressed intensity and expressed resentment during the last weeks before their proposed departure for New York.

Althea's progress had continued. She had remained admirably calm. She had completed her Greek translations. She was rational, self-controlled and observant. A knowledge had gradually borne down on her, by many small incidents, by Ford's subservient anxiety to please and placate the Italian and by the Italian's increased surliness and often quite open insolence, that their relationship was far from being merely that of master and servant.

Althea had, in the opening months of her marriage, idolized Ford and had been wounded by his kindness and his indifference. Far from being a vain woman, she was sadly lacking in any feminine self-esteem. Ford's dutiful kindness was not what she had hoped for in a husband. Assuming that it was due to her own defective charms, she made a great effort on their honeymoon to please him. She had taken pains to dress well, to make a good public appearance, to compliment him, to praise his paintings and share his tastes in art. She was acutely aware of her awkwardness, her lack of social grace, and of the uncomfortable fact that in certain areas she was more knowledgeable than he. She had tactfully concealed her erudition.

It was a source of anguish to her that both her mother and Ford treated her like an invalid even when she was well. On the periphery of her mind was the constant apprehension that they might take any normal sign of nervousness or fatigue as evidence of a coming relapse. She was aware of her mental instability and dreaded its recurrence. She was painfully conscious that they watched her, wrongly diagnosing symptoms and exchanging danger signals when none were needed. This caused her, when she was perfectly self-possessed, to blurt out the wrong things, to laugh stridently, to behave against her will as they expected her to behave. She knew that Ford did not love her and that her marriage had been engineered by her mother. But she nonetheless struggled to win his approval, to make herself worthy, not of his care and solicitude which irked her, but of some awareness of her as a woman. This, she felt deeply, would do more than anything to banish the specter that had haunted her all her life. She wanted to be loved.

Her collapse after the Brewster party and the ensuing horrors of her recovery weighed on her far more than the agonies she had herself endured. She was mortally ashamed. She felt that it was now impossible for Ford to consider her as a normal woman and that he would always regard her as a freak. But little by little during her convalescence she had been made aware that Ford was not primarily concerned with her recovery. He was prolonging it deliberately because he wanted to remain at Fairlawn. He performed his duties to her in a perfunctory way, but his mind and motives were elsewhere. He had refused her suggestion that they should hire other servants and instead took to assisting Antonio with his household chores. They were constantly together. She felt herself to be quite sound again and was eager to depart, but Ford delayed and again delayed, offering one excuse after another. She did not like to antagonize him by an open argument, but she could not avoid reaching the conclusion that he wanted to stay on, not on account of her health, as he pretended, but for reasons of his own.

His reasons could only revolve around one thing: Antonio.

She watched Ford as he had for so long watched her. Every indication that he strove to conceal betrayed him. He treated Antonio in her presence with a forced offhandedness, but she could detect his fear that he might thereby offend and antagonize the Italian. Day by day the situation between the two men became clearer to her. Ford was in love.

Althea found that she was not altogether as shocked by this discovery as she no doubt should have been. It even, to some degree, exonerated her from being so woefully lacking in allure.

Because of the frequent references to it in Greek classics, Althea was not unaware that this type of love existed or had existed long ago. The high regard in which those noble minds held the love of an older man for a younger had not revolted her. She had accepted it as part of a classical morality different from her own.

She wanted to understand what this obsession was that gripped her husband, and observed Antonio closely as he came and went. He was undoubtedly good-looking, his head was finely shaped, his nose well sculpted. His eyes, in their brooding blackness, had a kind of beauty. But he was common. It was this that most disturbed her. She could stretch her comprehension to the point of accepting that Ford had been in some way dazzled by the outer attributes of a classic age, but she was mystified that he was not offended by Antonio's crudeness, his lack of education, his all too blatant limitations of mind and manner. He was a servant who belonged in the stables. She wondered, watching Ford as he obliquely watched Antonio, if he had in some way been infected by her own delusions; if he could be, in some other fashion, no longer sane.

And what were they plotting? What was going on behind the scenes? What did they discuss when Ford excused himself and hurried from the room after Antonio? Althea strained to hear. There were whispers and little silences and surreptitious movements of approach and then withdrawal. She became a dedicated eavesdropper.

Once, darting silently from her chaise longue, she peered through the keyhole of the music room.

She was bewildered by the sight of her husband with his arms around another man, kissing him as he had never kissed her. It was passion. It was madness. But Ford had faced up to her own mental collapse and her outbreaks of violence which were now all blurred to her. He had stood by her through the worst. She thought, clasping her hands in an agitation of doubt and self-inquiry, that she must somehow find the courage to do the same.

This was not at all, Althea recognized, one of those exalted attachments extolled by Plato and Sappho. It was plainly and dreadfully akin to what she had experienced herself. Ford was in the grip of an aberration, as some people contracted consumption or bubonic plague. He was ill. He was infected and Antonio was the germ-carrier.

She must try to understand it fully and she must help.

She lay down on the chaise longue, pulled up the fur robe and tried to compose herself. If only Valeria were here! Valeria was so wise and calm and they could have discussed the whole thing in a rational manner. Valeria knew Ford so well and loved him and would sympathize. She had not commented adversely on those poems of Sappho that celebrated love between women; she would surely understand that Ford was in the grip of that malady which had caused the Greeks to commiserate with those so tragically afflicted. They had taken gifts of wine and fruit to friends in love and wished them a speedy recovery. Had not poor Sappho cast herself into the sea because of unrequited love?

Her mind was confused by all these classical illusions. Althea was aware that the house was isolated and that she was alone and had no one to turn to. It suddenly occurred to her that she might be the target of some plan that Ford and Antonio had been concocting. Were they planning to kill her so that they could escape together?

But she must not, *must not,* think ill of Ford. It was all Antonio's fault. She must stay absolutely calm and devise a plan of her own to help.

A little later, when Ford returned, Althea was lying rigid on the chaise longue with her great dark eyes staring at the door. Her questioning and frightened looks followed him to the fireplace where he put on fresh logs and poked the cinders. She watched the light of the flames on his face. How despondent and tired he looked!

It was the moment for her to act. She said with an effort to keep her voice steady, "Ford, I've been thinking; I truly believe it is time we left here. I am quite well and fit to travel and we should be back with mother in New York."

He glanced around without interest. "As soon as the weather clears. Next month perhaps."

"I should like to be there sooner. And I think you need a change. You have been so good and patient and looked after me so well. It has been a great trial for you, I know."

He sat down and replied, without looking at her, "I'm all right, Althea. Next month we'll go."

She said with the deliberate care of someone addressing a sick person, "I was thinking that we could go to Europe. To France, perhaps. To the south. It would do you so much good and I should enjoy that, too."

"In the spring perhaps." He was looking at the flames.

He seemed so beaten. Her heart yearned to console and strengthen him.

"Oh, but my love, we don't need to wait that long. We shouldn't. It's you I'm thinking of."

"I told you I'm all right," he repeated with the same tired indifference. "It's been a long winter, but it's nearly over—a few more weeks."

"But it's not over," Althea insisted. "And I am worried. I have been for some time. I do understand, Ford dear."

"Understand—what?" He looked at his wife, for the first time aware of what she was saying.

"That you have—not been yourself. It is not your fault. That's why we must go." She said with an abrupt firmness, "We must send Antonio away."

He frowned, taken aback.

"Antonio—What has he to do with it?"

"It's Antonio. Not you. I know that. He has made you ill. It was like me," she faltered, unable to make herself clear without offending him, "when I became ill—I couldn't help it." She broke off lamely.

He was now looking directly at her, his face hardened by shocked suspicion.

"What are you talking about, Althea?"

"Well, it *is* that, isn't it?" she plunged. "You're lovers. That's why you're ill." She said rapidly, "I've known for some time. I watched and heard things and I *saw*. I don't condemn you any more than you condemned me. We have both been ill for different reasons and we must go."

Ford got up, startled and appalled, and came over to her. He stared down at her in confusion in which there was an element of fear. Althea shrank back against the arm of the chaise.

"Don't look at me like that, Ford. I am not upset except for you. I have read about such things. He is a very base and common person and he's infected you. You must send him away—for good."

Her pathetic attempt at strength drained from her. She contrived to whisper, "I'm sure Valeria would agree."

"Have you mentioned this to her?" he asked sternly.

"No, of course not. But I wanted to. If you send him away now it will be all right. Please, Ford . . ."

He stood there unable to decide how to confront her knowledge of his absorbing passion which he had never imagined she would see.

"You have no idea what you're saying. It's an absurd delusion. I forbid you to mention it again."

Ford turned away to hide the fear he knew would betray the truth.

"You must!" she repeated. Althea managed to stand up. With a weak defiance, some vestige of her authority as a wronged wife, she announced, "I don't want that man in the house. I won't have him here."

At this moment Antonio came in with her evening glass of milk and some crackers. Ford turned quickly, alarmed that Althea might pursue the subject and precipitate a scene. He took the food from Antonio and signalled him to leave.

But Althea stood her ground and in a suddenly strident voice declared, "Antonio, I want you to leave Mr. Hollister alone."

Ford swung 'round savagely, "Be quiet, Althea. Sit down and *just keep quiet.*"

But she saw in despair that she must fight for him and deliver him from the cause of his sickness. "I want you to leave this house," she insisted. "You are to have nothing more to do with my husband. It is a very evil thing you've done to him."

Ford tried to avert a crisis by ordering the Italian to go. But Antonio was standing there, his first amazement turning to anger.

"She doesn't know what she's saying," Ford assured him.

"You tell me to go?" the Italian demanded, thrusting Ford aside. *"I* should go?" He came toward Althea. "I leave your husband alone?"

Ford held him back. "For God's sake, can't you see? She's ill."

"I'm not ill. I'm not ill," Althea protested. "It's you —because of him."

The Italian's eyes blazed. He shouted, "You— madwoman! You tell me to leave your house—after months of him day and night. Me?"

He smote himself operatically on the chest. A tempest of pent-up rage and contempt swept through him.

"I am the evil one? Ask him what he does. What he wants with me. You are the evil ones! You and him and this house—everything you are. Pigs!"

He spat in Althea's face. She fell back in this blast of animal rage.

Ford fruitlessly attempted to pull the Italian away, but Antonio, now beside himself, shook his fist in Althea's face.

"You want to know what he does? You like to know what I do for him? What I do for your money— what he steals from you to give me when you back is turned?" Again he threw Ford off. "Show her. Let her see. Let the madwoman see why I am sick, sick of you and this house and what I do for your filthy money!"

Possessed by a lunatic rage, he seized Ford by the

throat and forced him downward. "You shall see. You shall see what he does—the pig married to the mad-woman."

Fighting for breath, Ford struggled to wrench the Italian's hands from his throat, but his strength failed. He fell on his knees.

"Show her, pig. Show her what pigs do when their wives don't look. Eat, pig. Eat what pigs eat."

He forced Ford's head against his groin.

That night Antonio moved quickly.

There were two clothes hampers in the laundry room. He dragged them into the kitchen. He opened a large box of silver flatware and tipped out the draw-ers. Knives, forks, spoons clattered into the hamper. He ran on stockinged feet into the dining room, snatching up sterling candlesticks and trays, dishes and salt shakers. He flung them into the hamper.

He darted back into the hall. The music room door was closed. She was still there. He sped upstairs, three at a time, past Ford's door into Althea's room.

He ransacked the drawers of her dressing table. In a Venetian leather case he found the few jewels she had with her; the garnet and diamond necklace, ear-rings, the jade ring, and the pearls.

He went to the stables, harnessed the horse to the buggy and dragged them out to the back door. He could hardly lift the hampers inside. He had no set plan, only escape.

He ran back into the house, into a small room where wood and kindling were kept with kegs of ker-osene for the lamps. He picked up the flammable items and went back into the hall.

The door of the music room was open. Good! She had gone upstairs.

He sped to the first landing and streaked the kero-sene down the stairs, emptying the keg in a large pud-dle on the marble floor. He brought bundles of kindling and paper and built a fire at the foot of the stairs. The horse whinnied outside in the cold night air. He snatched up Ford's fur lined coat and Ford's hat and ran back to the kitchen. Antonio reappeared with a lighted torch of paper and flung it into the kerosene. It burst into flame and spread, licking the kindling, following its train to the stairs. The flames danced upward, with a greedy crackle.

Antonio, bundled in Ford's greatcoat, climbed into the buggy, whipped up the horse and clattered round the side of the house. He could see the glare of flames through the long window above the stairs.

Ford was woken by the acrid stench of smoke. He listened. The house was alive with the rumbling of burning wood. He ran into the passage and saw the flames climbing the walls. The whole staircase was ablaze. The smoke billowed in suffocating clouds. The curtains on the long window were suddenly swept by sheets of flame. He ran back into Althea's room. She was lying face down on the bed.

He shook her. "Althea, get up. The house is on fire."

He pulled her off the bed. She was dazed and unresisting.

"We can't go down. The stairs are burning."

They were cut off. There was no means of escape. There was no other way down.

With that electric clarity that precedes panic, Ford pulled her to the window. "The roof of the music room."

He dragged up the window and climbed out.

Reaching into the room, he shouted, "Do as I tell you and don't give way."

Like a mechanical doll, she climbed out beside him. A dreadful thunder filled the air and a sickening smell. It seemed that the whole house shuddered.

"Stay there!" Ford edged his way along the roof. There was a twenty foot drop to the gravel path below. The one hope, he saw, was the old ivy which had gnarled its way up the side of the house. There was no use in wondering if the main root would hold. At the worst it might break the fall.

Althea was standing very still, not even shivering, waiting to be told what to do. She was convinced that she was dreaming and that nothing could really happen. When Ford held out his hand, she meekly took it and allowed herself to be led to the edge of the roof. The void to the ground did not frighten her.

"Do exactly as I say," Ford cautioned her. "I will go first. Kneel down and watch what I do."

She knelt and watched as he lowered himself over the side. His foot found a precarious hold among the twisting branches.

She heard him say, "Turn around and give me one leg. I'll put it where it's safe and hold on."

She did as he bid. It was easy to obey orders in a dream because if something went wrong she would simply awaken and find herself in bed.

Ford set her foot in a knot of ivy.

"Keep it there. Now the other," the muffled voice told her. "Hold on to the gutter."

Her fingers grasped the gutter which cut into her flesh. Someone was grasping her other leg and placing it among the jumbled tendrils.

"Wait there. I'm going down."

And then something in the dream cracked and she woke. She heard Ford cry out and the thud, far beneath, as he hit the ground. She clung to the ivy. It was making an ugly wrenching noise like the pulling of giants' teeth from their gums. She felt the whole house swaying. But she held on, He had told her to hold on.

The roar of the flames and the billowing smoke filled the night as she hung there.

The whole earth swayed in a sickening arch. The wall was coming away.

For an instant she swung through space. The trunk of the ivy tore from the wall, bent, wavered and crashed, but did not break. She fell through a chasm of burning air and hit the grass.

Was she alive? She could hardly breathe. Althea disentangled herself, and crawled away.

Ford was moaning. "Althea . . .?"

She inched her way toward him and fell across him.

"I can't move. My leg's broken."

Somewhere she heard a horse whinny. Through the high music room window she saw the furnace raging inside. Outlines of furniture flared brightly for an instant, a painting, a mirror, before they vanished in flames. The chandelier was swaying, a cascade of angry rubies.

She pulled herself to her knees.

"You must get up."

"My leg's twisted under me."

"Hold on to me, Ford."

She struggled up and, holding him under the arms, somehow dragged him onto the grass. He twisted onto one knee, his broken leg stuck out behind him. With one arm pressing against the ground and the other 'round Althea's waist, he managed to hoist himself up. Althea did not give way.

Clinging to her, he hobbled to a tree and leaned against it. The pain was excruciating, but it was localized. His mind remained very clear.

As they stared at the burning house, Althea declared, "I'm glad it's burning. I hope it burns to the ground."

She again heard the horse whinny and perceived in amazement, through the drifting smoke, the buggy marooned in the driveway.

Althea stumbled toward it. The air was alive with floating cinders, black snowflakes that drifted in and out of the smoke. The front of the house was a mass of flame, shooting straight up into the darkness.

She did not ask herself what the horse and buggy were doing there, dragged off to the side of the drive with the reins tied to the branch of a tree. She noticed, as she untied the reins and pulled the resisting horse onto the lawn, that there were two laundry hampers in the back. The horse stopped, shuddering, and screamed, terrified by the glare of the flames.

"You must," Althea shouted. "You must come with me."

With a strength she had never before possessed she dragged the horse toward the tree where Ford was leaning.

It was three o'clock when Valeria was roused by a knocking on the front door.

She had been reading in bed, unable to sleep. At

the insistent knocking, she got out of bed, threw on her night robe and ran downstairs. "Who is it?"

A woman's voice answered.

She unbolted the door and Althea fell into her arms.

It was Tripp who, roused from the stable attic, carried Ford into the parlor and laid him on the sofa where he fainted. It was Tripp who, in his night shirt with a rug thrown round him, drove the Haverfield buggy to rouse Dr. Mortlake who had had few undisturbed nights that winter.

Valeria took the blankets and pillows from Sam's bed and fetched some brandy. When she returned Althea was standing like a sentinel before the mantelpiece, strangely calm and triumphant.

Ford opened his eyes as Valeria laid the blankets over him.

"Oh, Val," he murmured. "What a nightmare!"

He drank a little brandy and lay back. His face was blanched and shriveled.

Valeria poured out a glass of liquor for Althea. "Drink this, dear. It will steady you."

"I am quite steady, thank you," Althea replied firmly. Her great eyes were shining. She felt that for the first time in her life she had proven her worth.

It was dawn when McGiver rattled down the drive to Fairlawn with the antiquated contraption that was the pride of the Arcadia Volunteer Fire Brigade.

The fire had burned itself out. The house was smoldering like a great burned cake.

McGiver and Arcadia's bravest penetrated into what was once the hall. It was completely gutted. The staircase had given way. A pile of charred rubble impeded their further progress.

They went to the back of the house and made their way into the kitchen. It was there that, amidst the wreckage, they discovered what had been the body of a man and was now a large twisted cinder from which blackened bones protruded.

Halfway down the drive Antonio, with a start of horror, had remembered the Venetian jewel box. It was not in the buggy. Where had he left it? In those last mad and terrible moments, he must have left it in the kitchen. He remembered leaving it on the table as he dragged out the second hamper of silver.

Cursing himself and ill luck, he had raced back to the house and forced his way in.

The kitchen was filled with smoke. The baize door which led to the front of the house was burning.

He felt his way, coughing and spluttering, his brain pounding with heat, his lungs bursting, to the table. Was it there? Was it there?

He was driven back by the smoke. But the jewels! He wanted the jewels! They were his prize. The acrid, poisonous smoke poured into his lungs. He staggered, groping for the table. The smoke and the heat engulfed him and he fell, retching and blinded, to the floor.

The flames, so merry and eager, danced from the door to a pile of newspapers left on a shelf and raced up the kitchen cupboards. In a burst of comradely delight, they were joined by the main conflagration. The flames pirouetted and leapt and twirled in a balletic inferno, crept with sly malice to the rug under the table, grasped a leg and spurted to the cloth, devoured the table at a mouthful, gobbled the Venetian box, melting the silver settings, scorching the stones, raced down another leg to the rug again on which Antonio's arm had conveniently fallen. The flames, investigating Ford's coat, lapping and nibbling, pounced in gluttonous joy on the fur lining.

Chapter Twenty-seven

THEY WERE SITTING in the restful lilac-decorated room, these three who had been through so much together, who had survived so many crises, whose memories entwined back to their dim beginnings. Ford, with his leg in a cast, leaning thoughtful and despondent on his cane, Randolph already bearing on his face the marks of experience that would soon rob him of his youth, and Valeria, startlingly white in her widow's black, too thin now, the bones of her face too pronounced, the purple shadows beneath her eyes accentuating their troubled depths. She was steeling herself for the last ordeal, resisting with ebbing will any fresh problems or decisions.

Once they had played as carefree children; now they were embattled voyagers on the high seas of life.

The parlor, for a span so bright and original, after three months of infiltrating smoke and grime was turning gray. The great bowl of Josiah's dark red roses seemed to burn like a challenge from the outside world which none of these three, for their various reasons, felt inclined to face.

Valeria had existed since the funeral in a state of numbed unawareness. She moved like a somnambulist through blurred and fragmented days. Ford faced with a gnawing but helpless dread the resumption of his married life and Randolph was apprehensive of what he had hitherto regarded as a blessing.

"Whatever else you do," Ford cautioned Valeria, "don't hand over anything. You were his wife and you have a perfect right to anything he chose to leave you."

"Have I the right?" she queried. "We were only married for seven months."

"Wills are a matter of legality and not of sentiment."

Poor Ford! All his worldly calculations had proved mistaken. They had resulted in tragedy and the death of that conniving servant with whom, Valeria knew, he had been in some unpleasant and reprehensible way, involved.

"I have done what I thought was right," she closed the subject.

"What about Nancy?" Randolph asked.

"I want to put her in a finishing school either in New York or Paris— wherever I decide to stay. Anyway, she will stay with me. Unless her parents object."

"It does not seem likely that Ida Brewster is in a state to object to anything," Ford said tartly. "It's a mystery how she ever contrived to give birth to anything as human as a child."

Althea came in wearing a dress and coat that Valeria had lent her which, being a size too small, exaggerated her angularity to the point of caricature. She was unnaturally bright and positive, playing to the hilt her new role as her husband's chief support and nurse.

Valeria had observed how galling Ford found his wife's ministrations, and how Althea, in her odd shrewd way, was aware of this and in consequence redoubled her efforts. Her solicitude was her revenge. Each time Althea bent over to kiss him or arrange the pillows or inquire what she might bring him, Ford detected a hard, ironic gleam in her eyes that struck straight at his shame and reminded him of her knowledge of it. He was forced to endure her kindness as a penance for a sin that would never be expiated because she would never allow it to be. This torture, so subtly and smilingly administered, was the reinforced foundation of their marriage.

"Well, we are actually leaving," Althea exclaimed. "At last we'll be free of this dreadful town. Even you, Randolph. I suppose now that Josiah's elected you'll go with him to Columbus. I have a feeling he'll make an excellent governor. He has all the requirements for leadership and no scruples which is such a help to a politician. I shouldn't wonder if we'll live to see him in the White House. It would be nice to have such a handsome president. Are you ready, Ford?"

Ford drew in a martyr's breath. "Give me a hand, Randy."

Althea swooped forward to help him up.

"We'll see you on the train in the morning," Althea said with the brightness that Valeria had begun to find so tiresome. "I've brought the cards so that you and Ford can play solitaire. It is so vexing that my Sappho went up in smoke. Fortunately I worked so long on those translations I'm sure I can remember them when I get another copy. Do be careful, Ford dear. We have heaps of time."

She embraced Valeria at the door. She was destined to become a thoroughly annoying woman, Valeria thought as she watched Althea follow the two men down the path. She wished that she had not been forced to invite them to share Sam's private car to New York. There was always another obligation, another duty, another care.

Monsieur Emile emerged from the kitchen in his natty traveling suit, with D'Artagnan under his arm in a smart tartan coat that matched his master's. He bowed over Valeria's hand.

"Are you sure that Madame does not need me further?"

"No, Monsieur Emile, I have a few last things to see to. Just look after Mr. and Mrs. Hollister."

"Bien sûr, Madame. I am always happy to be of service."

She was grateful to the little man who had proved himself such a loyal and tactful friend. He had altered his plans to stay with his dear Mademoiselle.

"You have been so kind."

"Oh, Madame," he exclaimed as he took a last look round the dismal hall, "I am so glad, so very glad, that you are leaving here."

He proceeded down the path, handed D'Artagnan up to Tripp and climbed up beside him.

Randolph rejoined Valeria.

"Well, I must be going, too. I don't envy you having to face the family, but I suppose wills will have to be read."

"When are you leaving?"

"That depends on Josiah. There'll be a hiatus now before the inauguration."

"I'm glad you're staying with him. You like each other and he will need someone. I don't suppose he has many friends in Columbus."

"He'll have even fewer once he's governor. Will you come out and visit me when I'm settled?"

"My plans are so indefinite. I'm too tired to make any decisions. If later on you get tired of politics, you can join me—wherever I am."

"You think you may stay abroad?"

"I don't know, Randy. I don't know anything at this point. I just need rest."

"A sea voyage would do you good."

There was a curious formality, even a certain embarrassment, between them. The rift that had occurred had never been completely healed.

Randolph was disturbed and a little awed by his sister in her new role as a wealthy widow. She was moving into another sphere and he was conscious of being left behind. With her beauty and distinction, backed by money, her life would be entirely different and might have no place for him. He was merely the adjunct of a politician, the victim, he now felt, of his own futile and unproductive cleverness. Even his rebellious idealism was flagging. He had seen during the campaign that idealism has little place in politics and that expedience is everything. He was learning the bitter lessons of compromise.

"Write Nancy a note," Valeria suggested, as he lingered. "It will please her so."

"Perhaps I should marry her," Randy suggested, with the unconvincing irony of a man who would never marry, "and keep the Garvey millions in the family. I suppose she will get her share."

"Why don't you?" Valeria kissed him. She had revealed nothing about the size of her inheritance and he had lacked the courage to ask her directly.

He put his arms around her. "Dear Val, I hope you'll find the happiness that you've wanted. You so richly deserve the best."

He was begging her to reinstate him in her confidence as she had once begged him to stand by her. But she was a woman of secrets now—including the number of red roses Josiah had sent her.

They kissed and parted.

Valeria watched him, a brilliant failure. She was glad that he would be with Josiah. Randolph would always need someone to lean on and Josiah was generous and strong.

She went back into the parlor. She needed a few moments to compose herself before the Brewsters came and the inevitable storm of protests and accusations broke over her head.

Josiah's roses!

She could not bring herself to think of him or to ask herself if he played any real part in her life. He had written one brief note saying that he would call on his return. She was not sure that she wanted to see him or had the strength to endure another confrontation. She had just enough stamina to get through what lay ahead.

The roses had an overpowering scent, but they were flowers from the outside world. Beyond her departure the next day Valeria could think of nothing but sleep and rest. She was drained, by something deeper than fatigue, of any capacity for further feeling.

Nathanial Shawcross arrived with his briefcase, precise and deferential. Valeria greeted him with cold formality.

"You must not be shocked by Mrs. Brewster's condition," he warned her. "She is still a very sick woman. In fact I was doubtful if it was wise for her to come today. I think," he added tactfully, "that you have made a very equitable arrangement, very generous—well, under the circumstances—"

Shawcross cleared his throat discreetly and sat

down at the table she had set up for him. He opened his briefcase and, with elaborate precaution, took out his papers which consisted of two documents. He took as much care placing them correctly on the table as if they had been sheafs of statements, accounts and codicils. They lay there, white and fatal, two epitaphs that marked the span of Sam Garvey's life.

McGraw arrived, trying to look as impressive as the executor of a large estate should look. He greeted Valeria gravely. He did not like Mrs. Garvey and was perhaps, to some degree, afraid of her, but he respected her as a woman of integrity and will. She had not once asked for his advice or deferred to his judgment. She had simply informed him of her wishes. A cold and forceful personality. Easy to see how she had come to dominate the old man in his decline. He would love to have known what part she had played in the making of Sam Garvey's extraordinary will.

The banker and the lawyer stationed themselves, sentinels of rectitude, as befitted the occasion. They eyed the tall, stately woman in the austere black dress as she stood beneath her portrait, staring into the fire. She was still young, but already she had the authority of middle age. They warily recognized her as their superior, not merely in wealth but in strength of character. Valeria made them feel uncomfortable because she disregarded them, as though they were no more than functionaries required by law.

The bell jangled. Valeria steeled herself to face this final ordeal.

The door opened and Henry Brewster came in, supporting on his arm an effigy swathed in black. Valeria completely failed to recognize her.

Ida was bent double and moved with the painful and uncertain steps of a centenarian. The big frame had collapsed into gaping hollows and sharp angles. Bones protruded alarmingly as though from a cadaver. A wide-brimmed hat added a funereal heaviness to a head unable to support itself.

She seemed unaware of where she was. As she drew near to Valeria the head contrived to raise itself. The dead eyes, in their gloomed sockets, glared for a moment and went out. Henry assisted Ida to a chair where she sat bent over.

Valeria barely noticed Hank and Nancy who had followed their parents in and were standing uncertainly by the door. Such a sense of horror and disaster emanated from the draped body that had once been Ida Brewster that Valeria forgot to greet them and retreated in shock to the far end of the room. She seated herself on a small chair in the shadows where she could watch Mr. Shawcross without having to look at Ida.

"I shall try to make this as brief as possible in order to spare the feelings of the family," Mr. Shawcross announced in a flat dry voice that sounded like a machine. He picked up one of the two documents. The Brewsters tensed with apprehension because whatever was on it had been condensed to a single page. This couldn't be the will. Wills were bulky and contained clauses and legacies, embedded in lengthy and involved paragraphs, and the will of Sam Garvey would surely be a tome, considering the fortune he had made. An empire could not possibly be confined to a single page.

"This is the late Mr. Garvey's will. It was signed on the tenth of January of this year in my office and witnessed by Richard Malcolm, foreman of the mills, and Jim Pryor, whom you know. I can testify that it is in all respects a legal document. It is, I may add, the shortest will in my experience. Mr. Garvey would not have it any other way."

A silence of impending doom fell across the room.

"I, Samuel Garvey, being of sound mind and of my own free choice, do desire and decree that the undersigned statement be my sole will and testament. Any former will of mine is hereby null and void.

"I leave everything I die possessed of, together with all future revenues, emoluments or other increment derived from investments, bonds or savings in any account, together with any cash sums in any place whatsoever, to my wife, Valeria de

la Pagerie Lee Garvey for her sole use and bene-
fit and to do with as she sees fit."

"It is signed, as you see," Mr. Shawcross pointed
out, "Samuel Garvey."

The Brewsters looked aghast at Ida for a sign, an
outburst, protest, a scream of outrage, some pronounce-
ment of opposition. None was forthcoming. Had she
heard?

If the dead could be stunned by any news from the
world of the living, so were the Brewsters. The expectations on which they had counted all their lives
crumbled like a cliff under a charge of dynamite. Was
it conceivable that they had nothing? *Nothing?* The
Garvey millions, on which their entire futures, their
position in the world, their immortal souls, depended,
had vanished like a glass of water whisked into oblivion by a magician's wand.

They were penniless.

And there, motionless in the shadows, was Valeria who had robbed them of their hopes, their security, freedom, rights, everything that belonged to
them. Every single dollar that was theirs she had.

From everything to nothing because of that single
page.

Mr. Shawcross replaced the death warrant of the
petrified and paupered Brewsters and picked up the
other document. It was not on a single page. As the
Brewsters reeled into outer darkness these pages
seemed to them the seal of their annihilation.

The machine that worked in the throat of Mr.
Shawcross was turned on again.

"The sole legatee was made aware of the contents
of Mr. Garvey's will shortly after his death. She has
decided, as it is within her rights to do, to add certain
provisos and make certain amendments. These have
been incorporated into a statement which has also
been duly signed and witnessed. It is a legal document
of which both Mr. McGraw and myself approve."

"I, Valeria de la Pagerie Lee Garvey, have
decided to amend the will of my late husband in

the following way. I hereby renounce and relinquish all claim to the Garvey Steel Mills and all shares and income derived therefrom in perpetuity. I desire that the Garvey Steel Mills and all shares and income derived therefrom be held in trust for the grandchildren of my late husband, Nancy and Henry Brewster Junior, and that, during their lifetime, provision should be made for my late husband's daughter, Mrs. Ida Brewster and her husband, Henry Brewster, to the amount of one half of the said income derived from the said shares in the said Garvey Steel Mills, the remaining half to be equally divided between Henry Brewster Junior and his sister Nancy Brewster. Upon the death of their parents, the entire income derived from the said shares in the said Garvey Steel Mills shall be equally divided between them. I desire that this trust shall be set up and administered by Mr. Charles McGraw and Mr. Nathanial Shawcross and that this trust shall be irrevocable."

The united Brewsters, arrested on their plunge into the financial void, shot back, with a gasp, to earth. From being penniless, they were rich. From being outcasts, they were members of society. The magician had waved his wand and restored their rights, hopes, security, their very lives.

Ida alone evinced no reaction to this breathtaking reprieve. She was staring at the pattern on the carpet, bent double in the shadow of her lugubrious hat.

Mr. Shawcross continued.

"From the monies in my late husband's various accounts, I desire a second trust to be set up and administered in the same manner with the inclusion of Mr. Fletcher Jones as co-administrator with Mr. McGraw and Mr. Shawcross. This trust is for the education of the children of employees in the Garvey Steel Mills and for their medical care and that of their families. I desire that the house in which Mr. Garvey lived be handed over as part of this trust to be used as a meeting place and library and for general recreational and social purposes. I appoint Mr. Fletcher Jones and any employee of the Garvey Steel Mills he may designate to act as administrators of this center. I desire that a sum be set aside from this trust for the purchase of land and the erection thereon of a school with adequate space and facilities and for the salaries of such teachers as may be deemed necessary.

"I will retain for my own use the shares and perquisites pertaining thereto left to me by my late husband in the Mid-Western and Pacific Railroad, together with any cash sums left in my husband's safe, together with any items given to me by my late husband during his lifetime. Signed. Valeria de la Pagerie Lee Garvey."

Mr. Shawcross looked up. "The details of these trusts and the amounts involved are open for inspection at Mr. McGraw's office at the bank. I think that's all."

"I should like to say," Mr. McGraw pontifically added, "that I consider Mrs. Garvey's decisions to be remarkably fair and just. They were entirely her own. We merely carried out her wishes."

Hank murmured thankfully, "Bravo, Valeria!"

Ida was still staring at the carpet, but her lips were moving. Henry touched her arm. She raised her head and looked vaguely about.

"I want Mister Emile," she said in the tones with which, in her former incarnation, she had given orders. "There are twelve. For the stained glass window. I must decide—because—" Her voice lost balance and slurred into a threatening whisper. "Jo-die Pack-er. Jo-die Pack-er. You can't escape because of your career."

Henry forcibly raised her and took her arm. Step by small difficult step, the shattered skeleton, dragging its black weeds, made its way to the door and passed outside.

Here Ida abruptly stopped and drew back, as

though struck by some dim recollection of her surroundings. She asked fearfully, "Where are we going?
I don't want to be here."

Henry reasoned with her softly. A convulsion of
nervous rage passed through her. She tore away her
arm.

"I don't want to be here." Her voice rose. "It's all
filth. All of them—that woman!"

Henry gripped her arm. "Do as I tell you, Ida."

Hank shut the door.

The full implication of her mother's madness hit
Nancy like a blow. With a stricken sob, she covered
her face.

Valeria forced herself to the surface of this nightmare and went to her. "She's very ill. You must be
brave and patient." She took Nancy in her arms and
said in an unnaturally matter-of-fact tone to Hank,
"When are you going East?"

"As soon as I've shut up the house. Nancy's going
to help me. There's a lot of stuff to pack."

"Come straight to the Fifth Avenue Hotel."

Valeria led them into the hall. Nancy was shivering.
She had barely considered Hank. She saw that he was
no longer a brash and inarticulate youth. He had
matured and looked very attractive, upright, and en-
dearing.

"I hope that we shall be good friends from now on,
Hank." Valeria offered him her hand.

Hank wanted to say something profound and heart-
felt, but what had happened had been so overwhelming that he could not find adequate words. He had
always known that Valeria was far above him, a
woman of wonderful qualities. He felt suddenly proud
that he had loved her.

"I think what you've done—well, it's magnificent."

"It was the only thing to do." She kissed him. "Look
after Nancy."

The weeping girl threw herself into Valeria's arms.

"We'll be together soon," Valeria assured her. "It
will all be much better and easier now."

When she returned Mr. Shawcross and Mr. Mc-
Graw were standing where she had left them.

"Thank you, gentlemen," Valeria said. "I am very grateful for all you have done and for your patience. I hope that nothing that happened here will be repeated. It is best forgotten—by all of us."

They nodded in agreement. They were impressed by her dignity and self-control. They shook hands and were gone.

The room seemed contaminated by Ida's presence. Even Josiah's exquisite flowers seemed like a funeral tribute. Their perfume was the stench of death. She never wanted to set foot in the room again.

It was over. It had passed off with a calm she had never anticipated. In the lull of anticlimax she thought, I have only to empty the safe, spend a last night in this house and be on my way.

Valeria had bought a black tin trunk. It stood gaping on Sam's abandoned desk. She unlocked the safe and opened it. It was a ghoulish procedure, this robbing Sam of the last of his hoarded wealth.

As she untied the canvas bags and removed the bundles of notes, in fifties and hundreds, she thought of the ragged boy trudging along the wintry road to Pittsburgh. A cardboard shoe box and a black tin trunk. Those were the span of Sam Garvey's life.

She remembered vividly the night that seemed a century ago when she had stumbled into this room and demanded Sam pay her five hundred dollars. It had been while he had been counting out notes like these that she had fallen asleep and the strange whim had entered his heart to marry her.

He had given her all he had. A bitter harvest. Death had prevented her from fulfilling her share of the bargain that had become so strangely an act of love.

Unexpectedly, Valeria heard the bell and tensed. Was it Fletcher Jones come to say good-bye or Mary wanting to offer some final help?

The other mechanical self that had been acting for her since Sam's death crossed the room. That other half-dead woman who was not herself opened the door.

Josiah's actual presence conveyed nothing special to her. He was there in his big coat with the fur collar. He was there himself, handsome and imposing, the man of authority, the man of power. She was glad to see him as much as a half-dead woman could be glad of anything. He looked tired, she noted. He, too, had gone beyond the point of being spontaneous and alert. Perhaps this was not the real Josiah, but a substitute who had been sent to call on a substitute Valeria Garvey.

Tenderly, he kissed her on the cheek and handed her another bunch of the long-stemmed roses.

Why had he brought her more of these sickening flowers when she was going away?

She must look more worn than she even felt, judging by the way he was staring at her.

"I had to see you. Randy told me you were leaving!"

Randy and Josiah—friends now!

"Come in," Valeria said. "I am finishing up the final things."

He took off his overcoat lined with sealskin. Very rich and ostentatious. He looked older, but grander, more commanding. There was an aura about him of achieved success.

"Congratulations," she held out her hand. "I was so pleased. I'm sure everyone must be."

"Not everyone. I won by such a narrow margin. My opponents have asked for a recount."

"Will it make any difference?"

"No, but at this point I hardly care."

He must understand how she felt, then. Why had he come to vex her further?

Valeria brought out some whiskey.

"Please help yourself." She closed the tin trunk and closed the safe.

"This must have been an ordeal for you. I hope the family behaved—or as well as could be expected."

"They had no choice," Valeria said with seeming indifference. "Sam left me everything."

"The mills?" He was amazed. "What about Ida and the children?"

"We've set up trusts with the steel money. They're all taken care of. I kept the railroad. It's far too much for the little time we were together."

"You gave back the mills?" he asked, incredulous.

"It wasn't a question of giving back. I had no claim on them."

Josiah said after a shocked moment, "You're certainly amazing, Valeria, though I guess I might have expected it. My God, the Brewsters should thank their lucky stars Sam married you!"

"He knew I would see to the children. He didn't care about Ida. Something happened between them—apart from the rift over his marriage—something I never knew."

He did not intend to enlighten her. "Even so, you'll be a rich woman."

She shrugged, as though this made no great difference to her. "I suppose."

"What will you do now? You're not staying on here?"

"I'm going to New York first. I have to get Nancy settled. And then—a long rest somewhere—to sort everything out. I can't see anything clearly now."

"You're worn out. Poor girl!" He took her hand. "You should go on a sea trip. To Paris, maybe."

"Do you know," she said unexpectedly, "there were only six people at Sam's funeral; Nancy and me, Jim Pryor and Mr. Murdock, the new manager of the mills, Mr. Shawcross and McGraw from the bank, who were the executors of his will. And of those six, I was the only one who cared. Nancy never knew him and the others were just men he paid."

Valeria wished, as she told him, that she could cry, but she felt only this weight of numbness in her. "A whole lifetime and one person. He'd only known me a few months."

She sat down behind the desk.

"What did it all mean—all his achievements? What did they do for Sam or any of them? All that his money taught them was to hate each other, Ida and Sam and the children, and all the others. She was here today for the reading of the will. She's utterly destroyed. She hated me to the point of wanting to kill me and she meant nothing to me—nothing! Out of all his money she never said or did one kind thing—not one simple, decent thing. He spent thirty years alone shut up in this dismal room."

He said quietly, "Darling, what else could Sam have expected? He never put himself out for anyone or cared what anyone thought. You were the only person who was generous enough to overlook all that."

"I wasn't generous. He was good to me. Do you realize, Josiah, he never knew how to tell me what he felt about me? He left that to a lawyer and a bank manager. Sam had never learned to express feelings of any kind—except arguments over money. He was just starting to understand . . ."

She leaned her head on her hands. If only the tears would come!

"I didn't want all this money—or the railroad. I have no right to any of it. All I wanted was what he promised and what I could have given him—a little joy in life. It's all tainted—all of this. They're infected—all of them. It has infected me."

"He left you all he had because you were good to him. You were the only person who ever was."

"But why, Josiah? That's what I've been asking myself ever since he died. He had brains and energy and vision. He was an extraordinary man. What was it in him—in this town—this absence of any joy?"

Valeria was searching in her dry distress for some answer to this mystery that seemed to her far more tragic than Sam's death. She got up suddenly. "You'd better not stay. I'm no use for anything."

"Come, sit down," Josiah said gently. "It's no use wondering why people in towns like this are as they are. I've seen thousands of them in the last few weeks. They're conditioned by the narrowness of their lives. You must have been a revelation to Sam. You opened windows. You did for me. It's your special gift, Valeria."

"Is it so unusual," she demanded, "to believe that there is something more in life than money and greed and all this suspicion and double-dealing? The Brewsters are no better off than the Shacktown people. Worse! And they have such opportunities!"

"You'll see it all in perspective later on."

"I never had much perspective," she admitted bitterly. "I have none now."

She found a handkerchief and blew her nose. "I'm a disgrace and I wasn't expecting you. Even that isn't true. And thank you for all those roses." She tried unsuccessfully to laugh. "You really should go away."

She put away her handkerchief as though she had finished crying. "Don't you want a whiskey? There's a siphon there."

Josiah waited until she sat back and something of this desolate mood subsided.

"I'm afraid I'm going to add another burden to your list. I don't expect an answer now. It's something for you to think over—on your way East or wherever you decide to go. You can send me a postcard from Paris. "Dear Josiah. In reference to your suggestion . . .'"

Valeria knew suddenly what was coming. Every instinct in her rebelled against it.

"I must say it now because you're going away and I don't know when I shall see you. I want you to marry me, Valeria. I have thought about nothing else for a long time."

"Please don't, Josiah." She recoiled and shut her eyes.

"I'll wait. I'm not pointing a pistol in your direction."

"Don't!" she said sharply. "I can't think about anything more."

She got up and leaned against the mantel with her back to him. "I can't—even contemplate—I may never want to. What happened between us was an impulse because at that moment I was desperate and unhappy." She turned to Josiah with a sort of irrational authority, "You have a whole new career, responsibilities and work. You have no time to think about that either. And you must not."

"My dear Valeria," he said patiently. "I have had plenty of time to think of it. I shan't change my mind."

"I don't want to marry again. I may never want to. I have always wanted to be free."

"We won't discuss it," he enjoined her, as though pacifying a rebellious child. "I've made the offer and it stands."

Josiah seemed then to emerge out of the general confusion of her feelings. This was the man she had dreamed of and who was offering to share his life. She wanted to want him as she had before. Valeria needed that former need because it had brought her back to life. He was vigorous and restorative and sane. He could blot out the sickness of Sam's death, Sam's money, Ida's madness, and bring back her mind and body that were barely alive. She had too many guilts and regrets and the mechanism that had kept her going was running down.

She was aware of her inconsistency and could not control it. "Don't ask me to think of the future, Josiah. I am so tired."

She sank on her knees beside him and, like a drowning person, put her arms 'round him and was dimly glad he held her.

An hour later they went upstairs.

Into that mean little room she no longer noticed, this half-dead woman who needed to feel and could feel nothing was led, unresisting, because he guided her.

Valeria undressed without shame, hardly aware of what she was doing. She was sitting on the side of the bed when he stood before her. He was magnificent in his nakedness, a godlike giant who embodied all the urgency and potency of life.

His manhood stirred in tribute to her. She drew him to her and it hardened between the softness of her creamy breasts. There surged up in her the desire to abandon herself totally, to be reawakened totally as a woman, to be relieved of this deadening weight inside her.

They made love like lovers who found their bodies to be instruments of a fulfillment beyond pleasure. And that wonder of being penetrated by the force of life after so many months of alienation filled Valeria with a relief deeper than her body's joy. It was what Josiah had longed for on so many journeys, in so many empty rooms. It was everything she had been so cruelly denied.

They made love slowly. She was grateful for every movement in her, for his bodily heaviness and strength. She was borne with him on that slow pulsation until, rising like a wave, it broke and her inner self dissolved and she was free. She pressed against him, not wanting to relinquish him because, through him, she was once again linked to life. Nothing that had happened to her had been real; only the knowledge that she held this man within her salvaged her dream of finding peace.

She fell into sleep from a great height on outspread wings, not fearful of falling because his arms upheld her.

Long afterwards Valeria drifted into partial consciousness. Her hand moved along the smoothness of his hip and up his side. He murmured, "Oh Val, we could be together like this always. Remember? I asked you to stay with me before."

Words marred and deceived and there lay between them a wilderness of deception and illusion as vast as the nameless territory she had traveled through with Sam on that last journey from nowhere into nowhere. A cardboard box and a tin trunk. There was nothing beyond that and only this between.

She wanted to possess this one reality that was immune to doubts and to delusions. She held it and it swelled in recognition and, throwing back the covers, she laid her cheek against it, glorying in this root of godhead that was the only true salvation. It was Man and his triumph and his defiance and his survival.

She was aware, beyond whatever hours had passed, that he was bending over her. Josiah was speaking to her in a language she no longer wanted to understand. "I will meet you in Paris. Will you stay there till I come?"

She heard herself say, "How can you? You have no time."

"I can take a month. Go over on the first boat. To the Crillon. I will join you as soon as I can."

"I hadn't decided . . ." Valeria roused herself, "I don't know where I'm going yet."

"I have decided. Book a passage on the first boat. If I can't make that—I will be there soon after."

"Paris—?" What was he saying? What chance was there of meeting?

He was shaking her gently. "D'you understand what I'm telling you? The Crillon. I always stay there. Take a suite."

Josiah was kissing her glossy hair. "I love you, Val."

She sank back into the desertion of her former self. As he went to the door, she asked across the gulf that was already widening between them, "How can you go to Paris? You've been elected."

"Not till June. We can have two weeks at least. Do what I tell you, Val."

He had gone. Why had Josiah left her? She drifted back into sleep. She had not slept without dreams in months.

Just before dawn she woke. What had Josiah said? Paris? He had left because he had been elected and must guard his reputation. She was alone because she was Sam Garvey's widow and owned a railroad.

This was the morning she was leaving. They were waiting for her on the train. She must finish packing. They were going to New York where Nancy would meet her at the Fifth Avenue Hotel.

Had Josiah really meant that he would meet her? Valeria could not decide that now. There were still too many things to see to.

To get up, to dress, to go downstairs, seemed monumental efforts. She had no intention of going to Paris. It had been London. She had booked rooms at some hotel. They were going to find all the places he knew from Dickens. The Old Curiosity Shop and Portman Square—the Deadlocks. It was utterly thoughtless, utterly inopportune of Josiah to have proposed at such a time. It would be years before she could think of that. Independence at thirty-one. Sam had promised her that. Their bargain. She must keep her word.

Valeria must try first to accustom herself to the awareness of being rich. It would require a profound readjustment toward herself and her relation to the world. She would grow into it slowly like adopting a new and complex faith. For the first time in her life she had no one to consider—Nancy was no problem. Nothing that Josiah could offer could compensate for losing this opportunity for freedom. She would live for herself, for the present. Years of peace and calm and security to heal the wounds that went back to White-briars and the War. Wasn't it independence that she had fought so long for and endured so much for? Wasn't that why she had married Sam?

She got up after a while and in the dim owl light of eclipses, washed and dressed. What was it she had decided to travel in? She was tired of black. It was a constant reminder of what she most wanted to forget. But she had packed everything. The widow's dress and the black velvet hat with the widow's veil. The trunks were on the train. She hardly felt up to entertaining Ford and Althea for four days. She would make excuses and stay in bed.

As Valeria bent before the mirror to arrange her hair, she was confronted by a stranger. Eyes stared at her with a haunted, hunted look. Althea's eyes or Ida's. Was she going mad like them?

Try to concentrate. Remember. Her bag. Her furs. She had given the keys of the house to Mary. No, there was nothing else.

A bare little maid's room she had slept in for seven months. She left nothing of herself behind.

She went downstairs. The house and all it represented no longer existed for her. It would become a place for strangers. She went into the study and methodically packed the rest of the money. It was a fortune, she supposed. And it was hers.

As she dropped the key to the trunk into her bag, Valeria said to herself, "I will take this money to Thaddeus Brownlow and ask him to invest it. One day when I am rich enough in my own right, I will give back the capital to the Brewsters, the exact amount. And then nothing pertaining to them will have any further part in my life at all."

Was there anything else? Why did her memory not respond when she questioned it?

Mary came in with a cup of tea. Standing in that dim vacuum, Valeria took the tea and sipped it. It tasted bitter.

"Thank you. Not now."

There was still something of importance, something she didn't want to face.

"There are some canvas bags left in the safe full of money in coins. Give one to Tripp and take the others to the farm. You can spend the money as you need it. And take care of Mr. Garvey's desk. I may send for it when I'm settled. And the portrait too."

"Yes, Ma'am. You told me. I remember all you want done."

"Oh, did I tell you? And you will see that Mimosa is moved carefully? I'm relying on you to give her everything she needs."

"Oh yes, Ma'am, we'll take good care. You needn't fear."

She said undecidedly, "That's everything."

She put the sable stole about her shoulders. Something she had forgotten? Some last ordeal?

"You will come back, Ma'am, won't you?" Why did Mary keep crying when it was all over? "You will come back to see us? I don't know how we shall get along without you."

"You'll manage very well. And take Matthew to Dr. Mortlake regularly for the treatments. When are you moving to the farm?"

"Tomorrow. It's like a miracle what you've done for us."

Tripp emerged from the mysterious hinterland he dwelled in. "Please take this trunk. I want it with me on the train," she said.

At least Tripp did what she told him and didn't cry. He didn't try to pull her back into what was all past and done with.

"Well, that's all," she repeated without conviction.

She did not want to say good-bye. She had already parted with everything pertaining to the house. She kissed Mary swiftly and went into the hall.

Suddenly she remembered. It was Mimosa. The one thing she most dreaded, the last thing she most wanted to avoid. Had she the courage to leave without seeing her? She owed it to that loyal creature who had saved her life.

She went out by the back way, through that kitchen in which she would never again cook food, boil water, try to wash in that inadequate hip bath.

It was dawn.

As she opened the stable door, Mimosa heard her and stumbled to her feet. She could stand now on her three good legs, with the fourth slightly crooked beneath her.

Valeria turned up a lantern and, as the yellow light brightened the stable, she saw the dear brown head with the cocked ears and the great patient eyes filled with tenderness, thrusting towards her.

She thought in an agony of heart that she loved this creature more than anything on earth.

As Valeria wrapped her arms round Mimosa's neck and felt the moist nose nuzzling her shoulder, the stone that had lain across her heart splintered.

She broke into a passion of weeping. She had never in her life wept like this before. She did not even know what she was crying for. Her whole life poured out of her in a storm of convulsive tears. She was weeping for Whitebriars and her childhood and Randy and Ford; and for Sam dead and Josiah gone and for all the loneliness and futility and pain and wasted effort. There were not enough tears in the world to wash away this immense and pitiless grief.

When Tripp, some time later, came in search of her, he found, to his amazement, Mrs. Garvey lying in the straw with her head against Mimosa's side. To see Mrs. Garvey, always so cool and collected, in this condition, in this utter abandonment, was the most shocking thing he had witnessed in all his years.

Her hat had fallen off. She had dropped her bag. She lay there in the dirty straw sobbing as though her heart were shattered and could never be whole again.

⁊ EPILOGUE ⁊

VALERIA PUSHED OPEN the French windows of her
sitting room at the Crillon and looked out over the
Place de la Concorde.

It was a perfect morning. The chestnut trees along
the Champs Elysées had lit their pink and honey-
colored candelabra. The smart, shining carriages with
the immaculately groomed horses were rolling by.
People stepped along the pavement in a brisk and
carefree way. And the great fountains thrust their
shining plumes against the sky. This silvery city was
more beautiful than she had ever dreamed it could
be.

She drew in deep breaths of the unique and sparkling air. Oh, she could understand why Monsieur
Emile so deeply loved this most romantic of cities!

She had been there five days. Each day was a tonic,
a reaffirmation, restoring her confidence, like the per-
fumes and hats and gloves she bought in the smart
little shops along the Rue St. Honoré.

She still could not believe that she had actually
emerged from the long dark tunnel of her existence in
Arcadia. It all seemed to her like some remote and
ugly dream. She had come close to the end during
those last days, but now, with each walk she took,
each drive along the avenues, each meal lingered over
beneath the trees, she felt that she was coming to life
again like a plant that had almost perished for want of
light and water.

Monsieur Emile was coming to lunch. Afterwards
he would escort her to the proposed location of his
restaurant—*Valeria*. The little man was beside himself with delight at being back in his beloved capital.

His gallantries had become absurd. He bowed and
kissed her hand and presented her with posies in lace
paper, tied with ribbons like a bridesmaid's. Even
D'Artagnan frisked along the boulevards with the
perky self-satisfaction of a bon vivant.

She stretched. It was so easy to allow oneself the
luxury of happiness when everything one touched or
ate or saw contributed to the euphoria of simply being
alive.

There was a knock at the door.

That would be breakfast. She relished the thought
of sharp French coffee and warm brioches.

The door opened.

It was Josiah.

It could not be Josiah!

He stood there, smiling and triumphant, with a
great basket of spring flowers.

He saw the tall aristocrat against the sunlight in the
diaphanous lilac robe, with the luminous white skin,
the level, shining jade eyes, the ebony hair falling so
lightly about her shoulders. Everything about her,
elegant and distinctive, belonged in Paris. A perfect
wife for a politician, subtle, intelligent, able to keep
secrets, able to beguile. But there would always be
something enigmatic about her, just out of reach.

Valeria saw, in this instant of appraisal, a man of
worldly assurance who might be guided toward greatness, with persuasive charm that masked aggression,
ambition tempered by a natural hedonism that
would save him from becoming a fanatic. And, in his
love for her, apparent simplicity and trust. But he
would try to dominate, try to build fences. She would
have to defend herself. He had the weapon of his body
and she the armor of her mind.

That flash of objective vision passed.

Valeria ran across the room into Josiah's open
arms!

ABOUT THE AUTHOR

EVELYN HANNA is of Irish and French extraction, and lived mostly in Britain and France before moving to America in the late 1930s. She married an English sculptor and they have a son named Nicholas.

She loves travel, collects Chinese antiques, and is fascinated by Oriental philosophy. Miss Hanna also has a passion for gardening, but she has to guard her flower beds carefully against the activities of Mr. Pompidou, her pet Pekinese.

As a child she wrote limericks, but she put her writing efforts aside for a while to pursue an acting career and to work for the British diplomatic service where she was the first woman to be in the Foreign Office.

After World War II Miss Hanna took up her pen again, but only wrote for herself. Her son became a play and screen writer. After watching him struggle with scripts over the years, she finally decided to try her hand at a full-length novel and to try and get it published. *Stolen Splendor* is the result.

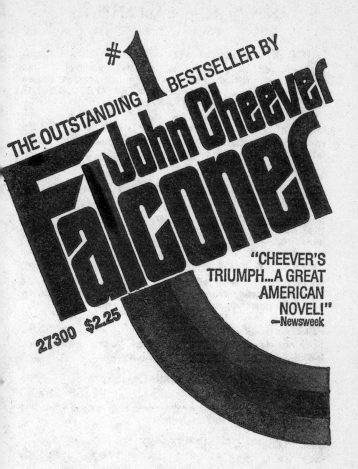

THE OUTSTANDING #1 BESTSELLER BY

John Cheever

Falconer

"CHEEVER'S
TRIUMPH...A GREAT
AMERICAN
NOVEL!"
—Newsweek

27300 $2.25

Also Available from Ballantine Books

BULLET PARK

27301 $2.25

NEW FROM BALLANTINE!

FALCONER, John Cheever　　　　27300　$2.25

The unforgettable story of a substantial, middle-class man and the passions that propel him into murder, prison, and an undreamed-of liberation. "CHEEVER'S TRIUMPH . . . A GREAT AMERICAN NOVEL."—*Newsweek*

GOODBYE, W. H. Manville　　　　27118　$2.25

What happens when a woman turns a sexual fantasy into a fatal reality? The erotic thriller of the year! "Powerful."—*Village Voice.* "Hypnotic."—*Cosmopolitan.*

THE CAMERA NEVER BLINKS, Dan Rather with Mickey Herskowitz　　　　27423　$2.25

In this candid book, the co-editor of "60 Minutes" sketches vivid portraits of numerous personalities including JFK, LBJ and Nixon, and discusses his famous colleagues.

THE DRAGONS OF EDEN, Carl Sagan 26031　$2.25

An exciting and witty exploration of mankind's intelligence from pre-recorded time to the fantasy of a future race, by America's most appealing scientific spokesman.

VALENTINA, Fern Michaels　　　　26011　$1.95

Sold into slavery in the Third Crusade, Valentina becomes a queen, only to find herself a slave to love.

THE BLACK DEATH, Gwyneth Cravens and John S. Marr　　　　27155　$2.50

A totally plausible novel of the panic that strikes when the bubonic plague devastates New York.

THE FLOWER OF THE STORM, Beatrice Coogan　　　　27368　$2.50

Love, pride and high drama set against the turbulent background of 19th century Ireland as a beautiful young woman fights for her inheritance and the man she loves.

THE JUDGMENT OF DEKE HUNTER, George V. Higgins　　　　25862　$1.95

Tough, dirty, shrewd, telling! "The best novel Higgins has written. Deke Hunter should have as many friends as Eddie Coyle."—*Kirkus Reviews*

LG-2